THE HUNTER AND THE OLD WOMAN

THE HUNTER

AND THE

OLD WOMAN

PAMELA KORGEMAGI

ANANSI

Published in Canada in 2021 and the USA in 2021 by House of Anansi Press Inc.
www.houseofanansi.com

House of Anansi Press is committed to protecting our natural environment. This
book is made of material from well-managed FSC®-certified forests, recycled
materials, and other controlled sources.

House of Anansi Press is a Global Certified Accessible™ (GCA by Benetech)
publisher. The ebook version of this book meets stringent accessibility standards
and is available to students and readers with print disabilities.

25 24 23 22 21   1 2 3 4 5

Library and Archives Canada Cataloguing in Publication

Title: The hunter and the old woman / Pamela Korgemagi.
Names: Korgemagi, Pamela, author.
Identifiers: Canadiana (print) 202102220ox | Canadiana (ebook) 20210222018 |
ISBN 9781487008253 (softcover) | ISBN 9781487008260 (EPUB)
Subjects: LCGFT: Novels.
Classification: LCC PS8621.074 H86 2021 | DDC c813/.6—DC23

Book design: Alysia Shewchuk
Typesetting: Laura Brady

*House of Anansi Press respectfully acknowledges that the land on which we operate is
the Traditional Territory of many Nations, including the Anishinabeg, the Wendat,
and the Haudenosaunee. It is also the Treaty Lands of the Mississaugas of the Credit.*

 Canada Council Conseil des Arts
for the Arts du Canada

 ONTARIO ARTS COUNCIL
CONSEIL DES ARTS DE L'ONTARIO
an Ontario government agency
un organisme du gouvernement de l'Ontario

With the participation of the Government of Canada
Avec la participation du gouvernement du Canada | Canadä

*We acknowledge for their financial support of our publishing program the Canada
Council for the Arts, the Ontario Arts Council, and the Government of Canada.*

Printed and bound in Canada

For my father

THE HUNTER AND THE OLD WOMAN

The boy stood staring at the paw print stamped in blood on the wooden floor. The mark was still red, as if made only moments ago, and it burned with an internal light visible to his eyes alone. He knelt to study it closer, memorizing its shape so he could recall it later, whenever he wished. His heart beat with a sudden intensity as he laid his hand on the print, in awe of its size.

He watched as the woman stood next to the basin, leaning over it, gently plunging the wool into the hot, soapy water. She pulled out the bundle wrapped in cheesecloth, letting the water drain, then she handed it to the girls to unpack. Already, damp tendrils of wool hung to dry, like a white fungus spreading on the air from tree to tree.

The dead sheep had been stacked together, like a tree of bones, out behind the house. The men cast fuel upon the pile, throwing it in high arcs so it reached the top. Then they stood back as one man struck a match and touched it to the dry grass. A blue flame seared over the earth, then bloomed, and the mound of dead was imbued with fire. The remaining wool ignited and blazed like glowing filaments before turning to ash, and the legs of the sheep blackened, and the skin began to bubble and curl.

The men stood watching the flames in silence. A stream of black smoke crawled into the sky, coiling in on itself as it rose and dissipated into the clear air.

I

HARBINGER

→≻

THE COUGAR STEPPED OUT of her lair into the cool dawn followed by her three cubs. As she passed from one shadow into the next the low light reflected off her eyes in weird, green flashes. She noticed a pronounced quiet in the forest around her. Then she heard the rustling of leaves behind her, and turned to look.

When she saw the lean, silver cougar stalking toward her through the grass, she knew it was too late. He could have struck while she was out hunting. She would have returned to her lair to find the cubs slaughtered and only his scent on the earth. Instead, he chose to come to her in the light of day, as she was leading her cubs out. He had chosen this moment among many. He had meant for her to see him. This was how she knew him as a harbinger of

Death. Her cubs stumbled against one another, the fur on their narrow backs bristling. The Cougar retreated, herding them behind her, and the Harbinger followed her for each step, head to the ground, level stare for her so she could not look away, only hiss at him to be gone.

The Harbinger gave a scream that cut through the Cougar like ice water, and she responded in her own worried voice. He was an old cougar with yellow eyes, a pale face, silver fur along his sides. Though lean, he was not thin with age, merely pared down to muscle and bone from years of hunting. His hide was smooth and unscarred, with the exception of his tattered right ear.

He reached out to catch the Cougar's face in his claws but she swatted his paw away with her own. She hissed, ears folded back against her head, eyes flashing. Her kittens would never outrun the Harbinger, and she was bound against leaving them. Though strong in her own right, she did not have the physical strength to defeat him. So while she knew she had already lost, she could not bring herself to turn and flee.

The Harbinger reached out again, this time catching her shoulder with his claws. She felt the sting of air against her raw flesh, an unbearable touch. The Harbinger pounced and the Cougar rose onto her back legs to meet him. They stood wrapped in each other's front legs, jaws open, each trying to sink a bite into the other's neck, that vital passage. The Cougar struggled with the Harbinger, trying to get in, but both cats saw they did not have an opportunity and broke off from their embrace, swatting each other away.

The Harbinger rushed her again and the Cougar stood to fend off his attack. He nearly knocked her over, her feet digging into the earth, but she withstood him. The panicked hissing of her kittens sounded far away, though they were right behind her. The Harbinger twisted left, then right, trying to get his bite in. His teeth had been yellowed by age, but were no less sharp. His breath was rank from the flesh of some kill he had eaten before coming to meet her. He reached up and grasped her head in his paw to pull her close but the Cougar slipped out of his hold and jumped away.

Alarmed by how close he had gotten, distracted with protecting her neck, the Cougar strayed too far from shielding her kittens, and the Harbinger took his moment, leaping past her and snatching the nearest cub in his jaws. The Cougar turned in time to see him shake the life out of the kitten. Then it hung like a dead snake from his mouth.

As the Harbinger pounced on the second kitten, the Cougar leapt to the third, snatched him up, and ran. When the Harbinger looked up from his work and saw that the Cougar had fled, he set after her.

With the kitten clutched between her jaws, the Cougar ran into a field of tall grass, taking it in long strides, a true run, devouring the earth, her heart beating fast, heavy beats. A wind brushed the grass into waves. She heard the Harbinger in pursuit behind her, his feet pounding the ground.

She saw the river through the trees, the bright water coursing between stony banks. When she came to the bank, she leapt. For a time her golden body held in the air parallel to the water's surface, the kitten in her mouth curled up against the sensation of weightlessness, before she plunged into the river. The cold was crushing. Then she was treading water. When she broke the surface, the kitten mewed and fought to keep its head above the surface. The Cougar swam, breath coming in gasps. Behind her, she heard the Harbinger crash into the river. She was not halfway across and she was struggling. The current rushed against her, pulling her down. The kitten squawked and squirmed. She forced herself onward, sinking slowly as she went.

When her feet found the bottom on the other side, her breathing came in tremendous gasps. Her body was heavy as she pulled herself out of the river. The kitten felt limp and when she released him he sagged to the ground. He lay, eyes closed, thin and wet, unmoving. Her heart pumped in her chest. She could hear the Harbinger splashing through the water behind her. She ran into the trees.

As she charged through the forest, the Cougar heard a strangled squawk rise up from the kitten she had left on the riverbank. She stopped and turned. One ragged breath and the Harbinger burst into view, running straight for her.

The cougars tore through the trees, leaving a trail of snapped branches and upturned leaves in their wake. The Cougar came to a deep chasm in the earth and leapt over the gap in a smooth, solid leap, landing with barely a sound. Moments later, the Harbinger made the same flawless jump.

In a moment, she would have to stop and stand, and she knew she would be defeated with ease. Then she noticed the silence in the forest around her. She stopped. She stared into the trees, searching for the Harbinger, heart pumping in her chest, but she was alone.

She slunk away, one unsteady step at a time. She slipped under the low-hanging branches of an evergreen, curled up against its base, and sat watching the forest as her heartbeat began to slow.

The silence of the forest rang loud in her ears. She made a pathetic yowl, as if it would lessen the weight of her loss, but it did nothing to subdue the sudden emptiness. She noticed then the stinging claw marks on her shoulder, the blood that had stained her chest, her front leg. She began licking the blood away until the only signs of her wound were three bright claw marks torn into her golden fur.

The Cougar stayed beneath the tree as the sun ran its course across the sky. Night came and with it the moon yet still she stayed, unwilling to rise and move on.

T HE COUGAR'S FIRST MEMORY was of meat. She and her sister had just begun to notice their mother's absence when one day she returned clutching a leg of deer in her mouth, the flesh bright and bloody, the hoof smeared with mud. The Cougar and her sister sat in rapt silence as they watched their mother, paws clutching the disembodied leg as she stripped the meat from the bone, rasping it clean with her tongue, the white fur around her mouth becoming stained with blood.

It was not long after that they left their lair for the first time. The Cougar and her sister followed their mother along the lakeside, through tall grass. Molten clouds hung above the horizon where the sun had made its descent. A dampness crept into the air as darkness cooled the forest. The cubs stayed close to their mother as she led them through the shadowed trees.

The Cougar was amazed by her own ability to see into the dark, as if everything produced its own light. Aside from this distracting power of sight, she did not understand the many sounds coming from all around her. She tried to pinpoint a single source, but there was too much at once and she became afraid. The Cougar stopped and yowled, but her mother continued on, calling for her to come.

They followed a path worn into the forest floor, a sheer

rock face at their side. The air was damp. Ahead she heard the sound of crickets. The rock came to an end and they were at the edge of a thicket of dense bush. The Cougar smelled it on the air, then she saw the deer on the ground, looking as if it had merely lain down to rest. She saw the set of antlers like branches sprouting from its head. Its body was enormous. The Cougar herself was barely the size of its rump. She believed her mother must possess great skill and cunning if she could convince such an animal to lay down its life for her.

But when the Cougar and her sister stood before the deer they saw the nature of its death; its head thrown back, its neck ripped open, shredded tubular matter glistening in the moonlight. The Cougar knew then it had not been as simple as commanding the deer to lie down. There was something dangerous about this exchange and she was struck with a sense of awe at the strength and mastery this would require.

Their mother stood waiting, watching into the trees as the cubs ate quietly, distracted by the sounds in the surrounding night, their ears twitching at every snap and skitter in the dark. It was difficult to apply focus in such chaos. But their mother stood by, unmoved. It seemed she was not afraid.

When the Cougar and her sister had eaten their fill, their mother began scraping up dirt and twigs to cover the deer. She retrieved a fallen branch from nearby, its dried leaves rattling as she dragged it over. The Cougar and her sister watched, taking note of this strange ritual. In the end, the deer was not completely covered, but it seemed the point was not to bury it, only to mark it as claimed.

They walked along the lakeshore on their way back to the lair. An owl hooted as the cougars passed. The Cougar's Mother turned, looking toward the trees where the owl perched on a branch. The Cougar looked into the trees, trying to see the owl, but she could not find it. She was displeased that the owl could see her but she could not see it, that it would call out, alerting others to their presence, and she decided then that birds were not to her liking.

A crowd of hazy mountains hung in the distance. Steam rose from the surface of the lake and glowed in the cold autumn sunlight. The Cougar and her sister followed their mother through the trees. They had stalked the forest all night but found no sign of the herd of deer. The Cougar had been with her mother two winters. Their lairs never strayed far from the glistening body of water, its gentle shore luring prey into the cougars' reach. They trekked around its border, they drank from it, they even swam in it.

IN WINTER THE COUGAR had ventured out onto the frozen surface of the lake as far as she dared. A ring of frosted trees stood still and silent, surrounding the lake, guarding it — a centre of some significance. From where she stood, seeing what the lake saw, she imagined what it meant to be eternal.

Their mother stopped in her tracks, watching ahead, her daughters likewise paused. Sunlight came down through the branches, churning in upon itself, the movement of the air made visible. Each cat sat within the shadow of a tree.

The Cougar saw her mother sniff the air, then step in one fluid motion from one shadow into the next.

Six yellow eyes stared through the bush into the forest beyond. A deer with her two fawns stood in the grass. Nearby, a herd of deer grazed, the males watching into the trees, antlers raking the air.

The Cougar's Mother waited, eyes on the mother deer and her fawns. The sun climbed higher in the sky but the air kept its crisp edge. A breeze plucked the leaves from their branches and sent them gliding to the ground. The deer and her fawns made their way closer to the cougars hiding in the bushes.

Without a sound, the Cougar's Mother rose and stepped through the bushes. Her cubs followed. They paused, waited to see if they had been spotted, took another step, waited. The deer and her fawns stood grazing. One of the fawns lifted his head to snatch the grass out of his mother's mouth.

Again, the Cougar's Mother advanced, this time quick over the cool, grassy earth. The Cougar and her sister followed. They fanned out, encircling their prey. When their mother stopped, so too did the cubs, eyes raised just enough to see above the grass. It was a pale golden colour, warning of the coming of winter, the perfect shade to mask a cougar.

As the Cougar crept closer to the deer she was conscious of her shadow. It could give her away, something she had learned through the pain of failure. But this morning her shadow was cast behind her, and the deer were still unaware of their presence.

The mother deer lifted her head, searching the grass.

The Cougar had noticed this while hunting. They could sense she was there, like they had felt a shift in the wind. At this moment, stillness was imperative. She forced herself to wait and not give herself away, to allow the deer to relax. If she leapt too soon and the deer was given the chance to run the hunt would be spoiled. She had learned to force herself to wait until the moment the deer believed she was alone.

The cougars rose out of the grass, claws out. The deer flew backward, but the Cougar's Sister was right there with her, tackling her to the ground. Startled, one of the fawns bolted right into the Cougar's Mother's reach. She caught it with one paw, brought the flimsy neck toward her jaws. The Cougar was left with the fawn who had fled. Three long strides and she jumped—for an instant she thought her jump was short, but the fawn faltered, a dip in the earth she had not anticipated, and the Cougar descended upon her.

The fawn hung from the Cougar's mouth, her legs sprawled on the grassy earth. The Cougar stood a moment catching her breath, then dragged the fawn over to where her mother and sister were busy devouring their catches. The Cougar's Mother had torn into the fawn's chest, and the Cougar's Sister sat with her head buried in the deer's rump. The Cougar began tearing the skin away from the body of the fawn to get at the meat.

She was well into the fawn when the sunlight hit the mountains in the distance. The Cougar looked up, her eyes two glowing points in a mask of red gore. The mountains rose up from the dark land, the snow gathered in the folds of the rock as bright as the sunlight itself, contrasted by furrows of deep shadow; these places hidden from sight, a mystery. The Cougar sat staring. She felt a sudden urge to go there, to see them for herself, called by a voice that seemed to come from deep within the earth.

The Cougar and her sister followed their mother as the sun rose higher in the sky, casting their shadows long on the pale grass. When they were about to enter the trees, the Cougar looked back toward the mountains. Though they were out of sight, she could still see them, sunlight casting them in a golden glow, in her mind. The image followed her all the way back to the lair, and even pestered her as she settled down beside her sister for her day's sleep.

WHEN SHE AWOKE THE next evening, she was thinking of the mountains. She sat staring into the darkening trees, but she could see the mountains in her mind, and hear them calling to her. She went with her mother and sister to hunt the night forest, all in silence. Everywhere they went, she heard that subsonic summoning. She heard it in the barrage of crickets as the cougars stalked through the grassy fields; in the breeze as it passed through the trees overhead; in her own heartbeat, pumping madly, as she stood watching the horizon.

The cougars returned to their lair by the light of the rising sun. The Cougar did not sleep. Instead, she lay with her mother and sister, listening to their breathing, the muffled beating of their hearts. She found herself unwilling to move, to rise and leave them, but the sound of the mountains was calling her out.

She stepped out of her mother's lair and stood squinting against the sunlight. A nighthawk called from somewhere in the trees. A breeze touched her and the leaves at once. She turned and saw her sister had crept out of the lair, and sat behind her, waiting in silence. They held each other's gaze, each looking on the other's face.

They set out into the trees, side by side, two golden shadows streaking across the land in full daylight. They raced along the edge of the lake, the water glistening in the cold sunlight. Then they cut through a flat, grassy bog toward the mountains, the Cougar leading the way.

A SOUND LIKE BRANCHES knocking together in the wind echoed through the forest. The Cougar and her sister crept through the trees, following the sound. They came to a rocky hillside and crouched in the bushes.

Through the scant leaves they saw two bucks standing, facing each other. They were matched in size, but the buck with the harem scattered along the hillside behind him had more silver in his hide, his face somehow sharper—whereas his opponent boasted the advantage of youth in his dark glossy hide, his proud chest. They stood in perfect stillness, sharing an intense gaze. The Cougar and her sister sat watching, tails flicking.

The bucks broke from their pose and charged. They drove their heads together, each trying to turn the other into the ground with his antlers. They were so close, almost touching, but neither could look into the other's eyes, staring fixedly at the stony earth. The deer parted and circled. The bucks shared another deep gaze, chests heaving, breath spewing into the chilled air from their wet noses.

The Cougar heard the breathing of the young buck, watched the motion of his rib cage, and she felt a great desire to stalk and hunt such a fit young deer, to run him down, and devour him.

Again the bucks lowered their heads and charged, their antlers clattering like branches. Though they seemed like branches, the Cougar knew antlers and branches were not alike, having tested both between her teeth. The branch would break apart, where the antlers would not. She had also tested the bones of deer and found they did fall apart between her jaws but only after some worrying.

The bucks stood locked in their stance, each trying to overturn the other. The younger buck adjusted his footing, trying to gain purchase on the ground, but the older buck drove him back. Stones skittered down the hillside. The younger buck steadied himself, hooves digging deep into the earth. The other deer, the young fawns, the slender females, wandered the hillside, seeming to ignore the duelling bucks, as if they could hear the noise of the battle and were seeking its source among the trees.

The bucks broke apart and stood, watching one another, waiting. The Cougar's Sister rested her head on her paws, eyes closed, but her ears were turned toward the bucks, twitching at the sounds of their exchange. She could hear what they were doing and knew exactly what transpired on the hillside and she would not raise her head until the challenge was over. That was her way. But the Cougar did not know how she kept from watching.

The older buck trumpeted into the air, black eyes shining in his skull. The two deer rose up on hind legs to gain force and crashed together again. For a moment, it seemed as if their antlers had become stuck and the battle turned from the question of supremacy to trying to separate themselves from each other. The older buck shook violently and the younger one was set free with a sharp snapping sound. They stood apart, heads lowered.

The older buck was not tiring. Likely he had defended his harem before. The Cougar saw this, and if she could see this she had no doubt the young buck could too.

Unceremoniously, the younger buck broke from the fray and fled down the hillside. The older buck took chase, galloping after him, but when he saw that the younger buck meant to retreat, he knew he had won the challenge and halted his pursuit. He lifted his head and trumpeted after the young buck, already out of sight.

When the Cougar rose, her sister roused and followed. They stalked after the defeated buck. A covering of damp leaves lay on the ground, masking the sound of their steps. Soon they heard the young buck ahead, his heavy footsteps through the wet leaves. The cougars stayed low to the ground, creeping forward one slow step at a time.

They saw him through the trees. He had spent his strength and now stood exhausted. They need only be wary of the deadly antlers and his heavy hooves. The Cougar's Sister left her side. They would approach him from both sides, a trusted tactic. The Cougar crept forward.

The buck stood, chest heaving, his breath curling into the chill air. The Cougar heard his heartbeat from where she crouched, concealed in the bushes beside him. His eyes, watery and watchful, reflected the green forest around him. A warbler's call shot through the air. The sun emerged from behind the clouds and the cold, wet forest was flooded with sunlight.

The Cougar rose out of the bushes, her sister emerging from the trees opposite. The buck froze. The Cougar's Sister was upon him, front legs wrapped around his neck.

The Cougar landed on the deer's back. All three came crashing to the ground like a beast of many limbs and different hides. The buck had time to make a stifled cry before the Cougar's Sister tore into his neck. They heard the gurgle of blood being sucked into his lungs, sputtering out again.

The Cougar's heart pumped no more than three beats in the time it took this action to unfold. The Cougar's Sister drew her claw down the deer's belly and reached inside for the warm, tender organs. They sat side by side, as they had as kittens, their faces becoming stained with blood as they ate. First they ate the deepest organs, the richest meat, then they started on the deer's rump, pulling back the deer's hide with their claws as they went. Soon the carcass was picked clean, the rib cage exposed to the air. The Cougar and her sister lay together beside the body, tails flicking, cool eyes staring into the forest as night fell. Once in darkness they rose and disappeared into the trees, leaving the carcass to the scavengers.

THE SUN MADE ITS approach behind an overcast sky, the whisper of its light turning the wet darkness a murky blue, then grey. The Cougar and her sister came down rolling ground covered in damp leaves and slushy white snow. A thin mist floated over the ground, so as the cougars walked it broke upon their chests, like the ghost of a sea unwilling to retreat.

They felt the vibration in the earth and heard the rumble before they began to see, between the trees, the rise of spray into the air. As they made their way through the cold trees the rumble in the air grew louder. The trees fell away and the sisters found themselves standing on a cliff, a raging waterfall coursing over slick, jagged black rocks. The cougars stood watching the white water rushing over the edge, crashing down into the pool below. A billowing mist surrounded the base of the waterfall which afforded occasional glimpses of the dark, churning water.

The Cougar stood rapt. The sight of the endless falling water held her gaze with a power she could not explain and the great sound of the rushing water pulsed through her body, a fascinating sensation she had never felt before. The waterfall fed a river that flowed into the land below. In the distance the mountains stood large and blue in the near light. She would follow the river toward the mountains. Even after she had come all this way, they still called to her, that she come yet farther.

The Cougar stepped down to follow the river. She glanced back and saw her sister looking down on the land before them, sniffing the air. Then her sister looked behind them, in the direction they had been heading before encountering the waterfall. Then she looked back at her sister.

The cougars stood staring at each other, the sound of the raging waterfall at their side, spray wafting through the air between them. Then the Cougar's Sister turned and walked away into the trees.

The Cougar watched her disappear, back into the forest. When her sister was no longer visible, the Cougar yowled after her, her voice cut down by the constant waterfall. From a distance her sister yowled back, and then the tremendous sound of rushing water resumed and the Cougar stood, unmoving, watching the waterfall.

T HE COUGAR SPENT THE winter wandering the forest night after night, until she had worn paths through the snow with her own feet. The river drew her to its icy banks, too wide and fast-flowing to freeze, the sound of its passage accompanying her as she sat listening through the night, through sunrise, and into the day. She grew hungry, so preoccupied with her observation she almost forgot to hunt.

Then the thaw of spring washed away the snow, revealing the pale land beneath, and the Cougar saw the face of the valley she had come to for the first time. She visited the places that had become familiar to her, yet seeing them anew, blooming with fantastic growth, seeing what the snow had hidden from her all this time. Birdsong and the constant drip of melt accompanied her day's rest. The river swelled, the leaves unfurled, and the tender buds of early flowers poked through the damp forest floor. The smell of earth, of old leaves and mud, was thick on the air.

It was in this spring that the Cougar awoke to the sunset in a state of agitation she had never known before. She thought she had been awoken by a sound and sat listening, but nothing indicated the presence of another animal. She left the lair, sniffing over the earth, but the forest stood in silence. Within the trees, the shadows grew thick in the light of the descending sun. The Cougar ran into the forest trying to flee the unrest within.

The sun vanished and the darkness lit her blood aflame. The rustle of leaves was the only sign of her body in the night. She slowed her approach to a whisper when she heard the quiet conversation of water over rocks. A gathering of crickets called to one another from their perches along the stream. As the Cougar approached, they fell silent. She sat down, settling in to wait.

The night crept on. Sitting and listening into the darkness was not enough to take the Cougar's mind from the point that had been distracting her focus since she had awoken. She felt a restless desire to run, but there was nothing to do except what she was doing now. She forced her attention to the stream.

The waiting was interminable. It seemed the deer would never come. Until they did.

The Cougar glided out of the shadows toward a young fawn drinking at the stream with its mother. She landed in the water with a splash and pushed off again so she was at the deer by the time they heard her. Even as her embrace closed around the fawn's slender body, the Cougar could not forget the strange anxiety distracting her attention, occupying her entire body. She retreated from the stream, the fawn clutched in her mouth. The mother deer made a solitary flight through the trees, only to stop, breathing heavily, and stare into the darkness that had come alive and snatched away the fawn drinking at her side.

The Cougar stripped the meat off the fawn with disinterest, and her hunger vanished. She covered the half-eaten carcass with some grass and a fallen branch that still had a few brown leaves clinging to it. It was not a well-hidden cache, but the Cougar had already forgotten it. She wandered the night, walking the paths she had walked many times before, but it did nothing to relieve her of the restlessness within her.

She stopped atop a rise in the land and looked down on the river below, snaking through the forest. The horizon simmered with the approach of the sun. The Cougar found herself agitated that the daylight should find her wandering around, mindless. She answered a sudden urge to call into the fleeing night; a piercing caterwaul that shattered the silence of the early morning forest. She called again, her voice reaching deep into the lifting darkness.

She made her way down the hillside with no specific destination in mind, compelled to make her call as she went. It seemed to release something within her, casting the madness out onto the air. Her cries travelled through the forest, exiling the other animals to pockets of silence wherever she went.

Her calling subsided as she grew tired. The rising sun shot through the surrounding trees. She thought of seeking shelter in the earth, where she would sleep, and be freed from this torment, at least for a time.

Then she smelled a scent that set her on guard; the scent of another cougar. Movement out of the corner of her eye—she turned her head and saw him coming out of the trees toward her. The Cougar stood staring as he stepped into the sunlight, waiting to see the reason why he showed himself to her, ready to run.

In the opening light, the cougar's eyes flashed an irides-
cent red as he stood, tail flicking, studying the Cougar. He
was young, a marauder roaming the forest. He had a wide
face, a bright chest, massive paws. The clear symmetry
of his body implied a balance of strength and skill that
signalled to the Cougar in a way that was somehow familiar. His fur shone like an evening sunset, with distinct
redness which she found alluring.

They shared a tense gaze, watching for any sudden
movement. They had been so long away from the company
of other cougars that they had grown wary of their own
kind. The Cougar stayed still, interested but ready to run.
The Marauder mimicked her posture. Sunlight lit the
leaves on the trees around them and turned the pollen in
the air to motes of gold, and the two cougars stood facing
one another, their hearts like tiny suns sending light pulsing through their veins with each beat.

The Marauder tried to approach the Cougar, but she
shrank back and gave a low growl. He sat, tail slashing
over the grass. She waited to see what he would do. She
did not trust him up close. He took a step toward her and
when he came too close she swatted him away. He sat
back, but after a moment he tried to approach her again.
She allowed him to touch his cheek to hers, but when he
swept his teeth close to her neck she swatted him again
and hissed. He sat back, blinked, and looked away, then
he began to purr.

The sound emanated from the dark centre of his body
and the Cougar felt her anxiety pushed aside. The sight
of him glowing red in the sunlight replaced her wariness

with curiosity. The Cougar's purr was much quieter, only heard up close. The cougars met noses, pressed their cheeks together. They investigated each other's faces, careful to guard their necks, until they were convinced neither would turn their claws on the other, a hesitant truce.

The quiet of the forest was interrupted by their shattering growls, almost indistinguishable from those made by battling cats. The forest stood frozen for a moment, then the drone of cicadas rose again through the trees. The cougars curled up in the shade of an evergreen and went to sleep, hearts beating one after the other, a call and an echo.

T HE COUGARS WOULD ACCOMPANY each other for days, finding that they must even hunt together, so thorough was their affliction. The moon rose, and the Cougar and the Marauder crept out of the lair they shared and into the fresh night. The sound of crickets was thick as they crossed a field of long grass drenched in moonlight, the cool air breathing across them with a sigh. The earth was warm from the stay of the sun.

The Cougar followed the Marauder as they stalked through the night. He led her through the grass, into the steep foothills where he hunted, a part of the forest the Cougar had never been to. It seemed he spent his time here. He had climbed these rocks before. He knew where to step. They navigated through a tangle of bushes until the ground dropped and they stood at the edge of a rock face, observing the forest below.

The Cougar lifted her head, licking her red-stained chops. They sat side by side eating through a deer. The sun burned below the horizon. The Cougar rose and stretched. When that did not get the red cougar's attention she sauntered over and swatted his face, making a low growl. The Marauder leaned back and began to purr.

Afterwards, they slept hidden beneath the low-hanging branches of an evergreen. During the day the Cougar opened her eyes and saw the sun high in the sky through the needled branches. The Marauder's breathing was steady and deep. She listened to the sound of the air rushing in and out of his body, the gurgling of his insides, his heart pumping his blood through his veins reminding her of the river, its continuous journey. She thought of the Marauder alone, wandering the wilderness, the many nights he had lived, the many days he had slept; his lonely life now entwined with hers.

The Cougar yawned and stretched her front legs. The sun blazed through the branches above. She resettled herself next to the Marauder, closed her eyes, and returned to the strange oblivion of sleep.

AS THE SUN BEGAN to set, they went out to hunt. The Marauder sauntered along beside the Cougar as they stalked through the forest; the only sound that betrayed them was their light footsteps on the soft grass. The Cougar followed her normal path, to the fields where she found her deer. When she entered the trees, she heard that the Marauder had not followed her. She looked back and saw him sitting in the grass, and she knew their time together had come to an end.

Seeing him from afar, so small amid the sea of grass, reminded her of her own solitude, and thinking of it now she could not believe how she could have forgotten it. Whatever had taken possession of her had now fled. She looked back once and saw the Marauder, a red shade through the trees, and then he was gone.

The next evening, she awoke in a new lair and noticed the absence of the Marauder's scent. She went out into the warm evening, the air muggy as she walked through the dark trees. The last flashes of the sun flared in the twilight. Night hurried across the forest and the Cougar ran, silent, a shadow through the trees. She returned to her life before the madness had overtaken her, her time with the Marauder fading, recalled as if from a dream, watery and long ago.

THE COUGAR EMERGED FROM the trees, the mountains pure blue behind her, the air like the ghost of water. The forest had seen through its wet spring and now bloomed lush and green with the approach of summer. The Cougar found the will to take down a fully grown buck, devour half the meat on its case, then sleep beside the haphazard cache.

Upon waking, the Cougar ate what remained of the deer and left the carcass to the scavengers. She was drawn to the river, stalking its banks with no real purpose in mind other than wanting to see what it looked like here, and here. On this meandering journey her appetite returned.

This was how she knew.

Standing by the moonlit river, staring into the black depths of the rushing water, she remembered the Marauder, the time they had spent together, the strange invocation they had been compelled to repeat, the way their union had come to an end once it seemed its purpose had been fulfilled. Some change had occurred within her, and though this seemed natural to her she did not know what it meant for her life to come. But there was no stopping it now.

AFTER THREE FULL MOONS the Cougar sought out a new lair. She waded through the dense bush where the forest met the mountain and found a fall of rock surrounded by tall grass. She squeezed herself inside. Fragments of bone lay among the leaves on the ground, but the remains were old. The lair had long been abandoned. She scraped out the leaves and bones, uncovering the moss beneath. She was careful never to walk in the same steps when coming and going from the lair, so that no path was made through the surrounding bush, no sign of her presence was left. She buried her feces and covered the spot with pine needles so even her scent would not be detected.

After this preparation, a day passed, then another. She went out in the early morning, before the sun rose, and caught and ate a deer, then returned to the lair. When she awoke next, she prowled around the small space but did not leave. She began to groom herself with an obsessive thoroughness, as if it were of great importance for what came next.

The sun set and she felt a great calm preside. All the forest around her receded. She heard nothing except the beating of her own heart. In darkness she surfaced between waves of pain, charged with bearing these slumberers into the waking world. Three kittens met the dawn. That they had spent three turns of the moon inside her was incredible enough. Now that they were in the world it seemed like one of her dreams had emerged into life.

The Cougar licked them clean, careful around their tiny faces. She held them next to her chest, all three of them encircled in her front leg. Then she laid her head down and slept the sleep of the exhausted.

Later she awoke and watched the kittens as they slept, their eyes sealed to the bright day. She could hear their hearts fluttering like moths trapped inside their chests. The size of them sparked fear into her own heart. How small they were. How easy it would be to wipe them away, their grasp on life was that precarious. She was entirely devoted to them. A sudden and permanent shift.

in, unseeing, and after a few breaths she turned away. She retreated to the trees, unable to fight the current pulling her forward.

The clouds shifted away from the full moon and the forest bloomed with a silver light. The Cougar looked up at the bright face of the moon in the night sky. Even the touch of this dim light exposed her body, removing her from the night. The moon slid behind the clouds again and the forest was plunged back into darkness.

She walked along the river, the constant rush of water loud enough to mask the sound of her steps and drown out her thoughts, and she went farther along the river than she had ever been before. Here, the river swelled out, wide and flat. The moon emerged from behind the clouds and revealed an Outcropping of Boulders. Something about the arrangement of rock, its sudden presence by the side of the river, caught the Cougar's attention.

The boulders seemed to have been cast off from the nearby mountains. But how they had arrived here from so far away was a mystery. The shards of rock had been smoothed down by rainfall, nights of howling wind. She sat and watched as clouds overtook the moon again and the boulders lapsed into darkness. She saw their shadowed outline and stayed, watching, as the moon emerged and retreated and emerged again, the rocks blooming white, fading into shadow, emerging again, until the moon had made its course across the night sky and the air around her simmered with the approaching sun.

She stayed as the sun winked over the horizon, casting sunlight into the tops of the trees, and watched as the pink light slid down onto the boulders, casting new shadows, and the rocks were revealed anew.

When she came out of her thoughts, the boulders sat in full sunlight. The Cougar blinked and stretched, then set out into the trees, seeking the shadows, to sleep away the day until the return of night.

T HE COUGAR STALKED THROUGH the night, announcing herself only to strike, and, having consumed the living, returned to darkness. She stayed sometimes for days in shadow, unwilling to let herself be touched by daylight, wandering the forest in silence. The heat of summer faded and the chill of autumn crept into the nights. The leaves on the trees turned bright yellow, fell and were swept along the forest floor by the wind.

She awoke to a cold sunset and found herself afflicted by that strange madness once again. She went prowling through the night forest, her thoughts pushed aside, her calls warning of her presence and summoning that which would match her terrible disposition. She ran through the trees, as if she might outrun what had taken possession of her, though she knew she would not rid herself of it until her call was answered.

It was the Harbinger who stepped from out of the shadows. When she saw him, she knew there would be no threat to any cubs sired by this cougar. Their safety was assured. She felt her anxiety disappear and she saw the sleek silver fur of the cougar standing before her, his golden eyes. His body signalled to her and she was powerless against whatever revulsion she might still feel toward the cougar who had slaughtered her first brood.

They stood, eyeing each other in the cold. The Harbinger's

silver coat gleamed in the faint moonlight, the Cougar's shone like muted gold. He tried to walk beside her and the Cougar yowled. Then she smelled him. He had found her scent raked into the earth and covered himself in it, to alleviate the tension that was sure to arise between two such deadly hunters. He tried again to approach her, but she swatted him away, again and again, until she was satisfied he would not attack her. The Harbinger was an old hunter. He knew how to wait.

THEY STAYED TOGETHER, SLEEPING in the depths of the earth, or out in the cool, open air beneath the star scattered sky. The Harbinger submitted himself to being swatted in the face whenever the Cougar felt the desire, and she was relentless. But he was familiar with such treatment from his mistresses.

Otherwise, they would hunt.

They crept, silent, through cold trees. A wind riffled through what leaves remained on the branches overhead, sending them floating to the ground. The cougars found a knot of trees where they settled down to wait, watching the field of grass before them. The Cougar stole a glance at the Harbinger, his silver face in the moonlight. He sat with his eyes closed but he was not asleep. The slightest sound roused his attention, his ears searching the field beyond, and he knew what was there without opening his eyes.

The darkness was lifting just as the deer emerged through the trees, and it seemed the Harbinger had known this was where they would appear at this exact moment. Soon the cougars would be visible to the deer. The Harbinger stepped away through the grass, silent as a shadow. The Cougar crept forward, one slow step at a time. The deer were walking toward her. She wondered, if she sat still, if they would walk by without even noticing her.

The two cats struck at once. As if they could sense each other's movements on the air, the Harbinger's intentions transmitted to her, so the Cougar knew it was time, adjusting her back paws upon the earth, measuring the distance between her and the deer.

In a moment they stood panting over the lifeless bodies of their deer as the sound of the retreating deer faded. The sun rose as they feasted. Afterwards, they lay down next to one another, and fell asleep.

They slept as the sun passed overhead, then they awoke and sat beside each other yawning, the bodies of their kills lying in shadows of blood. The Cougar rose and wrapped her tail around the Harbinger's neck until he submitted to her and they performed their invocation in the bright day, next to those eviscerated bodies, the cry rising up from the both of them cutting through the clear air and echoing through the trees.

As she lay with her head resting against him, she heard the Harbinger's heart in his chest, its deep, steady beat. Her own heart hammered in her chest so loud she felt certain he must be able to hear it. But if he could, he gave no indication. He gave no indication that he considered her presence at all, reserving his energy for only what was essential. She saw his focus and knew this was the key to his success.

THE COUGAR AWOKE AND the Harbinger stood before her. She heard the slow, deliberate beating of his heart across the short distance between them. Seeing that she was awake, he turned and walked away through the trees. The Cougar sat up, watching him. When he looked back at her their gaze touched across the distance between them. They were released from one another. Now if they met in the forest, it would not be as lovers.

The Cougar lay down to sleep, grateful to return to her solitude.

AS THE FIRST SNOW dusted the forest, the Cougar brought two kittens of the Harbinger into the world. The first time she led them out of the lair, it was snowing and a white forest stood all around them. The kittens huddled close to the Cougar's legs, black spots on their golden fur, eyes squinted against the white world. Snow like a fine powder fell in silence, coating the fresh fallen leaves, the naked grey trees, the evergreens. The Cougar's daughter looked up and jerked when a snowflake landed close to her eye. She meowed.

Memories of her first brood haunted the Cougar, like memories of a dream — watery and fleeting. When thoughts of her union with the Marauder threatened to rise from the depths of her mind, she retreated from them in haste. There was always distraction to be found in watching her kittens. The Cougar raised this brood with a distance brought on by the loss of her first brood. She was reminded of those lost kittens when she least expected it and she knew these kittens could be lost just as easily.

The winter dragged on and the kittens grew into cubs. Soon they would switch from milk to meat. Deer were sparse at this time, not having had their spring courtships yet. She would have to start the cubs out on hare, which were plentiful regardless of the season.

As she fell asleep, the sound of the wind running through the cold winter forest, her cubs nestled beside her in the warmth of their lair, she thought of hunting hare with her sister, those first months on their own. They had spent many afternoons chasing those bounding targets, their path erratic through the snow, sometimes letting one go when they caught it just so they could catch it again. Running through the snow, her beating heart, the taste of the blood in her mouth.

I T HAD BEEN SNOWING for three days when the Cougar emerged from her lair. The afternoon was not her preferred time to hunt, and her chances of finding anything were slim, but she had been confined to her lair for days and while her hunger could be negotiated with, the urgent mews of her two kittens could not and the sound of their voices had begun to wear on her.

She stalked the forest amid snowflakes that seemed to float rather than fall to the ground, like the ghostly spores of dandelions. The snow was so thick the forest was hidden from sight. Only a small realm of trees was visible to her; beyond that, the great white world stood in silence, unseen. But the snow did not impede her hearing or erase her memory of the landscape. She walked through the solid white day, the trees and bushes emerging as she encountered them, then fading back into the whiteness as she passed.

The Cougar crept beneath the branches of the evergreens where the drifts were not so deep. At the edge of the trees she settled in to wait. She sat listening to the crystalline sound of falling snow, loud through the frozen air.

When she heard them approaching through the snow she opened her eyes. A group of foragers, digging through the snow for roots, their footsteps slow and heavy. They travelled together because the greater their number, the less likely they were to be chosen. There was some sense in this.

The Cougar emerged from beneath the evergreens and headed toward some snow-covered bushes. She slid inside, disturbing the snow on the branches, which rained silently to the ground. Then she was concealed from view, the footprints she had left behind softening as the snow vanished them.

Though she could still not see them, she knew how many they were. A ragged group of elk, all males, too old or too young to defend their own harem, banded together to survive the winter. As they came closer, they coalesced out of the white day into snow-encrusted beasts, the thick fur upon their shoulders blanketed with frost, ice coating their nostrils and dusting their eyelashes. The Cougar watched as the procession made its way toward her. As the elk drew near, the Cougar was impressed by the size of the animals, noting the heavy muscles, the meat on their frames. Their feet were enormous. As large as her head.

When the Cougar moved to follow the elk, two starlings erupted from their perch in the tree above her. She lay flat in the snow. Though she was hidden from the elk, the group tensed. A few turned their heads in her direction. The snowfall continued like a slow downpour. The largest of the males, his head bare of antlers, took a step toward the Cougar. This would be the one. He chose himself.

The elk stood before her, unsuspecting of the terror hidden at his feet. The Cougar could hear the faint beating of his heart. She thought of his long life through the forest; an endless pulse, a continuous breath, his massive frame running through the cold, wide open, a river of blood coursing through his veins. Until this moment. His coat was blond along his side and grew darker and thicker around his shoulders, for warmth perhaps and to protect his neck — that vital passage. He was twice the size of the Cougar, but his size only enticed her. The smell of him, the smell of one who lived outside, not within a lair, like a wind on the ember of her desire.

The Cougar burst from out of the bushes at the elk's feet. He was fast. He called to his brethren and they sprang from their positions, fleeing into the trees. The elk flew back with an agility that seemed unnatural for his bulk, but the Cougar pursued him, upon him in one leap. She caught his back leg in her mouth and crushed the bone between her jaws. The elk kicked at her and she leapt away, out of his reach. The strength behind one hoof was enough to kill.

The elk made a panicked retreat, the Cougar close behind. It was a short chase. Away from the shelter of the trees, the drifts deepened and the elk, already awkward from his injured leg, stumbled, trumpeting at the Cougar to get away, thrashing through the fallen snow as if through water.

The Cougar jumped onto the elk's back and wrapped her front legs around his neck. The elk bucked, trying to throw the Cougar, but she hung on with her claws as he stumbled and fell to the ground. The fur around his neck was too thick for her teeth to penetrate. The elk twisted wildly against her. The Cougar hung on, trying to work her jaws into the right position.

The group of elk gathered around the Cougar and the elk, locked in their death struggle. She could not see them but knew where they were by the sound of their footsteps in the snow. They began to call, growing louder as more joined in, like the cawing of a flock of panicked birds. Despite their number, they would come no closer. She held on to the elk struggling in her arms, her claws sunk deep, her hold unwavering.

With a great heave the Cougar pulled back her head and ripped out a mouthful of flesh from the elk's throat. The elk cried out and writhed against her. The Cougar held on. The swarm of elk began to bleed into her field of vision, bleating and snapping their teeth, their breath spewing into the air in hot, hurried gusts. Their black eyes and black noses burned through the falling snow. There were more of them than she had realized. They edged closer, surrounding her. The elk in her embrace thrashed against her. The Cougar waited.

Blood pulsed out of the elk's neck, striking the snow in bright red sprays. The Cougar's face and chest became stained with blood where he struggled against her. Her eyes, blazing gold, stared ahead into the white day. He would bleed to death, writhing in the snow, until he was too weak to fight. Then the Cougar would begin to eat him while he was still alive. Later, she would bring a portion to the kittens awaiting her return. All this she saw before her; all she needed to do was wait.

From out of the forest came a harrowing growl and the Cougar froze.

The Harbinger emerged from behind white veils, eyes

levelled at the Cougar, breath trailing from his open mouth, as he stalked toward her.

A wave of dread crashed against her. There was no mistaking the silver coat, the tattered right ear. Hunger had driven him out into the snow, the same as her. He must have stumbled upon her by chance, attracted by the calls of the elk, and seeing an easy opportunity lying under the Cougar, he was not likely to look elsewhere.

He stepped forward and growled, head low to the ground.

She let go of the elk and screamed. Released from the Cougar's hold, the elk stretched out a weak leg but could not rise. The Harbinger was not intimidated by her and stepped forward, swatting her face and pushing her back. The Cougar screamed again, but she saw that she inspired no fear in the old hunter and she knew the elk was lost.

The Harbinger glared at the Cougar until she retreated a few steps, lowered her head, and hissed. The Harbinger ignored her. He tore into the elk's belly and began devouring mouthfuls of dark meat. Unable to accept her defeat, the Cougar remained, watching.

Perhaps distracted with keeping one eye on the Cougar and one eye on the group of elk that hovered around them, the Harbinger could not spare any attention for his surroundings. The sound of his hurried eating carried over that of the falling snow. Then, the Cougar watched as the Harbinger's ears snapped toward the direction of a sound from somewhere close by. He raised his head and stared into the white world.

The Marauder came charging out of the snow toward

him. The Harbinger hissed, his mouth and teeth red with blood. He stood on his back legs, ready to embrace the Marauder. The red cougar tackled him, and they went tumbling through the snow, tails whipping around.

They parted and stood, eyes flashing, their fur dusted white with snow. A silent moment passed as the cats stood studying each other. The Cougar had retreated, but stayed watching. The Harbinger broke the silence with a terrible growl that tore through the vast whiteness and could be heard as far away as the frozen riverbanks. So too called the Marauder, their cries mingling like threads of lightning in a storm. They stood in the tremendous silence afterwards, the snowfall seeming loud for a long, still moment. Then the Harbinger charged.

The red cougar dodged the silver cougar's tackle, swatting him away, staying beyond his reach. The Marauder's youth gave him strength. He would not tire as quickly. But he did not have the lifetime of experience behind him, as the Harbinger did. If he could avoid a fatal mistake long enough to exhaust the Harbinger, then he might prevail.

The Cougar watched them through the falling snow, two cats on their back legs, front legs wrapped around each other, each trying for the other's neck with their jaws wide open. The group of elk edged around the battling cougars. They called to their fallen brother lying in the snow who responded in his wavering voice, his blood spreading beneath him like a growing shadow.

The cougars broke off and stood, catching their breath, eyes locked. The Harbinger was not so fast to throw himself back into the fray. He saw now the Marauder was a serious challenger. The Marauder would not have chosen this moment by chance. This was the moment he had chosen at a previous time, then awaited its arrival. Now was the culmination of this effort, his patience, his will.

The Harbinger rushed in, reaching out with his claws, trying to grab hold of the younger cougar, but the Marauder jumped beyond the Harbinger's reach. In his movements, in his pursuit, the Cougar saw the Harbinger begin to tire.

The Marauder rose onto his back legs, his lean red body in the white air, the sound of his scream sending an icy breath against the Cougar's heart. He stood grappling with the Harbinger. It seemed he had an endless store of strength within him while the Harbinger was beyond his strength, slowing, growing clumsy. He made a desperate lunge, perhaps to try for the neck, his only hope, and it was the wrong move. He had stepped into this moment by his own choice. The Marauder grasped the Harbinger in his paws, caught his neck in his jaws, and crushed him, ending their struggle.

The Marauder stood, the Harbinger hanging limp from his mouth. With a sudden tremor, the Marauder shook the old cougar to ensure he was dead, and the Cougar saw by the lifeless response of limbs that his life had left him.

The Marauder released his hold on the Harbinger and the old cougar's body sagged into the snow. The red cougar walked to where the elk lay and knelt beside him. He paused a moment, catching his breath, then he sank his bite into the elk's neck. So it was neither the Cougar nor the Harbinger but the Marauder who granted the elk his death. At once the Marauder began to make feast of his claim, tearing into the elk's torso, fetching out the organs that steamed when they hit the air, blood striking his face. So he did not notice the Cougar spirit away the Harbinger's body into the darkening forest.

The group of elk parted for her as she disappeared into the snowfall. She cached the body but took with her a hindquarter, clutched between her jaws, the ragged flesh staining the snow with the whisper of blood. Darkness fell and the faint fear that her absence from the lair would provoke disaster swelled within her.

When she entered the lair, the kittens awoke at the sound of her steps, making angry mews even as they came forward and sat beside her as she began to eat. The three of them bloodied their faces in the Harbinger's flesh, eating the meat from the case that had called those very kittens forth. In this way, the kittens entered the first spring of their lives.

II
THE SMITHY

W HEN JOSEPH WAS BORN his father sent him to
live with his aunt. She had written on hearing of her
sister's death, offering to take the child. It was no
trouble, she wrote. She had three children of her own and
the youngest had finished nursing, so it was a convenient
time. While no duration for Joseph's stay was set, the offer
was made with the understanding that one day Joseph's
father would take him back.

August Brandt packed up his infant son and set off
on horseback into the cool autumn morning. As he rode
in silence, the baby slept. None who passed him on the
road would have suspected the cargo he transported, or
the assignment he was on. Only he himself thought of it
as getting rid of the child, tucking him away, out of sight.

When he saw his wife's sister for the first time he suffered a grave shock. Of course they would look alike. But he had not expected it to be such a true likeness, aside from the difference in age. The strangeness of the moment was not lost on her, and she smiled at Joseph to get past it. August handed his son to a woman he had just met and rode away, not even staying the night, knowing he would not be able to sleep in that house, wanting to distance himself from the exchange. After that, he sent money every month to soften the cost of feeding and housing the boy and to ease his conscience of the relief he felt at not having to see him.

Once he had deposited his son, he tried to forget him. He returned to work at the forge, disappearing into flame and smoke, the heat a sort of comfort. But no fire could burn away his memory of the woman who had loved him, had a child by him, and died. He was haunted by his last memory of her — hair matted with sweat, like a nest of crushed snakes; the cruel bloodstained sheets; her white face lifeless in death, inseparable from that terrible squalling in such a silence, the sound of Joseph's voice a reminder of what had been lost in order that he may live.

His neighbours came to him with trivial work, mend this, shape that, things that were not really urgent but were done for the visit, to keep him from retreating into the darkness of solitude that they seemed to know, or at least know of, and he found he did not mind. He was grateful for the company, for the distraction from his own thoughts.

Winter came and went. So too spring. He walked around a hollow man, conversing with other men, and on the inside he was nothing. Slowly, he set himself against the loss, rebuilding himself from the inside out. While his outer shape remained the same he could not erase the mark of the event upon him, like a newly exposed rock face, rugged and sharp. Enough time passed that he could separate the two in his mind, so when he thought of his son it was not of the total loss his existence signified, but of the money he must send next month.

In the next winter, the boy's aunt wrote to tell August that she was expecting and he would have to take back his son by the end of summer because she would not be able to manage the three children and a newborn and Joseph. It was not a question of money. She would gladly have kept him for though Joseph was somewhat clingy, he was quiet and easy to manage. But the boy needed to be in the care of someone who was devoted to him alone. She used these words, *devoted to him alone*, and they stuck in August's mind for three days until he wrote back to say he would collect his son before the end of the summer. He used this word intentionally, *collect*.

It was a great shift from having his son far away, in the care of a capable woman, to having him underfoot, in a home that had never yet seen a child. The thought of it filled him with certain dread. Nevertheless, he began to prepare his home for the boy. It was numb work. He swept. He tidied the clutter out from the corners. He was loaned a child's bed and bedding by his neighbour Mrs. Daniels. By the end of his preparations, he had created a space for Joseph that seemed to him bright and glaring and out of place in those solitary quarters.

Once the impassable mudways of spring had dried up in the summer heat, August set out again on horseback to collect his son, the whole way thinking of this child that was his, what he had looked like when last he saw him, a sleeping baby who had barely opened his eyes. The time between then and now, which had only been but two years, seemed like an insurmountable distance, and he felt diminished against the sudden reality he was travelling toward. Thinking of the many years ahead of him spent raising the boy threatened to overwhelm him, send him galloping home. But he pressed on. There was nothing he could do now to change his course.

When finally he saw the boy, he could not believe it was the same child he had left those two years ago. He was all limbs, aggravated by his clothes, like he was trying to wriggle out of a skin it was time to shed, red-faced and squalling—the noise of him! *A creature*, was August's first thought. But when the child stared teary-eyed upon him, his heart stalled. He had never seen his son's eyes to know that they were blue, and the colour hurt him in this initial look, that it should so resemble his mother's.

When Joseph was introduced to the man who was his father, he had no more than a handful of words and would use none of them in greeting, instead turning his head away, fighting against his aunt's hold to be let down. Later, when sat on August's knee at the supper table, Joseph was never more bewildered in his life. He was suspicious of this man, who was not the man he knew, suspicious of the food he offered, looking at his aunt who he knew to be his mother until she came and picked him up and set him on her hip. He ate the food she gave him. She was round-cheeked and her apron tied over her dress boasted the advanced state of her pregnancy — already it seemed an infant could be born — but she was no less deft in her movements; only August saw when she put her hand under her belly as she reached for a tin on the highest shelf.

Though Joseph did not fully understand the conversation between his aunt and his father, now putting on his boots, now donning a hat, he noticed that his aunt was preparing him for travel, getting a pack together, lacing his shoes, but she was not preparing herself. He became concerned, asking with his eyes the questions he did not yet have the words to manage. And all the time there was this man, standing with a grim posture, observing the proceedings, looking at him. What this look meant he did not know, but it seemed his heart concluded it for him because a desperate wail rolled out from within him.

August sat atop his horse as the boy's aunt passed Joseph up to him, his legs beating the air, a mournful bawling bubbling out of his mouth. The horse stood bewildered, shuffling as the child was sat upon its back, blinking at the sound of him. Joseph's aunt gave August a small pack containing the child's belongings and another pack containing some food for the road, then stood in the doorway of the house and watched as they rode away.

On the road, Joseph sat in front of his father on the saddle, his screaming calling out their position for all to hear. August tried to ignore the stares of the man driving his cart, the mother and her daughter on their way into town, as they passed by. The farther they went, the more determined Joseph's crying became, and August began to worry he would not be spared a single moment of this warbled screaming the entire trip back to his cabin, where he would be sole protector of the creature seated before him.

August felt awkward, unaccustomed to cooing to a child, and so tried patting the boy's back to soothe him, which seemed to him a formal, inadequate gesture.

He was very near to turning around and begging the boy's aunt to take him back, but Joseph eventually tired himself out from crying, and then was sullen for a time, making half-hearted yowls to express his outrage. Then he slept, cradled in the crook of his father's arm.

The light had fallen from its afternoon apex and shone behind him, warming his back. He looked upon the sleeping child and he did not think of the hardness of it, of the work, saw only a child alone. Just a beating heart in the delicate scaffolding of bones. For the first time since his wife's death he had a thought that was solely devoted to the boy, not shared with or haunted by the memory of his mother. August found that he did not want to look away from that sleeping face, peaceful now that he was at rest, and then he noticed how the light had fallen and suddenly they were nearing home, and he marvelled that he could have come all this way without realizing, as if he had just now awoken from a dream. Such was the spell cast when looking upon the child.

AT FIRST JOSEPH REGARDED his father with a fearful, wide-eyed look, constantly searching for his aunt.

August had to steady himself the first time Joseph called out "Mum!" in a sharp, insistent tone. He had not known that Joseph had been calling his aunt "Mum," though of course with the other children doing so it was only natural that Joseph would do the same. The first time he said it, the assuredness in his tone, shouting, "*Mum!*" as if he believed she would appear, had sent a wave of panic through August. He found it distressing that Joseph would call for her here, to the woman who would never come. He did this for some days, calling out to see if now, perhaps now, she might hear him, and when she did not appear he lapsed into a forlorn silence. August went to him, speaking softly, smoothing his hair on his brow.

The blacksmith's visitors were delighted by the boy's presence, bringing him apples, coaxing smiles by telling stories when they came to the smithy with their injured tools, even praising Joseph to August, which he found peculiar at first—*such a strong grip, what a handsome boy, he'll be taller than you for sure*—as if he were in need of hearing such things. But soon he found himself talking about the daily matters of raising a child, a subject thus far unknown to him, having rarely discussed parenthood with his visitors until now. He found in them a wealth of knowledge and he came to rely upon their experience. Entirely new ground to cover that seemed like it could never be conquered, no matter the depth or length of the conversation.

JOSEPH SAT WATCHING A hot coal, mesmerized by the bright colour, too bright for the world. August saw him looking.

"That's hot," he warned.

Joseph turned to look on him. By the angle of his glare August knew he would defy him. They shared a silent stare, each trying to will the other to concede, until the boy turned to the orange coal and before August could say another word he reached out. He did not even touch it and was burned.

Joseph wailed, furious. His accusing stare fell on his father.

"What did I tell you?" August said, but his words were lost against the boy's outraged cry.

For a moment Joseph was inconsolable, more angered at the consequences of his actions than at the pain itself, upset because he had done it to himself. A hard lesson.

His father sat him on his workbench. As one who worked with fire, he was familiar with the searing lick of flame. He reached into one of the cluttered shelves and pulled out a small metal canister, and Joseph's crying was subdued by his interest in the canister. Seeing the boy's reaction, August took care with his actions, exaggerating for the benefit of some distraction. He unscrewed the lid to reveal the honey-like substance within. Then he applied the salve to Joseph's hand, an area that seemed too small to cause such pain, and Joseph watched, unsprung tears sitting in his eyes.

When he was finished, August turned, screwing the

lid back on the canister. Joseph made an urgent sound, like the shrill call of a bird, absent of syllables, and held out his little finger.

"This one too?"

Joseph nodded. August applied the salve to this smallest of fingers. Then he took down some bandage and wrapped each of the four fingers, then wrapped the hand together, Joseph watching him work the whole time.

He gave Joseph a cup of cool water to hold. Joseph sat, teary-eyed, amazed at such a severe reprimand, resigning himself to the pain. August rubbed his back and Joseph turned to hide his face in his father's chest.

JOSEPH WAS CROUCHED NEXT to a small mound of ash. The size of the mound convinced him; this was meant for him. He reached out, trying his palm high above it to feel if it was hot. The texture was unlike anything he had ever felt before, so fine it was barely there. He picked up a handful, let it sift through his fingers, saw the white stain left on his skin, and knew what he had to do.

August noticed the silence, felt a prickling on the back of his neck, and the sudden urge to check on Joseph bloomed in his mind. He found the boy crouched by the garbage out back, playing in a mound of ash, his face, arms, even his clothes smeared with ash, like it was natural to do so.

Joseph turned to see his father towering behind him and read the expression on his face. He made to run but August grabbed him and carried him, like a sack under one arm, to the pump at the side of the smithy, where he sat him under a stream of cold water, washing the ash off him with a rag. Joseph unhappy, shivering and yowling.

SOON ENOUGH JOSEPH WAS sent to school. He took to this confinement with a sort of morbid glee, as an opportunity to torment those condemned to suffer alongside him. A strange mania came over him. He found he could not contain himself. It was too much to overcome, this temptation to antagonize his classmates and his teacher. Finally, only the thought of his father's anger at being pulled away from work was enough to curtail Joseph's unnatural urge to torment others, and keep him in the realm of good behaviour.

After class, Joseph was put to work to keep him out of trouble. He was given jobs like fetching water, sweeping out the ash, stacking firewood, until August's work was done for the day. Joseph spent many afternoons watching his father at work in the smithy, the explosion of sparks under the blows of the hammer as they landed in the hay underfoot, languished, then died; plumes of steam as blazing metal was cast into water; the subterranean glow of heated metal upon his father's face, intent on his work, shaping the glowing material into whatever he was thinking, mending tools so they were restored, creating tools as if by sheer will, summoned not by fire and water but with his thoughts.

When August had first arrived, the smithy was little more than a shed next to a single-room dwelling, just a man and an anvil, shaping and mending. At that time the blacksmith lived down the road from the cluster of dwellings, the general store, and the post office that made up the town. The smithy was separated from these buildings by a swath of bush yet to be cleared, but every year the edge of town crept closer, like a shelf of ice on a slow migration.

By the time August took over as blacksmith, the edge of town was visible through the trees. The smithy had been given its own structure and there was space enough to accommodate two men at work, though there remained the single anvil. There were two long work tables, one against each wall, a central fire, a rack of rough shelves on the back wall for tools. A constantly replenished pile of wood was stacked outside the smithy and beyond that the frame of an old cart sat rotting in the long grass.

The smithy held less and less interest for Joseph as he grew older. His thoughts strayed into the forest. August had noticed Joseph's disinterest in playing with other children, his preference for private acts of destruction, and he worried the boy might be violent. He tried to encourage him.

"Where's your friend Lewis today?"

Joseph stood with his shoulders drawn up, a familiar pose, refusing to answer.

"Alright, stay where you can hear me," August said, meaning for Joseph to stay where he could hear the pounding of the forge so he might find his way back in case he got lost.

Joseph's penchant for venturing into the forest often provoked a familiar warning from the townsfolk.

"Don't stray too far. The Old Woman might be stalking about."

Joseph did not know when or how he first learned of the Old Woman. His knowledge of her had come into the world with him and had grown as he had. She was spoken of only in hushed voices, as if she might hear any talk of her that was said too loudly. The forest was a dark and cursed place, a malevolent presence in all their lives, suited to and occupied by the Old Woman, that fabled panther who stalked the wilderness surrounding their town.

She was known by many names: cougar, panther, mountain lion, catamount, vermin, scourge. How she had been named "the Old Woman" was as much a mystery as the panther herself. Who had dubbed her so was also unknown. Presumably someone who knew the sight of panthers, which was rare for they were rarely seen, and who knew her to be female, and elderly in years. No matter where the name came from, this was how she had come to be known.

There were countless tales from men who had found themselves alone in the forest and experienced the feeling of being watched. Once the Old Woman had leapt into their thoughts they could not banish her until they were safely behind closed doors, staring out their windows, so unsettled by the notion that she might be there.

"The Old Woman catches children to eat and if she catches you, we shall never see you again."

August had cautioned the men against filling his son's head with such nonsense, not wanting Joseph to be influenced by what he considered an irrational fear. The forest was only to be feared as much as rain, or lightning. He disapproved of spreading false attitudes around one such as Joseph, who might take them to heart. There were real reasons a child should not go wandering into the forest alone: there were indeed dangerous creatures to beware, the chance of injury from tripping on upturned roots, or plants that caused the skin to blister by a mere touch, and the very real possibility of getting lost in the indecipherable wilderness.

"Oh, just a bit of teasing," was usually the reply. But there were those who would lower their voice, look Joseph in the eye, and say, "It's a fair warning, mind you. I've seen her."

Stories from men who had seen the Old Woman were highly regarded. Some men had seen her outright, that was clear. Based on the similar details shared by separate speakers, the Old Woman's appearance and a few of her attributes were solidified in the minds of the townspeople. Then there were the stories from men who believed they had seen her but could not confirm the notion due to poor weather conditions, the mischievous nature of shadow, or impairment. These stories were still listened to but given less regard. Finally, there were those who had not seen her and, even so, claimed to have been in her presence. These stories were listened to but generally disregarded.

When it came to her appearance, there was some general agreement. She wore a jagged scar across the left side of her face. Her fur was a tawny, golden colour. She was small in stature and this was only mentioned to indicate that she was indeed female. But when it came to describing her abilities, never had a more controversial subject been up for debate. On the extent of her power, there was little to no consensus. She had been accused of everything from the failure of crops, to bad weather, and even stranger things: sickness, rashes, preoccupation of the mind.

Once Joseph had stepped into the trees behind the smithy, he felt as if he had travelled deep into the forest. The sun streamed down through the green canopy overhead. The covering of old leaves and shed pine needles muffled his footsteps. He had spent many afternoons climbing trees, investigating the highest branches. He had fallen out of trees, and hidden the incident, and been found out. The trunks of fallen trees were sites of investigation, dusted with moss, as if the forest floor were growing over them, reclaiming the material at an imperceptible rate.

He crawled beneath the low-hanging branches of an evergreen. He pulled a brigade of army men from out of his pocket and set them up into two fronts, pulverizing them against one another until they lay bleeding and moaning on the battlefield — all but one man, who remained to continue the fight against an invisible horde. He crawled out from beneath the branches, aiming an imaginary rifle, and played as himself a soldier, shooting enemy men as they came into his sights, calling out the sounds of the bullets with his own voice as they tore through the air. He was greatly proficient at this killing, and it assured him that one day he would be a great hunter. For a long time he forgot himself in this game, the number of dead lost to him, running deeper and deeper into the forest, along narrow paths, through dense bush, cutting down his enemies with ease. Eventually the frenzy of his blood-lust passed and he walked, breathing deeply, gazing at the endless variation of growth all around him.

Then he noticed the slant of light through the trees and knew it was past the time his father would be finished work. He looked around himself, suddenly aware that he did not know which way to go back. He chose the opposite direction he had been walking in and started back, but after a few steps he did not feel confident it was the right way. He walked faster, jogging now so that he might get back before his father worried. But as he went, he knew the distance he had come was greater than the distance he could cover in that short a time and now the light was growing dark.

Soon he was running outright, without thought, hoping in some way that it would bring him home. The trees blurred into a single plane, the earth into another, and in between all the impenetrable air, and he was hurtling through, trying to get to the end, but it just went on and he found nothing familiar, nothing that told him where he was, and even so he could not stop himself from running.

Finally, he stumbled to a stop. It hurt to breathe and he stayed, hands on his knees, gasping against the pain. He began to walk, a great urgency to return to some place familiar, to return to his father, overwhelming him, but no tree, no rise of land looked familiar to him and the light was growing darker all the time.

Though he had been warned against becoming lost, he could not recall what he was meant to do if he became lost. The shame of this failure burned on his cheeks, for while he knew the failing was not totally his own, he also knew that he had done this to himself, however unknowingly. A cruel mistake. He did not know what to do by himself. He had never been completely on his own before, and now the danger of being alone in the forest was becoming all too clear. It was not a place that excused mindlessness; certainly no place for a child alone.

He went on through the darkening forest, around him the day's silence giving way to the chirping of crickets, the transit of squirrels, the calls of nightbirds, a cold, distant version of their daytime kin. The trees came to an end, and Joseph entered a clearing of long grass where some trees stood in clusters, thick trunks, low-hanging branches brushing the top of the tall grass. He thought if he climbed the branches of one of those trees, he might be able to spot a house by the smoke coming from its chimney. He would be saved. They would certainly help a child lost in the forest. He hoped they might give him something to eat because, thinking of food, he realized he was hungry.

As he waded toward the tree, the land dipped and the grass reached over his head. He picked his way through the bushes at the base of the tree. Standing on one of the tree's roots, he reached up, then hooked his leg around a branch, and hauled himself up. He reached for the next branch and pulled himself through, scraping his forearms, his knees through his jeans. He looked out around him.

All he saw were the trees surrounding the small clearing, nothing beyond. He searched the sky for the sign of smoke that would lead him home but found none. He felt remote, as if he had travelled beyond the reach of other men. He could not believe that with all the men there were, he could so quickly come to a place without them. He had believed that his home, the town where he lived, was enormous, but now he saw that it was all so small. A small domain upon the vast face of the earth.

He felt a sinking feeling, as if he were falling through the earth, that he could not ignore. Sitting alone in the tree, Joseph did not know what he should do next. He stayed, watching the clearing below, the sun sinking into the horizon. A breeze rose up and ran over the grass, shifting it in waves. When Joseph decided he should get down from the tree, he remembered the Old Woman, and then he wondered if she was there, hiding in the grass, in perfect silence, waiting for him to wander into her reach. And as he watched the grass shifting in the breeze, he believed he saw where it did not flow with the rest, where it was pushed aside by the weight of a body, and he believed she must be there, wading toward him, hidden from his eyes.

He tried to convince himself it was not true; there was nothing lying in wait for him. But each time he decided to get down from the tree, his will faltered and the fear that she might be there, waiting, rose up within him, rooting him in place. So he stayed on and on in the tree, trying and failing to will himself down, until the warmth of the sunset fled and the air grew chill around him.

A dim haze settled over the clearing. The sound of crickets rose like a sudden rain. The cry of an owl sent his heart crashing against his chest, triggering a slow dread that did not dissipate but grew as the night closed around him. The chill in the air deepened as the sky grew darker.

The mosquitoes came out in earnest and made a feast of him. Joseph tried to hide his neck, rounding his shoulders, squishing his head from side to side, but it was no use. The mosquitoes were too many, a horde of them devoted solely to him; and now, aside from being alone and afraid, he became unhappy. He could no longer make out the line of trees surrounding the clearing. He felt truly small, lost against the darkness, and he began to cry. He clung to the trunk of the tree to know that it remained, his sobs carrying through the night, but there being no one to hear him there seemed no point in it. Once his tears were spent, he sat, despondent, listening into the night.

He dried his eyes on his sleeve. When he looked up, he was shocked at the change in the landscape. Above, the sky was crowded with stars. By the dim light of the stars he saw his hands, the grass below, the treeline around him. The forest was just the same, drained of its light, but unaltered, merely in shadow. The wind sighed through the leaves on the trees, and he listened, thinking into the space around him. The sound of such an open space impressed him. It was not empty; the opposite. There was an indomitable presence all around him, too large to be seen. He felt this for the first time.

Then he heard the calling.

At first it seemed like the faraway cry of some strange beast, and he hoped it would stay away. It came long and mournful, unintelligible. He could not imagine what it was, but he watched into the forest, waiting to see. A trail of ghostly orbs travelled through the trees. As he focused on these points of light in the distance, the forest he had been looking at a moment ago collapsed and his dread returned to him like wings folding over his body. He was frightened of the approaching beast as its calls grew louder, and he sat waiting, astonished, not knowing what nocturnal event was unfolding before him.

As it drew near, Joseph saw that the trail of lights was a procession of men carrying lanterns, calling into the night. Yet still he did not move or make a sound, for he did not know who they were, or what their purpose might be, searching through the forest, calling some command into the night.

Harsh lantern light fell upon him and he squinted against it. The lantern bearer, concealed by the corona, yelled to the others: "Here! We got him!"

There was a growing commotion as the men converged, all bearing lanterns, until the brightness rose to an unnatural pitch, and Joseph covered his eyes to shield himself from the glare. Then someone grabbed hold of him, and by the smell, the manner of the touch, he knew it was his father. His heart seemed to leap into his throat so that he was unable to speak, only reach out and grasp his father around his neck. Secondary to the relief he felt, in the back of his mind he marvelled that his father was tall enough to pluck him down from the branches of the tree that he had believed to be so high.

His father set him on the ground.

"Why'd you run away?" he demanded.

Joseph looked around at the huddle of stern-faced men looming over him.

He shook his head. "I didn't—"

"Why didn't you come back?" His father's panic had still not faded from his voice.

"I don't know," Joseph said, somehow unable to explain what had happened.

August saw then the boy's pained expression, his shoulders drawn up like he was shivering, and thought of him having sat half the night in the cold dark, all alone, and his anger faded, his dread forgotten.

"It's alright," he said, picking Joseph up and carrying him away.

Murmured conversation drifted up from the men as they wound their way through the dark forest, their bodies yawning toward sleep. The shadows of the trees were made manifold by the parade of lanterns into the darkness, throwing movement into the otherwise still forest. The trees themselves glared white in the harsh light, the leaves shifting yet remaining static. Joseph watched the forest's moving shadows but he fell asleep long before they reached home and was not at all disturbed when his father laid him in bed, took off his shoes, and pulled the covers over him. He smoothed the hair away from Joseph's brow. The boy's expression was peaceful now that he was asleep. August sat watching him and fell into an exhausted trance as if his mind had already wandered to sleep. Then he shook his head and, with a bewildered sigh, rose and turned down the light.

III

NEIGHBOUR

➤➤

T HE COUGAR AWOKE, THE light at the opening of
the cave telling her it was daybreak. Quietly, she rose
and headed outside. In sleep her son and daughter
readjusted position, so they were cuddled up next to each
other, unaware of their mother's departure.

Her cubs sired by the Harbinger had begun to mimic
hunting behaviour, stalking and pouncing on each other,
wrestling until one caught the other in their jaws. Her
daughter was a graceful, watchful cougar. While not yet
capable of hunting on her own, her skills were there, waiting to blossom. Her son was sensitive to noise, his ears
twitching at every sound, ducking his head as if to avoid
a bird in flight. She had yet to see capable skill in him, but
he was young. There was still time.

When the Marauder usurped the Harbinger's territory, the Cougar had believed he might seek her out and try to destroy the Harbinger's cubs, as had been done to his, so she had been vigilant. She changed lairs at whim, keeping her cubs on the move, careful that her mark remained unseen, her scent undetected, no evidence of her passage left behind. Sometimes she abandoned entire hunts if she felt she might be exposed to the possibility of attack, determined to protect the lives of these two cubs. But the Marauder never appeared and as the cubs' spots began to fade, so faded her concern that the Marauder would appear seeking blood.

The Cougar sat blinking in the sunlight, watching the trees hitching in the breeze, their leaves hissing and glinting in the sun. She set off into the trees, toward the mountains. The sun had reached its peak by the time she climbed into the cliffs. From among the rocky heights, she looked on the forest roof stretching into the distance, the tops of the trees like clouds in an inverted sky.

As she sat watching the forest below, she spotted a stream of smoke rising into the blue sky. It seemed unnatural to her, this single column of smoke in the clear air. Her curiosity was too great to be ignored. The Cougar picked her way down the mountainside and into the trees. The daytime sounds in the forest around her, the call of birds, the whine of cicadas, went on uninterrupted as she walked through the trees, careful, silent. In the sunlight, the bright green forest looked almost unfamiliar, a place she sometimes dreamed about.

By evening, the stream of smoke had disappeared from

the sky. Instead, mountainous golden clouds rode by overhead. Staring up at their changing shapes, the Cougar forgot her fruitless search. The cubs would awaken soon. She swallowed her curiosity and returned home.

On the riverbank she stopped and sat watching the water, listening to the sound as it rushed past. The trees behind her hissed in the breeze and for a time she lost herself to thinking about the stream of smoke, what may have caused it, but she could not imagine a reasonable explanation and she considered this a bad sign.

On the other side of the river, some branches shuddered with movement and the Cougar awoke from her trance. She crouched to the ground; the wind was running against her so she knew her scent would not betray her. She strained to hear any sound over the passage of the water.

A thin blond cougar stepped out of the trees, scanning the riverbank. The Cougar watched as the other stood listening for a long moment, studying the scene before her. Once she was satisfied, she sauntered down to the river's edge, leaned down, and drank. After lapping up a few mouthfuls, she turned and looked into the trees. The branches twitched as, one by one, four full-grown cubs emerged from the trees and walked down to sit beside their mother to drink from the river.

The Cougar had never seen one of her neighbours before. She was modestly amazed. The skill required to provide for four cubs seemed supernatural to her. The blond cougar was small, but even from this distance the Cougar saw that she was nothing but muscle and bone. Her cubs were of a similar size so the five of them might be mistaken for a pack of cougars, roaming the forest, terrorizing the deer population.

Her Neighbour looked across the river to where the Cougar hid in the bare bushes, and though she knew she was concealed, her fur bristled at the touch of that direct gaze. She watched, eyes wide, as the blond cougar stood scanning the far shore, sniffing the air. Then her Neighbour turned and headed back into the trees. The four cubs followed their mother, entering the forest at the same spot they had come out of, in the very footsteps their mother had made. Once the branches they had disturbed stood still, only their paw prints in the mud remained as evidence of their fleeting presence.

The Cougar rose and set off through the trees. As she made her way back to her lair, she thought of that blond cougar. The sight of her Neighbour and her four cubs drinking at the riverbank remained with her, their five heads lowered to the water. She felt an unreasonable desire to turn and pursue this cougar through the forest, to see her up close, to watch her hunt. She wanted to know what quality she possessed that allowed her to be so successful.

By the time the Cougar returned to her lair it was dusk, the sun had set, but there was still light in the sky. When she entered the cave her son lifted his head, eyes barely open. The Cougar settled down next to him. The cub turned over and went back to sleep with a short sigh.

A S THE COUGAR ROAMED the night, sometimes she would remember her first brood, taken from her so suddenly. Her cubs now were older than the ones gone and while she knew this should be satisfying enough she felt the weight of those lost kittens dragging behind her as she made her nightly stalk.

The Cougar returned to the place where she had seen her Neighbour drinking at the river's edge and entered the trees in the very spot her Neighbour had. She stepped through the undergrowth, imagining these were the exact steps her Neighbour had taken. If she walked where her Neighbour had walked she would see what the blond cougar had seen.

She knew it was not wise to seek her Neighbour out. Though she was careful with her movements it was impossible to leave no sign of her presence. Another cougar would know how to look for these signs. But still she went on, pulled by a curiosity she could not ignore, however unwise it might be.

She slid through dense bush, silent, then waited within the trees on the stony banks of a stream. Aside from the wet stone and the mud, the Cougar smelled something that gave her pause. The scent was familiar, yet unknown to her. She knew it was her Neighbour and a secret thrill washed through her.

The Cougar saw the claw marks dug into the papery bark of a silver birch. The claw marks were recent, sending the scent of the birch into the air, and beneath that the earthy scent of her Neighbour. The Cougar stood on her back legs, leaned close to the claw marks in the tree trunk, and sniffed. She breathed in deeply, trying to memorize this specific smell, this mark. The Cougar rubbed her cheek against the tree so that the smell might be transferred to her.

There was another tree, scratched and scented, and the Cougar went to it and stood on her back legs, put her paws on the tree where her Neighbour would have, and breathed in the elusive smell. She lowered her head to the ground and sniffed the paw prints. Her Neighbour had stood here, walked through the trees to stand here, marking this tree with her scent. The Cougar rubbed her nose into the ground, that she might always know the scent, and by knowing it, know something of her Neighbour's life in the forest.

She glanced into the surrounding trees, her face stained with earth, then she set off, back the way she had come.

THE COUGAR STEPPED OUT of her lair, followed a moment later by son and daughter. The bright sunlight stunned them. They looked around, blinking, sniffing the air. The Cougar rubbed her cheek against their heads, first one then the other. She would not bring them far, ever wary of the possibility of attack. The cubs followed her along a narrow trail through long grass. A mild wind brushed through the grass and the cubs flicked their ears back and forth, trying to discern the source of the sound.

A gust of breeze floated some dandelion spores across their path. The cubs watched them on the air and murmured between themselves. The Cougar strayed into the long grass. Then she stopped and listened. It took her a moment to discern the smaller sound, the tiny scrap and skitter of mice scurrying to their burrows within the grass. She could hear their footsteps, the perfect size for cubs to practise their hunting skills.

Her cubs stood watching her as she paused mid-stride and waited. She stood still for so long they grew curious as to what it was they were meant to be watching. But they did not move or make a sound.

The Cougar pounced on the earth close by her feet. She was so fast the cubs flinched at the sudden movement. When she faced them they saw the brown mouse hanging by its tail from her teeth. The cubs looked to the ground for more mice, intent on what was hidden in the grass. The Cougar crunched the mouse between her teeth in two bites and swallowed.

Their first attempts were unsuccessful, they made far too much noise, they pounced too soon, but it was only after these failed attempts that they learned how to antici-pate the mice. The Cougar's daughter pounced but her jump was short and the mouse escaped. The cub searched her paws to ensure the mouse was not concealed therein. When she jumped again she jumped beyond the mouse, catching it beneath her oversized paws and snapping it up in her teeth. The cub chewed and licked her chops. She looked over to her mother and squawked.

When her son caught his first mouse he carried it to his mother and laid it down before her. The mouse still lived and as soon as it was laid down it tried to dart into the grass but the Cougar caught it beneath her paw, crushing it into the earth so it would not escape when she lifted her foot up. Then she rubbed her cheek against the cub's head and he set off to catch another mouse.

The Cougar watched, quiet, mindful of the forest at their backs, as the sun simmered across the sky and the breeze sent a wave of dandelion spores through the air and into the forest beyond.

THAT NIGHT THE COUGAR dreamed she was staring into the river where her cub had drowned but it was not the same river as the one that ran through her valley. The surface was smooth instead of flowing, reflecting the black, starless sky above and the treeline on the other side, and for some reason the Cougar was afraid to look into it.

She saw herself walk into the river, then she was beneath the water. Dark fish swam past her and she tried to catch them in her mouth, but she moved slowly while the fish were able to dart away. When she jumped through the water and her feet hit the bottom, great circular clouds of sand rose outward and dissipated around her.

She emerged on the other side and when she looked back across the river she saw that it was a lake, wide and deep. This confused her and she did not understand how she could have travelled so great a distance in such a short time.

Beside her the Cougar saw her mother leading four pale cubs, the offspring of her Neighbour, down to the water to drink. They stood in a cluster on the shore, their tongues lapping at the clear water.

Then she awoke.

A GAIN THE COUGAR HAD strayed into her Neighbour's territory, her curiosity compelling her with a strength she was powerless against. If she did not give in to her desire to investigate, to seek her Neighbour out, she knew she would be tormented by that unfulfilled desire.

As she walked through the dark trees, the half-moon rising overhead, the Cougar smelled a familiar scent on the air and she knew it was her Neighbour. By now she knew the scent well, having smelled it on the claw marks the blond cougar left on tree trunks throughout her territory. The Cougar stood considering, torn between moving on and giving in to her curiosity. It was a short idle. She went into the trees to seek out the source of her Neighbour's scent.

At the edge of a clearing between the forest and a rock face, the Cougar found a massive buck slumped on the ground. Covered by leaf-bare branches, its rump had been eaten from and its torso gaped open, a dark yawn, where her Neighbour had reached in and made her feast. As the Cougar sniffed over the earth she detected a scent other than her Neighbour's, and she found the paw prints of cubs muddling the paw prints of that blond cougar. She realized her Neighbour had a new brood to care for. There were two, perhaps three cubs, their tracks overlapping so it was difficult to discern between them. They were not yet old enough to hunt for themselves, but had stayed, watching from the trees, as their mother carried out her grisly work.

The Cougar sat away from the body, studying the site where the buck lay, the grass beneath it, the placement of the branches, absorbing all the details so she might recall them later. The carcass still had meat left to offer. No doubt her Neighbour would return.

The buck's head lay at an unnatural angle, its mouth open, tongue lolling out. Its eyes no longer liquid black, now glazed over, like a skin of ice had formed over them despite this warm, breezy night.

It was dangerous to be in the vicinity of her Neighbour's cache—where her scent was found that blond cougar was certain to be close by—but the Cougar could not pass up a chance to study her Neighbour's mark. She had not seen the blond cougar since that evening on the riverbank, only signs, only hints of her in the forest, her scent, her paw prints, marks of her passage.

As she sat considering the cache, the Cougar saw a ghostly vision of her Neighbour upon the back of the great buck, jaws clamped onto his neck, her front paws wrapped around his head, while the deer danced in panic, trying to dislodge her hold. Her claws had raked the hide on his back, where she hung on to him. The Cougar saw these marks now, dark in the moonlight.

Her Neighbour must have ambushed the buck from the branches of a nearby tree. Her tracks were nowhere to be found, as if she spent her bouts of waiting in the air. The Cougar marvelled at this feat. She had tried to follow her Neighbour's trail through the forest, but she could never stay on it for long, her path was so erratic, her habits unpredictable, even more paranoid than the Cougar, it seemed.

The Cougar searched the trees surrounding the cache for a good vantage point. She sauntered over to a massive evergreen and leapt up into the branches, out of sight. Once nestled in her perch, her view was partially obscured by the needled branches, but she could still make out the clearing below, the body of the buck.

The night rolled by and the Cougar remained in her perch, unmoving, awaiting the approach of that blond cougar whom she so desired to see. The dampness in the air vanished as the sun approached. The light jostled the sleeping creatures of the forest from their slumber. Birds roused and sat chirping in the trees. Cicadas whined through the air — no surer sign of day. The buck lay as it had all night. As sunlight inched across the clearing, a mouse arrived to pick at the bugs that had begun to crawl over the body.

The Cougar fell into a light sleep, wherein she believed she was awake. With her eyes closed she saw the clearing before her, the buck covered in leafless branches. There was no sound. Even the trees, though shifted by the breeze, were mute. Then she saw the sudden wingspan of an owl, massive, white wings outstretched. The blazing gold eyes standing out against the quiet trees.

The Cougar jolted awake, the daylight around her and the sound of the leaves in the breeze greeting her all at once. The clearing lay as before. Her heartbeat stammered in her chest. She let out a deep sigh.

The day grew long and then it was dusk. The crickets rose as darkness fell. The Cougar thought of her Neighbour, somewhere in the trees, waiting, likewise experiencing the growing night, and she wondered then if her Neighbour was thinking of her. As the moon climbed into the sky, the Cougar's patience came to an end. She stood, feeling the hours of stillness in her limbs, and stretched, first her front legs, then her hind legs. She jumped out of the evergreen and landed on the leaf-covered ground in silence. A single branch shuddered then settled as evidence of her passing.

The Cougar sat looking at the buck. She knew the reason her Neighbour had not appeared was because of her presence. She had known of her somehow, known she was there, waiting.

The smell of the meat on the carcass set her mouth watering. As she stood, in her Neighbour's paw prints, she felt her Neighbour's presence, as if her eyes were upon her even now. The Cougar cast a hesitant glance into the trees, searching for the blond cougar. But the forest stood silent, revealing nothing.

SHE RETURNED THE NEXT day in daylight. The remaining meat on the buck had been eaten and the remnants had not been cached. Already scavengers had been at the deer's eyes, into the cavity of his body. Before the body, her Neighbour had left a pile of earth, scraped into a mound with her claws, scented with her urine.

The Cougar thought about how it was she who had been hunted as she sat in the evergreen awaiting her Neighbour, believing herself to be secret. She marvelled that her Neighbour had such a mastery of silence and patience. There was a depth to her understanding of the forest that the Cougar had yet to reach.

A dragonfly hovered above the eviscerated remains of the buck. It flew toward the Cougar's head. The Cougar snapped at it with her teeth. The dragonfly reeled and hovered away, into the great expanse of air. The Cougar watched it go, growing smaller and smaller against the blue sky.

THE NEXT NIGHT THE Cougar pushed aside the thoughts of her Neighbour that ambushed her as soon as she awoke. This night she would take the cubs with her to watch her hunt. She would carry on with her life, ignoring her interest in her Neighbour. She would retreat into the forest, devote herself to silence. She would become a ghost.

She led her cubs out of the lair, bracing herself for a night of hunger, for though the cubs might be attentive they would surely be loud, scaring away any astute prey until they learned the brutal necessity of silence.

They had not walked five steps from the lair when the Cougar smelled a familiar scent on the air and stopped, heart thudding in her chest.

There were fresh claw marks in the bark of the silver birch. The marks were deep, aggressive, the bright new wood shining through, even in the dark light of dusk. The Cougar stepped up to inspect the mark, her Neighbour's scent reaching into her nostrils.

A short distance ahead was another tree scratched bare of its bark at the height of a cougar standing on her back legs, working at the wood with her claws. The Cougar followed this mark and soon saw another. She stopped. Her cubs stood behind her, unaware of the marks on the trees or what they indicated.

Her Neighbour's scent on the air was so powerful the Cougar could taste it in her mouth. Finding these marks so close to her lair, it worried her that the blond cougar might know where she and her cubs slept.

She should have left her Neighbour's cache alone, she should not have investigated her marks and drawn attention to herself, she should have stayed hidden in the forest where her Neighbour would never disturb her. They could have lived their entire lives separate, never having seen each other. Now her Neighbour knew of her and there was no erasing that knowledge. She was not a secret in the forest and this made her feel unhappy as well as unsafe.

Her daughter yowled impatiently and the Cougar snapped out of her thoughts.

She would lead them away from these marks, away from her Neighbour and her territorial warnings, deeper into the forest, where they would be hidden from that blond cougar's watchful eye. But even after they had crossed the stream and were heading toward the waterfall in the cliff where she had first entered the valley, she believed her Neighbour would be able to read the earth of her steps and find her wherever she was.

T HE COUGAR AWOKE IN darkness. Her son and daughter slept in a pile of limbs atop her. They had grown to nearly their full size and their weight was heavy as she pulled herself out from the tangle of their embrace.

A dry wind prowled the night forest. The cool air was a welcome contrast to the close confines of the lair, the humidity of sleeping bodies. She felt the heat of the day still locked within the earth. The smell of pine and sap carried on the wind. She saw a sudden flash of lightning. Her heart beat four times before the rumble of thunder sounded. Far away a storm was raging.

The wind pummelled the treetops overhead. The conversation of leaves was loud enough to drown out any sound the Cougar made as she ran through the night. Lightning flashed and the Cougar squinted against the sudden wash of light. The trees bloomed white, the leaves and earth drained of colour. Then the forest faded again into darkness.

What a strange thing lightning was, its whole life in a single moment. Or perhaps the lightning was an extension of a larger whole, each arm that reached down to the earth a part of the same, single being that lived for a storm, then died.

Roaming the chaotic forest, it seemed to the Cougar that only she and the wind were out tonight, and she would not find any prey unless the wind died down. She walked through the loud night, listening to the trees.

Then the Cougar smelled a familiar scent on the tumult of the wind.

Lightning flashed again and as the glare faded the Cougar saw the black tip of a tail slipping into the shadows.

The wind was carrying scents all around her. Such a wind meant her scent might be available for her Neighbour to smell. The Cougar knew this and she followed anyway, unable to stop herself.

The wind howled through the trees. As lightning revealed the forest once more, the Cougar caught sight of her Neighbour through the trees. The blond cougar sat absolutely still. The wind around her, the shaking trees overhead; nothing distracted her, as if the forest were in the depths of calm. The Cougar waited, mimicking her posture, to be as still as she was, though she felt the urge to stretch, to glance into the surrounding bushes, to lick her shoulder. Her tail flicked in agitation which she tried without success to calm.

By the brief flash of lightning the Cougar watched her Neighbour rise onto her hind legs and then she was gone. The Cougar was amazed by with the suddenness of the movement. She had been looking right at her and still she had missed it.

The Cougar crept to the place where her Neighbour had disappeared. She leapt between two trees, almost on top of the eviscerated remains of a hare. The carcass was not yet cool but the hide had been pulled back, the meat torn out, and the remains left to the scavengers.

The Cougar glanced around but there was no sign of her Neighbour. She walked along through the wind-torn forest. Having hunted, and eaten, her Neighbour must be on her way back to her lair. How thrilling to have encountered her in the forest, to have seen her as she hunted, to witness this in secret. Her heart was beating hard as she went on, aimless, through the trees. She could not get the memory of the blond cougar out of her mind. As if she had glimpsed something forbidden.

Thunder boomed overhead. Lightning lit up the night forest and the Cougar saw her Neighbour sitting before her, no more than a leap away. Her pale face and chest were bright with blood, the rest of her washed white by the lightning. In the flash the Cougar saw the scars that crossed her Neighbour's arms, and her eyes, burning gold, levelled at her.

The Cougar jumped back before the forest returned to darkness. She crashed through the trees, ripping off branches, as she chewed up the earth in her haste to retreat. Lightning flashed and she almost feared her Neighbour would be revealed again, before her, leaping toward her from out of the shadows. The Cougar ran until her legs grew heavy and her breath was ragged, though she knew she was not pursued.

She stopped by the river's edge and stood, panting.

How her Neighbour had glared! She must have known all along that the Cougar was following her and she had lain in wait for her, to show herself to the Cougar so she would know that her watching had not been secret at all, in fact was known about and considered clumsy, to remind her that only a superior cougar could stalk and hunt in secret.

The blond cougar had stood like some part of the tree, like one able to take on the properties of anything around her and project them so she could blend into her surroundings until the time came for her to announce herself. The scars on her arms meant she had fought, and been the one to come out living.

Only once inside her lair, next to those still-sleeping cubs, did the Cougar's fear began to subside. She lay awake, eyes open to the darkness, thinking of her Neighbour. The image of her bloodstained face burned in the Cougar's mind.

Overhead, thunder rushed in like a great wave rolling through the forest. Beside her the cubs slept soundly, their hearts beating one after another, a sure and steady rhythm.

T HE COUGAR SAT IN the naked grey trees, her cubs beside her. They knew silence was integral to their success, and while they had yet to master the art of stillness — yawning, licking a patch of fur they had forgotten earlier — they did their best to imitate their mother, her grave countenance. But even the Cougar battled the urge to stand and go stalking through the night, to pursue her prey rather than lie in wait for it.

Though she had not seen her Neighbour since that windy spring night, she had to remain vigilant to ensure their paths did not cross. Once her Neighbour's brood made the switch to meat, her Neighbour was out hunting almost daily. Training the cubs to hunt, despite the constant fear of encountering her Neighbour in the forest, had been a difficult task. Wherever she smelled the blond cougar's scent upon the air, she turned back. At least the forest warned her of the other's presence. Sometimes it seemed impossible to avoid her, and the Cougar began to suspect that her Neighbour might be seeking her out, in order to push her away.

So the Cougar hunted during daylight, on unfamiliar grounds, sitting and waiting in the rain, sleeping in the inadequate shade. Often her cubs would nap beside her, unable to maintain an interest during these long waits.

But as the chill of autumn arrived, they seemed to develop more patience, sitting beside her, watching and listening, though still not stalking or pouncing.

Having lain in wait all night, the Cougar noticed when the light shifted a degree and knew the sun was about to rise. The sun came into the sky like a blade of light, and the forest awoke around her. The Cougar grew weary of the brightness. It sent a drowsiness into her which she fought to ignore. She sat still, the chill breath of the wind rifling through the trees. The Cougar set her thoughts on waiting for just this morning. This was how her cubs would spend their waking hours. Let them see the patience they would need for the occupation that would employ them until death.

Sounds of the approaching deer carried to her on the wind. They had wandered all through the night so that they might come to her now. She tried to calm the beating of her heart. Now she could see them between the grey trees. Three males wandering the forest. Their coats had thickened in preparation for the snows of winter. One of the deer had already shed his antlers, giving him a somewhat naked appearance, but the Cougar knew this made him no less dangerous.

The Cougar waited. The deer took their time, grazing over the earth with the thoroughness of one with endless patience and nowhere else to be. She listened to their slow steps through the dry grass. The sun cast the deers' shadows long beside them. The fallen leaves gathered on the ground were bright yellow, the perfect shade to hide three cougars in their golden coats.

The deer stood at ease, poaching a bush.

When the Cougar burst from her scant cover a host of sparrows erupted from the branches overhead. Two of the deer reared and ran for the trees. The third deer was trapped in the Cougar's jaws. His legs snapped out, trying to gain footing, but the Cougar was resolved. Her jaws clamped tight around his neck, her front paws wrapped around his shoulders, she stared ahead with a wild, wide-eyed stare. Her determination was so ruthless she would wait until nightfall, she would wait as long as it took, for the buck to give up his life to her. However much he wanted his life, she wanted it more. She adjusted her bite, trying to find that place in his neck which would sever the connection between his body and his life.

Still, the buck twisted. The Cougar held out, making an immovable weight of herself. She would not let go now, not so close to taking the life she needed. Finally, she sunk her teeth in deeper, wedging apart the bones protecting that vital passage, and the deer's body went limp.

The Cougar opened her mouth and the deer fell to the ground with a soft thud. Her breath was revealed by the sunlight as it rose from her mouth in ragged plumes, into the cold air. She drove her claw down the deer's belly, the secret smell setting her mouth to water. She began to eat the deer as she heard her cubs creeping out of the underbrush, her heart beating thick in her chest.

From out of the corner of her eye the Cougar spotted movement. She looked up, a thread of blood hanging from her mouth.

Her Neighbour appeared from out of the scant yellow

forest, as if called by the Cougar herself. The Cougar was torn between noticing her Neighbour's skill and noticing her terrifying appearance.

The blond cougar growled and the Cougar hissed, her eyes drawn to the dark scars on her forelegs. Her Neighbour approached, head low to the ground, the white silhouette around her eyes like a crane flapping its wings, rising from a bog. She was thin, muscle and bone, all sharp edges. She walked with a confidence, a knowledge that showed in her posture, in the stare she aimed at the world.

She began to growl again but the Cougar cut in with her own baleful scream. Her Neighbour hissed and crept closer, but the Cougar stayed her ground, the dead deer beneath her. The Neighbour struck out and batted the Cougar's face. The Cougar retreated in an instant, springing back beyond her Neighbour's reach, and her Neighbour leapt onto the open deer, letting out a scream.

The Cougar watched the blond cougar standing on her hard-won kill. She hesitated, trying to find her way in, but it was lost. She heard her cubs behind her, pacing and hissing. She could not face their deaths.

The Cougar turned and fled through the trees, her cubs following.

THE COUGAR SAT BENEATH snow-covered bushes, her cubs beside her, watching some deer on the other side of an open field. The air was bitter despite the sunlight. On such a cold day sound travelled farther, making silence imperative. As the cougars waited, their breath rose into the clear air like steam venting from the earth.

It had been a dry winter with little snowfall. Though the forest remained under a covering of snow, the snow-storms of previous winters, when it would snow for days without end, were absent. During this time the Cougar was occupied with teaching the cubs to hunt. It was a hungry process. In order to learn they needed to fail and often their impatience, lack of silence, or inability to sit still, spoiled the hunt. The Cougar suffered their failures with them. Hunger was a punishing teacher.

The Cougar had not seen her Neighbour since their altercation before the winter, but she had found her Neighbour's paw prints, unmistakable since she knew her scent, and seen the imprint of her cubs' prints within the larger paw prints. They were accompanying their mother to watch as she hunted. Now the cougars were both careful to avoid each other.

Like clouds drifting across the sky, the deer had made their way over the frozen earth to where the cougars sat, hidden in the bushes. They need only wait and they would have their prey. Thinking of the moment when she would pounce, catching the deer in her claws and bringing its neck to her mouth, the Cougar felt the hollow feeling in her stomach swell.

The Cougar saw the deer tense and shift their bodies to jump away and she knew instantly what had happened. Her son ran out into the deer, sending them scattering into the trees. The Cougar's daughter took off after her brother, not wanting to miss her chance, running full speed toward her target.

The Cougar remained where she was, knowing immediately that their attempt would be in vain. Her son had alerted the deer to their presence and struck too soon. He had not yet learned the importance of patience. It was best not to have to deal with a deer on the run, to surprise them before they had the chance to run; otherwise, it was best to abandon the chase altogether and try again.

The Cougar's son was confused by the bounding targets and could not choose one among them; he had already failed, though he would continue with his failed attempt. He twisted to follow one, then another, losing ground with each moment he hesitated. His decision, and his devotion to that decision, must be total and immediate. Once he learned this, everything else would follow.

The Cougar rose and followed her cubs down into the clearing where the deer had been grazing, which was now empty. She could still hear the sound of the retreating deer through the snow. The sun cast a bright light into the clear air, causing her to squint. She wanted to retreat from this failure, to leave this vacant field. They must go now if they were to hunt again.

Her daughter sat patiently beside one of the bushes, hiding neatly in its shadow. She had an aptitude for caution, which the Cougar could only attribute to being a natural gift. When she saw her mother she stayed where she was but gave a low call. The Cougar's son had a brazen attitude when it came to caution, which might help him defend himself but would not ensure he was able to feed himself. Perhaps this was typical of male cubs. She did not know.

The Cougar searched the abandoned field. Her son appeared from the trees on the other side. She called to him. He approached, sniffing the ground. He looked up at her. She was stoic. He rubbed his face against her front leg. She remained still a moment longer, then lowered her head and ran her cheek along his.

The cougars set out. The sun reflected on the snow like fire, so bright at times they were blinded by its glare. They came to a pond fed by the river. A cluster of bushes stood encased in ice in the middle of the pond, the water frozen around it. How strange to be a tree, to be rooted to the same spot all its life. The Cougar wondered, if she had stayed in the same spot her whole life, what then would she know about the life of the forest?

She sat here in view of the icebound bushes, beneath the drooping branches of an evergreen, to await her prey. Her cubs sat down beside her, the snow squeaking slightly as they settled in.

As the sun climbed higher in the sky, she felt the air

warm, and from this she knew it would snow. First the snow came like a light dusting, glistening in the sunlight as it fell to the ground, then the snow came in volume. Snow drifted down in silence, lighting up the air like a bright fog. She could barely see the bushes on the water before her. The cubs sat alert, watching into the snowfall.

Then the snow stopped all at once. The sound of it hitting the ground ceased and a still silence prevailed. Through the trees that lined the river's edge they saw the slow, quiet herd of deer, wandering toward them.

Even the Cougar's son flicking his tail through the cold air seemed to make a sound.

The Cougar suppressed a sigh.

THE COUGAR AWOKE. SHE could sense a difference in the space of the lair, the absence of bodies. When she looked she saw she was alone and she knew that her cubs had left her. During the winter they had become capable hunters and could have left her at any time, but they had lingered until the drip of spring thaw sounded throughout the forest. Now, despite having known they were due to leave, awakening alone, the Cougar felt this sudden loss.

She left the lair, staying within the trees, unwilling to step out into the sunlight. When she came to the river, she walked along the sodden riverbanks until she found a place where the trees grew up to the water's edge. The Cougar sat beneath the overhanging branches of a silver birch, watching the endless flow of water in the sunlight. The sound of the rushing river filled her ears, the movement of the water holding her attention for a long time. When she looked up, she saw by the slant of the light that half the day had passed.

She noticed a trail of dark smoke rising into the sky. She recalled the last time she had seen one of these columns of smoke, how her curiosity had been denied. This one was much closer than the last. She turned and snuck back into the dark hold of the forest.

The Cougar raced over the land. Without light in the

sky, the trail of smoke would be lost. For once, she wished the day were longer. The descending darkness spurred her on and she ran over the forest floor of wet leaves, damp pine needles.

There was still light in the sky, though the sun had dipped below the horizon, when she began to smell the smoke upon the air. As she drew near, it was not the smoke but another odour, foreign but unmistakably animal, that caused her to stop and listen. There was no movement, no sign of anything ahead. Even so, the scent of something she had never smelled before made her cautious.

A chickadee called through the darkening light. There was no sign of any other animals nearby. The Cougar stepped into the clearing, eyes casting about.

A ring of stones lay on the ground, embers still smouldering in a pile of ash in the centre of the ring. When the Cougar saw this formation, she stopped. This seemed a strange arrangement of rocks. She had never seen them so organized before. She approached the ring of stones. A fire had burned within. The trail of smoke she had seen earlier, no doubt. The Cougar snorted. It seemed as if the rocks so arranged had called a fire from the earth to burn in this area alone.

She sniffed the ground and smelled the sharp scent of charred meat. She was deeply suspicious that an animal should leap into the fire. It must have been lured there. There were other signs to be read but she did not understand them.

She found the bones of a rabbit scattered over the area.

Their placement seemed arbitrary and she pondered over this, the possible reason for it.

The foul smell of waste reached out to her from nearby. She did not care to wait and see what animal might return here. The Cougar glanced over the mess once more and then turned, stalked into the trees, tail flicking.

On her way back to her lair, the Cougar ran until she could no longer run and then she walked, panting as she went through the dark forest. She could not leave the memory of the site she had just visited behind her. If she were to produce such a stench, make such obvious signs of her presence in the forest, she would never get close enough to her prey and she would starve.

An owl called as the Cougar snuck past, ululating in a low sweep, and she looked into the trees to find it but could not see where it sat, watching from among the branches.

When she returned to her lair, concealed by the shadows of night, she found no sign that the cubs had been there in her absence. She had known in her heart that they had left her but seeing the lair empty now she knew it was certain.

She looked out the entrance of the lair into the night, wondering how far they had travelled in one day, whether they had gone together or set out alone. The discovery she had made earlier had set a fear into her heart. She hoped her cubs did not encounter whatever animal was responsible for that strange ring of stones in the forest — but she would not know, whatever happened to them.

The scent of those cubs lingered on the ground and she worried that she might awaken confused the next day but she did not have the will to seek out another lair tonight. She settled down in the thin crevasse of rock which now seemed rather large and soon fell asleep.

THE COUGAR RETURNED TO her solitary life, her sense of urgency revoked. It was late in spring, a cold rain fell for days and filled the river until it swelled up over the banks, running grey and fast. The earth soaked up the water, creating a landscape of mud. The rain made no difference to the Cougar. She heard the space where the rain did not hit the ground and so knew a herd of deer stood nearby. She could hear the void made by even a single animal as it travelled within the darkness, whether it was a fox, a deer, or one of the lumbering bears that now roamed the forest, seeking out their first meal after awakening from their winter-long slumber.

It rained all through the night as she stalked the wet forest in darkness. She sought the riverbanks and listened to the rain as it hit the surface of the swollen river rushing steadily onward. She hiked up into the rocky cliffs at the base of the mountain and listened as the rain hit the bare rock and ran in rivulets down the stone pathways. She sauntered through a field of tall grass, the soft hiss of rain all around her.

The sun rose behind a white sky. Still it rained. A dark day. But the Cougar did not return to her lair. Instead she wandered, unwilling to admit herself to sleep. Throughout the day a fog crept through the trees. The Cougar travelled its depths, the forest swallowed up in the gloom.

She spied the deer as shadows wading through the fog. The Cougar sat, heart beating slow, and waited to see if they would wander into her reach. They took slow steps, their heads lowered to the grass here, then here. She crept out from beneath the thin branches of a spruce and made her way from tree to tree through the dense fog.

She moved with such slow, deft movements that at any moment she could sink into hiding, so even when one of the deer glanced up, and the Cougar paused mid-stride, she blended into the pale grass, the murky air, and the deer, unable to see her in that hazy landscape, lowered its head again to graze.

The Cougar sprang out of the grass and dug her claws into the back of a doe, bringing her to the ground. The other deer fled through the rain, their feet whispering over the wet grass. The Cougar sat breathing hard, deer in her jaws, the rain falling upon them. She tore open the deer's belly and buried her head in its case, unaware of the slight sounds behind her.

Though the appearance of her Neighbour was not unexpected, the Cougar was nevertheless amazed at the blond cougar's ability to conceal herself, to appear from nowhere. She had not seen her Neighbour since their alter-cation last autumn, and the sight of her body moving through the fog filled her with a cold dread.

The Cougar dropped the deer and hissed. Her Neighbour let loose a chilling growl that unnerved the Cougar but it was not enough to move her from her kill. They stood, heads low, eyes locked. The blond cougar stepped forward to push the Cougar off the deer but the

Cougar did not retreat, instead she growled in her own terrible voice and swatted at her Neighbour's face when she came too close.

The blond cougar jumped back. She seemed to hesitate and the Cougar saw that she was surprised by the Cougar's resistance. The Cougar stood, tail slashing the air. Today she had no cubs huddling in the bushes to defend. She would not retreat.

Her Neighbour circled her and growled. She tried approaching the Cougar from the side, but the Cougar reached out, trying to pull the blond cougar toward her jaws. Her Neighbour twisted out of her grasp with a scream. She tried to duck around behind the Cougar, but the Cougar turned and pounced at her Neighbour, jaws fighting for her neck, knocking them both to the mud-slick ground.

The Cougar rose onto her hind legs, prepared to meet the resolute strength stored within her Neighbour's solid form, but she met with no such force, only a frame of bones encased in thin layers of muscles. She felt the blond cougar's breath against her face and felt the rhythmic tremor of the beating of her heart. She was a cougar, like herself, and nothing more.

As they stood in each other's embrace the Cougar felt her Neighbour struggling to gain footing in the mud. Her Neighbour could not overthrow her by brute force alone. With a scream her Neighbour put forth a renewed effort, trying to pull her to the ground, but the Cougar remained where she stood, as if her Neighbour fought against the earth itself. They were together now, gone into this like sisters. Nothing but Death could separate them.

The rain, the mud, the fog receded — only they two existed, nothing else entered the Cougar's thoughts. She was vaguely aware of a rustling in the bushes, but it was forgotten as she tried to avoid her Neighbour's jaws. Their breaths mingled and rose above their heads, like the ghosts of their screams trailing through the air.

They rose to meet and threw each other off and rose to meet again. At no point did the Cougar perceive her Neighbour's growing fatigue. She would not let the older cougar rest. Finding that her strength matched her Neighbour's filled her with a kind of unstoppable fury, and she pushed herself further, drawing from some hidden recess of strength within her.

Her Neighbour twisted out of her hold and turned to face her but not fast enough — the Cougar latched on to her Neighbour's neck. Growling, her Neighbour tried to thrash loose, but the Cougar forced her down and held her still. She adjusted her hold, working her jaws into the right spot. Her Neighbour yowled, a pitiful, injured sound, and tried to struggle free, but the Cougar was immovable. The Cougar sank her bite further into that connective passage and felt the tension in her Neighbour's muscles release, like a sudden breath vacating her body, and the blond cougar went limp, slumping to the ground.

The rain fell hard. The Cougar stayed on top of her Neighbour, unwilling to move, her breath swelling out into the cold air. She could not believe her Neighbour's death, that she was capable of bringing about this death, as if she had altered the very landscape around her.

Finally, the Cougar rose from her Neighbour's body,

each step slow, careful. She felt as if she had been running for days. She had one deep claw mark across her right front leg, blood showing red through her covering of mud.

She looked back upon the blond cougar's muddied, lifeless body. One amber eye remained open, staring, unseeing into the depths of the fog.

The Cougar smelled them through the rain. She tensed and turned toward the treeline. The shape of three cougars darkened the fog like unbidden shadows. But as they emerged the Cougar saw that though they were fully grown they were still young, not yet ready to leave their mother. They glared at the Cougar, six blazing eyes in the cold rain.

The Cougar lowered her head, growled low in her throat. She feared she would not survive another confrontation, especially not against three cougars, no matter what their age. But she could not give them that impression. If they sensed she was weak, they would strike because they were likely hungry, waiting in the bushes for their mother.

The Cougar summoned her breath and with a throat raw from calling sent forth a loud and piercing growl, ears flat against her head, eyes flashing in the dark day. Her heart beat hard in her chest and at her temples. Before the echo of her call died out, she charged her Neighbour's cubs.

The two males raced into the forest, the sound of their retreat fading the farther they went, but her Neighbour's daughter stood, wide-eyed, deliberating, before backing up a few steps. Then the young cub, who wore those same white wings upon her face, turned, eyes flashing at the

Cougar, and screamed, her voice high and thin with youth.

The Cougar rushed her, bounding over the earth between them in one leap and coming within a claw's reach of her, but the lithe cub flew into the trees, branches snapping as she made her escape. She sent a scream into the forest that rang so loud and so long that the silence that followed seemed to ring with an equal strength. Then, the hiss of the cold rain resumed and the Cougar stood panting into the fog.

She returned to the deer for whom her Neighbour had risked her life. As she sat eating out in the open, her weakened state seemed irresponsible to her, dangerous even. The fog obscured her vision and though she listened into the rain and heard nothing, she felt the prickle of unknown eyes watching her.

She rose, red gore dripping from her mouth. The rain had washed her back of its covering of mud, but her lower half remained the colour of stone, her face stained with blood, her eyes burning through the fog. She reached the river and walked down into the cold water and stood as the mud lifted off her torn and beaten flesh. The air grew brighter around her and the Cougar felt the urge to hide from the light.

She returned to the mountain, climbing into the rocky foothills until she spied a shadow in the rock and headed toward it. The Cougar entered the cave, glanced over the interior, then turned and sat in the opening. From here she could look out on the roof of the forest below, shrouded in fog.

Though she was tired, and the day was bright, the

Cougar did not sleep. A nervous energy flowed through her that kept her heart pumping in her chest. Instead she kept watch from the mouth of the lair, as the fog flowed past, washing through the trees, climbing up the mountainside, like a slow river, and all the forest drowned.

IV

GORMLEY'S FARM

→→

J OSEPH WAS AWAKENED BY a gentle shake of his shoulder. His father insisted he wear a sweater, for though the days were warm, the mornings had grown cool. Then he gave him an apple, which Joseph ate, eyes closed. They stepped out into the morning sunlight. Joseph held his father's hand as they walked down the shaded road to the footpath that would lead them directly to Gormley's, where August was expected for the day. In the trees, cicadas called to one another, like a wildfire spreading from one tree to the next, rising as the heat grew.

Joseph found a gnarled piece of branch that resembled a sword and wielded the weapon before him, slaying bears and mountain lions as he went, severing limbs and skewering heads, so that his father who followed could walk in safety. Soon Joseph was far ahead of him.

"Hold up!" August called. "You're going to leave me behind!"

"Walk faster!" Joseph commanded, but he saw his words had no effect and stood waiting until his father caught up. He took his father's hand and walked along beside him.

"How come you walk so slow?"

"I've got a bad knee."

"Why?"

"I fell off a horse. Well, the horse threw me off. Snap!"

"Why didn't the doctor fix it?"

"They did. But sometimes when you fix something it's never as good as it was before it was broken. Besides, some things can't be fixed."

Such a statement directly conflicted with Joseph's understanding of his father as the man other men came to when something needed to be fixed.

"What do they do, if they can't fix it?"

"Oh, I don't know. They might . . . cut it off."

"They *wouldn't*!"

August shrugged. "It depends."

Joseph was shocked.

"You keep that in mind when you're running around the forest like some kind of berserker."

They continued walking, quiet for a time.

"Pop, how old are you?"

"Fifty-three."

Joseph considered fifty-three years against his eight.

"That's old."

August nodded. "It's starting to feel that way."

They stepped off the road and into the forest. A narrow footpath traced through the bush. Joseph looked back. His father followed, eyes shaded by the brim of his hat, his beard catching the sunlight. The call of a warbler floated through the trees. The scent of pine and deep sunshine and beneath that the cool, dark scent of earth.

"Did you have a forest like this where you grew up?" Then he added, as he had heard his father often say, ". . . in the old country?"

"Well, there are forests there. But I grew up in the city. With streets and streets of buildings. Buildings taller than these trees. And more people than you can imagine."

"You lived there when you were my age?"

"Yes. And when I was your age, I spoke a different language than we are speaking now."

"Like Mr. Petersen?"

"Yes, but Mr. Petersen was born farther north and spoke yet *another* language when *he* was a boy."

Joseph considered this. "How many languages are there?"

"Oh, I don't know. Maybe thousands."

"Thousands?"

August laughed. "What? You seem dismayed."

"I didn't think there would be so many."

"Oh, yes." He nodded. "That is the way of all things. Trees, mountains, people. More than a man can count."

They walked along in silence through the sunstruck forest. Joseph remembered his sword and the horde of invisible beasts barring their path. He turned on them with a yell, to clear the way, slicing through the air, his voice echoing through the quiet forest, calling their position for all to hear.

They emerged from the trees into a clearing where there was a cabin and behind it a low, squat barn. The dark forest surrounded them on all sides, the cleared land sloped up toward the trees, resembling an amphitheatre. As they walked up toward the barn, the call of a warbler pulsed through the still air. Joseph saw Gormley's daughters staring out at them from a window in the cabin.

The woman of the house stood in the doorway, arms crossed, squinting against the sun, observing Joseph and his father as they made their way toward the barn. Joseph's father nodded, and she nodded in return. There was something about her response, the slow nod of her head, that signalled to Joseph something was not right about this morning.

As they approached the barn, Joseph noted here as well the grave posture of the four men in conference. Even Gormley's dog regarded them with a weary stare. The entrance to the barn stood open, the interior made darker by the bright sunlight.

They entered the low barn. When Joseph's eyes adjusted to the darkness, he saw the corpses of countless sheep lying in disarray.

"Goddamn—"

"Joseph!"

Joseph fell silent, eyes wandering over the wreckage of dead sheep.

August greeted Gormley, nodded greeting to the two men, Donald Mavis and John Gunn, nearby neighbours, and the boy, John Howland, who worked for Gormley. They nodded in return, calling him Gus, which was how he was known to some men. Gormley's neighbours, Mavis and Gunn, had been drawn by the sound of the shot earlier that morning. Fifteen-year-old John Howland worked on hand for Gormley and he often stayed the night and ate with the family.

"What has happened?"

"A massacre. That's what's happened," muttered Gunn.

"I never seen anything like it," Gormley was saying, as if he hadn't heard the other two and was just talking to himself. "What kind of creature comes in the night, kills thirty-nine sheep, and then leaves them to rot? Barely ate from any of them, just tore them apart and left them. Doesn't make any sense."

Joseph felt a prickling sensation crawl across his skin as he gazed upon the bloody work around him. Dozens of sheep lay slumped on the hay-strewn floor, dark red wounds on their white coats, like a lurid garden in full bloom. In the darkest corner of the barn, the remaining sheep huddled together, shivering into the hot day.

"You didn't hear?" August asked.

"I heard too late. Came out here, seen them running back and forth in the lantern light. Couldn't figure out what in the hell was going on until the light caught her and I saw these glowing eyes flash by in the darkness."

Joseph, standing nearby, pretending not to listen, feigned a sudden rapturous interest in the floor.

"When the light hit her, she stopped. I don't think she could see me behind the lantern but she was looking right at me, eyes burning like green fire, and her mouth was all"—he gestured with his hand—"just pure red from all the blood."

The other men stood in silence, watching Gormley as he remembered the moment when he latched eyes upon the Old Woman.

"The dog was there, barking like a lunatic. Like that would do it, that would send her away. I was worried she would get a hold of him. He doesn't know any better. He's never seen a panther before. I never saw one myself. It's truly strange . . . seeing an animal like that, like a true *creature*. Not like animals you live with.

"I fired a shot but I missed. She was right in front of me and I missed her and then she was gone. Probably took off into the trees. I went back to the house and didn't come out until dawn."

The men stood staring on that stale violence, arms crossed. The sheep had been cut down where they stood. Some appeared unharmed but for a small wound at the throat, a red stain on their side, as if their assailant needed but the slightest portion, a different part from each, collecting the ingredients for some nefarious recipe.

"You want to go after her?" This from Gunn. Rallied by the shot, now he was up for blood. Like it was a pastime. August had noticed this about him. It was not true of every man. But it was true of this one. Mavis looked between Gormley and Gunn. He would go with whoever stood strongest.

"I don't have time for that," Gormley said.

The men stood in silence, looking inward.

"Might as well shear the dead," said August.

Gormley knew it. He did not pull his eyes away from the dead sheep but nodded as if listening somewhere else.

They left the barn for the sunlight and stood talking plans. They sent John Howland to fetch the insurance agent, Matthew Stokes. The boy departed immediately. He cut through the grass, stepping into the dark trees at a seemingly arbitrary point, but he knew the way through the bush that would lead him to Stokes's land.

Joseph walked deeper into the barn and knelt down before one of the carcasses, its eyes closed, its head twisted away at an unnatural angle. He could see into its open mouth, the dull glint of the teeth therein.

Then he saw the paw print of the panther stamped in blood on the wooden floorboard at his feet. He knelt and after a moment's hesitation laid his hand on the paw print. There was the floorboard against his palm, but there was also a subtle fire, an electric current, that he felt when he placed his hand there. By touching this mark in blood, he claimed it, and since no one had seen it, or cared about it, it belonged to him. Her paw print was larger than his own hand and it seemed fantastic to him that her paws should be so large.

He left the barn to find his father.

"—comes in the night and kills thirty-nine sheep?" Gunn was saying. "That's no ordinary panther."

Gormley did not seem like he would answer.

"Were you able to see? Did she have the mark on her face?"

Gormley's eyes slid to Joseph.

"Go on," said August when he saw his son watching them. "Why don't you go up to the house and see if Beth and Gloria need some company. They might be spooked after what happened."

Joseph's expression darkened. This was exactly the kind of thing he hated, being forced to socialize with other children, and worse yet, with girls.

"Just go see how they're doing. If they see you've been out here and everything's alright, it might make them feel better."

"Can't I just stay with you?"

"Joseph—" Said in a tone that was itself a warning.

Joseph trudged up to the house, glaring at the ground before him, arms at his sides. The door stood ajar. He heard the sounds of washing from within and his heart stuttered. Joseph felt he was asking a great deal just by announcing himself.

He made a quiet knock on the open door and peered in.

In a joyless voice he did not care to mask, he said, "Good morning, Mrs. Gormley. My father asked me to come visit Beth and Gloria and see if they were spooked from what happened last night."

But Mrs. Gormley was busy at her work and barely noticed Joseph's total lack of enthusiasm. She was bent over a basin, scouring a large pot in such a ferocious manner Joseph wondered what it must have done to displease her so. Mrs. Gormley was wire-thin, tall, made slightly mena-cing by her dark dress. Her apron reminded Joseph of the apron his father wore as a blacksmith. For some reason this unnerved him and he found himself unable to act reasonably in her presence.

"Oh . . ." She seemed to be thinking. "Very well, come in."

Joseph entered the dark house, his eyes adjusting from the brightness outside. He smelled fresh bread, the scent of soap and that of coffee, all mingled with the heavy aroma of smoke. Two girls sat at the wooden table. Beth, the elder, was darning a sock. Gloria, the younger, had a book open on the table in front of her and was looking up at Joseph, waiting, as one just interrupted. Both girls wore their blond hair in braids, Gloria with her cap on, the strings untied as if she were about to go outside. Both watched him with wide, dark eyes.

Joseph took a breath and spoke to the ceiling. "My father asked me to come see how you both were doing after the uh terrible incident that occurred here last night."

Gloria looked to her sister to answer for them both.

"Thank you for asking," said Beth, perfectly earnest. "We are very shocked by the horrible news of our killed sheep. But we are both doing fine."

Joseph had not thought of what to say beyond this initial conversation. He could feel Mrs. Gormley looking at him, her eyes on his back.

"Want to go look at the dead sheep?"

"Joseph Brandt!"

Joseph winced at the sharp tone she used to say his name, like a terrific clap of thunder had come out of her mouth.

"Can we?" Beth asked. Mrs. Gormley relented with upward-cast eyes.

The three children emerged into the sunlight, the two girls in their skirts, Joseph in his dusty jeans, small boots. Gloria had tied the strings of her cap under her chin. Beth was bareheaded, the sunlight shining off her hair like spun gold. They approached the barn, its door open onto shadow.

Inside, the smell was thick, and the reality of the sheep lying dead on the ground made Joseph doubt his asking the girls if they wanted to see them. But they looked without fear upon the destruction inside, and he was impressed by their resilience.

Joseph marvelled that, in a single night, in mere moments, a stealthy cougar had come and laid waste to the sheep by one sweep of her deadly paw. The efficiency, the number of dead, made a grave impression on him. His heart was certain that this was the work of the Old Woman. He dare not share this thought with Beth and Gloria though, or even his father, for he knew they would doubt.

"Poor sheep," Gloria said in a plain tone devoid of sentiment. She looked to Beth to confirm her assessment.

Beth nodded. "Poor sheep."

Joseph, feeling obliged to comment, could not think of anything more to add other than, "Yep. Poor sheep."

Joseph and the girls stood, looking on those lifeless bodies.

"I hope that mean old mountain lion never comes back here," said Beth.

"I'm going to hunt that old mountain lion," said Joseph. The words left his mouth before he had time to think what they were but as soon as he said them he knew they were true. By speaking these words he had tapped a vein deep within himself, out of which his desire arose like a great beast called forth from the earth, standing tall and indomitable in his mind. Standing beside the two girls in the dark barn, he was stunned into silence by his vision, by its intensity, and by his sudden and total commitment to this fearsome beast, regardless of the consequences.

Gloria said nothing to Joseph's declaration but looked to her sister.

"No, you won't," said Beth, not looking at him, looking at the sheep. "That mountain lion would kill you."

"No, it won't," said Joseph. "I'll hunt it and bring it back here for everyone to see."

To this the girls said nothing. Joseph could see they were not impressed by his promise of vengeance. Instead, they looked around at the dead sheep with sad eyes, as if surveying the left-behind belongings of a friend they would never see again.

The two girls and then Joseph emerged from the barn, taking backward steps, hands held out, trying to coax the remaining sheep out of the darkness. Gloria had the most success. A bulky lamb, thick with wool, stepped out into the sunlight, reaching with its mouth for her hand. Gloria took another step backward, and the sheep stepped forward to meet her.

Joseph did not have as much luck convincing the sheep to come out of the barn, but he did not mind. They knew Gloria and Beth better. He mimicked their calling, *here lamb, come along, that's a good lamb*, and in this way they helped the remaining sheep past the bodies of their fallen kin and into the field beyond.

The men were busy gathering the dead, hauling the bodies down to the area by the side of the house. They worked in silence, shearing the slaughtered sheep, stacking the bodies in a neat tower. Gormley's dog stuck to his side the whole time, as if he were afraid to be on his own, despite the daylight hour.

Joseph reached the shade of the trees and sat looking down on the Gormley stead, the forest at his back. He could see in the darkness as the Old Woman came out of the trees, through the long grass, and into the clearing. She would have leapt up to the open window on the side of the barn with ease. It was no barrier to her. Then he watched, a gust of breeze touching his face, as the massacre began. The sheep fell like cut wheat. And he saw the glazed look in the Old Woman's eyes, flashing in the lantern light, face bright with blood.

He tried to imagine if she had died, if Gormley had shot her and he and his father had come that morning and seen the Old Woman dead. But he could not conjure the image to mind. It would never happen like that. Joseph watched in his mind as Gormley fired a rifle into the dark and the Old Woman raced through the long grass, back into the shadows of the forest, leaving the ruin of sheep where they lay. He tried to see her, what she would have looked like as she slipped back into the darkness, but he was denied. She existed in a darkness that he was not able to see into.

Mrs. Gormley's voice broke through Joseph's thoughts,

coming from across the field, calling him and the girls into the house. He rose, as if in a trance, the vision in his mind still vivid as he walked through the bright sunshine toward the house.

Gormley and his neighbours worked against the sun the whole day. The sunlight on their backs, reminding them of the finite amount of time they had before sunset. Their work must be done before then. A natural, non-negotiable deadline.

John Howland returned with the insurance agent. They arrived in silence, coming around the corner of the house unannounced. The men stopped their work. Stokes nodded to Gormley, Gormley nodded in return. From out of a bulky case, Stokes took various parts and began to assemble the whole while the men stood watching. When the camera was loaded and ready, Stokes hid beneath a blanket attached to the camera and raised his hand to indicate the process was taking place. They all stood quietly in the hot day, as the machine captured the image of the men's work before them.

After a moment Stokes undraped himself and nodded to the men and began disassembling the camera.

Joseph was put to work assisting Mrs. Gormley and the girls to wash the wool the men had shorn. He helped her to pack the stained wool into bundles wrapped in cheesecloth and then watched as she soaked it in hot water. When she gently wrung out the bundles there was a slight pink twinge to the sudsy water that dripped back into the basin.

He wandered to the side of the house and looked around the corner to see the men watching the flames envelop the pile of sheep they had gathered. A dark plume of smoke slowly rose into the air. The bright fire seemed diminished by the glaring sunlight, yet still it raged with a blistering intensity.

As they were leaving, Joseph glanced back. All evidence of the Old Woman's work had been erased, as if even the suggestion of her presence was too much to bear. He saw the dark column of smoke still rising up from behind the house, down where the men and his father had been at work.

August placed a hand on his son's shoulder, drawing his attention to the road before. They stepped into the trees and onto the path that would take them home.

JOSEPH THOUGHT ABOUT HIS sudden devotion to hunting the Old Woman. Standing at the edge of a field staring into the long grass; at the dinner table, silent, as his father placed his plate before him; even as his teacher was speaking to him, then calling his name, then calling his full name; shrouded in his own thoughts, seeing and hearing another realm. It was a serious affliction, touching as close to spiritual experience as he had ever felt. He could see himself going into the forest, finding her mark among the trees, and he imagined what she might look like, how they might meet.

He thought that if he killed the Old Woman the entire town would know him for this deed. Shop owners would cut him deals. Men would nod and tip their hats to him as he passed. Women would smile at him wherever he went and know who he was. He believed this achievement would remain with him for the rest of his life and even as an old man he would be considered a great hunter by those who knew him.

It was not long before he shared this ambition with his sole, trusted adviser.

His father sat on the veranda slicing a green apple into sections with his knife, eating the slices from the blade. Their one-room cabin stood against the quiet trees. The door to their home lay open to let out the heat from the stove, light from within spilling out into the evening. All around them the steady thrum of crickets sounded.

"Why don't you leave that poor old panther alone?" his father asked once Joseph had revealed his intention to hunt the Old Woman.

"It's not a poor old panther. It's a mean old sheep killer. And I'm not going to let it kill any more sheep."

"Oh, you're not, are you?"

"No, I'm going to hunt it, and kill it, and then I'll bring it back here for everyone to see, and they can stuff it and put it in a museum and put a sign next to it that says, *Killed by Joseph Brandt*."

His father offered him a slice of apple on the blade of his knife. Joseph took the slice from the blade, popped it in his mouth, and chewed furiously.

"And just how do you plan on accomplishing this great and noble task?"

Joseph swallowed and took a breath. "I just need to find where she sleeps," he said. "Then I can hunt her." That he would be the one to do this remained constant in his mind.

As important as the idea of hunting the Old Woman itself was his belief that he alone was capable of doing this, that it must be him. He believed that all he needed was to know where she slept. Everything that involved stalking and killing her would follow, after he learned this single detail.

August sat, considering in his thoughtful way, thinking of what he was going to say before he said it. Joseph waited.

"Why find where she sleeps?"

Joseph shrugged. "That's what you do when you hunt something. You find where it sleeps. And then you hunt it."

"Well—" August was caught. The boy was right, which was what concerned him. He thought Joseph was too young to know this, but then perhaps age had nothing to do with it. He did not like discovering such knowledge in his son, and he marvelled that things could be born within him secretly, like mushrooms in the dark.

"You don't go poking around in any caves," August warned him. "The last thing you want is a bear chasing after you, I can tell you that."

"Okay."

"You hear me?"

"Yeah, yeah, I hear you," Joseph said as he took another slice of apple from the blade.

V

APPRENTICE

 ⤞⤚

THE COUGAR SCALED THE trunk of a great tree
perched on the edge of a cliffside. Her claws sank
into the bark with ease and she noticed how dry the
tree was. No sooner had she had this thought than she
heard a sharp rip and in the next moment she was falling
through the air. She reached out, trying to catch one of
the branches but already they were out of reach.

Open sky, the dark spread of trees below, the ragged
rock face, slid past in a confusing jumble. Using her tail,
the Cougar spun around in the air, and just as she corrected
herself she caught the side of the cliff. A sharp pain dug
into her side but she forgot it as she hit the cliffside again,
then tumbled down the steep scree.

She came to a sudden rest at the bottom. A ring of dust

rose up around her. Small stones skittered down after her. She took a breath and all her pain came to her at once and buried her. She had to fight to breathe, trying to force air into her lungs, as if some solid thing now occupied that space. It seemed as if time was not passing, she was stuck in this moment. She rolled onto her side and coughed, and somehow she took a breath, and another, each one a struggle.

When she tried to raise her head she was struck down. A wave of pain pressed her against the earth. She shut her eyes and lay still, sucking in hot breaths like shards of stone. She made a long, angry yowl, but realized that the sound of her distress might attract some unwanted attention that she could not defend herself against.

She forced herself to lie still, trying to ignore the fear roiling in her gut.

Her thoughts returned to the tree that had submitted her to the sky. The bark had ripped off under her weight and sent her sprawling through the air. She had noticed it was dry even as she climbed it. The bare branches, the withered trunk, she should have known this tree meant Death.

She was covered in dust, scratched and bleeding from where she had been cut. A throbbing pain coursed outward from her injured side, forbidding her from moving. As the minor cuts and bruises faded to a dull ache, the pain in her side remained and she could not deny what this meant for her. If she could not stalk, if she could not pounce, if she could not hold a struggling victim in her embrace, then she would die.

The sun climbed the sky and the air grew hot. The Cougar lay crumpled at the base of the cliff, a tawny smear on the rocky white landscape. The heat smothered her under its heavy hand. Her thirst grew into a wild animal. She tried to ignore the pain in her side, to wait for it to diminish, but as time passed and her pain did not subside the grim truth of her situation sunk in.

A fly buzzed around her head. She jerked away, repulsed. She knew the fly as a companion of Death and she would not allow it to touch her.

The Cougar fell asleep and when she opened her eyes again, the evening air was cool around her. Her thirst was like a hot hand gripping her throat, yet she shivered. Pain and thirst—two creatures at work within her. Her body was a tree of pain, its roots growing into her limbs, digging its claws into her side, and squeezing with every beat of her heart. If she breathed too deeply, a sharp pain stabbed her side. If she moved, the pain shot down her front leg. She commanded herself to remain still and wait.

She could not help but make a long, annoyed whine into the air but she soon gave it up. The evening grew into night. The sound of crickets rose up from the fringe of grass below. The Cougar listened, her heart beating slow. She heard indistinct footfalls coming from the forest and though she knew this must be the skittering of rodents she began to fear something else would come for her from out of the darkness.

———

WHEN THE COUGAR AWOKE, the darkness was lifting, the pulse of crickets throbbing in the grass. From within the trees an owl made its call into the dark blue light. Her heartbeat was slow and hard. A mad thirst prowled within her. Though the sun had not yet risen she felt the heat beginning to build within the earth, on the air. She could not lie another day with the sun crushing her into the unforgiving stone.

Still, when she tried to move her front leg, she was granted a sharp stab. She took a breath, braced herself, then rolled to her right side and rose onto three legs. A bright flash dazzled her and she fought to stay standing as colour and dimension faded back into the world. She stood, breathing hard. The tree from which she had fallen clung to the rock, high above her. She was briefly amazed that she had not died falling from such a height.

The Cougar crept along on her right front leg and two hind legs toward the shade of the forest. The sun simmered below the horizon. She stood, leaning against an oak, recovering from the short walk. Her heartbeat fluttered, light, insubstantial. Her balance was unsteady. The pain in her side barked with every breath, however shallow. But somehow her thirst was a greater torment than her physical pain, forcing her through the trees, toward the stream.

She kept her left front leg up close to her side, but it was no protection. To cover even a short distance was a great struggle. Creeping along, she was reminded of the vastness of the forest, the great amount of it she had not even seen. The magnitude of the earth's surface, which had so impressed her in her youth, had been forgotten. She considered it now, feeling lost in its expanse.

She approached the stream a howling beast, sending her terrible cry before her to warn of her approach, to ward away anything she might come upon by accident. She collapsed by the stream's edge and submitted her head to the water. She could not drink fast enough, the sound of her drinking louder than that of the stream itself. She stopped, lifted her head to listen, water dripping from her parted mouth. The steady flow of the stream was the only sound through the sunlit forest. She drank again.

The Cougar hobbled on through the forest as the sun made its passage across the sky. By nightfall she had reached the base of the mountain where she kept her lair, hidden in the rocks. She kept her eye on the entrance as she made her slow ascent, the incline, the rocky terrain impeding her progress, feeling that if she lost sight of it now she would lose her way completely.

When she entered the lair, her cubs clamoured forward to greet her. Their meows were insistent; they had noticed her prolonged absence and meant to convey the ferocious hunger they now suffered. They had transitioned from milk to meat, had gone to watch their mother hunt, so it was clear she had nothing to give them. They rubbed their heads against her legs, their voices like claws at her neck, for they did not yet know the grave fate that awaited them.

The Cougar collapsed in a corner of the lair, wanting only the oblivion of sleep, even if it meant she may never rise again.

The cubs stood, making angry yowls, tails slashing.

The Cougar lay staring ahead, her heartbeat heavy in her chest. When they saw she would not move, they relented. They curled up beside her, settling down to sleep. But the Cougar did not sleep, despite her exhaustion, fixed on the terrible path before her. Though she tried, she could not banish the black shadow darkening the entrance of the lair.

T HE COUGAR AWOKE TO the yowling of her son and two daughters. If she rested long enough, she might be able to hunt. But even as she lay there on the bare earth of her lair, she knew that the time she needed might be longer than the time she had before she was too weak to hunt. The grip of hunger had grown unbearable, her other injuries diminished against it, and tomorrow would bring no difference. She would waste away in a shallow pit of rock, and her cubs as well. She considered all this as they clamoured around her, squawking and mewing, prodding her with their paws, their noses.

She had lived a solitary summer after she vanquished her Neighbour. Then, in the midst of the following winter, she and her Marauder met once again. Two daughters and a son had been born by the time the snow had melted. Now, unable to look at their faces, the Cougar laid her head against her paws and closed her eyes. Her cubs gathered around to rub their heads against her face and paws and lick at her ears. Their meowing had grown frantic, as if they only had to do it loud enough and she would arise and give them what they wanted.

The Cougar watched into the dim haze of the lair, trying to get comfortable around the pain in her side, the nag of hunger. Eventually she slept.

EACH TIME THE COUGAR surfaced from the grip of sleep she felt its growing strength over her and wanted nothing more than to return to its hold. Outside, the sun was setting. She could smell it on the air. Another day had passed. She felt a cool breath against her body—

She awoke to find her cubs licking clean the blood from the scrapes on her front legs. At first she would not let them, giving a dull hiss when they approached, but she became tired of sending them away and their persistence won out. She lay as they licked her wounds of their gore.

She saw it now: the three of them, waiting until she was weak enough, then they would come to her, eyes glinting in the dark, and feast on her flesh out of mindless hunger, tearing her open, messing their faces in her blood, then once every morsel was consumed, setting off into the forest.

She opened her eyes and saw them, asleep as before. As the sun set in the sky and again the lair was plunged into darkness, the Cougar stayed awake, watching those cubs, the sound of their breathing seeming loud in the close confines of the lair.

THROUGH THE HAZE OF weakness, the Cougar thought of eating her cubs. The small meal might be enough to sustain her until she healed and was able to hunt again.

The cubs lay beside her. She opened her eyes a sly degree. As she lay watching them, her daughters opened their eyes and raised their heads to look at her. Though fatigue weighed them down, she could see them assessing her, trying to see into her eyes.

There must have been something in the stare she gave them, some indication in the dull gleam in her eye, or perhaps they perceived it through the air. Her eldest daughter mewed, a thin whisper in the dark lair. The sound of her voice broke the Cougar's focus and she sank back into sleep.

ONCE THE THOUGHT HAD been born inside her head, she could not send it away. It sat with her in the darkened lair. It was no longer a question of whether she would but when she would. She would take her first opportunity, commit herself to the act when the time came. She lay for a time in mock sleep, having made this decision, awaiting the right moment.

When finally she roused herself from sleep, she opened her eyes and found the lair was empty. She was alone beneath the mountain. Now she knew she would die. They must have sensed what she was planning and abandoned her for the unknown. Death was now sitting, waiting outside the entrance of the lair. What had been a glimmer on the horizon now burned as brightly as the sun and the Cougar shrank from its terrible light. She closed her eyes against it and lay down.

———

SHE BEGAN TO FEEL so sick from hunger that she grew impatient with Death. The pain in her side was now outmatched by the pain in her gut, chewing her in its jaw. She regretted and did not regret having not taken her chance to eat the cubs, whatever bleak existence it might have gained her. The thought of her cubs alone in the wilderness only filled her with gloom. They did not yet have the skills to survive on their own. They may already have died. She would never know.

Her head swam and her breathing grew fast. She saw a lake before her, glistening in the sun. Outside, she heard the wind and knew it would rain. The smell of wet sand was sudden — those smooth stones catching the sunlight like a path of daytime stars.

She felt like her body was sinking into the earth.

She thought of those cubs who had died.

She thought of her mother, whether or not she had died.

SHE AWOKE AND SAW a single cub standing in the entrance of the lair. A dim, early morning light seeped in so that the cub stood in shadow. At first the Cougar did not recognize him. She did notice that he was soaking wet. Seeing this, it became clear that this was her drowned cub, come to fetch her. The sight of him here did not surprise her and she was not afraid as he approached.

The dripping cub paused mid-stride and watched her. He gave a quizzical meow and his voice confused her. It was not the voice she remembered. The cub meowed again and his call cut through her confusion. She saw it was her current son, standing in the entrance, yowling at her.

The Cougar croaked in response, her voice weak from disuse. He came forward and rubbed his head against her face. She began licking the water from his face, his shoulders, and his sides; the fluffy fur carried a few mouthfuls of water. Though the Cougar was not fully restored, she felt her head clear.

She lay back down, tired from this small effort, and before falling asleep she thought, it must be raining.

AGAIN THE COUGAR'S SON awoke her by standing and yowling in the entrance of the lair. He stood as before, dripping wet, and the Cougar thought it strange that it was still raining. She licked away the water from his face and neck and slowly her thinking restored, her thoughts no longer trapped under the weight of her thirst.

It was not raining. The cub was venturing down to the stream and soaking himself in the gentle current, then returning to the lair. He came back twice more and each time the Cougar drank a few mouthfuls of water. Then there was a long pause during which the cub was absent. The air grew dark and the Cougar began to grow fearful. How quickly the slight feeling of wellness could vanish. But as the last of the sun's light bled from the sky, the Cougar's Son returned, clutching a brown mouse between his jaws. He laid the body before his mother with care, an offering of great importance. The Cougar snatched it up whole, bones snapping in her mouth as she chewed. It was barely a mouthful, but it was an entire meal for a cougar who had not eaten in days.

For the first time since her fall from the sky, the Cougar was not ruled by the burden of hunger. She felt a comfortable sleep washing over her, and she lay down her head not out of resignation but of true fatigue. A tiredness that required sleep—but with the promise of awakening, renewed.

Seeing his mother settling down to sleep, the Cougar's Son curled up next to her side, where he could hear the beating of her heart. Then the cougars slept, breathing deep breaths, as the day passed around them, growing into night.

THE COUGAR'S DAUGHTERS DID not return. They might already be dead—there were too many dangers to account for, too many things they had not been prepared for and would not understand. A heavy sadness engulfed her when she thought of them—that they had left to save themselves from her only to die in the unknowing forest.

Soon, the Cougar's Son devastated the mouse population in their area.

The Cougar felt her true hunger return, and for the first time in days she had a lusty desire to bring down a deer, crush its neck between her jaws. The thought of it made her mouth water. But while she could entertain these visions in her head, she knew she was too weak to attempt this yet. She would have to start small.

The Cougar emerged from her lair for the first time since she had returned to it expecting to die. The day shocked her with its strength, as if she had not seen daylight for many years. She stood blinking in the sunlight. If ever she had believed the night superior, all she had to do was spend a moment in full sunlight to see that the day had power equal to the night—equal but opposite.

The Cougar's Son ran ahead as the Cougar took her first shaky steps out onto the stony earth. Her heart beat hard. Never had she been closer to Death, and yet she felt an unrelenting strength within her, compelling her to go on. She could think of nothing else but water—the stream. They would go to the stream to sit and wait. Her son led the way.

T HEY SAT FACING THE wind so their scent would not be driven into the thicket before them. The Cougar's Son sat beside her, eyes scanning the trees. His ears flicked toward sound independent from his line of sight. If he was restless, it did not show in his posture. He sat, squinting into the wind, with perfect patience.

This was a strange summer compared with the summers she had known. The grass had turned yellow and brittle in the heat. The river ran low, exposing submerged rocks to the touch of air, turning them bright green where the algae had dried into a scaled skin. The wind pulled the dry earth from the ground and sent it through the forest, staining the trees, the leaves, the same vague colour on one side. But these things, which concerned the Cougar, did not seem to concern the Cougar's Son. He could not compare this summer with summers past. He seemed to take the world as it was, unburdened by the conflicting perception that divided the Cougar's attention. His attention was whole. And the Cougar wondered when her attention had become so distracted.

They wandered through the dry summer, clouds blooming from the earth as they stalked by. Grooming was a constant effort. They coughed up grimy hairballs, gritty with sand, and never felt like they had fully accomplished the task. The whine of mosquitoes crept through the forest, a nocturnal sound that invaded the day and proclaimed desolation wherever it was heard.

Because the Cougar was hesitant to take down the larger prey she was used to, she and her son took to killing small animals. They lived on the move. Once they had devoured their catch, they left to hunt elsewhere, in another ambush spot, because there was no telling how long they would have to wait until some prey came their way.

Both of them remained thin. The Cougar worried about her son, that he was not eating enough during this time, the most important period of growth in his life. They did not keep a lair. They slept where they killed, on the riverbanks, beneath the low-hanging branches of evergreens, concealed within the hollowed trunks of trees, then moved on. They did not leave caches. Between the two of them, they could strip a skeleton clean of flesh and organs in a single sitting.

Even if the Cougar were at her fittest, she would have to be vigilant to contend with this summer. She was wary of other cougars desperate for food and watched for their signs in the forest. If she found another cougar's mark clawed into the bark of a tree, she would turn and head back the way they had come. Her son might glance into the trees in the direction they had been heading, but he always followed her guidance.

The Cougar thought of that blond cougar. What an easy kill her Neighbour would make of her if she came upon her now. What strange luck it was that it had been then that they had quarrelled and not now. The Cougar wondered at the inflexible nature of time.

Despite these conditions, the Cougar found comfort in watching her son investigate the forest around him. He was content to sit gazing at the shadows of clouds as they slid over the earth with the speed of melting ice. He was intrigued by the calls of birds, the sound of the leaves whispering on their branches, the scent of other animals' droppings. The river was a mystery and the creatures within it were awesome, sleek, gleaming, as if made of water themselves, or dark, spiny, from a hidden realm.

An owl watched them from the trees as they stalked by. The Cougar's Son stopped and stared. The owl returned his stare. The Cougar called her son away, continuing on at her slow, determined pace. He stood, transfixed by the owl's white face, its bright, sharp eyes that seemed to devour his own stare. The Cougar called to him again. He turned and ran to catch up with his mother, glancing back at the yellow-eyed owl once, then again.

Though providing for three cubs during this time would have been a task, the Cougar dwelled on the death of her daughters. She regretted it for them and she regretted it for her son, who had no siblings to play with, for in play lay the practice he needed to become a successful hunter. Still unable to run, never mind entertain the boundless physical energy of a growing cub, the Cougar played the only game she could.

There was no need to introduce the game. When they were not hunting, sitting next to the remains of a kill, or travelling from one place to the other, either the Cougar or her son might disappear into the surrounding forest. Once the other had noticed the disappearance, it was necessary to go in search of the missing cougar, to hunt them down.

It did not always require a lengthy pursuit. Sometimes the prey was easily found and the point of the game had been for the surprise of it. But sometimes there was a long, quiet stalk involved. If the disappeared party could not be found, it became obvious they were lying in wait, even now stalking their stalker. They traded the role, so each played the hunter.

At times she saw him, hiding, inadequately, behind the thin trunk of a tree, tail flicking in anticipation, and she would pretend she did not know he was there. It hurt the Cougar when she tried to go along silently, these soft steps took more effort than she realized, but she did it for the sake of the game.

Soon the time came when the Cougar's Son surprised her out of nowhere, appeared as if from out of the air itself, silent and sudden. Her heart leapt and she stumbled back, an abrupt pain stabbing through her side. She was impressed. And when she looked at him again in this light, she saw that his spots were barely visible, his face and shoulders had grown wider, and all of a sudden she felt like she was staring at the very likeness of the Marauder.

When she blinked the vision faded, and it was her son staring back at her, waiting for her to lead the way.

She had seen her Marauder last in the winter before the birth of her son and two daughters. She had awoken to the sunset experiencing that now familiar feeling which sent her out of her lair to go screeching through the forest, seeking with a mad desire. She seemed a terror even to herself, the forest plunged into a frozen silence wherever she went. Until finally, called by her wailing and the scent she had left along the river and into the mountains, the Marauder came to her from out of the naked trees.

The stark winter light lit his fur like red gold. His eyes were devoted only to her. It had been so long since she had seen him. Just the sight of him seemed to dampen the tumult within her, and once in his presence the pull that drew her to him was as strong as the governing force that kept all things locked to the earth.

The Cougar yowled and swatted his face. The red cougar sat back, tail flicking. He knew how to wait.

They made a lethal duo. At the edge of a clearing, the Cougar and the Marauder sat side by side, awaiting their prey. They could hear the elk within the trees on the other side of the clearing. He waited a long pause before advancing a quiet step, then waited again. When he felt all was clear, he began to graze. The cougars watched the elk as he made his way deeper into the clearing, coming closer to where they sat, hidden in the pale bushes. The sky shifted from dark grey to white.

As the elk stood chewing, the birds went quiet.

The Cougar and the Marauder ambushed the elk from both sides. The elk hesitated, unable to pick a direction of retreat, reared up, lashing out with his front hooves. The Marauder twisted aside, but the edge of the elk's hoof caught him on the side of his face. Meanwhile, the Cougar had dug her claws into the elk's back and was struggling to stay in place. With a leap, the Marauder rose into the air and came down upon the elk's back opposite the Cougar.

The Marauder and the Cougar used their united weight to bring the beast down. The Cougar held him in place, jaws at his neck, while the Marauder tore into the elk's throat and sank his bite home.

As the sky brightened overhead, the cougars feasted on the ample meat on the elk's case. Once their bellies were full they sat grooming, using their paws to wipe the blood from their faces. Then they curled up next to the remains and went to sleep.

When they awoke in the light of the setting sun, the Cougar saw that the wound on the Marauder's face had bled on him in his sleep. The side of his face, his shoulder and chest, were veined with dried blood.

The Marauder submitted himself to a cleaning from the Cougar, squinting his eye as her coarse tongue picked up the dried blood from his fur, grunting when she got too close to the wound. When she had licked clean all the blood, she saw that the wound still bled. A bright gash like a crescent moon upon his cheekbone, beneath his eye. It would heal but the Marauder would have a scar in that place. The Cougar, having been with him when he had gotten it, would be a part of this mark.

Like two ravenous birds, they ate the rest of the elk until they were scraping the bones with their tongues. They left the remains, spread out to the sky, for whatever scavenger might come by to claim them.

THEY HAD BEEN STALKING all night, and mated out the last of their half-hearted lust, and then, just at dawn, they came to an impasse; the Marauder heard the nearby rushing of water and sauntered toward the river. But the Cougar was not interested in the river and so continued on the path that would lead her back to the mountains where she so often sought her lairs.

She glanced back and watched the Marauder's sleek form disappear through the bare trees. She would not see the Marauder again for many seasons — but after a week in his constant presence that notion did not particularly trouble her. At times she would think of him as she travelled through the night and see him as if before her eyes — stalking the forest, sitting and waiting — and it was enough to think of him this way, believing that he was there, until they were called together again.

T HE COUGAR AWOKE TO the sunset. Sometimes she stirred during the day because her side was hurting and in a half-conscious state she would turn her back on the light and return to sleep. But on this day she awoke, not in pain, but to a clarity and calm, as if she had been called awake and now that she had awoken the voice was silent. She sat listening into the day, growing suspicious.

She rose, favouring her injured side. With a limp that lessened as she went, the Cougar left the cave in the mountainside where they had slept through the day and stood on a stone ledge overlooking the forest. A breeze hitched the branches to one side and on that slight wind the Cougar smelled the sharp scent of smoke.

She searched the cloudless sky, but the mountain forbade much of her view. There was still no sign of the foretold smoke. Doubly suspicious since her accident, she had learned to trust her instincts when it came to danger, to heed the signs, and she did not doubt her sense of smell. It did not seem unnatural to her that she might be smelling smoke which was yet to be.

Still, it had not rained. The leaves were yellowing on the trees. The sun had faded the forest roof so instead of the usual lush green, a mottled yellow and gold canopy stood before her. The Cougar shunned the daylight hours, preferring to appear only after the sun had set, but even on her nighttime forays the heat hung in the air, refusing to vacate the forest. The smell of moist earth was a distant memory.

The Cougar noticed her son sitting behind her. She had not heard him approach but it pleased her that he had learned the importance of silence. He sat searching the trees, sniffing the wind. He too sensed the strange air around them. The cats shared a glance, as if the same thought passed between them, from one eye to the other.

The sky was aflame with the last light of the sunset as the cougars made their way down the mountainside. The scent of smoke greeted them once they entered the trees. Tall spruce towered over them, blocking their view of the sky so they were not able to determine the origin of the smoke.

The light fell and they were blue cougars in a blue forest. The sound of their cautious footsteps seemed loud to them, magnified by an unnatural silence that occupied the forest around them. Then, through black trees, they saw an infernal glow coming from the earth. The cougars stopped and stood, staring. The Cougar's Son grunted. But the Cougar was hesitant to investigate. Such a disorienting angle of light was not to be trusted. She turned and headed around it. After a moment, she heard her son following over the crisp leaves.

They came to a clearing where they could see the open sky, the ominous presence of smoke rising up from behind the trees around them. The Cougar searched her memory of the landscape around them and knew which way to go, but she was not certain now of what they would find.

The land rose, the trees grew sparse, and they saw the forest below; fire crackled along the ground like a slow flood, crawling up the trees, spreading across the leaves so the trees bloomed, each in a flare of light that burned and diminished. The sound of so many trees burning was a dull roar, the violent opposite of the sound the trees usually made.

The Cougar's Son called out and the Cougar gave a low response but did not stop. They went on as smoke wafted through the trees, driven by the wind.

The air grew hazy. In all directions the earth glowed with that infernal light. They tried to retreat from the flames, but it seemed that everywhere they turned the fire was already there. Soon they were surrounded.

They kept their heads low to the ground, but the air was becoming hard to breathe. They began to see the flames licking toward them through the haze, the menacing glow between the black trees, and they picked up their pace. When the crackle of burning grew louder, and they could feel the heat on their bodies, they broke into a run.

As they ran the fire seemed to chase them. The hiss and pop of trees burning outmatched the roar of the flames. The Cougar found what path she could through the trees. They could not turn back for the fire had consumed their trail, and they could not stay where they were for the very earth beneath their feet would soon be devoured. They went on, finding the places to set their feet as they went.

The sound of splintering wood cracked through the air. The Cougar's heart leapt as a flaming tree came crashing to the ground before them, its branches breaking off in a shower of sparks. The cougars stalled, their path barred by this blazing heap, their backs harassed by fire. They had no choice but to jump.

The cougars rose into the air, the flaming tree lighting up their white chests as they leapt over, a moment of heat hotter than the sun, then they were clear. The ease with which she jumped surprised the Cougar for she had not called on her body, tested it in such a way, since her injury, and though her landing sent a bolt of pain through her side she did not falter. She heard her son land behind her, then they went on through the burning forest.

Again the fire was behind them, but it was impossible to know where they would encounter it next. Already the Cougar was tired from running. Breathing the smoky air gave her sharp pains in her chest. The wind pushed the fire on and the dry forest passed the flames along like an urgent message. Then, despite the disorienting smoke, the trees ablaze, the Cougar recognized where they were and veered toward the river.

They began to see the river through the trees and as they approached the Cougar felt the coolness of the river's presence before her. They stood panting on the riverbank, the roar of the fire behind them. The Cougar felt the heat upon her back and stepped down into the cold, black water. The Cougar's Son hesitated on the bank, uncertain of braving the depths at night. Hearing him hesitate, the Cougar called to him, trying not to allow her own dread to be heard in her voice. The Cougar's Son looked into the water as he stepped into it, as if hoping to see what lay beneath. The Cougar called to him again and he followed.

When the water was at their chins they pushed away from shore. The gentle current pulled them out onto the river. Behind them the fire showed through the black trees with a menacing brightness, like a beast of fire prowling the forest, watching them as they passed by.

They floated downriver, the roar of the fire dampening as they moved away, and they were plunged into darkness. To keep themselves afloat the cougars trod water or rolled onto their backs. The current pulled them along. The Cougar noticed the mess of stars overhead, her own heartbeat sounding loud to her own ears. Then she saw the light glowing through the trees around a bend in the river, the sickly yellow smoke rising above the black trees. When they came around the bend, the cougars saw the forest ablaze on both sides of the river.

The fire had jumped the river and was at work eating away the trees on the other side. The river reflected the fire in the trees like a river of molten flame. Smoke rose into the sky like mountains above the raging flames, billowing and convoluting, lit by the fire below.

The Cougar felt the heat on her face as they floated by and dunked her head under the water, then continued watching, the fury of the flames reflected in her eyes. The wind picked up leaves ablaze on their branches and sent them floating out over the river like fireflies, slowly coming to rest and extinguishing as they hit the water's surface.

The sound of the inferno was constant, all around them. They floated on, past the raging flames. The mountainous clouds of smoke climbed upward, pummelled by the wind. When the Cougar's Son, struck by the strangeness of the sight before him, uttered a yowl, his voice was barely audible, cut down by the roar of the fire. The Cougar mirrored his sentiment but remained silent, watching as the forest was consumed in one terrible breath.

Even from afar they could see the smoke from the wildfire as it coursed into the night sky. The Cougar wondered what could survive such devastation, what the forest would look like after it had all burned.

They drifted until dawn, the sky fading from black to deep mauve. Before the sun rose, they pulled themselves from the river, exhausted. With limbs like waterlogged branches, they climbed up the bank, one heavy footstep at a time. An owl hooted as the cougars slipped through the trees, the sun crawling into the sky, the faint smell of smoke wafting through the air.

PLUMES OF BREATH ROSE around their heads as the Cougar and her son awaited their prey. Winter had plunged its icy hand into the earth. The cold air snaked around them. It was impossible to move and not be reminded of its presence. The Cougar enjoyed the sensation of taking a deep breath, the cold air filling her lungs, though it sent a stab of pain into her side. She was rediscovering her appreciation of many things now that the trauma of her injury was behind her. Mundane things like cold air, the sound of snow falling, which now seemed marvellous again, which she had forgotten.

Fleeing the wildfire had reminded her of her younger self. It seemed her survival was never certain, yet now more than ever she wanted to live. She wanted never again to become trapped in her lair, close to Death. Let the end come swiftly, not creeping toward her, not staring her down.

The sun was setting but the clouds overhead were too thick for the light to penetrate. The Cougar and her Son rose, twin shadows in the dark day, and stalked through the snow on light feet. They came to a rocky ledge. A tree had toppled over the edge, pulling the earth away with it, leaving a tangle of stone and dead limbs. Covered in snow, it was impossible to tell when the scene had occurred, this winter, or some winter long ago. The cougars jumped down from the ledge next to the tangle of roots, landing in silence.

Two cougars leapt through the deep snowdrifts, one following the other. They cut through the trees, leaving a slim corridor through the snow behind them. The Cougar's Son had surpassed her in size and while still lean he was nothing but muscle. His paws outsized her own. So like the Marauder in his movements — which the Cougar found strange since they had never met — the way he stepped and paused, sniffing the air, one paw held against his body until he deemed it safe to set it down. And so like herself in colour and appearance, a gold lion with stoic patience.

They heard a sound across the air, from the trees upon the rise before them. The Cougar stopped. Indulging her curiosity had proven dangerous in the past, when it had attracted the unwanted attention of another cougar, when she had fallen out of a tree and down a cliff, and with her son watching she was conscious that her actions were being studied, absorbed, and she knew she must always act as one whose survival depended on constant vigilance. Nevertheless, being cautious had served her well and she decided it was best to learn whatever she could about the territory in which they now lived.

She headed toward the trees. As the cougars crept over the rise, they saw the sharp orange brightness of firelight casting the dark blue shadows of the trees against the snow, rising and fading like a heartbeat.

There was movement across the flames. They heard the sound of chattering ahead. She smelled the scent of smoke coupled with that of charred meat, and refuse, and the Cougar grew wary, yet more curious still. She stopped, about to turn back. The firelight flickered against the bare, frozen trees, reminding the Cougar of the wildfire that had torn through the valley. The Cougar's Son stood rapt. He would not take a step until she did, but he stared, intent, yearning to know what lay beyond the trees. Finally, the Cougar sunk low and crept on toward the firelight. Her son followed, obliterating her paw prints with his larger ones in silence.

The cougars stayed within the trees, hidden in shadow, and peered into the small clearing. Another flash of memory jolted the Cougar when she recognized the ring of stones wherein a small fire crackled and sputtered. Two creatures, the nature of which she had never seen before, attended the fire. One man stood on his back legs, the other man sat gazing into the flames.

The one standing was like a squirrel, rummaging through their sacks, collecting items, travelling back and forth to the vessel suspended over the fire. It seemed like a conscious decision to the Cougar that he would walk about on his back legs, exposing his belly to attack, but she could not imagine a reasonable purpose for doing this.

The wild hair on their heads and faces seemed warning enough, but the lack of hair around their eyes, exposing the skin around that delicate juncture, seemed somehow shocking—perhaps meant to distract—and the Cougar found the sight of that bare flesh somehow unsettling, even inappropriate.

The thing most immediate about the men was their peculiar scent, which she could smell from where she sat within the trees. The Cougar saw her son sniffing the air. Let him memorize the scent, so that he might know it for next time. She wondered if allowing themselves to smell this way was the means by which they lured their prey to them, or whether this was how they warded off their predators.

The men called back and forth to one another. Their conversation sounded to the Cougar like the chattering of birds. Their smell, their unassuming appearance, led the Cougar to wonder how these animals had the ability to call fire from the earth. There must be something more to them, perhaps something not easily perceived, and she knew she must not rely on her vision alone when it came to men. By their soft, flimsy appearance, the Cougar believed she could snap their necks just like a deer. But the presence of the fire was a sign of something else entirely, something she had no knowledge of.

The man sitting before the flames began to speak. The one standing watched him, expressionless. The one sitting threw a shout into the air between them. There was a pause. Then a convulsive sound erupted from them both, their faces contorted, flashing their teeth so the Cougar thought they were challenging each other to fight. She hunched down into the snow, waiting to see what would happen. But nothing came of the display. The men returned their attention to the flames, the simmering pot suspended above it. The Cougar wondered if the two were mates.

The Cougar lost interest in the men and rose, taking a silent step back the way she had come. The Cougar's Son sunk low to the ground. He took a step forward, meaning to engage the men. But the Cougar was walking away. They had not observed these men at great length. There was no telling what they would do under threat. It was not worth the risk of learning.

The Cougar's Son looked after her, then back to the men. He took another step toward them. The fire seemed to have a strange power over him, calling to him, but when he saw that his mother did not intend to join him, he hesitated.

The Cougar went on through the trees, the slight sound of the snow crushed beneath her feet diminishing as she vanished into the darkness, and when the Cougar's Son could no longer hear her, he relented. He cast a last look at the men sitting around their fire, then followed his mother's paw prints until he caught up with her and they went on through the starlit night.

I N THE TWILIGHT BEFORE dawn, two cougars sat side by side next to the ravaged body of a deer. The Cougar was neck-deep in the rib cage while her son worked at the flank. The Cougar lifted her head, a beard of blood upon her face as she sat chewing, staring into the trees.

They had not eaten in three days, seeking through wet snow, sleeping for short bouts, then moving on, when they came across the tracks of a lone deer. The tracks were melted into the snow so it seemed they were stalking a giant deer through the forest. As they followed the prints, the Cougar imagined, in her hunger, what an enormous deer might look like, antlers scraping the branches overhead, legs like the trunks of trees. But when they found the deer he was of normal size.

The deer sniffed over the frozen ground, believing he was alone. He looked up, drawn by something, a current on the air. The darkness had gone quiet.

The Cougar was at the deer's side, reaching out with her claws. The deer reared back; a gust of breath trumpeted from his nostrils. Eyes on the Cougar, he did not see the Cougar's Son, who stepped in from out of the darkness and wrapped his front leg around the deer's neck as he brought him to the ground, jaws at his throat.

They were ravenous and ate with no intention of caching the remains. Otherwise the forest was still. Through the cold air, the call of an owl interrupted the crystalline sound of melting snow.

The Cougar's ears turned toward the trees. She heard nothing in the surrounding forest but silence. Then she stood as she realized she was listening to the distinct silence that preceded a horde.

The sound of their feet over the damp forest floor came through the trees. She could not tell how many they were. The smell of them, a complex aroma, indicated a pack, and she knew there was a dangerous number of them even before she saw the swarm of glowing eyes gathering in the dark.

The wolves began to emerge from the trees. The Cougar's Son hissed. The Cougar stood unmoving, head to the ground, eyes on the wolves, the deer at her feet forgotten. Their proportions looked odd to her, with such large heads on those thin bodies, the long legs above their heavy paws. They were full black and pure blond, some a silver grey. There were ten or twelve in all. But none of these wolves drew her attention. A large male with black fur on his shoulders and white fur on his chest stepped out of the shadows but remained in the back, white muzzle, black mask over his yellow eyes. This was the leader of the pack. The Cougar let out a warning scream to show him she was not afraid of their number.

A wave of dread passed through her. The Cougar recoiled at the swarm of them. She had heard the howl of wolves through the forest, seen them hunting from a distance, but she had never seen an entire pack up close before. There were too many to keep an eye on. She knew it would be wisest to withdraw. But if they ran, the wolves would give chase. Wolves were mad for a chase. A cougar survived by stealth and surprise, by expending as little energy as possible. A wolf survived by its ability to run its prey into the ground. Though fast in its own right, a cougar could not run forever.

The Cougar screamed again, to send them away. The wolves shivered back at the sound of her voice, but were not deterred. Instead they began to circle the cougars, prancing and chattering. The Cougar wondered if they were communicating, or if this was done merely to intimidate, and she was determined this would not distract her. The cougars stood, backs to each other, watching as the wolves ran circles around them.

The Cougar was willing to sacrifice the half-eaten deer to the pack, but it barely seemed of interest to them. They wanted the cougars to run. The Cougar maintained her initial posture, eyes on the wolves. Let them see that she was not frightened by them. She would reveal nothing else. The wolves ran with their mouths open, gusts of breath rising into the air, their tongues lolling out, in anticipation.

The Cougar screamed again to silence the wolves, but now it seemed this did nothing but excite them.

The alpha remained in the back, eyes on the cougars, as the other wolves circled. The sound of their unnerving chatter, their mad behaviour, aggravated her. Though they might still convince the wolves they were not worth dealing with, her heart beat hard in her chest. The number of wolves concerned her. The Cougar's Son shifted on his front feet, eyes jumping from wolf to wolf as they ran by.

The Cougar growled again. This time her son joined her. She had not heard the sound of that growl in full force until now. Being fully grown, agitated in earnest, his voice ripped through the air, sending an icy breath across even the Cougar's body. The wolves faltered, as if pushed back by a sudden wind.

A wolf danced close enough for the Cougar to reach out and grab, and she hissed, ears back, eyes flashing, outraged that it would come so near. She was beginning to think they would have no choice but to run. The Cougar's Son swatted at a wolf who came too near, but the wolf twisted away, barking. The alpha stood behind his circling wolves, waiting, watching the cougars.

The Cougar felt her son tense against her as a grey wolf rushed toward him. The Cougar's Son reached out, catching the wolf in his claws, and pulled him into his jaws. In the next instant, the wolf hung limp from his mouth, and the Cougar knew now there was no retrieving the situation.

The Cougar twisted and leapt over the wolves, their heads moving in unison as they followed her flight through the air. When she touched ground she set off running. She did not have to look back to know that her son was with her, she could hear the sound of his footsteps just behind her.

The wolves ran after them, the rumble of their feet hitting the ground like the sound of distant thunder. One of the wolves let loose a vicious bark, then one by one the others joined in the barrage of baying. The Cougar and her son cut through the trees, taking the ground in great leaps, yet they could not leave the wolves behind.

She heard the panting of the wolves and glanced back. They were close, in sincere pursuit, but they were not gaining. They were waiting. They would wait until the cougars were tired enough to turn and stand. This was the ending they anticipated. This was what they wanted.

The land dropped away, a rocky chasm yawning before them. The cougars leapt across the crevasse, catching the other side with a clean landing, then setting off again. The wolves followed, jumping as they encountered the gap, a dark horde spilling across the void.

One of the wolves came snarling out of the darkness at the Cougar's Son, driving him to the side. The Cougar's Son leapt away from her, and directly in his path stood a knot of fallen trees. He jumped and kept rising, over the wreck of tangled branches, and cleared the highest outstretched branch. The Cougar glanced back as he set down, noting his landing without pause, his leap forward over the ground, like he was made of air.

Ahead the Cougar could hear the trees come to an end, the open space beyond. They had to take cover or they would be forced to stand and fight. Weak from exhaustion, they would be overwhelmed by the wolves, who were frenzied by their bloodlust.

The cougars came out of the trees. The Cougar veered to one side, running along the treeline, her son like a shadow close behind. The wolves spilled out of the trees and tumbled over one another as they scrambled to follow the cougars. An expanse of meadow lay beside them, mounds of melting snow glowing white upon the black earth. The smell of the soil drew the Cougar's eyes. A giant tree stood in the distance, its bare branches grey against a sky burning blue with the imminent arrival of the sun.

The Cougar felt her limbs growing heavy. Pain shot through her entire body, striking out from her injured side. The Cougar's Son gained on and surpassed her. The wolves were barking at her feet, getting nearer.

The cougars turned toward the lone tree in the open field. It was not a permanent measure, it would only prolong their stand against the wolves, but they could not stop and fight now. Her skin crawled as they drew near the tree. Its leafless branches immediately brought to mind the tree that had sent her tumbling down the cliffside. This tree was older still, ten times as thick, its massive grey branches like claws clutching the bright sky.

The cougars leapt into the tree's branches, leaving the wolves foaming and snarling below, angry puffs of breath rising into the cold air. The Cougar and her son climbed the tree as far as they dared, chests heaving around their worried hearts. The Cougar looked to her son, his body twisted around a branch, gripping it with his claws. He watched the wolves below, a stoic expression on his golden face.

Anguished howls rose up from below. The wolves jumped, trying to reach the lowest branches so they could get at the cougars above. The Cougar and her son felt around with their paws, settled into more comfortable positions. Soon the howling below dwindled to the occasional whimper. The sun broke the horizon. The cougars curled up and the wolves settled in to wait out the time until their inevitable encounter.

THE WOLVES SLEPT IN a tight knot at the base of the tree, huddled together for warmth against the stark, white light of day. Always one of their number sat up, watching, standing guard among the sleeping, keeping an eye on the surrounding land, the cats in the tree above. Eventually this wolf would yawn, lower its head, and return to sleep, and another wolf would raise its head and take up the guard. Thus, a system of continuous surveillance was created, so no member of the pack lost out on sleep.

All day the Cougar feigned sleep, watching the wolves below. She was surprised to learn that, like her cubs, they dreamed, mimicking the action of running, making half-hearted growls, soft whimpers in their sleep, and the Cougar wondered what events transpired in those dreams, and marvelled that two such dissimilar animals would share this mysterious affliction.

Later in the day some of the wolves perked up and between yawns watched the cats perched in the tree, staring up with great and knowing patience, as if at any moment they fully expected them to step down. But most of the wolves ignored them. It was as if the wolves had forgotten their siege on the cougars and were merely waiting for an interval of time to pass before moving on.

The Cougar maintained her posture of sleep. Now every breath must be devoted to her survival. Every action cost energy and with no way to replenish their reserves, they had precious little to spare. Above all, they must act upon their first available opportunity. To hesitate would mean death.

THE SUN BEGAN TO set, casting long shadows over the thawing earth.

The wolves roused themselves from sleep and rose together, stretching with quiet yawns. They began stepping lightly around the tree, restless, aimless movements. They circled the tree as if this were some requirement they were familiar with that they had done many times before.

As the sun sank behind the trees, the wolves began to howl. They stood, their faces raised to the sky, their eerie voices rising into the air. Then they quieted down, returning to their former state as if nothing had occurred.

The Cougar looked to her son, who met her stare with a reflection of her own bewildered expression.

Once it was fully night, the wolves roused again, and went about their familial rituals. They greeted one another with affectionate licks. They sat together in twos or threes, in what seemed to be personal preference, bonds forged through season after season of hunting and sleeping together. There was also play-fighting, done not in earnest, but rather as a daily requirement, or to entertain the others, as the alpha looked on. Even when two young males started to tumble around, jaws at each other's throats, snarls unleashed, their bites were never meant to injure. They were expressive animals. Though the Cougar did not fully understand the nuances of their language, she understood the broad meaning of their interactions. Everything was a form of communication, the noises they made, their movements, even where they looked. It was forbidden to make eye contact with the alpha. Only the alpha female was given leeway in this regard. The Cougar observed all of this from the branches.

The half-moon slid out from behind white clouds. The Cougar and her son watched as four wolves made their way across the snowy field and disappeared into the trees. The pack returned to their leisurely posture, as if they were not out in the open waiting on a tree of cougars but relaxing in the privacy of their den.

Hours passed. The Cougar and her son moved among the branches when they became uncomfortable; as they did so, the wolves below followed their movements, licking their chops. The Cougar was pained by the strain of supporting herself on her injured side, and there were only so many suitable places among the gnarled branches. She stood to stretch, extending her front legs one at a time, stretching out her back. Then she stood on her back legs and reached up, shredding the bark with her claws. First the Cougar then her son; one took up the ritual as the other was ending.

The silence of the night was broken as the faraway cry of the four absent wolves reached their ears. Three more wolves rose and set off for the trees, toward the call from somewhere within the forest. Later still, they heard the howls of those wolves and the responses from the first wolves, guiding them. The Cougar marvelled at this communication, their ability to function as a pack, all attended by a dominant couple.

Close to the morning, the first four wolves returned. Three more departed and then the reason for their coming and going became clear. They were hunting and feeding and in this way could guard the cougars indefinitely, or at least until the forest cats fell out of the tree from starvation. The Cougar saw that the wolves would not abandon them; instead, they would replenish their energy and wait for whichever gave out first: the cougars' energy or their resolve.

As the Cougar watched, the wolves went about their business quite naturally. They would tell her how she could escape them, she need only wait, though she knew her time was running short. She would have to act before hunger overpowered her strength and she was too weak to cut down even a single wolf, let alone an entire pack.

ASIDE FROM THE PHYSICAL discomfort they endured being confined to the tree, the cougars found themselves battling not just hunger and fatigue, but also boredom. Both mother and son had scratched the trunk bare of its bark, their claw marks revealing the bright wood beneath the weathered, grey exterior. They stretched often, as if their sleep tired them out rather than restored them. There was always the lengthy process of grooming, but they found they could not give themselves completely to this ritual under the watchful eyes of the wolves below.

It seemed the wolves also suffered boredom. One of the younger wolves made several attempts to get into the tree's branches. He would run and jump up off the trunk of the tree and twist around, snapping his teeth on empty air. But even the lowest branches were out of reach. It seemed a waste of energy to the Cougar. Even if the wolf was successful in grasping the branch between his jaws, he would not be able to pull himself up. This would be easy for the agile body of a cougar, whose front legs could embrace, but wolves were not capable of such a manoeuvre.

The wolves could run great distances, which the Cougar recognized as a definite advantage. If she could run as long as a wolf, as well as possess her strength and skill as a hunter, she would be unstoppable, pursuing prey until they collapsed from exhaustion. No prey could escape her.

She noticed too their superior sense of smell. At times, one of the wolves would raise its head to the wind and the Cougar would see its nostrils working at the air when she herself could detect nothing. She wondered what this told them of the world, what knowledge was gained by this specific ability that she herself lacked.

The wolves respected a strict order of command under the alpha. The Cougar saw the subordinate males licking their legs to make their fur sleek, their legs appear thinner, almost feminine. No wolf ever raised its head higher than the alpha's. No teeth were ever bared before him. He was the centre to which all was devoted. The Cougar was intrigued by this dynamic, for such an order would never work among cougars.

A pack of cougars, if such a thing were to exist, would never submit to a leader. Each cat was alpha of her own domain. But supposing such a thing did exist, this pack would quickly decimate the prey population. After a brief period of gluttony, the cougars would begin to starve, only to turn on one another — a grim vision.

THE COUGAR LAY BETWEEN sleep and waking, cradled in a branch. Her son slept in a similar position, head resting on his paws. Suddenly, the tree began to quake. A low rumbling sounded below them. The Cougar started, dug her claws into the branch, looking around for some explanation. The top of the tree shivered as if in the midst of a violent wind, but the Cougar felt nothing except the tremor. When she looked to the ground, she saw the wolves running in circles around the base of the tree and the earth was slowly getting closer — the tree was sinking.

The Cougar climbed to higher branches. She looked above her and saw that her son had already climbed to the top and clung there, looking down at her. Below her the wolves were jumping, trying to catch the lowest branches in their jaws. Soon one of them would jump into the branches and then they would all swarm into the tree like ants overtaking a fallen hatchling.

———

THE COUGAR LIFTED HER head to find her son watching her. He yowled at her, a deep sound now that he was grown. Her heart was beating as though she had been running. She looked around in the heavy orange light of sunset and saw that the tree was as it had been when she had gone to sleep.

Below her she noticed the alpha sitting, also watching her. The Cougar exhaled sharply and lay her head in her paws and closed her eyes. Her son too settled back down as the sun set on the third day of their standoff with the wolves.

T HE COUGAR SAT THE whole day, unmoving. Her
son likewise slept. The wolves prowled below as the
sun ran its course across the sky. The day was at its
warmest as the light began to fade. In that time before
sunset, the wolves were up, anxious, dancing around the
tree. There seemed to be some tension in the air.

She did not see what happened, only heard the sudden
snarling from below.

A young black wolf stood growling, the alpha growled
in return, fur bristling along their backs. Even as he was
challenging, the subordinate male never lifted his head
higher than the alpha's, instead keeping his head low to
the ground, the whites of his eyes visible as he looked up
at the alpha, teeth white against his black fur.

The alpha rushed the smaller wolf, barking louder than
any sound the Cougar had heard from the wolves so far. He
had his jaws at the black wolf's throat. The black wolf lay on
his back, exposing his belly, absolutely still. The alpha stood
over the subordinate, breathing hard. The rest of the pack
sat watching. It was all for show. A way to alleviate tension,
to express frustration more than anything else. The Cougar
sensed the restlessness in the pack, the cost of a long siege.

The alpha sent out his female and two adolescents to
hunt. Before departing, the alpha and his female touched
noses, licking each other's chops, and the Cougar spied

on them from her perch in the tree. Her eyes followed the female as she raced across the barren field flanked by the younger wolves, then disappeared into the dark trees.

The alpha looked up at the cougars sitting in the tree as they watched the sunset. Then he too sat and gazed upon the sunset blazing on the horizon. All the wolves quieted and watched the fiery performance, the flare of colour spreading out into the sky, blooming and withering in one slow movement.

Night fell and the air grew damp. The sky was clear and the starlight was more than enough for a cougar to see by. The wolves slept together in the dark, snoring, growling at dreams. A call came through the air. Two of the wolves rose and set out across the field toward the trees.

Once they had gone, the Cougar stood and was immediately struck by a wave of dizziness. She felt she had been here before. She could not help but notice this weakness, this closeness to Death, as a familiar feeling. It was almost a comfort. The cold air was thick with the scent of mud. A deep breath made her head swim. She took another breath, despite the pang it caused in her side. Then she leapt out of the tree.

The Cougar and her Son each landed atop one of the wolves below. Startled, the wolves had time to cry out to their sleeping brethren before their necks were crushed between their assailants' jaws, then they fell dead at the cougars' feet.

A wolf sprang toward the Cougar. The Cougar's Son caught him by the head and threw him to the ground. The Cougar felt certain the wolf would lie there, dead, from such a rough blow. But instead he scrambled up, shaking his head.

Two wolves tackled the Cougar, jaws at her neck. She felt one of them torn off, its whimper cut short. The Cougar's Son tossed the wolf clenched in his jaws to the side. The wolf hit the ground then lay in a heap. Another wolf sprang at him but he dodged the attack and caught the wolf in his claws. His bite nearly severed the wolf's neck and the wolf's head lolled back against its body as it slumped to the ground.

The Cougar tried to shake the remaining wolf off her back. Another latched on to her, the two of them trying to bite into the thick muscle around her neck. She saw the alpha before her and she growled and twisted, trying to shake the wolves off. The Cougar reached out and grabbed a wolf leg and brought it to her jaws, crunching into the bone. The wolf yelped and hobbled away on three legs. She threw herself against the tree's trunk, crushing the wolf upon her back. It did not make a sound but let loose its grip and slumped dead at her feet.

The Cougar's Son flew out of the darkness toward the alpha. The alpha met him, jaws snapping, twisting away from the young cougar's reach and right into the Cougar's waiting grasp. She pounced on him, pinning him to the ground. He let out a surprised yelp, astonished, cut short as the Cougar tore into his neck.

The alpha lay on the ground, a wheezing breath escaping his torn neck, gurgling through the seepage of black blood, then he joined the rest of his pack felled by the Cougar and her son.

The Cougar cast a deadly look at the remaining wolves. They saw their leader cut down, the two forest cats, lusty and blood-splattered, glaring wildly. The wolves turned and ran across the muddy field, all the way to the trees.

The Cougar and her son stood panting, clawed and bitten. In the weak light, their wounds appeared black upon their blue bodies. The wolves had defended themselves with resolve, as a pack would, and the cougars bore the marks of their fearlessness. The only sound was that of their ragged breathing, their working hearts.

The fallen wolves lay like shed limbs cast off from the tree above. Exhausted from their days-long struggle, drained by their ambush on the pack, the Cougar and her son became possessed by hunger. Each fell upon the nearest body and tore into the fresh meat. The Cougar reached out and drew her claw down the belly of one of the wolves, the insides still warm in their case. The Cougar felt on the verge of collapse even as she began to eat, her heart beating fast, her head pounding.

The sun rose, revealing the Cougar and her son wearing red masks. They squinted into the growing light. Some of their injuries were superficial and would heal and disappear, while others would scar. The Cougar's shoulder throbbed where she had been chewed. Her son's ear was torn, a shard missing. He was marked for life. They were united by these wounds, the story told by these marks, each a part of the other.

They rested in the warmth of the sun and slept a true, deep sleep for the first time in many days. During the day the Cougar awoke and scanned the treeline. Four lupine heads watched them from the edge of the field, just within the trees, but she knew they would come no closer. She could not discern from this distance which one was the alpha female but the Cougar had no doubt she was among them. With the death of the alpha, the female would choose one of the subordinate males and together they would lead the diminished pack through this reduction in numbers. But for now they retreated to the shadows of the forest.

When the sun set, the Cougar and her son rose and headed into the trees. The scent of damp earth in the air reminded her of the valley. Spring would have taken root there as well. She had not thought of the valley since they had come to this territory and suddenly she longed for it, curious to see what spring would look like in a forest ravaged by wildfire. She wanted to see those familiar places, walk those familiar paths. Thinking about this, she felt somehow relieved.

NOW THE FOREST LAY muddy and moist, awakened by the heat of the sun. The smell of the earth hung heavy in the air. The cougars made their way back toward the river, pausing to hunt, replenishing the store of fat sacrificed during their long standoff with the wolves. They slept side by side next to the eviscerated remains of their kill, the restful sleep of the unguarded.

They found the river and travelled along its mindless bends and indulgences until finally they came to the place where they had climbed out of the water the night of the wildfire, recognized by the view of the mountains hovering above the treetops in the distance. The familiar sight sent a current through the Cougar's body and awoke in her a sense of urgency. She felt herself called to the mountains, just as she had been when she first set out toward them alongside her sister, so long ago.

The Cougar sat within the tall grass on the riverside. A thatch of grey trees stood behind her, their branches reaching over the water's surface. She caught her reflection in a small recess where the river had eaten away the land and the water was calm. Her face was changed, sharper than when she had last looked upon it. The whiteness on her chin seemed brighter, her golden cheeks leaner, and her eyes bore the haggard look of one pursued. Her face struck her with its gauntness, the softness of youth had been worn away. How sudden, she thought, though she knew the change must have been gradual, a process of many years.

As she watched, her reflection rippled with the movement of something beneath the surface of the water. Then she shook her head and pushed this vision aside.

When she did not hear the sound of her son's footsteps behind her, she turned. He sat, a flick of his tail when their eyes met. She called for him to come, but he remained where he was, giving her an impartial gaze, and then she saw he meant to leave her.

He would stay here in this territory and carve out a life for himself. She had almost forgotten he must leave her. He had lingered, while they investigated this new territory, and had seen her through another disaster. She saw him then, not as her son, but as a fully grown cougar, a hunter, about to strike out on his own, and her heart ached at their imminent parting. She stood, unable to bring herself to turn and go on.

The Cougar's Son turned and slipped through the trees, a golden shadow in the evening forest. When she could no longer hear his footsteps, she made a short growl. His response came to her from within the trees, low and nonchalant, and then even the sound of him was gone.

The Cougar sat, rooted to the earth by the heaviness in her chest. She could not move, unable to leave this last place they had been together, her desire to return to the mountains diminished. She stayed, waiting, until the light collapsed around her and she disappeared into shadow.

The sound of crickets and toads, the flow of the river, the fluttering of wings surrounded her. Time passed, measured by the steady beating of her heart. Like the river, it would not allow her to pause even for a moment, it just went on. Once in darkness, the Cougar moved from her spot, her side aching dully as she took the first few steps. She continued along the river back to the valley, grateful for the rushing water at her side, loud enough to drown out her thoughts.

THE NEXT DAY SHE entered forest that had been scourged by wildfire. The land seemed bare, weighed down by so much sky. Black, branchless trees stood next to trees that had escaped unscathed. What had burned to ash had been crushed beneath a layer of snow. The snow now melted, she saw the face of the earth like never before.

The sun fled and the sky darkened to a smouldering lilac as the Cougar walked along paths that she knew to exist, though their contours had been burned and blurred. Tender green sprouts pushed through the black earth into the air. They lay like a thin green fog on the ground and as the Cougar travelled deeper, they thickened into a lush cover, soft against her feet.

The Cougar came to an older part of the forest, where the tree trunks were massive, and though many had been damaged by the fire, the bark on their trunks blackened, their top branches grew rife with tightly furled green buds. Here her eyes were drawn to the patches of blue and purple flowers that grew at the base of these trees. The flowers spread like blue flames between the great trees. The Cougar followed their trail through the forest and came to a hillside covered with pink flowers that seemed to glow in the dusk, the colour so intense it stung her eyes to look at them even in the falling light. The flowers had grown tall enough that they brushed her face as she waded through them, like a forest of small pink trees and she a giant cougar.

The Cougar stalked this strange, electric landscape as the air grew dark. Her body seemed to melt away, neither earth, nor air, but a mixture of the two. Her blood turned to fire and she felt invigorated, despite the pain in her side, despite her heavy heart, eager to return to the places she knew. She toured the paths she had once known to see all that had taken place in her absence. She went seeking through the night and in the waiting shadows of the forest she found her solitary self, silent as ever, and, once reunited with her shadow-self, disappeared.

VI

MAIN STREET

->-

A S JOSEPH GREW OLDER, he was a terror upon the wild things that lived in the forest around him. August would find his son in the midst of digging into an anthill; uprooting young trees, pulling them out of the earth with his bare hands; throwing rocks at squirrels whenever they scampered past. All sorts of bewildering behaviour.

August was perplexed by this obsession with the destruction of the natural world. He tried to remember back to being a boy of ten, whether or not he had been filled with murderous rage. He tried to think of what his father might have thought of him at that age, but he could not imagine this, obscured by the distance of time. He had grown up in the city, where the narrow streets were made of cobblestone, the buildings were carved from stone, and in the alleys each doorway was occupied by people smoking on their steps, as children played in brackish puddles. In that place, the danger was from the closeness of people, the threat of disease, of hunger. As a child, and growing into a young man, August had wanted nothing more than to get away from these people. But now he wondered if living among so many people had trained him to adapt himself to his environment. And he wondered if growing up surrounded by wilderness made a man feel as if he were custodian of his domain, and therefore could do with the forest as he pleased. Cut it back. Burn it. Waste it. Perhaps this imbued a child with a sense of violence, that he must battle against the world in order to live in it. Or perhaps this was just the way Joseph was, and always would be, regardless of where he grew up.

In truth Joseph was not obsessed with the death of all things, as his father suspected. He had but one prize in mind.

Tales of the Old Woman's exploits had been circulating through the town since long before Joseph was born. She was scorned and hated by the townsfolk, a common thread through their dark, wintry lives. Sometimes they did not think of her for months, then they would get a scent of her through the trees; someone believed they saw a set of glowing eyes in the shadows, or twenty sheep were killed in the dead of night, and the old tales were passed around again.

While there was a great deal of disagreement where the Old Woman was concerned, there were a few points on which most men could agree. She was older than any natural cougar had a right to be, thin as bone, sharp as a blade. Her eyes glowed like flames in the darkness. In sunlight, her fur shone like gold but her forelegs were crossed with the marks of many wounds and she wore a scar upon the left side of her face.

While out hunting, a man found himself in a sudden drop, pressed on all sides by waist-high grass. He noticed then all the birds had gone quiet. He moved to draw his rifle and out of the corner of his eye he saw her, sitting almost at his feet, staring right at him, ready to pounce. The hunter swung his rifle around and fired. But when the smoke cleared, she was nowhere in sight.

Two hunters were settling down next to their fire in the quiet evening. They had a hare roasting on a spit over the fire. As the rabbit cooked, their mouths watered at the scent of the cooking meat. Fat dripped off the spit onto the hot red embers below, sizzling softly. They heard a sound, the slightest snap of a twig, and turned to see, and there was that scar-faced cougar sailing out of the bushes toward them. She passed them, grabbed up the rabbit on the spit in her mouth, and without even touching the ground passed right through the camp and into the trees on the other side. The hunters sat, mouths open, not believing what they had seen.

Wherever there was talk of the Old Woman, there was Joseph. He listened to every story, weighing the facts, testing whatever he heard against the litmus of his heart, for he believed there was something to be gained from listening to every word, however obscure, however untrue. He believed that seeking out these stories would lead him to her, though he did not yet know how.

Prompted by Joseph's continued disinterest in school, and out of a hopeful notion that Joseph just needed an avenue to channel his lust for destruction, August tried him as an apprentice. It was an immediate and unmitigated disaster. Joseph was not attentive to his father's words, he did not listen, or chose not to listen, and then could not remember any instruction given him — an ingenious tactic — and it became clear he had no real interest in blacksmithing whatsoever. He could be trusted to do basic tasks — fetch water, sweep out the straw, build a fire — but he had no patience to learn anything shown him. He did not remember procedure. He had no instinct for the strength of his blows, no patience for the repetitive tasks requiring deftness of hand. He did not have a sense of timing, that delicate touch required, to know amid all those many moments when was the moment to strike.

August had believed these things could be taught. With enough repetition, a man could learn and understand. But he saw now there was one thing lacking: the will. A man must have a will to learn. And it seemed Joseph did not. The smithy was a dangerous place and there was no room for error or daydreaming. It was a place of smoke and flame and metal so hot it glowed with an infernal heat that could sear skin at the barest touch. These were elements that required a certain amount of respect. If they were not handled properly, they could injure a man, mark him with his own inattentiveness for life.

Finally, August became so frustrated with Joseph's unwillingness to learn that he dismissed him. Between father and son, the matter was dropped, and for the time being the question of what Joseph would do for a living was not up for discussion.

August worried that the boy was hopeless, and worried somehow that it was his failure, that he had done this to him. He tried to think around what he considered a grave obstacle. If a man had no interest in school, no interest in work at all, how would such a man provide a life for himself in the age to come?

THE TOWN HAD CONTINUED to grow with each passing year and, like a slow wave, eventually engulfed them and kept moving onward. The smithy was actually set back from the current road so it ended up behind the buildings lining Main Street, down a wide alley. Behind the smithy the scene remained unchanged: nothing but trees.

When Joseph was twelve, the smithy expanded into the single-room dwelling to facilitate the rising demand for work, so they were forced to vacate their cramped living quarters. They rented some rooms down the street, so August would be close to work. This meant Joseph would get his own room. He had never been more thrilled in his life.

Their rooms were on the third storey of a house on Main Street. They bought some shelves second-hand and lugged them up the two flights of stairs, father and son grunting and cursing the whole way. They had three large windows opening onto the kitchen and the front room. Joseph got the long, narrow room, a child's bed bookended by walls. He had a chest of drawers in which he kept his clothes. He hung his rifle on the wall beside the door, and his hatchet beside his rifle. The head of the hatchet had been forged by his father and given to him as a present.

His bedroom window overlooked the street, and he immediately forgave the room its awkward shape. This feature appealed to him a great deal. From here he could observe the people, the entire town, in secret. He spent many hours watching down into the street, fascinated by the activity of horses and men, each man with some purpose of his own, though they were in fact working together as a whole, even if they were not conscious of it. Joseph believed this insight, which he had come to on his own, to be of grave importance. Here was the centre of all things, here was a point of significance, and he felt the superiority of one who had been included.

The first time Joseph saw an automobile rolling down Main Street he was enamoured with this fantastic machine; its gleaming metal exterior caught his eye: the grille, the headlights, the glass windshield. He admired the structure of the body, and he was somehow envious. Not envious of the car's owner, envious of the car itself. It could withstand the world, a mechanical body made for the mechanical world.

He could not help but broach the subject with his father.

"Now that we live in town, we should get a car."

August turned a perplexed look on his son. "What on earth for?"

Joseph felt the notion was self-explanatory. "To drive around!"

"To drive from one side of town to the other? Sounds exciting."

Joseph was amazed by his father's dismissive attitude. How could his father not be astounded by automobiles? It mystified him — and he could not stop himself from trying to persuade him otherwise.

Finally, fed up with Joseph's continued harassment, August gave his definitive opinion on the matter. "There is no reason for such a clamorous, costly extravagance! You can just forget about it!"

Joseph was appalled. He detected what he believed to be a note of hysteria in his father's objection. August dismissed automobiles as one in total denial of the age to come, and Joseph considered this an ignorant and unreasonable attitude.

Joseph was given the task of looking after their rooms, and despite his best efforts their apartment maintained a shabby, unkempt appearance. He grew frustrated with the burden of his responsibilities. He had all the housework to himself, and he quickly learned there was an endless list of tasks that went into keeping house. Perhaps too much work for the boy.

Conflict started with a single word, an inconsiderate tone.

"After you're done with those dishes, the tub could use a scrub too."

Joseph threw his sponge into the sink. "I'm sick of cleaning up after you like some maid! Why don't you get a wife to do all this work?"

August tried to suppress a smile. "Wise words from one so young. I suppose I'll just pull one out of the air?"

"You couldn't get one! You're too old and ugly!"

"Well, I guess I'm stuck with you then."

Joseph growled through clenched teeth. He was annoyed that he was made to clean instead of being allowed to attend to his time as he pleased. It did not seem fair.

As if reading Joseph's thoughts, his father said, "Life isn't about shooting things and having fun. It's about work. And the sooner you get that into your head, the better."

Joseph turned back to his work, silent, outraged.

JOSEPH SAT ON HIS bed, window open to the cool evening air. He had been watching the street below for hours. At sunset, a man came to light the lamps that lined Main Street. The shops were closing their doors for the day. Now the street became busiest with pedestrians, people heading to the rough row of houses on the road leading into town while others arrived home from other parts. Two neighbours spotted each other and stopped briefly on the plank sidewalk to chat, hats on their heads, scarves about their necks, gusts of breath puffing out between them.

After the evening traffic, the street turned quiet. The street lamps cast a hazy light over the sidewalks, the mud road. Joseph heard the sound of someone approaching well before they appeared. A young man emerged from the evening, cap pulled down so the top of his face was hidden in shadow, hands shoved into his pockets. Joseph watched as he continued down the street, stopped at the entrance to The Black Hen, and went inside.

After dark, a man alone on the street was headed in one direction. Joseph could see the entrance to The Black Hen from his window. The sound of conversation, a few chords of music, escaped from the bar when the young man opened the door. It seemed like a warm, inviting place on a cold autumn evening. Joseph did not see what was so bad about that. His father was always disparaging toward the bar and its patrons in general. He had forbidden Joseph from going there. But that had never stopped Joseph in the past.

It was ten o'clock. Joseph sat drowsing in bed, the cool air reaching in through the open window. His father slept in the next room, the light sound of his snoring audible through the walls.

A shot rang out from the east end of town. Joseph jerked awake, confused. He heard a far-off yell, indecipherable, through the night air. The music in the bar stopped. It was so quiet Joseph could hear a baby squalling in one of the houses on the other side of town.

In the absolute stillness he heard "—that a shot?" when the door to the bar opened. A man stepped out and peered down the street. Others along the street appeared on their doorsteps, looking out into the night, listening. Joseph saw lights come up in some of the rooms across the street, people with their heads craned out their windows. He opened his own window as far as it would go and leaned out, the cold air raising goosebumps on his arms, looking into the darkness at the end of Main Street then back to the entrance of the bar where now a small gathering had congregated.

Another shot rang out, this time at the opposite end of town. People ran toward the second shot. Joseph laughed, shaking his head. What pandemonium all of a sudden. It could be drunks. It could be nerves, for the darkness was a formidable opponent even to the most stalwart of men. But he doubted these possibilities. Another answer sprung to mind.

"What is going on?"

Joseph jumped. His father stood in the doorway to his room.

"There's some shots fired in town," Joseph said.

August came and knelt beside his son on the bed and peered out the window, wild-haired and haggard-faced in his nightshirt.

"Drunks."

"Could be," said Joseph.

"Go back to sleep," his father said, ambling off the bed.

"Go back to sleep? But there's shots fired in town!"

"Then the best way to get a bullet in your brain is by poking your head out the window as soon as you hear a shot fired! Now—"

They both turned at the sound of hurried footsteps below. A man came quickly, half jogging, down the sidewalk. One of the men standing outside The Black Hen saw him and walked toward him. They began speaking before they met.

"What's the noise about?"

"Errol Robinson took a shot right outside the general store. Said it was a panther."

Joseph turned and saw the stern expression on his father's face.

"Alright, back to bed."

"I just want to see what happens," said Joseph.

"*What's* going to happen?"

"What if they catch her?"

"Her who?"

Joseph hesitated. "The Old Woman."

"Oh, for heaven's sake! And just *who* is going to catch her?"

Joseph paused to think, feeling the moment draw out and turn sour.

"Men in town?"

"Ha! They couldn't catch a cold!" His father made to leave but then turned back to Joseph and railed, "Now I don't want to hear any more about that godforsaken panther. Shut that window and go back to sleep!"

Joseph made an exasperated growl. He shut the window and got under his blankets but he kept an eye on the street. The crowd outside The Black Hen dispersed. Some men returned inside, some set off for elsewhere. When the street was again deserted, a single man walked down the entire length of Main Street, but he seemed in no particular rush, with no particular business in mind.

Joseph knew he would have to wait until tomorrow

to learn anything more about what had happened, but he could barely sleep for the thoughts cycling through his head.

FOR THE FIRST AND only time in his life, Joseph was early for school. The news was everywhere. Not only did Errol Robinson claim to have shot at a panther, so did Leslie O'Connor. And both men claimed to have shot the same panther, that fabled panther, the Old Woman. Two separate incidents, at opposite ends of town.

The children were full of reports.

"My granddad said it was an evil spirit because it showed up on one side of town and then on the other. No way an animal could do that!"

"My mom said she heard it on the roof—"

"My mom said she saw the panther herself! Right through the kitchen window!"

"Everybody says they saw her," said Joseph, the one person willing to admit he had not seen anything.

"She did too see her! She said she was hanging around the trash in the back when all of a sudden she bolted. Leapt right into the neighbour's yard."

"Oh, sure. That's a panther for you, rummaging through the trash."

"Panthers aren't interested in trash!"

"They want to eat children!"

"Maybe it was lost and came into town by accident?"

"It wasn't an accident. Panthers eat children because they like the taste! That's why she came into town."

Joseph could not abide this statement and felt compelled to interject. "Sometimes when panthers get old, they might break a tooth. If that happens, the panther doesn't have a chance against deer. So they hunt easier, less dangerous prey. Like rabbits and stuff." This he had learned from one of the hunters who had come into town and entertained Joseph for a whole afternoon with bear and panther stories while his father eyed the speaker as he worked at his forge. Joseph went on. "Children are just easier to hunt. They can't defend themselves. They're not strong enough."

The other children listened to Joseph and shared glances, raised eyebrows, barely hidden smiles. It was well known that Joseph fancied himself an authority on panthers, especially where the Old Woman was concerned.

Joseph had become an expert shot in the few years he had owned a gun. He went from shooting rats and squirrels to taking aim at rabbits and birds. The bird moved at whim through the air, just as the rabbit moved over the land, unpredictable, making them harder to shoot. But that made him secretly more satisfied when he was successful. Besides, there were hoards of them in the surrounding forest. In time, he was surprising even himself with the accuracy, the deadliness, of his shots. Though his father had often complained about Joseph's obsession with shooting, he could not object to the grouse, pheasant, rabbit, and duck they now frequently enjoyed. August prepared the meals they ate—Joseph seemed to have no interest in that part.

"What do you know?" demanded the boy Joseph had contradicted. "Panthers eat children all the time!"

"Oh, yeah? Do you know anybody who got killed by a panther?"

The children were silent.

"That boy who got snatched!" said one girl, unsure.

"What boy? What was his name? Anybody know?" Joseph asked.

No one knew.

The discussion moved on.

"My father said Errol Robinson said there was no way he could have missed that shot. She was right there in front of him, yet no injury came to the panther, as if the bullets had gone straight through—"

"Errol Robinson is a drunk!" declared another child, no doubt repeating something she had heard said. "He probably never even saw a panther, just made it all up so he wouldn't get in trouble for shooting up the town in the middle of the night!"

"Well, Leslie O'Connor's no drunk. My father said Leslie said he was coming home from shooting some geese—"

"Nobody comes home from shooting geese at ten o'clock at night! He was visiting Mrs. Fairborn—"

This drew a chorus of squeals and laughter from the children standing around in a loose ring, bundled up in hats and scarves. Joseph stood with his hands in his pockets, conscious of the holes in his mittens.

He sat through class, unable to think of anything the teacher was saying, thinking instead of the Old Woman, and his desperate need to hear confirmation that she had been here, in his town, so close. He could not even pretend to be paying attention, so when the teacher called on him to answer he just said, "I don't know," accepting his fate, instead of trying to finesse his way out of answering. He could not spare the thought.

Neither would he devote thought to feeling annoyed at being assigned some lines. While the other children were outside in the yard, he stood at the chalkboard writing out the words *I will pay attention in class* but seeing beyond the board, imagining that fluid golden body stalking through the shadows at the edge of town.

When the teacher dismissed them at the end of the day, Joseph set off running.

The afternoon traffic seemed lively despite the cold, grey day. Joseph dodged around the other people on the sidewalk. He stopped and stood in front of the general store window, looking at the display. A stuffed bear stood on hind legs in the background, a bright red tablecloth lay draped over a circular table, the objects laid upon it glinting in the dull afternoon light: a fancy oil lamp, a pair of scissors, bottles with handwritten labels, some boots, a mirror.

The bells above the door announced him. The shopkeeper cast a glance at Joseph, but he was in conversation with a patron and turned back to the gentleman with a patient smile.

Joseph picked up a paperback and pretended to read as he scanned the other patrons in the store. Three women stood carrying on a hushed conversation. The tallest was a pale, thin girl, perhaps only a year or two older than Joseph.

"Can't something be done about this sort of thing?" She made no effort to subdue the anguish in her voice. "What if it had gotten one of the children? I don't know what I would have done. How are we expected to live our lives if we don't feel protected in our own town?"

The oldest woman spoke up, glancing at the other two over the rims of her eyeglasses. "At the post office just now, Mr. Brawley told how he and a few others went into the forest early this morning to track the panther. They found its tracks leading up the road into town, but then the trail disappeared. They found no trace of it leading away from town, around near the bus depot, and they were forced to give up their pursuit."

"They should send someone out there to shoot the damn thing." This from the woman with a child sleeping against her shoulder. She stood stroking the child's head absently. "That way we can put our minds at ease."

The shopkeeper loomed at Joseph's side.

"Hey, Joe. You going to buy that?"

Joseph paused as long as he dared before shaking his head.

"Then get lost, will ya?'

The sky was growing dark. Scarf wrapped around his face, Joseph walked down the street toward The Black Hen. Every time he had gone into the bar, his father had found out. He knew this time would be no different. But he could not stop himself. He stood, watching the front door, listening to the muffled sound of conversation from within. He glanced over his shoulder but no one paid him any mind when he opened the door and went inside.

He waited as his eyes adjusted to the watery light, the smoky air. Everyone was smoking, including the bartender. The smoke rose to the ceiling, drifting around the ghostly orbs of the lights, their coverings filled with the dry husks of long-dead horseflies. The bar ran along one side of the room. Men sat elbow to elbow on stools at the bar. There were a few tables pushed up against the other side of the room. Every seat was taken. The sharp smell of beer just about masked the smell of stale perspiration.

Joseph pulled down his scarf against the sudden warmth. He pushed his hair away from his forehead and it fell right back in place, hanging in dark locks over his bright eyes. He was not tall for his age and remained slender no matter how he ate. He had a fair complexion that blushed red at the slightest provocation: exertion, embarrassment, wind.

The debate was well underway.

"Of course not! There must have been *two* panthers—"

"There were two shots fired, but it was the same panther."

"How could the same panther appear on opposite ends of town within seconds? No matter how fast—"

"It was Her. That villain whose name I shall not speak—"

"There's no way. Either there were two goddamn panthers in town last night or else we're talking . . . some kind of ghost."

"It's said the Old Woman's got round pupils like a man so she can shapeshift into a man and no one would know it were a panther walking around and not a man—"

"All panthers have round pupils like a man, instead of slit pupils like a cat. Panthers have eyes like men. It means nothing."

"How else do you account for her abilities? How would she get from one end of town to the other in the blink of an eye, except by magic?"

No one answered, most taking that moment to drink from their glasses.

Joseph moved deeper into the bar, away from the argument. He saw Leslie O'Connor seated at the back.

"—walking past the bus depot and there I saw her perched on the roof, just sitting watching the town. I raised my gun and fired." He gestured the motion, aiming an imaginary rifle. "And when I looked up, the panther was nowhere to be seen. Not running away, not falling dead off the roof of the bus depot as she *ought to* have been. Just nowhere. Now you explain that to me."

"What did this panther look like?" Joseph nearly had to shout to be heard, his voice sounding high and thin next to those of the men. A crowd turned to look at Joseph and suddenly he felt very unsure of his presence in the bar, but his resolve was firm and he held his breath and did not blink.

"Hey there, Joe." Leslie looked over the boy's shoulder. "Your father know you're in here?"

"Sure he does. He sent me to get him a drink."

The men laughed. Joseph smiled, more at ease.

"Come here. I'll tell you."

When Joseph got up close to Leslie, he could smell the man had been drinking. He could see it in the flush of his skin, the unfocused look in his eyes, and a flash of instinct told him to be cautious of the words he was about to hear. But his curiosity was greater than his unease, and he found he could sit down next to the man, place his elbow on the bar.

"When I found her, she was sitting on top of the bus depot. Just a little thing. The night was dark but I could see by the moonlight that her fur appeared black, like a sable cloak had been draped over her golden shoulders. Her ears moved about on their own, listening while she sat, watching the town. She would never let a man sneak up on her, but she was intent on the pandemonium she had caused, listening to the sounds of the men scrambling from one end of town to the other, like a bunch of idiots—"

"Hey, now!"

"—she wasn't watching her back. I knew I wouldn't have a chance if she saw me. But when I cocked my rifle, that smallest of sounds made her turn her head. She looked directly at me and I saw the left side of her face ravaged by a great scar and I believed then, as I do now, here was that fabled panther, the Old Woman, staring back at me."

At the sound of her name spoken aloud Joseph felt a wave of relief wash through him, crash against him, and he was submerged.

Leslie continued, "She had one good eye and one bad, and I could see in the moonlight the many scars along her front legs. When she looked at me, I was struck by the notion that behind those eyes was a terrible intelligence—"

"Smart enough to fool you!" called a man from down the bar.

The bar erupted into laughter, Leslie the loudest of all.

JOSEPH RAN HOME. THE sun had long since set and he arrived in darkness. He unwound his scarf from around his neck as he ascended the stairs.

"At last! He has blessed us with his presence," August said when he heard Joseph come in the door. "And where were you this afternoon?"

His father stood at the stove, turning the mechanism on the can opener he had clamped to a large can of stew. The lid came off, accompanied by the faint sound of tearing metal, and he dumped the contents into a pot.

"I went with Lewis to shoot some rabbit."

"Any luck?"

"No." Joseph thought quickly down this imaginary line. "Only Lewis brought his gun. He's a lousy shot," he said, sounding embarrassed for his friend.

"Maybe you should give him a few pointers."

"I tried to. He doesn't listen."

"Hmm," was all his father said to that.

Joseph took a seat at the table and watched his father at work over the small stove. His hair had grown more grey than black. Joseph noticed the rounding of his back, the slant of his shoulders. His right arm still outweighed his left from years of pounding away at the forge. He devoted the same attention to stirring the stew as he did to heated metal, his face locked in the same grave expression.

August placed a bowl of stew and two thick pieces of bread in front of Joseph.

"Did you hear anything else about that panther?"

Joseph tore off a chunk of bread, dipped it in his stew, stuffed it in his mouth, then sat, negotiating this huge mouthful, awaiting his father's answer.

"No," his father said, reaching for the salt. "I did not."

They ate in silence a moment.

"Agnes McConnell said her mother saw the panther going through their trash."

"Did she?" August replied, in a tone that suggested he was more interested in his stew.

Joseph knew if he said the right words, it would get his father talking.

"People are in disagreement, about whether there were two panthers last night or just one."

"Hmm . . ."

"But Leslie said the panther . . . he saw—"

His father was silent, watching him. Joseph felt the panic of having let oneself step into a trap.

"When did you speak to Leslie?"

Joseph took a breath. A perfect blank drew itself in his mind, and as he sat looking into the space above his father's head where he hoped some answer would appear, a robust pink bloomed upon his cheeks.

"For pity's sake! How many times have I told you to stay out of that bar? Some panther happened to wander into town. That's all. He's not trying to torment the lives of men. He's got better things to do than waste his time hanging around here. That's just talk, Joseph. A bunch of drunks spinning yarns because some old panther wanders through town in the dead of night. This is exactly the kind of thing that gets men riled up and into a mob and then someone catches a bullet in the back because people see panthers everywhere they look!"

Joseph was not sure what his father was referring to, some imagined future event or a memory from the past.

"Outrageous!" His father sat chewing, staring at some other scene entirely. "The problem with this town is not too many panthers, it's too many men!"

They ate in silence as Joseph thought about this.

"Don't you care if a panther shows up, walking around town as she pleases?"

"No, I *don't* care. I just want to go to work and eat my supper in peace and not have to listen to grown men chattering away all day like a bunch of schoolchildren!"

"That's not how everyone feels," he informed his father with the authority of one who knew. "It's dangerous having panthers wandering around. People don't like it. We have a right to defend ourselves."

"Against what? An animal who also lives here? Yes, panthers are dangerous. That is why we don't go poking into dark places in the forest, seeking them out!"

Joseph tried another approach. "People are just excited!" The entrance of mystery into their daily lives was too much entertainment to pass up, even if it was that solitary kind of entertainment called thinking. Joseph did not understand why his father was not likewise affected.

"People get excited when the wind blows." August shovelled a spoonful of stew into his mouth and a thread dribbled down onto his beard.

"But it's not just *some panther*, it's the Old Woman!"

August took up his napkin, nodding, and wiped his

mouth. "Oh, yes! How could I forget everyone's favourite panther? Those are just stories, Joseph. There is no Old Woman. That's just the name they give to whatever panther happens to stumble into town. I was hearing stories about the Old Woman as soon as I came here. That's almost twenty years ago now! Do you know how long a panther lives? Ten years. Maybe twelve. So how do you explain that?"

Joseph could not explain that, which he had already known and, in his musings, chosen to ignore. Though he could not discount his father's logic, he became angry that he would be so stubborn and dismissive. Why his father was not in awe of the Old Woman the way everyone else seemed to be was a complete mystery to Joseph. It made him doubt his own preoccupation. He could not explain his devotion, as strong now as it had been at the moment of its birth, so he had stopped trying. He only knew he could not reveal this devotion to anyone, and he knew if he was to remain devoted he must carry on in silence. He stared into his stew, considering this profound and solemn appointment.

"What's so wrong with hunting panthers?" he muttered.

"What are you doing it for? If you can answer that, you can hunt a panther."

Another silence hung between them.

After a moment, his father said. "A panther is just trying to live his life—just like a man. They don't know the difference between you and a deer . . . except the deer probably tastes better."

That pulled a reluctant smile from the boy.

August gave him a level stare.

"Have I ever told you the meaning of the name Brandt?"

Joseph's eyes grew wide. He had never encountered this question before, never even considered that a name could mean something other than a personal designation, that it might have some different meaning coded into it.

"It means 'to clear the land by fire.' Or to come from such a place. So your ancestors were men who came to a place and set fire to it. Burned down everything that was there before them, so that they could have their lives. You keep that in mind when you're dreaming about hunting down every wild thing that lives in the forest." He studied Joseph's face for a moment. Then he said, "You stay away from that bar and those drunks with their talk. You hear me?"

"Yeah, yeah, I hear you."

"I mean it."

"Okay!"

"Okay, what?"

"Okay, fine! Goddamn—"

"Joseph!"

AS NIGHT DESCENDED, A distinct stillness settled over the town. People took their steps lightly on the muddied sidewalk; children lay in their beds, eyes open; mothers and fathers sat up, each with one ear set to listening; even in the bar they played the music low and conversation never reached beyond a whisper. A great quiet prevailed, as if the town itself were waiting, holding its breath.

But the night passed without incident. Joseph fell asleep with his window open and awoke shivering late in the night. Teeth chattering, he pulled the blankets around himself like a cloak and looked out onto the street below. The street lamps burned low; the storefronts along the sidewalk stood in murky shadow. A dog barked on the far edge of town, breaking the silence. Joseph looked into the quiet darkness where the town ended and the forest began. Somewhere the Old Woman was stalking through the night. He thought of her running through shadow, the sleek movement of her body, the fluid steps, as she slid between the trees.

He knew there were mountains deep in the forest. He wanted to go there, to be on that dark mountainside and disappear into darkness himself, but he did not know how to bring himself there. He could not see how he would do it, but he believed it could be done.

The crisp air reached into his blankets and sent a shiver down his back. He was tired, struggling to keep his eyes open. He shut his window on the cold night, burrowed into his blankets, and fell asleep.

VII

STALKER

✈

THE SUN ROSE BEHIND the white sky, casting a dense light onto the yet-grey forest. A golden shadow picked its away along the cold, rocky ledges that reached into the mountain. If the day had been clear, the Cougar would have seen the forest roof reaching all the way to the horizon, interrupted only by the river. But today the fog blocked her view of the land below, as if the world had disappeared and all that remained was herself and the mountainside.

She took her steps with care. Her fall from the cliff had taught her that even the ground beneath her feet was uncertain, but knowing that had not robbed her of her curiosity. The Cougar had spent a solitary year hunting, seeking through the forest. The days rushed past like the unending current of the river, through the summer, autumn, and winter, until it was again spring. She had found the Marauder in that time, and they had accompanied one another as the warmth of summer drew near.

Though her figure did not betray it, she was again awaiting the birth of the brood nestled within her, the expected result of her time spent with the Marauder. Her kittens would be born by the time the moon grew full again, and then she would no longer have the time to go exploring the mountainside whenever the urge struck her.

The fog parted and the Cougar saw the earth below, an enormous shard of rock that had fallen, shed from the mountainside like autumnal leaves. The mountain went through the same processes as any living thing, only with a much longer life than any the Cougar could imagine. To the mountain, day and night were like the pulsing of some cold and distant heart. Death was possible as well, in some unknown future likewise unimaginable.

She was considering this when she spied the body of an animal lying on the rock far below her. She stood watching the still body. It appeared dead. Then the fog swallowed the sight from view.

The Cougar was displeased at being denied, and after a moment's deliberation decided to investigate. She made her way down the steep terrain, leaping where she saw solid rock. She had to retrace her steps whenever she came to a sheer drop with nowhere to land, not wanting to risk the fall. Once the ground came to a reasonable incline, her course had taken her far from where the body lay, but her memory of the land remained unchanged despite the fog drifting past like earthbound clouds.

When she saw the body through pale bushes, her skin prickled as though a wave of icy water had rushed against her. The animal she had spied from above was a cougar.

He was stretched out, his forefeet and hindfeet together, as if he had just lain down to sleep. As the Cougar approached the body, she saw that he had been dead, out in the open, for less than a day. He still retained his shape, but the skin was dried-looking, plastered to the bones, and though his fur was smooth there was a fine layer of dust covering him entirely: if ever there was a sure sign of Death in a cougar, it was this. No living cougar would go a day without grooming. The body had yet to be picked at by scavengers, and the Cougar concluded he must have died sometime yesterday and lain here all night until she found him.

She searched the ground, the rock face above, the body itself, for some sign that would tell her how this cougar had died. If there had been a struggle, it would be visible on his body. If he had fallen, signs of his fall might be read upon the rock. But there was nothing. She saw neither tracks bringing him here, nor bruises indicating a fall. It was as if he had dropped out of the air.

Then, looking into that sunken face, she realized with sudden shock that the cougar lying before her was one of her own. This face, aged by many seasons, was none other than the male cub sired by the Harbinger who had left her long ago.

The air suddenly seemed thin. She felt as if she were no

longer standing on solid ground but falling through the earth. The dead cougar lay, eyes closed, as if in sleep, as she had seen him so many times in life. She should not be surprised by this death. A cougar's life was a perilous one, and she had lost cubs before but those had been kittens. Not full-grown hunters.

She turned away from her fallen offspring to return to the forest.

The white light weighed upon her as she walked through the wafting fog. Though she put more and more distance between herself and the dead cougar, her shock did not diminish. The mystery of his death gnawed on her.

She thought of her Neighbour, that pale huntress, cut down by her own clumsy young claw. Her Neighbour had been an experienced hunter, yet even after a lifetime of success she had called forth the fight that led to her own death. The Cougar found herself troubled by this now though she had not thought of her Neighbour for many seasons, and after wrestling with the possibilities for a while she pushed these thoughts away.

By the time she returned to her lair, the fog had lifted to reveal the cold, wet earth. A grove of trees hid the entrance to a cave in the rock, the ground spongy with moss. This would be her birthing lair. She had chosen it just yesterday and spent time clearing out the old leaves, carrying out branches and bones between her jaws, scattering them afar so as not to betray her presence.

Now, as she entered the lair, she ignored its empty feel and settled down in the meagre shadows of daylight to sleep.

THE COUGAR DREAMED OF a day with a black sky. The trees, the leaves on the branches, the grass underfoot, all like smooth, white stone. Though it seemed like something that would be unnerving, she was not disturbed by it, because she knew in some way that it was not the actual forest but some other place. It occurred to her then that this was not the first time she had been here.

A hollow silence prevailed, unnatural for any other forest, but here there were no bugs, no creatures to create the hushed din of a living forest. Not even a wind to create the impression of movement. Above, the sky was flat black, no stars, nothing beyond the sky itself. Just this single, white realm where stagnation was the main event—Death did not exist, but neither did life.

The river did not flow. Its glassy surface was still, the water unmoving in its bed. When the Cougar stepped to the river's edge, she saw that the water was not black but clear. At first, she saw her own reflection on the surface of the dark water. Then she saw within—the cubs of her womb sitting below the surface. They were as they had appeared as kittens, but they were all white. White fur, white noses, white mouths, their eyes white, glazed over like frozen water. They were all the cubs she had, and the ones in the murk were those she was yet to have—

The cub below the surface of the water opened its white mouth, and the sound she heard was like wind through dry, autumn leaves.

THE COUGAR AWOKE. She stared ahead, the images from her dream disintegrating, and she saw the entrance to her lair, the needle-strewn earth outside. She saw that the sky was still brightened by the sun and she longed for the relief of darkness.

She settled back down though she did believe now she would return to sleep. At least her kittens would be with her soon. The thought of their coming presence consoled her. Then she would not be alone when she awoke from these disquieting journeys.

O N THE NIGHT WHEN the moon turned its face away from the earth, the Cougar gave birth to her kittens. Three daughters settled into the world, blind and mewling. When they opened their eyes and found their voices the Cougar felt the peculiar thrill of hearing her cubs for the first time. It seemed amazing to her that each would sound different from the ones that had come before, but she supposed this was the way with all things — trees, birds, mountains — so naturally with cougars.

As a younger cougar, leaving her kittens alone in the lair while she went out to hunt had sent a current of fear through her. The pain of that early loss was always with her. Now, as an older cougar, she tried to keep this fear to the side. She did not stare it in the eye, but neither did she let it out of her sight.

The night air was damp. She negotiated a rocky descent over steep ground, then cut into the thick forest. The river was ahead, hidden by the trees, but the Cougar turned and travelled parallel to its flow, toward the flat grasslands where she would find the deer.

She leapt over a fallen tree, the trunk bearded with green moss, and her side gave a sharp cry. Her feet touched ground, the sound of her landing a mere rustle of leaves, and a dull wave of pain throbbed through her front leg, into her stomach, and then faded. She would go days without being reminded of her injury. But sometimes she awoke to a howling in her side that could only be subdued with a long walk through quiet trees.

The Cougar went sniffing over the earth. She smelled some foxes, a mother with her young, long since departed. A rabbit now burrowed away in the earth. Then she found what she was looking for, that familiar scent which set her mouth watering, the grass bent where they had stepped. She set off into the trees to follow the herd.

As the Cougar followed the trail through the forest, her thoughts returned to that dead cub she had discovered on the mountainside. He would enter her thoughts unbidden, and stay with her as she made her nightly stalk through the forest. It was like she was discovering his body everywhere she went and living the discovery as if for the first time. She did not torment herself trying to envision how he had died. That she would never know. That he had died was what troubled her. Why had she not succumbed to similar circumstances? Why had she survived her accident only to go on in pain? And this thought led her to the inevitable thought: when would her own death come to her? She felt Death's eye focusing upon her. Where before it had been a glimmer on the horizon, now it shone with a final light.

By starlight she found a snug spot in the lee of a boulder and settled down in its shadow to wait. She listened to the slight sound of the wind through the trees. After a time, all listening ceased. In the darkness the moments bled one into another and only when the sky began to brighten did the Cougar realize the night had passed.

She knew of their approach by the impression of their

silence in the forest and she sat watching the spot where she knew the herd would appear. In the meagre light before dawn the Cougar saw the males, their antlers among the low branches, then the females, slender, white necks, white chests, walking in a living ring surrounding the fawns, their collective migration no louder than the sigh of leaves.

When she spotted a ghostly deer in the distance the Cougar's eyes went wide and she pressed herself into the earth. Through the gloomy trees, she saw an apparition glowing white in the lifting darkness. It was that stealthy deer who had eluded her catch once before, all of him white, like the bare branches of a silver birch. The sight of him set her heart pumping. Her tail flicked with a sudden vigour, which she tried and failed to stifle. The White Buck stood, sniffing the air in the clearing the deer were about to cross. There could be no other — it was the same deer she had seen before.

It had been only last winter when she first saw him. She had lain in wait through the bright, cold day until she heard the quiet sound of the deer digging through the snow. She sat watching them from the cover of a snow-laden evergreen, concealed beneath its branches. Then, when she laid a paw in the snow, suddenly the trees had shuddered and come to life. The White Buck leapt out from between the evergreens, his antlers like the branches of a small tree. The Cougar watched transfixed as the White Buck flew away with the rest of the herd, bounding through the snow with ease. His weight had meant nothing to him, as if moving through space was achieved merely by thought. He dashed through the trees and she had lost sight of him, indiscernible in the white landscape.

Now she lay watching him from behind the boulder, her heart beating hard in her chest. He stood in the murk of the early morning forest like a white flame, his shoulders broad and muscular, the lean bulk of his body atop those long legs. Black eyes like liquid night set in his skull. He walked with a confident gait the others did not possess. His focus was superior. It would have to be if he were to survive, white as he was, during the green seasons of the forest. The Cougar could not look away from the muscular line of his chest, his graceful walk. A lusty desire bloomed within her and none of the other deer mattered.

She crept from her hiding place and advanced in short bursts until she came to the line of trees bordering the clearing. The deer walked along on thin legs, a quiet procession. The Cougar kept her eyes on the White Buck. He watched into the trees, ears scanning for sound.

Again she advanced over the needle-strewn ground. The deer moved slowly toward her. The Cougar waited, watching. The forest had noticed the Cougar's presence and gone silent. In a moment, the deer would also notice.

The Cougar worked her feet into the earth until she found the perfect footing. She would not move from that posture until the moment arrived. A sudden pain needled her side, but she remained in her position, endured it unmoving. Her heart beat two slow beats. When the White Buck stepped into reach, she pounced.

Perhaps he had known she was there and only been feigning ignorance of her presence. Perhaps she had given herself away, however unlikely, in that last instant before announcing herself. As the Cougar leapt out of the trees, the White Buck jumped away. They were flying through the air, like birds, one chasing after the other. The Cougar reached for the White Buck, claws out. Both deer and cougar touched ground and pushed off through the air, and again the deer remained just out of the Cougar's reach.

It was this last jump or failure. The Cougar pushed off against the earth, summoning her whole strength for this final effort, reaching out, eyes ablaze, but still the deer remained ahead of her.

When she saw the deer had outrun her, the Cougar ended her pursuit. She sat watching the White Buck as he raced across the clearing and into the trees, followed by the herd, the echo of their retreat ringing out against the resuming silence.

What strength lay in that deer's body, the muscles that worked his limbs, the blood that coursed through his veins. A formidable deer. It was not by chance that the White Buck had survived in the dark forest bearing the glaring whiteness of snow throughout the year. Even in winter, the forest could be grey. To be unable to hide in his surroundings would have meant Death for a lesser deer. His existence, grown to adulthood, suggested a fitness, a capability, that not all deer possessed. Indeed, not even some cougars.

The hollowness in her stomach swelled and she turned back into the forest to find some rabbit or fox before returning to her lair. The sun was threatening the horizon. As she stalked through the trees in the growing light, her thoughts stuck on that White Buck. Her failure did not ease the anxiety that had been afflicting her since she had discovered her dead cub.

She sat down by the stream to wait. A pain stabbed her side as she took a deep breath and she felt the fatigue of her night-long stalk. She crossed her paws in front of her and closed her eyes but she did not sleep. The light grew and the sounds of squirrels and mice rose to what seemed like a commotion to the Cougar's ears. She grew impatient with this waiting. In order to live, to move on, she must sit still. The major action in her life was waiting. Even now, at her age, patience had not been mastered. It was still a constant effort, always sought, never possessed.

The cicadas made their call into the air, long and loud, and the Cougar gave a heavy sigh, settling in to wait.

THE COUGAR STOOD IN the entrance of her lair, squinting out into the bright summer afternoon. A warbler's call cut through the still forest. Behind her, three eager faces peered around her legs. When she was satisfied there was no threat awaiting them within the trees the Cougar emerged from her lair, followed by her three daughters. As she stepped through light, then shadow, then light, her fur glowed bright gold, then dark gold, then bright — the signal of a hunter in the daylit forest. The cubs with their spots did not shine so and were afforded better camouflage in the busy forest. They would lose their spots around the time they began to hunt in earnest, only once they became a real threat to their prey.

The cubs heard the sound of rushing water before they saw the river, and the Cougar saw them sniffing the air, ears working by themselves, trying to comprehend what lay before them. When they stepped through the grass onto the riverbank, the cubs crowded against her legs. They stood staring at the river, their eyes scanning the opposite bank, taking in the expanse of the water. One cub looked up at her mother and squawked. The Cougar walked down to the river's edge, and when she saw that her daughters did not follow, she called to them. She stepped into the bright water. One cub leaned down and sniffed the river's surface. The Cougar picked her up by her scruff.

She squealed, legs splayed, tail rigid, as she was placed in the river, and was silenced. The cub looked around her at the undulating surface of the water. One of her sisters mewed at her. The cub mewed back and then her sister came forward, touched a paw to the water, and jumped at the movement of the surface. The Cougar leaned down and ran her cheek against the top of the cub's head.

Under the watchful eye of their mother, the cubs grew bolder testing the water, walking out a few steps only to retreat to shore, looking back at the river, and then going out again. They made small noises to one another, a language of discovery. Soon they were chasing each other along the stony riverbank, mindless of the noise they made. One cub tackled another in the shallow water. The tackled cub mewed defeat and squirmed out of her sister's grasp, only to bat her sister in the face and try to tackle her once she was free.

As she watched the cubs, the Cougar's thoughts turned again to that male cub she had found sprawled out on the rocks. She had brought him and his sister to the river as well. She could see him as he had been in life, splashing through the water still in his spots, and see him as well ravaged by Death, his lifeless form, the unseeing stare.

The Cougar shut her eyes against that vision. She would not think of him today.

Though the air was still, the Cougar felt as if a cold wind had blown against her. She stood and glanced into the forest behind her, turned and looked across the river. Noticing her sudden, quiet posture, her daughters cast their own glances into the trees, sniffing the air. The

Cougar scanned the line of trees on the other side of the river for some sign of what had disturbed her, but the landscape was unchanged. The river rushed on. The birds in the trees had not silenced.

Nevertheless, the Cougar felt a prickling along her skin, as if some secret set of eyes were upon her. She called her cubs. They shook themselves, spraying droplets into the air like bursts of light, and scampered after her. She led them along the riverbank, but once they were within the trees she did not lead them back to their lair. Instead, she headed away from the river, toward the mountain. Even once they were well away from the river, and there was no sign that would suggest she was being followed, she still could not shake the feeling she was being watched.

The Cougar and her cubs emerged from the trees onto the disjointed land at the base of the mountain. On open ground she picked up her pace. They ascended the rocky scree, climbing around thatches of dead, leafless bushes. The Cougar glanced back more than once toward the treeline, to assure herself they were not followed. She spotted a shadow in the rock, an eye looking down upon the mountainside, and ushered her cubs toward it.

From inside the shadows of her mountainside lair, the Cougar sat, nose to the wind, watching the treeline for any sign of movement. The feeling that made her flee the riverbank had left her, but the anxiety it had caused remained, her heart beating as if she were in distress. Perhaps she had been hasty to retreat to the mountain. If there was no reason for it, if she had just imagined the threat, then there was no harm in seeking out a safe shelter among the rock. But if she had been watched . . .

She sat as the sun set and molten clouds bled across the sky. The drone of crickets rose up from the grass before the trees, calling on the night. Behind her the cubs slept, their breathing light and steady, but the Cougar did not sleep, unable to dismiss the fear that even now something lurked in the shadows of the forest, awaiting her.

THE COUGAR STEPPED OUT onto the quiet mountain-side. As she walked down toward the treeline, the wind went howling over the open rock, a different sound than wind through the trees in the forest. The late sunlight cast an orange glare over the rock and the trees below, which dimmed only once she had entered the blue shade of the trees.

The feeling of unease that had taken hold of her that day by the river had not left her as the summer progressed. It became a constant presence in her life, shadowing her throughout the nights, even infiltrating her dreams. She kept her lairs along the mountainside. The elevated vantage gave her full view of the forest below, and she would hear anything approaching over the stony ground. The rocky terrain did not betray her tracks or her scent as the mud of the forest might, making it difficult to trail her. She felt secure within these stone lairs, surrounded by rock.

Even so, she found herself unable to sleep deeply or for very long. She changed lairs frequently, sometimes for no reason at all. If something was stalking her, trying to learn her habits, she believed she would throw them off with random, even senseless, actions. That she would do this was most strange to her, that she was so moved by nothing, by shadow. But it seemed she was powerless against these whims and must submit to them or else suffer the torment of her paranoia. Better to alleviate herself of her anxiety, no matter how strange her behaviour became.

The warm day and the open air were a welcome change to the confines of her lair, but still she could not keep herself from casting glances into the branches overhead, hostile even toward the trees. Some days she would sit in the mouth of her lair, staring down on the mountainside while her daughters slept behind her. She had found no signs, no evidence, that suggested her fears of being hunted were correct. And yet her anxiety could not be banished.

The Cougar stopped and stood against a tree, reaching up with her claws and scratching the trunk until the bright wood beneath the bark showed through. When she was done, it looked similar to, yet still distinct from, every other mark she had ever left on a tree. It told of her presence and stood as a warning to others.

While this action seemed to relieve some of the anxiety she felt, she was overall disturbed by her own behaviour. She was not concerned with the possibility of attack. She had withstood many an altercation and could defend herself. It was the notion that some presence, some point of focus, was directed at her, stalking her from somewhere in the darkness as she made her way through the forest, that troubled her.

The Cougar ran over the dark forest floor, the leaves

muting the flurry of her footsteps. When she came to the edge of the trees, the river beyond, she took cover beneath some low-hanging branches to wait. After a moment, she closed her eyes. The sigh of the wind was a night-long conversation with the passage of the river. She smelled the approach of the sun even before the sky began to lighten.

When she opened her eyes, the trees were dusky grey shadows floating above the murk of the river. She could sense the heat building in the air and knew the day would be warm. Though she could not hear them, she heard the silence of the approaching deer. She watched the spot where they would emerge. First, they would wait within the trees, listening, until they believed it was safe to approach the treeline.

Then the silence grew and she knew they were there. The deer stood motionless within the trees. Still she could not see them, but she could hear the faint rustle of the leaves as they stepped slowly through the brush.

They began to emerge from the haze of shadow, their white chests glowing in the dull light. They took cautious steps, no single deer straying too far from the others.

The Cougar rose, set down a paw.

A low-pitched hum sounded all around her, growing like the distant rumble of thunder travelling toward her. She looked out on the open terrain, into the trees, but nothing was out of place, yet she could not move, forbidden by some unseen force.

The deer were passing out of reach, fading into the vague morning light. The Cougar let them go, watching as they crossed in silence.

The sun rose above the trees and a warm light flooded the field before her. The river in the background glistened like a fiery path. The Cougar turned her back on this bright scene and retreated into the shadows of the forest.

Not far into the trees, she stood on her back legs, reached up against the trunk of a tree, and raked her claws into its bark until she had scratched her mark deep into its flesh. When she was finished, she returned to all fours and sauntered away. But she had not travelled five steps when she saw another tree that needed to be marked. There was nothing unique about its appearance that required her to mark it but she felt compelled to do so, as if she had been commanded. She stood, scratching the bark with her claws, until her mark had been carved into the tree. Then she went on.

She made her way back to the dense forest surrounding the mountains, intending to return to her lair, but found she could not cross those barren rocks. The feeling of distress that had caused her to abandon her hunt was still circulating around her body and she knew she would not sleep. Instead, she prowled the forest.

In the bright morning she went on a slow trek, inspected the marks she had made in previous days, and everything seemed as it should be, as it had been when last she had visited. And yet she was not satisfied, unable to break from her search.

She stood on her back legs and carved her mark into tree after tree, without thought, a ritual performed more to relieve her of her troubled nerves than to warn transient cougars of her reckless attitude. The action was addictive, a pale brand made by her own claws. This was her sign, specific to her.

As she stood against a tree refreshing an old mark, her thoughts wandered to her daughters. They had begun to wrestle, pouncing on one another, jaws open. The Cougar would sit watching them, lulled by the endless energy, the constant activity, until a tumbling mass of fur knocked into her, bringing her out of her meditation. Though the cubs had grown long and lanky, they were still as clumsy and impulsive as kittens. Soon they would come hunting with her, spoiling hunts with their enthusiasm.

Thinking of their clumsy stalking, she was reminded of herself, the clumsy manner in which she had stalked her Neighbour. Those white wings flashed through her mind, that burning stare.

Passing by the stream, the Cougar returned to a tree she had made her mark on days earlier.

Here she made an alarming discovery.

At the base of the tree there were her old paw prints, softened with the lapse of a few days. But there were other paw prints, well defined, perhaps from only yesterday. She leaned her nose to the prints and sniffed; a distinct, foreign scent. New and unknown.

Her heart beat hard inside her chest.

She turned and ran through the trees. The sound of her hurried steps seemed a great racket to her ears. Her heart was beating in worry by the time she returned to one of the marks she had made earlier that day. It too had been inspected. Again there were paw prints in the mud where some other cougar had stood and sniffed at her scent, inspected the mark left by her claws. This was not extra-ordinary. The marks were put there for that very reason, to be inspected by others, to communicate her presence. But this was no passing curiosity. This was a thorough investigation. For here again she found the same scent that was on the other mark.

This was how she knew her Stalker's scent.

No mere delusion. It was a living cougar who hunted her. Learning this, the Cougar was not afraid. She was bewildered. Now she must accept that she was the focus of some unwanted attention. Her body had known but she had not understood, until now.

With this confirmation there came another fear, some almost remembered notion she could not place. The feeling itself was like something from a dream, distant, obscured by fog.

The Cougar sat staring into the trees, unseeing. Her mind was elsewhere, searching through the forest, seeking out her Stalker.

The low call of an owl rose into the air, seeming out of place in the bright day. The Cougar waited, listening for some indication as to why the owl had made its call, but none came.

THE BLACK RIVER RUSHED an endless course through the quiet night. The Cougar waded into the icy water and set off for the other side. Her Stalker could not follow her beyond this restless border. That stealthy cougar might follow her trail to the river's edge and know that she had crossed, but she would not be able to pick up her scent on the other side unless she went hunting up and down the bank for the place where she had emerged.

As she paddled across the river, her tail and head above the surface of the water, the Cougar glanced up at the sky. The slow pulsing of countless stars appeared to her then like a river of stars stood out in the sky, to mirror the river below, and the Cougar wondered why this should be. She heard the silence of the land before her. Her feet touched ground and she climbed out of the water. Once within the trees, she set off running.

She ran in a determined line, not the meandering course she usually took. She did not stop to investigate, as she often did, or sit and contemplate, as she sometimes would. Instead she tore through the night, her feet hitting the ground in a silent rush, the distance lost in the darkness. When finally she slowed her course, the Cougar found herself in an old part of the forest. Thick moss bearded the trees, their trunks wider than the length of the Cougar. That they would grow to such a size told her this part of the forest had not suffered the scourge of wildfire for countless seasons. The quiet was astounding. The Cougar looked up as she walked, in awe of the presence of the old trees.

The branches overhead blocked the sky from view. An owl hooted from within the branches and the Cougar looked and saw a muddy path cutting through the trees. A distinct silence occupied the forest and the Cougar stood listening, wary of such a deep silence. There was nothing. No rustle, no indication that even the smallest creatures were moving about. They either avoided this path, or lay quiet even in the dark of night.

The Cougar studied the muddy tract cut into the earth, eyes flicking from one spot to another, trying to determine what could have created such a deep disturbance, but the ground before her described something she did not understand.

There were many paths in the forest, created by the feet of the animals who trod them. But this path would have taken the feet of an enormous herd, as long as a river. The silence surrounding her caused her to wonder where these animals might be, and why now there was no sign of them at all, the forest around her abandoned.

Remaining in the trees, the Cougar followed the muddy path. She would have to turn back soon, her cubs would certainly awaken before she returned, but she felt herself lured onward. Her old injury sang to life then fell silent. She ignored it and went on.

She heard the rise of crickets floating through the air and knew there would be open ground, tall grass ahead. She came to the treeline, beyond that the land was completely cleared of trees. The Cougar looked out on this dark land, seeing it as if it were day. She saw the outline of a dwelling and smelled the scent of living beasts, the scent of rot and refuse, and hanging over it all the sharp scent of smoke. She found it strange that the dwelling would be out in the open. As if whatever lived here had no need to conceal itself.

She sat for a time, watching the dwelling, but she heard no movement within. The sounds of movement elsewhere pulled her attention to another structure in the background, obscured by darkness even for the Cougar's keen sight. She was hesitant to enter the open ground. The lack of cover was a bad sign. Nowhere to run but back into the trees. Everything was pointing her back the way she had come, but she went on, knowing her curiosity was overwhelming her judgment.

She set off across the field. Beyond the cover of the trees the Cougar felt the weight of the open air and she wondered how it came to be that there were no trees here. But then, she knew. Only fire could level the hardy growth of the forest. She wondered, what had kept the forest at bay since? The soft gathering of crickets surrounded her as she made her way through long grass.

She had seen elaborate structures constructed by beavers, nests by birds, but none like this. The design of the lair was flat and featureless. It smelled like a lair, one long occupied. And even here the scent of smoke.

She walked up to the barn and listened. From the rustling sounds she could not tell what was inside. An endless shuffling and sighing. She heard breathing, the breathing of many. There was an opening high up on the side of the barn, a window that led into darkness. She stood considering. Then she shifted her feet until she was satisfied with her footing, and jumped up to the window as if rising on the air, and landed without a sound. The darkness within was total. But her eyes soon adjusted. When she saw the ground below her, the horde of them, she froze.

Milling about within the confines of the barn, agitated by her presence, were dozens of small, white sheep. The Cougar was entranced. She had never seen anything like it, the group of them all confined to this small space. They walked around on little feet, which she noticed were similar to those of deer, but the sheep had bulky bodies, short legs no good for running. They were covered in a voluminous white wool, a perplexing feature. The Cougar felt this warranted closer inspection.

She jumped to the ground. The sheep bristled and pressed against one another, huddling together. They almost seemed to shiver. The Cougar sat looking at them. The sheep made alarmed bleating noises and moved in their huddle away from the Cougar as she circled around them, still careful to keep her distance.

What strange behaviour in response to her presence, that they should cuddle up to one another as opposed to spread out and make themselves into smaller targets. It seemed like the behaviour of an animal unaccustomed to danger, who had never had to defend themselves before.

She realized their docile appearance could be deceptive, and she must be mindful of the possibility of attack, but when she saw the sheep went to no great lengths to escape her as she tried to approach from one side then the other, she wondered what they might do when tested.

It was no task catching the first. She walked up and put her paw around its shoulders. The sheep almost relaxed, as if comforted by her touch. Then she pulled it close. The sheep in her grasp froze, waiting to see what she would do. She pushed the sheep over and into the ground and was mildly surprised that it died from the impact. The Cougar was distrustful of such an easy death.

She caught another and pulled it to her jaws. It squawked as she crushed its throat, dying in the next instant. Its death spurred her on, and she pounced on the next sheep, catching it in her jaws, snapping its neck before her feet had even touched the ground. She ripped open its belly with her back claw, buried her face in the fold, and foraged out the liver, so small she devoured it in a single bite. But before she had really eaten from her kill, the sounds of the other sheep scurrying around, frenzied with fear, pulled her attention away.

As she stood over the half-eaten sheep, another sheep ran by so close to her that she barely had to move, she just reached out and caught it. Neither did she pause at this one, merely tearing into its neck to ensure it was dead. She jumped and landed in front of a fleeing sheep and it stalled and started and fell dead before her. She pounced on another sheep and the force of being knocked to the ground was enough to kill it.

She could not stop herself. It did not matter that she had killed more than she could eat for the rest of the autumn and winter. Still, she went on, unthinking, cutting down another sheep, and another. She could tear through a thousand sheep, spreading her bloodlust over the entire forest, consuming, like a fire, all she touched.

Then, amid the wreck of bodies, the frantic sheep, there was a dog standing and facing her, which the Cougar confused for a small wolf. The Cougar froze, chest heaving, struck by the dog's strange appearance: long, shiny fur, white upon his paws and face, an undersized head, and compact paws, totally unlike a wolf—and yet so similar. It stood its ground, growling, black lips pulled back over his teeth. She was too puzzled by the sudden arrival of this animal, its stunted appearance, to feel threatened.

She had only paused to observe the dog. She meant to kill it as easily as she killed the sheep and she worked her feet into position, getting ready to pounce.

Unannounced, a blinding light crashed into the barn. The Cougar squinted against the blaze, not able to see what was causing it. It hurt her eyes to look upon but somehow she could not stop herself from looking. The dog was there, barking in its juvenile voice. But she could not see the dog, the light consuming and obliterating the physical realm.

She opened her mouth, red with gore, eyes blazing in the false light, and hissed.

A crack of thunder ripped through the air. The sound snapped the Cougar out of her bloodlust trance. She leapt up to the loft window she had come through and off the ledge, travelling in a great arc through the darkness, a great jump, a hard landing. Once she hit the ground, she set off running.

Before she reached the trees, another crack of thunder shattered the air.

Within the trees she stopped, heart beating in her throat, and looked back at the barn. At first the scene remained unchanged, the dark structure resting in silence in the still clearing. Then a man emerged from the barn. In one hand he held a hive of fire, in the other, a long, thin branch. The dog followed the man out of the barn, paused, sniffed the air, then stood barking against the darkness as if in triumph that he alone had cast the Cougar out.

The Cougar watched as the man walked across the field holding his glowing orb aloft, the dog at his side, two travellers within the corona of light as it floated through the darkness, toward the dwelling where now light was burning through the windows and a familiar chattering sound reached her ears across the air.

A wave of nausea hit the Cougar, flung her aside though her body remained rooted to the ground, and she felt like she would vomit. She stood breathing, each breath a struggle, her heart pumping wildly.

She turned to flee but the earth turned to mush beneath her feet. She fought against the nausea that threatened to engulf her. If she took enough steps, she could leave it behind. She stumbled a few steps through the dark, unfamiliar forest, the sounds of the men in their dwelling dwindling behind her. Hot saliva gathered and drooled out of her mouth in two clear strings. Then she stopped. Her body rebelled against her and her stomach lurched and all of its contents came rushing up out of her mouth.

Pummelling waves forced her to retch the portions of

sheep she had eaten onto the ground, hot and burning. When it seemed over, she stood panting. The revolting taste in her mouth, the smell steaming up from the ground, invading her nostrils so she could smell nothing else. Unnatural that she should bring up her food, unnatural that she should encounter so many sheep trapped in one place with nowhere to run, unnatural that she could cut down so many at once, unnatural all.

The Cougar burped into the quiet night, sparking a mild fear that she would vomit again, but there was nothing left to bring up. The walk back to her lair seemed an insurmountable, long distance. More than anything she wanted to sleep, but she could not stay here.

The night seemed longer than most. She did not take the road she had come in on for she did not want to encounter any more men. Instead, she traced a mindless path, following the slope of the land back toward the river.

By the time she reached the river, the sun had risen above the treeline. She stood on the riverbank squinting into the brightness. Her heart fluttered inside her chest, a very small moth. In the sunlight she was a red cougar, yellow eyes burning through her gory mask. Blood stained her chest, her front legs, along her sides. She licked at the blood on her paw, but even that effort was too draining. The sunlight on the water's surface sent reflections of light onto the grass, the trees, the branches above.

She stepped into the water and the coldness shocked her out of her exhausted daze. The blood staining her fur began to lift off. A haze of red surrounded her, shedding and drifting downriver, trailing away from her like a red shadow.

The current pushed against her. Her heart pumped slowly inside her chest. She felt hollow, emptied of her insides, and hungry despite the night's ordeal. She waded into the water, then set off for the other side, her limbs heavy as she swam. She thought of her daughters, asleep on the mountainside, as the sun crept higher in the sky. The new day caught her in its hold, and the night was left behind.

THE WHOLE WINTER SHE sought through the forest, searching for the one thing she needed to hunt her Stalker — finally, in the spring, her vigilance was rewarded.

While her daughters slept the Cougar left the lair to visit the Outcropping of Boulders. Through an evening filled with spring thaw, the Cougar trekked to the stone arrangement and watched the slow movement of its shadows as the sun rode past overhead. Upon her face a look of quiet concentration, as if she need only wait here long enough and some answer would be revealed to her.

As the sun began to set, she prowled along the riverbank. The sound of crickets filled the air, throbbing with a slow pulse. She entered the trees, the sound of the river fading behind her. Her ears twitched at the mosquitoes buzzing around her head. The Cougar took a running jump and cleared a shallow creek. As she landed, a stab of pain bloomed in her side, spread out, and was gone.

The light created deep shadows at this time of day. The

Cougar noticed a fallen tree, the shadow beneath, and she paused. The creek whispered behind her. A breeze ran through the trees. She stood staring at the darkness of this shadow; it stood out to her among the other shadows. Something about the fallen log, the incline of the land guarded by trees, called to her and she went toward it, her steps hushed by the grass underfoot.

When she stood looking into the entrance of the lair, she got a taste of the occupant's scent, muted, nearly lost amid the scent of earth. Until now the Cougar had smelled only traces of the cougar who had been stalking her. Now here it was, full, complete. The Cougar glanced behind her, scanning the stony creek, the trees beyond, then ducked her head and slipped into the shadow beneath the fallen log. She had to squeeze herself through the entrance, but once inside it was quite spacious. Ideal even; hidden in plain sight, limited access to the entrance, water close by. Her Stalker would have sat here, waiting, watching the creek, until something came to the water, then she would slink out of the shadows, the perfect ambush. The Cougar breathed in the smell soaked in the earth, tasted it, committing it to memory.

The light coming in from the outside was fading, red and slanted. The coolness of the earth beneath her matched the coolness of the stone roof above. A few bones lay discarded on the ground, small and delicate. No evidence of anything larger than fox, or rabbit. If she was not bringing anything back to the lair, she did not have cubs. The Cougar sat with this knowledge, considering.

The leg bone of a fox, stained with earth, rested by her

paw. She leaned down and sniffed it. She reached out and moved it with her paw, turning it over. At one time resting within the fox, at another chewed between her Stalker's teeth. The Cougar sat staring at the leg bone, seeing.

A DRAGONFLY DRIFTED INTO view. Tempted by its colour, the vibration of its wings, the Cougar's daughter lifted her paw to swat the dragonfly away. The Cougar shot her a stern look and the cub put her paw down and focused on the field before them.

They sat in the bright day, the cool autumn sun shining upon them, in an island of grass washed pale of its colour. Her daughters sat alert, beside her, blinking in the sunlight. On the wind, the scent of the earth. The herd of deer stood two leaps away, sniffing through the grass. The deer were congregated against the edge of the river with a clear view of the grass around them.

A young buck crossed the invisible threshold, into the cougars' reach. The Cougar rose into the air, her expression calm, paws outstretched, in total silence. She tackled the deer into the ground, crushing its neck in her jaws. The rest of the deer scattered into the trees, a low rumble that dwindled then vanished. She sat catching her breath. Her daughters stepped out of the grass, tails slashing. She tore open the deer's gut, a stream of blood bright in the afternoon sun, and they ate, side by side.

The Cougar and her three daughters were now alike in size and appearance. Viewed from afar they might seem like four identical cougars, but up close the Cougar was gaunt and scarred where her daughters were full of face, their posture unburdened, as if the air weighed less to them.

The cougars made their way back to their lair. Their hunt had stretched out into the day and her daughters had grown tired. She could hear how they dragged their feet as they walked. Once back in the lair, the three of them curled up and fell asleep almost instantly. The Cougar watched them sleep, the easy rise and fall of their breathing. She looked toward the entrance of the lair, the brightness of the day causing her to squint. Her curiosity called to her and she knew it was useless to fight it. Though she was tired, she rose quietly and left the lair for the trees.

She returned to the site by the river where she had hunted the deer with her daughters. She sat looking at the half-body of the deer lying in the bloodstained grass, its expression frozen in the chaos of its last moments, before the Cougar's bite sent it from this world, the long flow of its life interrupted by her jaws.

She began digging at the ground with her claws, pulling up earth and throwing it overtop the deer. A hasty job, though she took care to ensure the mess of blood was not wholly covered.

She rolled on the ground, coating herself with this specific scent, the blood from the deer, the upturned earth. Then she left the site altogether, cutting through the trees and travelling in a great arc, away from her kill, until she arrived back at the site from the opposite side. She jumped up into an evergreen, found a perch among the branches, and sat down to wait.

The sound of the river flowing along in its bed, together

with the wind through the leaves on the trees, created the sensation that the same moment was stretching out over the entire day. As the sun began to set, the Cougar noticed the shift in temperature and roused from her somnolent state. The dusk had gathered around her. She stood and began to stretch, first her back legs, one at a time, then her front. Her left side groaned as it was tested, and the Cougar grunted softly, then exhaled.

Night descended on the forest. The wind died, the trees fell quiet. Cued by the darkness, the Cougar felt herself grow more awake. Her heartbeat quickened, pumping her blood through her veins. She remained still, aside from the twitching of her tail.

The Cougar watched the deer lying on its side. She heard the buzz of flies circling its head. Another life she had devoured. This was a necessary exchange, destroying life so she could have hers. The Cougar sat watching the body of the deer she had torn open and eaten from and she felt like there was no difference between them, though she sat breathing in the dark and it lay dead on the earth.

Night too seemed to pass in a heartbeat. She could sense the coming of day before she perceived the shifting light.

She stood and stretched again, then settled back down.

At the moment when the darkness began to lift and the trees, the earth, the sky living in shadow emerged into colour, the Cougar saw a shade of movement in the trees across the clearing. Her heart skipped an entire beat, then came back twice as strong. Something was there, waiting in the trees.

For a long time there was no movement and the Cougar wondered if she had imagined it. The air brightened, though the sun had still not risen. The Cougar took a slow breath. Her tail flicked once, and again.

From out of the trees stepped a thin, young cougar, pale as flame in the dark blue light. The Cougar had never seen this cat before, but as she watched the sleek body, the lightness of step, she was reminded of another cougar and suddenly a dark cloud passed over her.

Her Stalker sauntered into the clearing, casting glances into the trees. The Cougar's own heartbeat filled her ears. A prickling sensation crawled over her face and traveled down along her back toward her tail. She knew there was some explanation for what she saw before her, but in her shock she could not think of what it was, only be astounded because for a moment she believed it was her Neighbour walking out of the trees, restored.

She did not understand what she was seeing, trapped in her own disbelief. Then she realized her Stalker was her Neighbour's daughter.

The young cougar stopped in front of the half-buried deer and sniffed the ground. Then she sniffed the air. She sat watching, unmoving save for her eyes flicking over the carcass, reading the signs. Her Stalker stood and made a slow circle of the deer, looking at the earth, sniffing at the Cougar's paw prints, then circled again, a ritual that made the Cougar nervous.

The Cougar had not thought of this cub since that day of rain and fog on which she had vanquished her Neighbour, but she thought of her now—the wretched screech she had flung into the air, the anger flashing in her eyes—and here she was grown, a dangerous cougar, stalking and hunting her.

She wondered what her Neighbour must have thought of her the first time she had laid eyes upon her. It must have filled her with a kind of dread, just as the Cougar was experiencing now. A hardness that set her against her Stalker. She felt a bit of her strength, that familiar secret, stir within her, rising.

As the Cougar watched, her Stalker turned her head and looked into the trees where the Cougar sat in her perch. The Cougar saw the dangerous look in her eyes, and she knew this cougar had come for annihilation. Its mark had been left on her and so her life was devoted to nothing else.

Her Stalker sat before the deer, looked up again into the trees, her neck and chest bright white in the morning light. She stood and walked a few paces and sat and again looked up into the trees. The Cougar sat stone-still. She had but to wait out her Stalker's investigation. To give herself away now would be a novice error.

After a long, breathless moment, her Stalker walked back over to the deer. The Cougar watched as her Stalker looked up into the trees, searching, and the Cougar saw her face plainly: the white wings were there, fainter perhaps, but there all the same, like an echo of those on her mother's face. The black tip of her tail showed against her nearly white flanks as she disappeared into the trees in silence.

The Cougar waited until the sound of her Stalker's departure had vanished and the crickets resumed to move from her spot. She stood gently, stretching first, and when she came down from the tree's branches her limbs were stiff and her left side seared with fire.

She stood looking at the deer in the dark pit of blood, its head twisted to the side, antlers turned into the earth, trying to see what her Stalker had seen.

F OUR COUGARS EMERGED FROM their mountain lair into the evening light. The Cougar made no sound across the rocky earth. As her daughters followed they dislodged stones that went tumbling down the scree, cracking through the cold air. She wondered if the noise was as aggravating to them as it was to her. Once they hit the grass, the sounds of their footsteps were hushed. As always, the cubs followed behind her in their same order, stepping into the very paw prints their mother made.

A thick covering of orange and yellow leaves lay throughout the forest. The sun had set and the light was fading. They came to flat ground sparsely populated by flimsy, young evergreens. The cougars picked up their pace through this area where there was little opportunity for cover. The sound of crickets emanated from the grass around them. The earth rose, the evergreens crowded in, and the Cougar and her daughters made their way up a rocky incline, then crept onto a ledge where they spied the herd of deer grazing below.

The deer stood together, nudging their noses through the fallen leaves, never straying too far from the protection of their circle. A few deer stood alert, watching the trees, taking turns to bow their heads to forage.

Within the bare trees the Cougar spotted the shadow of

movement, like the still branches of a tree suddenly come to life. In the almost darkness he seemed to glow.

The White Buck stood watching the trees, scanning across the field for signs of movement. The muscles in his chest, his shoulders, lifted gently with the motion of his breathing. His breath issued from his nostrils like gusts of smoke.

The Cougar was fixed, the other deer forgotten.

With slow footsteps she stalked him along the higher ground, her daughters following behind her over the uneven terrain. She paused beside a leafless bush to wait.

The Cougar had hunted and stalked many deer in her lifetime. Their appearance was so well known to her that she could picture them, the movement of their legs, the rhythm of their breathing, perfectly in her mind. But the White Buck struck her with his physical beauty. He was unique. The sight of him evoked an unreasonable desire within her. Perhaps it had to do with the fact that he had evaded her capture before. She knew she had a better chance with one of the other deer. But she ignored them.

The White Buck stood watching into the dark forest. The quiet shuffle of the other deer through the leaves could be heard across the field.

The shifting of a stone, even that slight sound, rang loud and distinct behind her. She looked and saw her eldest daughter paused mid-step. The cub stared at her, wide-eyed. The Cougar looked back to the White Buck, fleeing into the twilight. The small herd fled the field like a flock of birds lifting into the air. The Cougar watched the

White Buck loping over the earth, the other deer following behind him, into the trees.

The Cougar sat down, folded her paws beneath her, tail slashing the air. She watched until all the deer had disappeared, then she sat listening as their retreat faded and the silence resumed. The cubs sat waiting in the growing dark, yawning, but they would not approach her. They would wait as long as they were required to, recognizing her desire for a moment of solitude. It was not her daughter that concerned her. She did not care about the adolescent clumsiness. That was a phase. The failure would teach her a valuable lesson. It was her own fault more than the cub's. If she had not allowed herself to be distracted by her fixation on the White Buck they would be eating now instead of nursing empty stomachs.

They were alike, the Cougar and the White Buck. His success depended on the failure of others. He survived only if others succumbed in his place. She thought of all the many deer that had died in order to sustain her. She could not imagine how many. Countless many. But the White Buck would not be among them.

Instead, he would live on, perhaps to one day lie down upon a bed of pale grass, the cold of winter lurking in the air, and cease to breathe. Scavengers would come and feast on his remains until all that was left were his bones and the dusty white cloak of his hide. Later, even this would melt into the earth, wild brome growing over the spot to mark where he had returned to the earth.

Unbidden, the image of her Stalker came to mind, and once that ghostly cougar appeared in her mind she could not send her away. She had come to realize there was but one conclusion to her Stalker's obsession. Her Stalker would come to her from out of the forest. There was no way to avoid it now.

The Cougar could not allow herself to become confident of any outcome. Whatever she thought might happen between them was only a possibility. She knew she might die by her Stalker's claw. Her Stalker could surprise her while she was distracted by following some prey, drop soundlessly from above, having awaited her arrival. Or, even if she had announced herself and the Cougar was prepared, the earth might betray her. She could trip over a root, lose her footing. Or, her Stalker could be stronger than the Cougar outright, and easily defeat her by catching her in a deadly embrace, pulling her neck into her jaws. She saw her Stalker making feast of her organs, her own torso a black pit, the shadow of her blood surrounding them like a dark moon.

The Cougar's daughters waited patiently for their mother. They mimicked her posture, sitting with their paws crossed in front of them. The sound of a yawn brought the Cougar out of her thoughts.

The thick of night surrounded them. If they meant to catch a meal before sunrise, they could not waste time. The cougars followed the river after the trail of the deer. Overhead, the sky was bright with stars, the moon high above. Around a bend in the river they came across the Outcropping of Boulders. The Cougar recognized its form even by this meagre light but she did not stop to admire it today. Her daughters seemed not to notice the arrangement of rock, though to the Cougar it stood out like a blazing fire.

They searched for the deer all through the night but the herd managed to evade them. Close to dawn the Cougar tried the stream, hoping they might find something smaller. Even just a few bites shared between them would be enough to tide them over until the next night. But they had no luck here either. The stream flowed on through the growing light, undisturbed.

They would not make the trek back to their lair in the daylight. Instead, the cougars took refuge beneath the lush, low-hanging branches of an evergreen. They settled down together on the ground of green moss and fallen needles. Each of her daughters gave a yawn and shifted about getting comfortable, an interval she bore with patience. Once they had grown quiet she knew they were asleep. Before long the Cougar joined them.

AROUND THEM THE FOREST was wild. The Cougar lifted her head. A violent wind shook the trees. Her daughters slept as if the forest stood in the depths of calm. The sun was high in the sky. Despite the sunshine the wind was cold. The Cougar stood, careful not to disturb her daughters, and slithered out from beneath the branches.

She walked through long grass tousled by the wind. The brightness of the sunshine was overwhelming and she squinted, amazed by its strength, its power to obliterate. The sound of the wind through the leaves was constant. All other sound diminished. No birds made their call.

The Cougar paused and listened. She turned and looked into the trees. Beneath the wind, a pronounced silence had drawn her attention, pulled her away from her thoughts. She stood looking into the shivering trees, into the shaded understorey, waiting.

Her Stalker faded into colour from out of the daytime shadows, claws outstretched, reaching toward her, and the Cougar rose to meet her.

The force of her Stalker's tackle pulled her off her feet. They went tumbling down the hillside. At the bottom they stood and met each other with icy screams. The Cougar struggled to free herself from her Stalker's embrace, but the pale cougar held on, her strength like a rock. The Cougar kicked at her with her back legs, trying to catch her Stalker's soft belly with her claws, but her Stalker kept clear of the Cougar's attempts.

Her Stalker swept her claws across the Cougar's front leg and the Cougar screamed. It was not a mortal wound, but she felt the sting of air on her raw flesh and the warmth of blood seeping down her leg. They stood and met face to face.

Locked in an embrace, they each tried for the other's neck with their jaws. But the Cougar did not exhaust herself in unnecessary struggle. Once she saw that she did not have a decent grip, she threw her Stalker off and waited for the younger cougar to come to her again. The Cougar watched the pale cougar's reaction, believing she was close to learning the secret to her strength. Her Stalker hid nothing, openly demonstrating her strength, mindless of the Cougar's watchful eye.

She saw that her Stalker was trying to attack her on

her injured side, meaning she must believe this was the secret to defeating her. The Cougar pretended to protect her injured side so her Stalker would be distracted with looking for her moment to strike and, in doing so, give the Cougar hers.

Her Stalker was full of rage and her strikes were savage, but the Cougar had it within her to withstand these attacks. She threw her Stalker off but the pale cougar pounced and tackled her. They fell over, tangled in each other's embrace. Her Stalker slithered out of her grasp and they stood, breathing heavily, glaring at each other. The Cougar waited. Her Stalker began to prowl but the Cougar did not move, knowing the waiting would vex her. Her Stalker became frustrated with the growing pause and let loose a scream. The Cougar waited, standing perfectly still. In the sunlight her fur appeared like gold, almost too bright to look at.

Her Stalker grew still. The Cougar recognized the posture well and prepared to meet her attack.

They stood again to embrace, her Stalker's jaws wide open, reaching for the Cougar's neck. She felt her Stalker's sharp breath against her face, but the Cougar resisted, her strength rooted in the earth. Once her Stalker realized that she would not get her bite in, she threw the Cougar off.

When the Cougar and her Stalker separated, the Cougar raked her claws across her Stalker's face. She felt her claw catch within the pale cougar's eye socket, and felt the slight pop, and knew the eye was ruined.

Her Stalker danced away in silence. She stood stone-still, as if a distant cry had suddenly called her attention.

The side of her face savaged by the Cougar was a bright red mess, fingers of dark blood reaching down her neck, the eye screwed shut, absent.

The Cougar stood panting, staring at her Stalker. If she left now, the Cougar would give her leave to go into the forest to die, or live, with her half-sight, if she could. She saw no point in further endangering her own life if the contest was determined. But her Stalker remained, eye pouring blood. Her anger would not allow her to leave. She paced in an injured way, took an unsure step toward the Cougar, retreated.

Then the Cougar's daughters appeared, rising up out of the grass like smoke. They took slow steps, eyes levelled at her Stalker. Seeing their focused posture, their tactic of surrounding the injured cougar, she knew their intention. But she could not allow them to endanger themselves. An injured cougar might prove more dangerous than they realized.

The Cougar rushed forward with a scream, claws outstretched. Her Stalker stumbled back, and in one deft motion twisted and leapt away. She scrambled to gain her footing, then she ran. The Cougar watched her frantic retreat, the black tip of her tail visible above the grass.

Despite her warning, she saw her daughters meant to follow, already in the air. But the Cougar called them back with a piercing scream. Her daughters turned wide-eyed stares at her, bewildered.

The Cougar sat watching after her Stalker, thinking of her blind eye, evidence that she had escaped Death once but it had left its mark upon her.

Around her the wind rifled the grass, the leaves. Her

eldest daughter approached, slid her cheek along her mother's scarred shoulder, then she too looked after that pale cougar, into the trees.

THE SUN SHONE THROUGH the edges of the clouds so they appeared as if they had caught fire and were drifting aflame in the sky. The Cougar sat with her daughters in the tall grass, in the light of the setting sun.

The claw marks on the Cougar's front leg burned. Her legs ached and her back was sore but the pain was secondary to the sense of relief that circulated through her body, filling her with an irresistible desire to sleep. The fiery gaze of the sun cast the surrounding trees, and her daughters in the grass, in a blood-orange light.

The Cougar sat, eyes falling closed. A true calm spread through her, out from her body into the forest around her, along the river, and into the mountains. Once the winter had passed, after her daughters had left her, she would walk into the rocky cliffs, returning to the familiar comfort of her solitary roaming. She was the same cougar, as always. This was a great relief to her.

Two cubs lay next to her, yawning, while her eldest daughter cast searing glances into the surrounding trees. The warmth of the descending sun made her feel she was filled with sunlight. A slight breeze ran through the grass, whispering through the trees.

Her daughters did not disturb her when she began to snore.

VIII

PRECIPICE

->-

J OSEPH WAS WANDERING THE streets of town one
grey winter afternoon when he happened to see Vern
and Wesley Willis glancing over their shoulders,
heading in the direction of the smithy. This was not altogether unusual but something about their body language
signalled to him, and he decided to follow them.

It had been a quiet winter. The summer before, all the
able-bodied men had been drafted to fight in the war in
Europe, leaving behind the young, sick, and elderly. This
seemed to produce a vague sort of shame in the men,
resulting in an exaggerated desire to protect the town, to
seem useful.

Joseph heard the men gathered, the pack of dogs,
before he saw them. The smithy was surrounded by a

posse of men, standing in the snow in twos and threes, preparing to go on a hunt. Some had rifles, but others had crude-looking clubs, which stood out to Joseph as more brutal than the firearms. They wore heavy boots, fur-lined hats, their jackets tied up against the cold, and stood muttering to each other, casting glances toward the quiet section of muddy winter street visible down the alley. His approach warranted a few looks, but his was not the arrival that concerned them. Joseph approached the nearest group of men.

"What's happened?"

"Panther got a hold of Elmira Olsen, out by Shouter's Field. Her mother seen her being dragged across the snow and ran after her. Fought off the panther barehanded! Sounds like the girl got torn up pretty bad. They've taken her over to the doctor—"

"Her neck and shoulder was all chewed up, and some of her face. That ear is probably gone, by the sounds of it."

"Did anyone get a look at her?" Joseph asked, by *her* meaning the panther. He would not be the first to mention the Old Woman's name, though he longed to hear it.

"No. None of us saw her. We just heard," the man replied, by *her* meaning Elmira. "She's with the doctor now—"

Joseph pushed his way into the centre of the group, familiar faces all around.

John Gunn was there addressing the men, a stolid figure, rifle in hand. His dark, full-length coat concealed his body almost entirely. He wore a black hat and heavy deerskin mittens. There was no part of him left unprotected, exposed to the air.

Joseph spotted his father and leaned behind the bulk of a larger man, not wishing to be seen just yet.

"We'll lead the dogs to Shouter's Field so they can pick up the panther's scent from the scene, then we'll hunt her down from there." Gunn sounded certain. "We cannot allow these kinds of attacks to go unpunished. Not in our town."

Murmured assent rippled through the crowd.

Joseph saw his father's expression harden at these words. Then a flash of recognition crossed his face when he spotted his son and his expression darkened.

"Come to join the rabble?"

He said it low, but his voice carried on the crisp winter air. It seemed all other conversation had settled down and the attention of the gathered men was focused on Joseph. Despite the cold, he felt his cheeks begin to glow.

At fifteen, Joseph stood nearly a head taller than his father but was still a boy in frame, perhaps slight for his age. His dark hair he got from his father, but the blue eyes were from his mother, like blue fire in the clear, open air.

"Someone's gotta keep an eye on you," he said, trying to joke.

"Don't you have somewhere to be?" his father asked, implying that he did not; the same argument as always. Everything related to that. Joseph said nothing, feeling he had no way to defend himself here, in front of others.

"Let me come with you," he said, more to the men in general. "I'm a good shot."

There was no denying this. It was well known.

"We could use the extra gun," said one man, his face nearly lost in the folds of his scarf.

At first August shook his head, then, scanning the anxious faces of the men gathered round, he knew they would protest if he said no.

"Alright," he said. "But you watch out you don't get yourself shot, you hear me?"

"Yeah, I hear you."

"Go grab your gun and meet us at Shouter's Field," the scarfed man told him. "But don't attract too much attention."

Joseph could not keep from running.

Sunset was still a few hours away; even so, the air was dark, a blue murk all around. Joseph dashed up the stairs to their apartment. He put on thick socks, another sweater. He grabbed his rifle, took two rounds, and placed them in his breast pocket. He cut two slices of black bread and two pieces of salami and made a sandwich. One half he ate. One half he folded in a clean napkin and put it in his pocket. On his way out, he slammed the front door behind him with such force it pushed his bedroom door inward with a slow creak, the sound of his rushed steps down the stairs echoing against the walls of the empty rooms.

On the street he tried to look like he was heading nowhere in particular, casting glances like a thief to see if anyone was watching him. When he rounded the corner of the post office, he set off through a field of unbroken snow, toward the trees, beyond which stood the white plain of Shouter's Field.

The men stood, rifles and clubs slung over their shoulders, lanterns glowing dimly in the dark afternoon light. Joseph slowed to a walk, his heart beating hard, his breath trailing behind him like a banner.

At the scene, there was little to see but a muddle of prints, the whisper of blood upon the snow.

"When Mrs. Olsen found the beast at her daughter she took off her boots and threw them at the beast. And when that didn't work, she tackled the panther herself and started smacking it right in the face!"

"Is Mrs. Olsen hurt?" Joseph asked.

"Not a scratch on her. She carried Elmira all the way to the doctor's, screaming like a banshee. At first they thought she was the one hurt, what from all the blood."

"Did anyone see her?"

"She's with the doctor now—"

"No—did anyone get a look at the panther?"

They shrugged. This was not known.

The dogs howled and pulled against their leashes. The men followed, muttering and coughing, stomping along, rifles against their shoulders or at the ready. They stayed together, a dark horde on the white plain, though no threat seemed likely out in the open. Sensing the agitation from their masters, the dogs grew excited and menaced into the winter air, barking, almost confused, glancing about for the source of their anxiety.

Joseph caught up with his father trekking through the snow in his staggered gait.

"Here," Joseph said, handing him the sandwich.

His father took the offering and put it in his pocket.

Joseph noticed his eyes stray to Gunn leading them on, his black hat covering the top of his face. Gunn stopped, as the men went on, and stood surveying the field around them, as if the panther lay in wait somewhere close by.

"How'd you know to find us at the smithy?" August asked.

Joseph shook his head. "I didn't."

August eyed his son. "Even the faintest hint of a panther and there you are."

Joseph laughed.

"Well, so be it. You can try to keep these idiots from shooting each other in the backs!" He said it loud enough for others to hear. Some snorted a laugh, some ignored him, others shared a look.

Then his father took hold of his arm, forcing him to stop, and was speaking to him, his voice low: "Joseph, listen to me, if this mob actually manages to catch that panther, I want you to shoot it between the eyes before things get out of hand."

Joseph did not know what to say.

"Promise you'll do that."

Joseph glanced around them to see if anyone had noticed them pause. "They're not going to catch her—"

"You could make that shot, Joseph." His father was firm, looking into his eyes. "Promise me you'll shoot it before things get out of hand."

Joseph found himself unable to look away from his father's face, the whites of his eyes shot through with veins, surrounded by a web of wrinkles, not pleading, telling. Commanding him by some blood magic he was unable to disobey. Other men passed by on either side of them, paying them no mind, as a silent exchange took place between father and son there on the open plain. Joseph was compelled to nod, caught so in his father's stare, his father's grip on his arm like the roots of a tree clutching at the earth.

"Okay," said Joseph.

"Okay." His father let him go, lurching back into step with the other men. Joseph stared after him a moment, then followed.

Joseph felt as if he had been compelled to say those words almost against his will, wanting to pull himself out from under the weight of the old man's gaze. While he had no intention of letting anyone else shoot the Old Woman, he did not want to bind himself to this promise. He was confused by his father's adamance. He felt the authority that bound the Old Woman and himself together superseded any earthbound authority, including that of his father.

Still, the memory of his father's stare stayed with him and he was forced to see it again in his mind's eye. It was not the intensity of his stare but the sincerity. He felt it still, and tried to look away, to resist its influence on him.

He picked up his pace through the snow, not wanting to be left behind.

———

THE PROCESSION OF MEN across the white plain was flanked on both sides by black rock, black forest atop the sheer cliffs around them. The braying hounds pulled them toward the trees, the men holding lanterns that grew ever stronger in the failing daylight. The dogs were their guides, seeing on the ground, on the air it seemed, the trail of the cat, the mark it had left as it sauntered through their midst. The panther's signs were undetectable by human eyes. They needed the dogs to see, the fire to light their way. A meagre creature, man.

More than one man had brought a flask to fortify himself against the cold. These were passed furtively among the group. When one came to Joseph, he dared not hesitate. Careful not to let his father see, he threw back a hasty swig, nodded his thanks to the man, eyes watering. The man laughed.

After only a few steps Joseph was passed another flask. He took a drink and wiped his mouth. When he took his next breath, the air seared down his throat, into his lungs, like the roots of a frozen tree. He coughed, an icy fire at work within him, but when his breathing calmed, the air around him seemed clearer somehow and a jaunty smile spread across his face. Joseph felt his cheeks burn with a flare of heat he was helpless to prevent. He knew it was a sure sign to anyone who cared to notice, but he felt brazen as well. He pushed his toque back on his head, his dark hair out of his eyes. The cold air was welcome on his face, almost wonderful. Besides, anyone would mistake the colour in his cheeks as a result of the cold.

One of the hounds howled into the air, sudden,

urgent. The sound penetrated his euphoric mood and he remembered there was a panther stalking about. The men announced their presence for all to hear. They would ward off a panther sooner than ensnare one. He saw this and knew there was no way around it. Soon he was casting glances into the trees, studying their position, to see how he might slip away from the party.

He fell back among the stragglers of the group, allowing them to pass him. Then he stopped altogether, waiting to see that no one was watching him. He stood, a slow breath vacating his mouth. The group continued on. No one noticed his absence. Joseph waited, watching as the last of the men disappeared below the rise of land. Joseph turned and entered the trees.

He cut through the trees like a water snake, the snow impeding him no more than if it were air. The bark of a dog, then the indistinguishable exclamation of a man's voice cut through the air. The quiet commotion of a large number of men dwindled and fell silent. Away from the party, the forest was still, silent, his own footsteps through the snow sounding loud to him.

In an instant it seemed as if he were in the middle of the wilderness, though the town was only through the trees, and he almost laughed at the strangeness of this thought. They were always in the middle of the wilderness, no matter where they were. The position of the town made no difference. But in town, living and working with other men, one could believe the town was a place of importance when all that had happened was that collectively they had agreed *here* was a place of significance. The notion of shelter, of community, the world built by men, was suddenly brought to an end only a few steps into the trees.

He followed the land down through the trees. At the bottom was a stream, frozen over, the snow blanketing it as if covering some sunken pathway. Joseph ran and leapt across the stream entirely and went on.

A howl bled through the air. Joseph stood, listening. Other dogs joined the chorus. If the men caught sight of the panther, they would let the dogs go and the dogs would tree it, or bay it against the rock face. And the men would follow.

Joseph saw the sober sense in his father's appeal that he shoot the panther the first chance he got. To spare the panther being tortured to death. To show it mercy. As well, he sensed a desire to deny the other men their sport, to ensure they did not descend into cruelty. But somehow he knew no such scene would take place. The panther would avoid the hunting party. They would never see her. Perhaps the dogs would track her down, but there was no way the men would get close enough to take a shot.

He continued through the knee-deep snow, which made for heavy walking, but he charged through the unblemished snow like one possessed. It was not just the alcohol giving him an exaggerated, though perhaps false, strength that compelled him onward. He could feel something different in the air, and he believed it must be her.

In the dusky light the snow seemed to glow with a luminescence that emanated from within. An owl muttered its call to the approaching night. Joseph considered it strange that he would see an owl at this time of the day but spared it little thought. The earth began to rise and he climbed on steady feet, rifle slung over his shoulder.

The ground levelled and Joseph found himself looking down on the plain below. Before him, cut into the snow at his feet, he saw the fresh tracks of a panther. His heart stuttered at the sight. His mouth went dry.

He stared down at the paw prints in the snow, impressions of her very feet. The size of them sent a chill through him, dampening the fire in his chest. Joseph leaned down and sniffed the earth where the panther had laid her paw and smelled something other than snow — a dark, unfamiliar scent.

He took the glove from off his hand and pressed his palm into the icy mark. The snow burned against his skin. After a moment, he removed his hand and studied the superimposed prints: his long fingers reaching beyond the cat's paw, the points of her claws sharp even in snow.

Joseph rose and followed the tracks through the black trees, heart beating in his throat. The earth continued to climb, the trees thinned. He used the feathery branches of young evergreens to pull himself along. As he neared the top, he stopped to catch his breath. He had come to the edge of forested ground, the open air before him, a sheer drop below.

A shot rang out, breaking the spell of silence. Joseph heard the clamour of the men and their dogs down below, but was too far from the edge to see them.

Then he looked up and she was there before him, so unexpected that for a moment he did not believe his eyes.

The panther sat watching him, allowing him to see her.

He marvelled that if she had wanted to kill him, he would be dead. He had not seen her sitting in the gloom and only saw her now because she allowed it. The white fur on her chest seemed blue in the twilight, the rest of her coat like dark gold. But what caught his breath was the scar on her face which lay across the left side, cutting into her cheek, just missing her eye. This, coupled with her unflinching stare, fixed Joseph to his spot, unable to move.

Through his shock, he reasoned that she had not appeared from nowhere, but had jumped from below, the entire rock face in a single leap. He saw that the stories of her ability to appear from nowhere were no mere exaggeration. She had appeared in an instant, in a heartbeat. All the words, all the stories until now, were but shadows when compared to looking upon her actual body. He was so close he could see in detail the fine fur that covered her face like velvet. Her eyes, clear as glass; the pupils, round like a man's. Her gaze was strangely unbearable, and yet he could not look away.

It was plain she did not fear him. Her tail flicked back and forth, but otherwise she remained still. A wispy trail of breath issued from Joseph's mouth as he exhaled. The beating of his heart was so strong his body shook with tiny tremors. His stomach folded under the weight of her stare, as if he had felt her touch across the distance between them.

Joseph sank to one knee and raised his gun, catching the forest cat in his sights. She turned her head, mindless of him, listening to some far-off sound he could not hear. Her ears moved on their own, giving the impression they were separate from her, giving her instructions.

The Old Woman rose to her feet in one fluid motion and stood at the edge of the cliff, looking down. Joseph could hear the faint commotion of the men, the dogs below.

Now, he knew, was the moment he had waited for all his life — but he could not move, unable to pull his eyes from the Old Woman's body. It seemed impossible that such a creature would exist, moving through the world, a secret, yet seen here in truth. He could not explain the urge he felt to walk across the open air to her, and he was thankful for the space between them that barred such a crossing.

Another shot shattered the air and the Old Woman pulled back from the edge. The shooters were not at an angle to hit her.

Below, the horde of dogs barked and snarled. They could smell the panther, and her presence, denied them, drove them to frenzy. The Old Woman looked back to Joseph. That she would look at him so directly somehow unnerved him. He had her in his sights still — and still she stood so if he pulled the trigger now he would certainly make the shot. But she would not know it had been him. She would merely be gone and he realized that was not what he wanted.

The panther turned and slipped into the trees. For a desperate moment, Joseph thought of following her into the forest, so sudden was his desire for her he would leave everything without a thought, but he could not will himself to move. He blinked, still kneeling, clutching his rifle, stunned, his breath vacating his mouth in one long sigh.

Finally, he let his arms down and sank into the cold, blue snow. His heart hammered in his chest. Exhaustion gripped his body, as if he had run a great distance, and he did not understand how this encounter, the mere act of observation, had tired him so completely. He tried to slow his breathing, taking deep breaths. The first stars glimmered above the eastern horizon. He would have to get down from this cliff before he could not see his hand in front of his face but he stayed, breathing, feeling warm despite the snow. From below, the sounds of the men, laughing and swearing, the yawn of a dog, the words *good boy*, and *that's a good boy!*

HIS FATHER WAS NOT at home when he returned to their apartment. It seemed the others had convinced him to come for a drink. Joseph, who surely would have been allowed into the bar tonight, veritably snuck home, staying in the shadows behind the line of buildings on Main Street to take the back entrance into his own building, not wanting to be seen. In complete darkness he mounted the stairs and opened the door and in darkness went through the apartment to his room, not lighting any lamps, seeing by the diffuse light coming in from the street.

He opened his window to the cold and lay on his bed feeling hot. An invisible weight had wrapped around his head, turning his thoughts disjointed, without order, and he was powerless against them. He regretted the flasks now. If he closed his eyes, it felt like the room was slowly spinning around him. The Old Woman ran through his thoughts and he could not banish her. He could not believe that he had seen her, and that she had seen him. She had caught him in her gaze, and he had been unable to look away or even move, unable to command himself to shoot. Not even unable—unwilling. He had not wanted to. This he found most confusing of all.

The memory of her gaze sent a subtle current through his veins, and in the darkness he felt a renewed flush burn upon his face. To be seen by her, it was like being seen by the sky, or the sun.

He drifted to sleep but awoke when his father came home. He listened to his father light a lamp, take a drink of water, then walk unevenly across the apartment, floor-boards creaking in that spot before the hallway. August stood in the doorway but did not enter. The lamp, held to the side, sent a soft light into the room.

"Joseph?"

"Hey, Pop."

"What happened to you?"

Joseph could tell by his voice that he had been drinking. He could smell the smoke on him, and a wave of regret rode through him that he had not gone to the bar with his father and the others.

"Jacobs told me he saw you head into the trees . . ."

Joseph was silent, thinking about what to say.

August launched into his own retelling, his manner a bit more animated than usual because of the alcohol.

"I'm sorry you missed her, Joseph. I couldn't believe my eyes! The dogs tracked her down into that gorge.

They could tell she was around and all of a sudden they just lost it, barking like mad. We let the dogs go and they went howling after her through the snow. The boys thought they'd caught her then. Even I thought, *Oh, now I will have to save this poor panther.* But then we saw her come right up to this rock face," — his eyes, not in the room, looked up and saw the cold, sheer rock face again — "and without batting an eye she jumped straight up, like it was nothing. Made it almost to the top, then bounded off the sheer side of the cliff and up onto the top and disappeared."

Joseph considered his father's story. She had jumped from the earth below — the height of a tree — silent as a ghost. He shut his eyes against this impossible feat but saw it all the more clearly in the darkness of his mind.

"Like something picked her up and placed her on top," his father mused. "I've never seen anything like it. The men just froze, staring in wonder!" He laughed, thinking of it now. "After that, some wanted to go after her, but by then it was getting dark . . . and they were out of liquor."

He was silent for a moment, considering his story. Then he said, "Sounds like Elmira Olsen is going to be fine, by the way. Reports of her injuries were . . . somewhat exaggerated."

"Oh." Joseph had forgotten all about her. "That's good."

"Yes. Turns out her left ear or eye or arm or whatever it was is intact. She did get scratched up a bit but not near as bad as we were hearing. She'll probably have a scar or two to remember it by."

Joseph was silent, wanting nothing more than to calm the restless thoughts in his mind. He could not convey to his father what it had meant, the sighting he had waited for his whole life, because now it seemed ridiculous that he had anticipated this moment, that he had waited his whole life to see her. A few years ago, he would have confided in his father about the secret meeting from that afternoon. But he remained silent. He knew what his father would say, what he thought about Joseph's feelings for the Old Woman.

"Well, goodnight then," his father said.

"Goodnight, Pop," said Joseph, and he listened to his father's uneven gait as he crossed the floor to his room and closed his bedroom door.

THE NEXT DAY JOSEPH heard how John Gunn had gone with a few stalwart others by lantern light, to track the panther's trail. They discovered that the panther had stalked Elmira Olsen and her mother from their house all the way to Shouter's Field, and had waited, pouncing only once the girl had strayed from her mother's presence.

When news of this reached the townspeople, they were outraged. That a panther would stalk a man as prey was unacceptable, and people responded with true hatred, as what might be directed toward some long-standing enemy. Joseph shook his head at the violent nature of this reaction. People believed they had been attacked. They were offended. Joseph lapsed into silence in the presence of these ravers, seeing the anxiety written on their faces. He knew he would not convince them otherwise.

That the Old Woman had failed to take the child said to him that she did not want the child. If she had wanted to, she would have taken her; of this he was certain. Joseph believed instead that she had had another purpose in appearing. She was calling out the hunter who would accompany her down that dark road, calling in a serious voice to the one who would come to her from out of the forest and relieve her of her long life.

But if he had shot the Old Woman that day, what a failure it would have been; the cheering drunks below, the frenzied barking of the dogs, himself drunk, out of body. To drag home the lifeless carcass of an old panther for the townsfolk to jeer at? To show them what? It was nothing to them. She meant nothing to them. That would not be appropriate. He was troubled by how close he had come, how mindless he had been.

Having been drunk, being so far away from her, this was not what he wanted. Still, his desire to meet her pestered him with its constant presence, though its impossibility grew the more he thought about it. He did not understand where this desire came from, which now for the first time he looked on with suspicion.

Confused by his thoughts, the persistent desire he could not understand, the fanatic devotion he could not explain, disgusted by the town and its hysteria, he turned away from the visions in which he had drowned hours of his youth. He would not permit himself to think of her. He gave her no opportunity, no foothold to gain entry, and the sudden flashes and dreamlike messages began to dwindle and grow weak. He willed his obsessive notions away, until they left him completely, and as a result he did not think of the Old Woman for many years.

IX

TRANSIENT

T HE COUGAR SAT IN the fading sunlight, staring up into the cloudless blue sky, many breaths between slow blinks. A cold wind blew through the red leaves on the trees, lifting them off their branches and sending them scuttling across the dry earth. Three winters had passed since she had banished her Stalker and she had not seen her since. She had had a brood in that time and those cubs were almost ready to leave her. Her three sons were asleep in their mountain lair, the entrance hidden by a slide of rock.

Her sons would sleep the whole day through, exhausted from hunting the night before and from the hectic pace of their growth. Now that they were deep into their apprenticeships, the Cougar felt less the need to stay with them in the lair throughout the day. More and more she was called outside.

Often she would leave the lair to bask beneath the open sky, or lie cradled among the branches of a tree, opening her eyes at points throughout the day to see again the world around her. She would sit and watch the movement of the forest for long stretches, the breeze rustling the leaves of a grove of white birch, the endless rush of the river, slow clouds as they swept across the sky. Sometimes her contemplation was so intense, pulling herself out of her thoughts and back into the waking world was like stepping out of a dream, and she was slow to adjust.

Other times, she could not sit still. She wandered the forest, visiting the places she knew, reading the changes that had occurred since the last time she had been there. Her interest was drawn here, to studying the earth. There was nothing that did not interest her, however slow, however small: the spinning of a spider's web, the changing face of melting ice, the growth of moss. The more she saw, the more she wanted to see.

The sound of the leaves in the wind was like a dull roar all around her. The trees stood as they had all afternoon. Yet now she looked up, as if something had spoken to her upon the air. The Cougar rose, stiff-limbed, and headed into the red trees.

It was cooler in the shade. The Cougar walked through the fallen red leaves, the chattering of birds in the trees uninterrupted by her passage. She followed a path without signs through the bush, out to where the trees broke before a sloping field, golden in the late autumn sunlight. She sat watching the field for a sign of what had called her here. The field was quiet before her. The wind ran through the long, pale grass.

A dark cougar sauntered out of the trees, mindless of the daylight. The Cougar could tell from her shabby appearance that this was a transient cougar, too old to defend her own territory, forced to wander the fringes, eating what she could catch in a hurry or forage from the leftovers of others. But this cougar did not act like one trying to go softly through another cougar's territory. She walked out into the open, not bothering to hide herself, as if all the forest belonged to her.

The Cougar caught her scent on the wind. It was the smell of a cougar not concerned with concealing herself from others, the sign of a body and mind in decline. The Cougar could not help but be curious. She had never encountered such a cougar before. She followed the black cougar, keeping her in sight but staying well away. The wind rustled the fallen leaves, muting the sounds of the Cougar's slow pursuit.

The sight of the Transient, a dark shadow walking through the long grass, hypnotized her, and she did not realize at first that when the Transient paused and turned her head to look into the trees where the Cougar stood that she was looking at her. She found herself caught in the other cougar's gaze, unable to look away. But now that she had been seen, there was no sense in hiding.

The Cougar stepped through the trees and came within a few steps of the Transient and sat. Up close, the old cougar's smell was obvious. The earthy smell of one who had long been waiting in the shadows, a smell of darkness. It was a sign this cougar must not be taken for her physical form alone. Though she gave the impression of madness she would have to possess qualities that her outward appearance did not betray or else she would never have survived so many years in the forest.

The Transient's fur was so dark it was almost black along her back and her legs, her face white at the muzzle and upon her chest. She was smaller than the Cougar but the severity of her physique was no less intimidating, sharp as bone, pure hunter. Below her chin grew a thin silver beard and her eyes hung barely open, as if she were about to sit and take a nap on her feet. Her right eye was rheumy and clouded, blinking slowly, the left screwed shut by a jagged scar that started below the eye and reached up toward her ear. The Cougar could not look into either of her eyes. She considered this a bad sign.

The Cougar studied the scar on the Transient's face that twisted through her left eye. That she had survived such an injury was a testament to either her strength or her luck. This was no mere cougar. She was half-starved or she was mad. Her arms bore the dark scars of her altercations, her face was gaunt. She had begun to resemble Death. Death stalked behind her where she went, and the Cougar felt that presence like a crackling close by. The Transient stared on, as if she did not see the Cougar, nor the world around them, but something beyond that.

The Cougar affected an air of indifference. She licked her muzzle and pulled herself to her full height, showing her sleek coat, her strong chest, to the Transient. Her paws were giant, her eyes clear, her face symmetrical. True, she was no longer a young cougar, her body not unmarred by contest, but she was still strong. What scars she had she wore as an indication of her ability to evade Death.

The Transient's rheumy eye flicked over the Cougar vaguely, then with a sound like a bending branch, she opened her mouth and yawned.

The Cougar narrowed her eyes. She took a step to circle the Transient, push her back with the closeness of her body, but the Transient sat, looking away, uninterested. The Cougar came around to face her again, lowered her head, and hissed.

The Transient remained unmoved.

The Cougar pulled out her voice and gave a sudden, piercing growl. The Transient faced her, looking through her with her crooked gaze. The Cougar growled again and raised her paw to swat the Transient's face but touched air; the Transient jumped back with so subtle a movement she had not even seen it. The Cougar drew back.

They stood watching one another for a moment, a fraught pause, then the Transient turned and walked away.

How she turned her back! As if the Cougar were no threat at all, to be given no more thought than fog. And while she was impressed by such boldness, she was also outraged. She rushed the Transient, but the black cougar turned and met her embrace. They fell to the ground together and toppled one over the other.

When the Cougar regained her footing, she stood face to face with the Transient, who opened her mouth to show her teeth and from that death-dealing maw came the strangled whisper of a hiss. The raspy sound sent a shiver down the Cougar's body. She stood fixed, caught in the Transient's stare, paralyzed by the sight of her blind eye, her small yet deceptive frame, by the smell of her, almost horrible — and she had the feeling like she was trying to recall a dream she had had but could not remember.

The Transient turned and walked away at that same easy pace with which she had entered. The Cougar watched her go, her lean body, her shadow cast on the earth beside her as she crossed the field and disappeared into the trees.

The Cougar stood watching after her, suspecting the old cougar had not taken her retreat any farther than out of her field of vision and now sat observing her from somewhere within the trees.

The Transient was none of her concern, on some harmless crossing. That is what the physical events would suggest. But the Cougar was not convinced. Though she did not fully understand what had been shown to her, she knew to trust herself when she grew suspicious. There were too many signs to ignore.

The Cougar turned and entered the trees, to return to her lair.

HER SONS WERE STILL asleep when she returned to the lair, the sight of them at rest easing her anxious heart. The sun had not yet set. They would awaken on their own, signalled by the change in light. The Cougar turned and sat in the entrance of the lair to wait.

The three cubs were identical-looking, the gold colouring from her, the substantial size and shape from their sire. They were swift learners, attentive to her instructions. They seemed to have a natural sense of silence, an aptitude for patience, which she could not attribute to her teaching alone.

In the summer previous to the cubs' births, the Cougar had been walking the forest in the evening, the sun low through the black trees, when she came to a small clearing. A fallen trunk lay shed of its branches, growing fungus, slowly disintegrating. At first, she did not see the body. It took her a moment to discern the dark shadow sunken into the earth from the fallen leaves, the general disarray of the forest floor. It was not unnatural to find Death in the forest. She could see that this cougar had been involved in a fight. Claw marks on his shoulders, his sides. The hide torn back, torso clawed open, rifled through and robbed.

As she came closer she saw the cougar's face, recognized the scar marking his cheek below his eyes, and realized it was her Marauder.

A dark shadow had spread out beneath him where his blood had stained the earth and turned to ash. Scavengers had been at his eyes, picked away every scrap of meat from his case. The sight of his bones, open to the air, alarmed her most of all. His limbs and head remained intact, the fur on these parts a brutal imitation of the living thing. His remains were a mockery of their former state. Soon there would be nothing at all, he would disappear altogether, returned to the earth.

She had not seen the Marauder since before the birth of their three daughters, but she had believed him to be alive. Up until the moment she found him lying here, he had been hunting, stalking the forest, drawing breath. Yet here he lay, for many days it seemed, and the shock of learning this was like learning the sun would no longer rise.

An owl called from within the trees overhead. The sun had set and the shadows descended like a sudden shower. The Cougar leaned her head down and brushed the side of her face against the Marauder's cheek. Though still the same shape, the skull felt wrong, hollow, but she could not stop herself, compelled to repeat the action one last time.

She stood watching his remains a moment longer, unable to pull her eyes away from the dark eye sockets. As night swept over the forest, the distant song of crickets rose and murmured through the trees. Then the Cougar turned and walked on, leaving the Marauder behind to sink further into the earth.

She was shocked by the suddenness of the Marauder's death. Days were spent handling the numb feeling that swelled inside her. The loss of him almost confused her—that she had given this inevitable event no thought at all, not considered it once, seemed foolish. His absence became a presence in her life. She hunted and ate but she could not escape the lingering emptiness inside her. She sat on the riverbank staring through the river, unmoving. The Cougar retreated into the night and did not emerge until the heat of summer had been chased away by the chill winds of autumn, and when next that madness came upon her, the Cougar saw why the Marauder had been slain.

Under the spell of that infrequent madness, she stalked through the cold forest, the wind through the trees, her feet silent on the cold earth. The sound of her voice had become ragged from calling all through the night, and she was weary from her night-long trek, when she realized the forest was staring at her with golden eyes. She looked again and saw a young cougar sauntering toward her from out of the trees.

By the sight of him, she knew he was a usurper. He was lean but muscled beneath his smooth coat, the brilliance of youth shining all through him. He could not have been away from the care of his mother for more than two winters, and already he had staked his life in contest, and seen victory.

He came toward her in perfect silence. Then sat, glanced away. The profile of his face caught her attention. His bright gold colour, the symmetry of his shape, so fine, her attraction to him was immediate.

The Usurper had an open face yet unmarked by conflict. She did not have to see him hunt to know he was a successful hunter, and just by looking at him the

Cougar could envision the excellent offspring they would have together. She could see them in her mind, bright, golden hunters.

By winter she had three sons. She had not been wrong in her prediction. The three of them careful, serious, even in play. They seemed to learn from one another, watching each other's failures, so their progress seemed faster than that of any of her previous broods. Now fully grown, they outweighed their mother, their faces and paws wider than hers, but they still bent their heads to her so she might rub her cheek against their cheeks, and they still followed after her in their decided order as she led them on the hunt.

One of the Cougar sons raised his head, met her eyes, yawned. Noticing his brothers were still asleep, he lay back down and shut his eyes with a short sigh.

The Cougar turned back to the sky to wait.

FOUR COUGARS, RED IN the slanted light, came through the trees, heads low, eyes like fireflies. They crossed into a valley of young trees. The wildfire here had ravaged this part of the forest, exposing the land to the sky. She thought of her son who had fled the wildfire with her, who had followed her through this very stretch of forest. Now the thin trees stood sparse and the ground was hazy with bright green ferns. As she made her way across, the Cougar remembered the forest that had stood before the fire, the branches of the tallest trees mingling overhead, blocking out the sun. It occurred to her that she was older than these trees and that seemed strange to her.

They left the young trees behind and entered an older part of the forest, a deep silence surrounding them. They climbed the tangled landscape. Near the top of the incline, they slowed their steps. In cold air, sound travelled far and their prey possessed sharp hearing. Their skills must be just as sharp or else they would starve. The trees parted and the Cougar saw the deer slowly migrating toward them.

She leapt down the incline, her sons following in long, silent strides. In the red light, the cougars blended into the leaves scattered on the ground, giving them an added level of cover. The herd stood, red as well in the descending sunlight, grazing, watching into the trees, some asleep on their thin legs.

The cougars stayed low to the ground, advancing in bursts. They made their way over the short grass, with nothing obstructing them from the deer's view out in the open. The Cougar had become brazen with age, making bold attempts to get as close as possible before the deer noticed her. Sitting in plain sight, perfectly still, and letting them go by. Sometimes even walking along beside them before striking; so studied was her skill she could pass for a deer herself.

The cougars fanned out, bodies close to the ground. Though they would strike together, now they were each on their own. The birds knew of them. She noticed the deer tense, saw them studying the field. The cougars waited, held their breath. The deer were looking at them right now but did not even realize, so devoted were the hunters to stillness. The Cougar sat poised in the red light, within a single leap of the nearest deer. The deer had grown still, watching the trees. They had noticed the silence of the birds.

The cougars rose into the air as if on a wind. Surrounded on all sides, the deer did not know which way to flee and froze.

The Cougar wrapped her front paws around the body of a fawn who had not even tried to flee. She crushed his neck between her jaws, then sat, breathing steadily. Her sons had worked together to bring down a buck, which now lay on its side, his hide scrolled back, the shade of his blood lost upon the cubs' faces in the red light of the setting sun. The cubs had begun to forage out the inner organs, the most secret of meats. When they looked up from the body of the buck, their eyes flashed green in the failing light.

A cold breath blew against the Cougar's cheek. She looked into the trees and saw the Transient sitting in the shadows, the ragged scar through her left eye, the milky right eye staring out at her. There was no question: she sat there awaiting the Cougar, so the Cougar might see her.

The Cougar growled, drawing the attention of her sons. The Transient sat watching her; she did not even blink. Then she turned neatly and sauntered away through the trees. The Cougar's sons stood beside her, ready to face the foe their mother had addressed, but the Cougar would not pursue her now. Instead, she stayed, staring into the trees where the Transient had disappeared.

The Cougar turned her attention to her kill, that her sons would do the same, but she ate out of mechanism, her hunger forgotten. That black cougar stuck in her mind and would not leave her. Even when she closed her eyes, the old cougar was there, staring back at her.

THE COUGAR WATCHED HER sons as they slept. They had been hunting by themselves for days now. The Cougar's presence was superfluous. But they had yet to realize it. They would sleep the day, arise, and head out into the night, perhaps together, perhaps on their own. She could not see beyond these initial steps. Before the Cougar stepped outside, she cast a glance behind her. The faint beating of their hearts within their chests reached her ears, a quiet chaos.

An owl made its sombre call from the branches above, marking the Cougar's passage. Her side cried out and then was silent as she slipped through the underbrush. She returned to the site of the earlier hunt, the remains of their prey now a bitter red stain in the early morning sunlight. She entered the trees where the Transient had sat staring at her and found the old cougar's trail, her scent obvious amid the familiar scents of the forest.

As she stalked through the trees, the Cougar realized the Transient must have followed her all the way through the field where the wildfire had scourged the forest, perhaps even followed her from her lair. This was especially disturbing to her. But instead of warning her away, this compelled her to follow the Transient. She knew this was a dangerous curiosity, knowing it was unwise to follow so far. And she shocked herself that this did nothing to deter her. It seemed she had grown too old for caution—a bad sign.

A single crow sat perched on a leaf-bare branch. The Cougar eyed it as she walked past. The crow, roused from contemplation, put forth its jarring cry, the sound echoing against the surrounding trees. It stretched out its wings against the blue sky, like a black sunrise, and paused a moment, head turned toward the horizon. The Cougar was struck by this unusual pose and stood watching as the crow folded its wings back against its body and returned to its meditations.

The Cougar waited to see if there was more. The crow ignored her, as if nothing had occurred, and the Cougar wondered what it was she had just seen.

SHAFTS OF SUNLIGHT PLUNGED through the cold red forest. The Cougar's breath rose up around her head. Above, the treetops were brushed by a slow wind. The Cougar followed the Transient's trail, wary that the following should be so easy. The old cougar made no effort to hide her presence in the forest. This concerned the Cougar, but still she went on.

When the Cougar emerged from the trees, the river lay before her and she knew the Transient had crossed and was now within the trees on the other side. The river was a calm, dark vein. The Cougar stood on the river-bank watching the surface of the water, seeing within. The land was flat, the river wide, less violent here than it was upstream, its level low due to the late season. Though she could not bring herself to trust the river she knew she must cross if she was going to take her pursuit any further.

She could turn back now, forget the Transient, return to those sleeping cubs who may have yet to notice her absence. She stood a moment on the rocky shore staring at the other side of the river, deliberating. The sky was cloudless. The ghost of the moon hung above the horizon. She stepped down into the cold water, then pushed off. The cold was a shock, like she had just emerged into being. Only her head and tail appeared above the surface. She kept her eyes on the far shore, breathing steadily. At the midpoint of the river she wondered what might now be looking up at her from the depths.

She pulled herself up onto the rocky shore, shook herself in a spray of light, then cut into the trees after the Transient. She did not have to read the ground in order to find the Transient's trail. She could smell the wet cougar on the air.

The Transient was not trying to elude her. It seemed she did not have a purpose in the direction of her course, as if she were merely out for a walk in the forest and had nowhere else to be.

The whine of the cicadas rose up, stretched on into the cold autumn air, and faded. The Cougar stayed listening. She looked and saw the path through the trees she would take as if it were suddenly lit by the sunlight. Though there was no sign the Transient had been through here, the Cougar would follow this path to see where it led her.

The Cougar continued on her path without thought, a pure action of the body, and fell into a sort of trance. In this way she covered a great distance throughout the day. Sunset filled the forest with orange light, the trunks of the trees glowed the same bright red as the leaves on their branches, and the sky was set ablaze with the colour of flame. Then, like the sudden blooming of a flower, she smelled that earthy scent and knew the Transient was nearby.

She heard the absence of trees before her and saw the bare earth, and the fur on her back bristled at the sight. She smelled the scent of smoke on the air and then she knew—men. The domain of men was a place she was determined to avoid. This was a sure sign that she should turn back. She knew this. But she knew even now she would not turn back.

The Cougar peered through the trees. A wide path had been cut into the earth, hard-packed by the wear of many feet. She recognized this sign from the night she had killed those many sheep. She scanned the road, trying to see past the trees, but no one was there.

It was then the Cougar noticed the din of activity nearby. The source of the sound was just ahead. At first she had missed the low hum in the air, but now it was clear, beneath everything else a continuous humming. The Cougar crept through the trees toward the sound. As she drew near, she smelled a scent obvious and glaring, along with the smoke, which could only be produced by a herd of men. Its strength shocked her. Such disregard for conceal- ment. There must be so many of them that they did not mind their presence to be known.

She jumped up into a tree, silent as a breeze, and from her perch among the branches looked down on the town. The trees had been cleared away, a swath of wild grass lay before her, and beyond this a sea of mud stretching up to where the men's dwellings stood, clustered together like a troop of mushrooms, smoke pulsing from each one. The Cougar was amazed at their dwellings out in the open, shrouded in such obvious stench. She could hear them now, a great many of them, milling about, an invisible hoard. So many the sound was constant, reminding her of a hive. The murmur in the air, the sight of the earth, flat, exposed, unnerved her. These were signs, but their meaning was not clear to her.

She shifted her position among the branches and settled in to await the cover of darkness. As the light fell, a hazy glow settled over the town, like a mist hovering atop a body of water, concealing what lay beneath.

T HE COUGAR WAITED FOR the inhabitants of the town to settle down and go to sleep, but instead the men lit fires so the interiors of their lairs glowed, sending an uncanny light out into the evening. She reasoned that they slept at times during the day, like herself, or in shifts, like the wolves, and could not be expected to all be asleep at once, meaning there was no opportune time at which to approach the town.

She remembered the night she had killed the sheep; the sight of the man carrying that hive of fire through the darkness, accompanied by the smell of smoke. It had not been possible to discern his abilities based on his outward appearance. Everything about him was secretive. The number of men was unknown to her, but the sound of them reminded the Cougar of the bees' penchant for swarming, impossible to defend against except to run. An unnerving sound, warning her to turn back from this place devoid of trees, as if some unnatural wind had ripped them from the ground and carried them into the sky.

She began tracing the town's perimeter, her curiosity drawing her closer. The smell surrounding the town masked the presence of specific individuals, likewise that of the Transient. She was clever to come here, to lead the Cougar into a place where her sense of smell and sensitive hearing gave her no advantage.

The Cougar found a place where the forest grew right up against some dwellings, the shadows darker here where no unnatural light was cast. She peered through the wooden slats of a fence into the enclosed area within. She leapt the fence and landed in silence. Refuse lay piled in heaps, stored here for some reason she could not discern. The entrance to the lair lay open to the night, spilling light out into the darkness. She heard the sound of voices from within the dwelling. The Cougar took a step closer, sniffing at the air.

The Cougar's curiosity had her close to entering the dwelling when a chubby young child stumbled into the entrance. The Cougar froze. Their eyes met and she noticed the child's bright blue eyes, which she found vaguely familiar. The child stood staring back at her, neither afraid nor apprehensive, then the child opened its mouth to her and she saw that it had no teeth. An awed squeal escaped the child's toothless maw and the Cougar heard the approach of someone from within.

The Cougar leapt up over the fence and out of the yard in one silent motion. Behind her she heard someone murmuring to the child, then shutting the door. She padded along behind the line of dwellings, staying in the shadows, continuing around the town's perimeter.

The Cougar slid between two houses. From the shadows she peered around the corner, out into the open space of the road. The streets were lit by burning globes hanging from tall, branchless trees. The roads that crossed the town were nothing more than pathways of mud. The Cougar stared at the mess of the path/road before her in the faint light. There were so many tracks she could not trace the line of a single one. The openness made her nervous. That and the many darkened windows which seemed like eyes watching down into the street.

Then she noticed, standing in the shadowy lamplight, a fantastic beast she had never seen before. The horse stood tied to a rail by straps connected to gear fastened around his head and body. She was instantly in awe of his structure. The sturdy feet, strong legs, his smooth, muscular chest, the sheen of the lamplight on the horse's brown hide, its mane of black hair hanging to one side. She could smell physical exertion, the suggestion of his lived life upon the earth.

The Cougar crept through the darkness. She saw the look of fatigue in his dark eyes, the sway of his back, and she wondered at his age.

Then, for no reason she could account for, the horse seemed to know she was there. It snorted and trotted on the spot, pulling at the reins fastening it to the rail. The Cougar froze. The horse whinnied and kicked.

The door to the dwelling flew open and a man came out, his feet clattering loudly as he descended the stairs. The man took a cautious step toward the horse, holding up his hands to it, as if some effect might be produced by this gesture. The horse refused to be consoled but the man did not retreat.

The Cougar sat watching from the shadows as the man laid his hands upon the horse's neck, stroking its hair, speaking softly. His hands reminded her of claws, but he had a gentle touch. The man also seemed weary.

He too had a similar fatigue in his posture. The man's face was hidden in the shadow cast by the brim of his hat, he kept his hand on the horse's neck, speaking next to the horse's ear.

The Cougar slipped away, behind the dwellings. She looked around the edge of a house into the street. A line of flat buildings stood on either side of the street. It was a deserted place. It seemed impossible that the herd who made such a constant sound could remain out of sight. She wondered if the Transient was somewhere in the shadows also watching into the street, waiting for her to reveal herself.

In the dwelling beside her, there was a dark alcove covered by a pane of glass, with a clutter of objects in the darkness within. From where she sat in the shadows she could not make sense of the display. The Cougar scanned the street, the line of dwellings, in the gloomy light of the street lamps. Her heart beat hard as she stepped out onto the cold, dry mud.

She came up to the glass and stared in. An arrangement of objects stood gleaming in the shadows. The Cougar stood trying to unlock their meaning with her eyes, but nothing was revealed to her, their shapes were too obscure, too unlike anything she had ever seen. She laid eyes on the artifice of a man's feet, but she was hardly bewildered at this point by the things she saw in man's town.

Then she saw, lurking in the shadowed corner of the alcove, a bear stood on hind legs, and while a ripple of panic passed through her she immediately detected the bear was false. It was an illusion of a bear, she knew, and though startling in its mimicry of life, she felt its absence, like a void.

She tested the glass with her paw. It was cool to the touch. Her breath fogged out against the glass and she saw then a ghostly cougar staring back at her and leapt away, but even before she had landed she knew it was only a vision of herself. She sat panting, watched her shadow-self sitting upon a dark road in some sister realm.

She heard the fall of a footstep behind her and dashed back into the shadows. That familiar crack, like the sudden break of thunder, tore through the air. The Cougar ran around behind the dwellings. She raced through the shadows, stopping in a narrow alley. She held her breath, listening to see if she was being pursued. She could hear the rumble of footsteps from elsewhere in the town.

The alley was littered with trash. The smell was chaotic, overwhelming her ability to smell anything beyond the incoherent mess in front of her. As she stepped through she heard the faint rustling of movement. The Cougar froze, waiting to see what would reveal itself.

From out of the garbage rose some lanky cats, their fur rough and unkempt. There were three of them. One black, one mottled, and a striped tawny-coloured one, all with muddy paws and dingy coats. Their eyes flashed green in the dim light and when they saw the Cougar they arched their backs, the fur rising like grass, and they opened their mouths and she saw their tiny fangs and they made quiet hisses at her.

Their size was the most perplexing part. They were not small due to immaturity, they were fully grown. Their similarity to her in shape and feature was eerie. At once familiar and unknown. The sight of their angered faces, wrinkled up by their hissing, sent a chill through her body.

Another gunshot rang through the air. The cats scattered back into the trash and the Cougar fled into the darkness.

She remembered her search for the Transient. The Cougar ran toward the gunshot. The sound had rallied the attention of the men all around her. She heard them stirring in their dwellings, their voices carrying into the night air. It was time to flee. The Cougar leapt up onto the roof of the nearest house and crossed it, then leapt to the next house. In this way she travelled across town as the men began venturing out into the streets in pairs, clutching rifles, brandishing fire.

The distance between dwellings grew and the Cougar jumped to the ground. As she ran behind the dwellings she caught glimpses of the men gathering in the street. Their faces twisted in alarm, the expression passed from one to the other like wildfire spreading from tree to tree. She realized the men could not see into the darkness but they could still sense her presence, that she was among them, and this seemed to frighten them most of all.

She came to the edge of the town. Moonlight shone down on the frozen sea of mud, a bleak plain. Abandoned implements lay scattered in the mud, half-buried, like the skeletal fragments of prey animals slowly decaying. She stood waiting, her breath coming hard, watching the edge of the town.

The Transient sauntered out onto the sea of mud. She

turned and looked to where the Cougar sat in the darkness, her good eye flashing red as if an eye that were not her own stared out of her skull, then she turned to head into the trees.

The Cougar waited, letting her breathing return to normal. There was no urgency. Neither cougar was hiding from the other, as if by their passage through the town they had come to an agreement. She searched the open ground to make sure there were no men here, then she stepped out onto the mud, heading toward the place where the Transient had entered the trees.

ONCE WITHIN THE FOREST, the town of men faded from her mind, their commotion in the night forgotten, the quiet of the forest resumed. She could hear the passage of the Transient before her, the sound of her feet through the fallen leaves, and she followed. The Transient led the way as if she herself were being guided, remembering the path to a place she had been long ago.

The Cougar followed the Transient through the night. At times she could see the old cougar between the thin trees, walking in her determined gait, her ears twitching to the sounds the Cougar made. Other times she strayed so far ahead that the Cougar lost sight of her, but could always hear her light progress over the forest floor.

Thin, blue veins shot through the black crystal sky. The land sloped downward, the trees began to thin. The evergreens grew squat and spread out. The cougars emerged from the trees and before them stretched a sea of pale grass. The land beyond lay indecipherable, still in the murk of night. As they waded into the grass the crickets swelled, masking the sound of the Transient's passage and that of the Cougar as she followed close behind.

The grass grew short and the Cougar saw the bare face of the earth. Rock stretched on into the horizon as if they had come to the edge of the earth. The Cougar stopped and looked upon the stone passages snaking through the desert before them. The Transient did not pause. She went on, either not caring if the Cougar followed or knowing that she would.

The stone pathways which from afar had appeared like mere furrows now loomed over their heads. The Cougar eyed the walls, their rugged texture. She was tempted to pause and inspect the stone, as if she might uncover some meaning regarding the place they had come to, but the Transient went on and the Cougar did not want to lose her in the folds of the stone labyrinth.

The thin corridor opened up, the stone walls on either side fell away, and the Cougar followed the Transient onto a shelf of rock, the edges of the plateau barred by open air. Below them the desert stretched on into the distance beneath the deep sky.

The Transient sat watching the Cougar, sitting with perfect posture, waiting. In the distance behind her, the sun flashed above the horizon. The cougars faced each other as the sunlight crept over the stone toward their feet. The Cougar watched the Transient for any indication that she would pounce. But the Transient waited. The Cougar's heartbeat grew anxious and she felt certain it was so loud the Transient would hear it across the short distance between them.

The sunlight had reached their feet. The Cougar watched as the slow sun revealed the subtle contours of the Transient's body, the line of scars along her front legs, the slope of muscle down her chest. The Transient's black fur glistened with a ruby sheen. Her face bloomed in the sunlight, sharp and thin, the silver beard at her chin, her right eye golden fire, her left a dark hollow.

Still, she waited. In the full sunlight, the cougars' breath was lit like smoke, which rose curling from their nostrils, and dissipated into the cold air. The stone was pale and dusky in the daylight. Heat started to gather in the stone beneath their feet.

The Transient's posture revealed nothing. She seemed content to wait forever. Something about the pose, her unseeing stare, made the Cougar's patience snap and she rushed to meet the Transient.

She meant to tackle her, knock her to the ground, but the old cougar reached out and swatted her attack aside like she was batting away a wayward branch. The Cougar twisted and faced the Transient, hissing. She rose onto her back legs and the Transient rose to meet her, locked in an embrace, terrible cries rising up from them both. The old cougar was nothing but bones yet somehow she had the strength of rock.

The rising sun glared down on the two cougars as they wrestled on the stone, the Cougar flashing gold, the Transient's black fur gleaming, their shadows cast beside them. They threw each other off and stalked away, to the border of their arena, neither letting the other out of her sight.

The Cougar dashed forward, trying to reach in and catch the Transient's side with her claws, but the black cougar met her advance and threw her off. Her attacks were being evaded with ease. The Transient was no stronger than she was, yet she stood against the Cougar like a mountain withstands the wind, immovable no matter how the wind rages. Seeing her tactics were having little effect, the Cougar backed away, heart pounding.

It did not matter if the Cougar was the stronger. The Transient was hard to grip. She eluded the Cougar's embrace like water, not letting herself be caught. Behind the Transient's veneer of madness, her mind, when pressed, was as sharp as stone. Having this thought, a shadow of doubt descended upon the Cougar.

The Transient pounced, wrapped her forelegs around the Cougar's shoulders as she tackled her to the ground, crushing her against the stone. The Cougar was amazed that her weightless frame was capable of such strength. The black cougar's rancid breath touched her face and she did not want to breathe it in. She twisted out of the Transient's grip and stood, growling.

The Transient paced around the Cougar, yellowed teeth bared. Despite her uneven gait, it seemed she was not the least bit fatigued. Over the pounding of her own heart, the Cougar imagined the Transient's heartbeat as a dark, steady pulse. She knew the black cougar was waiting her out, harassing her until she was tired enough to give the Transient the moment she wanted.

The sun glared down upon them, turning the air to pure heat. The stone walls on the periphery of her vision began to shift and shimmer, as if affected by a slow wind.

The Transient sent forth a scream and the sound of her voice, dragged through the rough passage of her throat, sent a fine prickling over the Cougar's skin. Her own voice seemed somehow diminished by the other, and did nothing to terrify that steadfast hunter, so she refrained from using it but was unable to keep from hissing.

The sun was at its highest point in the sky. She began to throw the Transient off instead of attacking her, and the Transient spotted this retreat, as she would, and this seemed to energize her, allowing the Cougar no rest. The Cougar marvelled that this was possible for the old cougar and wondered how long her own strength could hold out.

The Cougar considered that she might die — and once she thought this, a terrible vision rose up before her. A cougar of enormous size, fur the bright colour of blood, climbed up from out of the earth and stood behind the Transient. The vision drew her full attention, and she stared, wide-eyed, and she knew she must not become caught in its gaze. The Cougar forced herself to look away from this terrifying, red figure, back to the Transient.

The sun burned white in the sky. In the distance, the air shivered over the ground. The heat weighed on the Cougar and she knew that soon she would be unable to stand, and still the Transient was relentless. The cougars stood locked in each other's embrace, waving their open mouths at one another, trying for the neck, their back legs struggling for footing on the hot, unyielding stone.

The Transient reached out and in her fatigue the Cougar did not move aside fast enough, so when she twisted out of the Transient's grasp, the old cougar's claws raked across the side of her face. The sting of the air at her open flesh was immediate. Two claw marks slashed through the Cougar's cheek below her left eye.

The Cougar stumbled back, never taking her eyes

off the Transient. Her left eye was intact, but the pain throbbed through her entire face, pounding with the beating of her heart. Blood dripped onto the stone beneath her, flashing in the sun. She glared at the black cougar, who waited, her tail flicking.

The vision of Death returned and this time she could not look away. The Red Cougar took easy, patient steps, the glow of her eyes like two small suns, as she paced, tracing the edge of their circle, not permitted to enter until one of them fell. The Cougar knew she must not look away from the Transient yet her eyes strayed beyond her, drawn to the indomitable presence of the Red Cougar.

She felt herself nearing the end of her strength. The Transient opened her mouth to the Cougar and she saw the old cougar's yellowed teeth — all the many hearts she had consumed throughout her life, a river of blood. The Transient circled around to approach her side and the Cougar was distracted by her black fur glistening in the sunlight. The walls of stone seemed to have pulled back and the desert below appeared as if she were looking on it from a great height.

The Transient swatted her with a paw and the Cougar met it with her own, casting it aside. The Cougar hissed but the Transient was unmoved. She wrapped her forelegs around the Cougar's torso, attempting to bring her to the earth. The Cougar growled and twisted, trying to escape her grasp. They fell to the burning ground. The Transient tried to sink her bite into the Cougar's neck as the Cougar struggled to break free of her.

The Red Cougar continued her slow circle, padding

along on silent feet. The Cougar felt those steps vibrating through the stone. She dare not look at the vision as she struggled beneath the Transient, whose mouth was so close she felt again that hot breath against her face and was repulsed.

The Cougar twisted around and caught the Transient in her embrace. The Transient thrashed wildly in the Cougar's grip. She tore away, and the Cougar's claws struck through the flesh on the Transient's shoulders. The blood was not visible against the Transient's fur, but when she took a step, her paw print was left behind, stamped in blood upon the stone.

The Transient rushed her with a growl but the Cougar threw her off. They stood watching each other breathe. The Cougar's bright gold eyes fixed on the Transient, scanning her body for the slightest indication of movement. The Transient's gaze was impassive, her clouded eye not seeming to see the Cougar, as if she stared beyond her—even her stare was deceptive.

The Cougar shut her eyes to the great loiterer on their periphery. If she could just bear these last desperate attacks, the Transient would make the fatal mistake the Cougar was waiting for.

The sun cast their shadows long beside them. They stood, exhausted, on guard, as the deadly pause stretched out, each waiting on the other to act. They stumbled close, waving their open jaws toward each other. The Transient stepped close and the Cougar made a low caterwaul, not even a growl, for she could no longer muster the strength, and twisted her body to face the Transient. The Transient's breath came in ragged gasps. She stumbled and leaned against the Cougar. They stood together for a moment, breathing. The Cougar felt as if her legs would collapse beneath her. She fought to stay standing, to push the Transient into the earth.

The low sun cast a dark orange light over the desert, raising valleys of shadows before them. In this light, the bloodstains from their injuries seemed to disappear, their bodies restored. The Cougar raised a foreleg and rested it around the Transient's neck. The Transient did not refuse. The Cougar pulled the Transient down, collapsing with her, the black cougar on her side, the gold cougar pinning her to the hot stone. They lay panting, their hearts pumping madly in their chests.

Out of the corner of her eye, she saw the Red Cougar sat waiting, tail curled up against her body. Now that her victim had been identified she was no longer restless. She could wait while the Transient breathed her last breaths.

The sun cast a flare of light into the sky where it sank beneath the horizon and then was gone. The heat fled from the air. The cougars' breathing slowed to an even rate. Beneath them, the earth began to cool.

N THE QUIET EVENING, the passage of the day seemed unreal. The Cougar felt hollow, as if she were made of air, stripped of all flesh and all that remained was her shadow. Beneath her, the Transient's body burned with the heat of exertion still in her limbs, her breathing ragged, trying to force air into her lungs even as her body was closing, growing dark.

It was then the Cougar realized her hunger. She had not eaten since she began her pursuit of the Transient. With her back claw she tore an inelegant slice down the Transient's torso, and the beating of her heart, though faint, seeped into the air. Blood spilled out onto the white stone, appearing black in the starlight.

She rummaged through the Transient's insides, to that deep, secret organ, the richest, darkest of meat. After the first bite, she lost herself to hunger and buried her head in the Transient's gut.

She felt a wind blow over her and then she saw a great void swell beneath her. The flat expanse of desert went on, endless. The shadows of clouds crawled over the stone ridges as the sun cut across the sky. She saw a slow flood over the land, the passage of the water cutting down into the earth, carving out the peaks and ridges, the stone melting beneath the spinning wheel of the sun. Then a dry wind ran over the barren plains, blowing smooth the ridges of stone. Despite the vast distance, this was all enclosed, all within something larger still, and far more silent, and way down below she saw herself sitting next to the Transient, eating from her body, blood spilled on the stone around her in a black circle—

She looked up from the Transient's body, her face darkened by its mask of blood. The desert plain lay white beneath the starlit sky. The moon looked down like a half-closed eye. Despite the moon's changing shape, she found its consistency a consoling presence in her life.

The Cougar's breath swelled out from her nostrils into the cold night air. Her body ached. Her wounds stung. The claw mark below her eye pulsed with a steady beat. Her skin felt like a case around her, the blood and dust that caked her fur like a skin she had outgrown and needed to shed.

With slow, tired movements she began the task of grooming herself, amazed at how long it had been since she had last done so. She started with her paws, dark with dust and blood. Then she used her paws to wipe clean the contours of her face, being careful around her injured cheek. After a time, she broke from this chore to eat again.

Then, at last, she slept.

THE RISING SUN AWOKE her. On the desert plain, there was no shelter from the light. For the first time in days, the Cougar thought about her lair and her three sons. She did not even remember how many days it had been since she had left them. They must have gone by now, knowing she would not return to them. She looked on the desert below, the stone ridges seeming like a forest of mountains. She could not look away.

By mid-morning, two vultures circled high overhead, tracing a silent circle in the sky. The Cougar watched these scavengers, grateful they would not come down as long as she remained. They too were patient hunters.

The wreck of the Transient's body lay beside her, the hide torn away, the insides ransacked. Yet still the Cougar found herself reluctant to leave.

The sun rose into the sky and the air grew hot and the Cougar sat on the baking stone, eyes closed, breathing slow. She felt through her injuries. The most serious were the claw marks on her face, but even these had faded to a dull ache. She thought of the river, plunging into the brisk water. But when the sun set on this day, still she had not left, and she stayed on even as the last rays reached out from the horizon and faded against the growing dark.

Finally, once the earth had cooled and her breath once again rose up around her head in the moonlight, she saw there was no reason to stay any longer. She had eaten all she would from the body, slept by her cache, guarded it against trespassers, was herself restored. Now she must leave the Transient to her decomposition.

The Cougar rose, stiff-limbed but steady. At the entrance to those stone passages, she turned and looked back. The old cougar was no more than a shadow on the rock, insignificant against the enormous landscape. The vultures who throughout the day had lingered, circling in the sky, would descend and have their feast of the

Transient's remains, raising their shabby black wings to the sky, beaks a mess with gore.

The stone passageways were lit by starlight, furrows of shadow and bright rock. She noticed the pronounced silence loud in the air. Her own heartbeat was a dark pulse that called into the night before her. When she heard the rise of crickets ahead and felt the moisture in the air her body surged toward that familiar feeling with actual relief.

She waded into the sea of grass and did not look back as she made her way across, the crickets falling silent as she passed, and resuming once she had gone.

THE COUGAR RETURNED THE way she had come days before. Though this was foreign territory, she had no trouble finding her way back. She no longer needed a path to guide her. She stalked through the trees, fascinated. It seemed impossible that anything should be new, that even after a lifetime in the forest there were still things that remained hidden from her; yet it was true, the forest remained unknown, even now. The leaves burned bright red, searing yellow, a river of light flowing through the air. Disturbed by the breeze, leaves lifted off their branches to scatter over the forest floor, a sensational distraction.

The days were cool even in sunlight. The cold air seemed new to her, as if it had not just been a few seasons ago but a lifetime ago when last she had felt it. If not for her body, she would never know the cold. If not for the cold, she would never know her body. In this, all things.

When she came again to the town of men, she followed

the fall of the land down, circumventing the entire area. If she saw even one man, she feared she might succumb to her own curiosity. She could not trust herself when it came to men; her senses, her hunting skills, her long life of experience meant nothing. Their behaviour was still confusing to her. She knew she must avoid them altogether.

The Cougar slept hidden beneath the branches of an evergreen. When she awoke she watched the slow passage of the shadows of clouds as they drifted over the mountains, spreading onto the surrounding forest. She decided she would wait until the sun had warmed the air a bit more, and closed her eyes to sleep.

She sat on the riverbank, caught by the sight of the water rushing past. The notion of endlessness struck her, the possibility of endlessness. She could almost think of it, but it slipped away, just out of reach. The Cougar stepped down into the river, walking until the water rose up to her chest. When the bottom dropped beyond her feet, she plunged forward, head and tail above the surface. The sound of her own breathing, deep but even, rushed loudly past her ears, the sound of the passage of the river diminished against it, a distant whisper.

By sunset, she had returned to the base of the mountain where she and her three sons had kept their lair. As she climbed, the trees thinned, their roots clutching the earth that had gathered in the folds of the mountainside. Shards of rock discarded from the mountain lay in her path so her route was meandering, indirect. She found the lair unoccupied, the bones of their prey scattered among the leaves, thrust to the side. The scent of her cubs had grown stale. She could not know for how long the lair had lain abandoned. She did not know how many days she had been gone.

A wind blew across the entrance of the lair, rattling the leaves within. The Cougar turned and sat, resting one paw on top of the other, and looked down upon the forest. The red trees pulsed like the beating of a heart before her eyes.

The sun drew behind the clouds. The low howl of the wind sounded as if it were emanating from within the lair beside her.

A dimness crept in at the edges of her vision.

It began to snow.

X

THE HUNTER

JOSEPH PULLED A BLACKENED rag from his back pocket and wiped his hands.

"Alright, try it now." He stood back from the automobile.

Lewis turned the ignition. The engine made a grating start, trying to turn over. Joseph waited, holding his breath. The engine coughed and rumbled to life, running loud and steady. He took a deep breath and exhaled. Lewis turned off the ignition. Joseph stared at the gleaming metal body of the automobile, his thoughts already turning away from it, toward the next task.

They left the garage and walked out onto the street. Joseph lit a cigarette, scratched his jaw, leaving a dark smear along his chin. He stretched, exhaling smoke into the bright air. The men stood in their blue coveralls, soiled at the knees, sleeves rolled up past their elbows, their hands and forearms stained with grease. They almost had to yell to one another to be heard.

When Joseph was sixteen, a garage opened in town and he had been there nearly every day since. He liked working with the other men. Though they varied in age there was a kind of brotherhood between them. He liked the work as well and he attended to it with a focus he had never given to any other work. He believed in the relationship between the moving parts in an automobile, something solid that could be relied upon. The world was becoming full of machines, and there was a need for men who could keep them in good working order. He believed this would afford him a key position in the world to come.

The sidewalk was busy with pedestrian traffic. The street was a dry tract in the late summer heat. An automobile rumbled past, sending out a slow wave of dust. Passing on the other side of the street was a man driving a horse-drawn cart, hauling a load of casks. The two, autos and carts on the same road, seemed woefully mismatched to Joseph. Soon the automobiles would outnumber the carts. He believed this would happen in his lifetime, a sudden and permanent shift. He felt that now was a particularly exciting time to be alive and he often thought how lucky he was to have been born in this time. What a disaster to have been born fifty years ago or more.

"Hey, Joe!"

Joseph turned to see an old friend of his father's, a man who had known him since he was a child. He had begun visiting the garage once he realized that it, like the smithy, was an unofficial meeting place and centre of information in the community. But the garage was not like the smithy in that the mechanics did not set their own schedules. There were double the amount of cars in town than there had been a year ago and Joseph imagined this would double again by the end of the year. The mechanics could not spare the time to chat. Time was money and they dare not waste a second.

"Hi, Mr. Clement. How you been?"

"I'm alright. Got a story for you."

"Oh yeah?" Joseph sucked on his cigarette, catching Lewis's eye.

"Volker Rux. Lives up on the Ninth Line."

"Out past Shouter's Field?"

"That's him. He come by the post office just now, said this morning on his way into town he saw a panther right on his property, where Nine meets the Third Concession. Just sitting in the trees, staring at him." The old man paused, searching Joseph's face, as if he were waiting to see whether Joseph would guess what he was about to say. "Said she was the Old Woman."

Joseph stood still, betrayed nothing, though the words lit a flame in his chest that seared outward, toward his hands, his neck, up onto his cheeks to his absolute chagrin.

"You don't say," said Joseph.

"Said she just sat there, staring at him. He ran for his gun, but she was gone by the time he got back." The old man laughed. "Walked into town with his rifle over his shoulder. Like a nut!"

Joseph forced a smile.

"Come on, we got to get back," Lewis said, trying to extricate them from what he believed to be a tedious conversation.

"How would he know it was the Old Woman," Joseph asked. "Has he ever seen her . . . to know it was her?"

"Well, that's what I wanted to know." The old man gave him a look over the rims of his eyeglasses. "Said she had that mangled-up side of her face. Saw it clear as day."

Joseph shot a stream of smoke into the air, his heart beating hard in his chest.

"Thank you, that's very interesting, Mr. Clement. We'll be sure to let people know Volker Rux seen a panther," Lewis said, trying to pull Joseph away.

He had not heard her name spoken aloud in many years. He remembered that winter day when he laid eyes on her, years ago, the blue light, her neat body in the unforgiving wilderness, the gun in his frozen hands as he knelt in the snow, trapped in her gaze.

"Just thought you'd want to know." Clement nodded his farewell, off to spread the news elsewhere.

Joseph and Lewis flicked their cigarette butts into the street and turned back to the garage.

"Just thought you'd want to know . . ." Lewis said.

Joseph laughed, shook his head, avoiding his friend's eyes.

———

THROUGHOUT THE DAY, JOSEPH was dragged through a course of uninvited memories. All his visions of her returned, taking him down furrows of contemplation he thought he had rid himself of. He remembered now the hours drowned in thinking about her, the intensity of these thoughts, and was repulsed that he should once again become possessed by such madness.

The end of the day found him seeking relief from the tumult in his mind. He convinced Lewis to go with him to The Black Hen. As soon as they walked in, the humidity, the sour scent, the smoke hit him, stinging his eyes, sinking a hand into his brain, and he felt at ease. The bar was packed. Not an unusual circumstance since the place was small. The two men made their way over to the bartender and each ordered a pint. It was not until after the second pint that Joseph was able to forget.

Joseph and Lewis had to shout to each other to be heard. They chatted with the men they knew, and some they did not know, who when seen sober on the street did not evoke any particular feeling at all, but when seen here, through the dim haze of intoxication, were their brothers, drinking side by side. The sharing of secrets with a stranger was not unheard of, as if the very nature of someone unknown compelled a man to reveal that which was most intrinsic to his being.

A young man Joseph knew was sitting down at the other end of the bar and for no reason at all Joseph did not like the look of him and he sneered into his pint glass. There were enough men that he did not have to speak with him directly. But soon the other men began to wander off, and they were coming closer and closer together. It annoyed him every time he glanced over and saw him.

Finally, Lewis had the sense to leave.

"One more, one more," Joseph urged.

"Joseph, goddamn! It's a Tuesday," and he departed, leaving Joseph staring after him into the crowd.

Joseph stayed on, knowing he should leave. He could keep his thoughts at bay here, in the warmth and light, amidst the company of other men, but he knew that protection would leave him as soon as he stepped outside. So he stayed, ordered another drink, until he was left talking with that man whom he seemed to dislike more and more the longer he spoke with him.

He did not know how it happened, but suddenly they disagreed. Standing too close, the proximity of the other man's body aggravated Joseph enough that he thought of pushing him away, grabbing him and slamming his face into the bar, all in an instant.

But when he looked into the other man's eyes, he saw there a fleeting likeness, a recognizable hesitation that may only have been the intoxication they shared, and then he remembered he knew this man well, had known him as a child and gone to school with him. His anger from a moment ago was forgotten and he began to apologize, though no incident had occurred. Apologizing seemed to confuse the other man, made less intelligible by the amount Joseph had had to drink, stumbling over words.

Eventually even this man left. The smoke seemed to lift and still Joseph stayed. He sat holding his drink, eyes falling closed. Unnoticed, the barman stood nearby, drying a glass, watching Joseph.

"Joe!"

The sound barely penetrated his thoughts.

"Hey, Joe!"

He looked around, confused. He noticed then the bar was nearly empty, down to a few men refusing to abandon their shadowy posts. The quiet rang loud. As if the scene from earlier had just now been interrupted, and he found himself suddenly here.

"Hey, Joe! Go home, will ya?"

"One more —"

"Get outta here!"

Out on the sidewalk, as soon as he stepped into darkness his thoughts ambushed him. He let himself think her name and she was there, taller than the houses along the street, an enormous panther, stalking the shadows. The Old Woman pushed out all other thoughts so that he could think of nothing else. He saw now that she had never left him. She had been stalking the dark hallways of his mind. Just as now she was slinking around in the shadows of the forest, awaiting him.

He pushed these thoughts away, but the only other subject that came to mind was the continued divergence in thought and feeling between himself and his father that had crept into their lives and held them hostage. As he saw himself coming into the world, he saw his father retreating from it. He found himself annoyed by this submission to fatigue, and his anger showed in his words so that conversation between the two was restricted to bills and groceries.

Any other talk devolved into an argument over perspective.

"You shouldn't be smoking all the time," August told him.

"Oh yeah?"

"It can't be good for you."

"Says who?" Joseph knew it was not good.

In response, his father grunted.

Many such exchanges.

His father's face was a storm of wrinkles. His silver hair stood awry on his head. When it was too cold, he did not leave the apartment as the cold bothered his knee. His work had slowed. His body had slowed. Even the thoughtful pauses he took before speaking now seemed endless, as if the man had become lost in thought; Joseph could not help but grind his teeth at the ever-increasing span of time before responses.

At nineteen, Joseph had grown to his full height, a head taller than his father. He had inherited his father's strength in his arms and shoulders, but he was lean and long instead of broad and bulky. He had his hands from his father. But his face was all his mother's. At this time, he so resembled his mother it chilled August to see his son in certain light, his face in profile, while he was reading or concentrating on some work and did not know he was being observed. His blue eyes, as bright as hers, the same shade of sky, seemed to laugh, which he had liked in her but somehow found grating in the young man. Still haunted by her, almost twenty years later.

Joseph turned into the gloom of the alley behind his building, groping along the brick wall. With seeking hands, he found the back door, opened it, closed it behind him, and was swallowed into darkness. His sense of balance fled. He lost his footing and swore and had to brace himself against the walls of the narrow staircase as he ascended, one quiet step at a time. The climb seemed to take longer than usual. Without the guidance of the walls, he might never have found the door to his apartment. He opened the door and looked inside to see what was there, but his father had gone to sleep. Light from the street lamp outside cast murky shadows over the apartment. The hallway leading to his bedroom stood in total darkness. As he crossed the living room, his head felt like it was floating above his body. Not a good sign for tomorrow.

He collapsed onto his bed, feeling the immediate comfort to a work-sore, liquor-weary body. This sensation accompanied his descent into sleep, where he stayed, unmoving, a deathly sleep, grey and dreamless, until the ring of his alarm clock thrust him into the unforgiving morning light, wearing the same clothes from the day before, mouth dry, head pounding, confused to be awoken in such a painful state until he remembered the night before and slumped back into the bed with an inward groan.

WHEN THE GARAGE WAS established, it had been located at the end of Main Street, but since that time a line of buildings had risen up and now the garage was right in the centre of town. Construction was at work behind them on another street. They were calling it Front Street. The hammering of nails, the sawing of wood, the sounds of auto traffic reached into the garage over the struggling of motors, the racket of tools, and the voices of the other mechanics in conversation with their customers. The combined noise pounded on the outside of Joseph's skull while his brain raged in private turmoil within.

Thinking was too much activity. Work required less thought, distracting him from his suffering. Concentrating on his hands, the pain could be pushed into the background. But any sudden movement, any direct stimulation, caused the pain to bloom inside his head. His mouth was hot. He drank water, trying not to be noticed. He could work quietly, but his expression betrayed him soon enough.

Lewis was laughing. Their eyes met.

"How are you feeling?"

Joseph did not have to speak.

"That's what you get," Lewis said, shaking his head.

He withstood the intermittent waves of nausea that threatened to overwhelm him by concentrating on the task at hand, taking one deep breath after another. By midday, his nausea was mild but his headache was worse. It was a great effort not to curl up on the floor and fall asleep. On his lunch break, he walked down the street to the store to get some aspirin.

The bells above the door to the general store clattered softly as Joseph entered. The scent of polished wood, lemon, and medicines hung on the air. In the back of his mind, he felt vaguely self-conscious at entering the store in his work clothes, greasy and smelling of the garage, but the pain throbbing in his head allowed him to overcome his anxiety.

A man stood perusing the shelves, perhaps waiting

to speak to the clerk in private. A woman paid for her purchases at the counter. Joseph stopped at a polite distance behind her, waiting to buy some aspirin from the clerk. The bells above the door announced the entrance of another patron. In the glass behind the clerk, Joseph recognized the short, greying woman in her sun hat.

"Oh, Mrs. Drinkwater," she said to the woman at the counter as she approached. "How are you?"

"I'm well, Mrs. Merryweather, thank you. How are you?"

"Very well, thank you. Joseph Brandt, is that you?"

"Yes, hello, Mrs. Merryweather." Joseph nodded, head pounding with every word.

"My, you are tall! Or maybe I've been shrinking! How is your father getting on?" she asked. "I haven't seen him in ages."

"He's alright. His knee bothers him some in the cold and he doesn't like going up and down all those stairs."

"Well, I hope you are taking good care of him."

Joseph's headache ballooned inside his head. "Yes, ma'am."

Mrs. Merryweather turned back to Mrs. Drinkwater, laying a gloved hand on her wrist. "I've just seen Mrs. Bagley. She told me that Mrs. Kenshaw told her when she was walking into town this morning, right before she took the turn onto Main Street from the First Concession, she saw a panther in the trees."

"*No,*" breathed the other woman.

"*Yes,*" a hissing sound. "By the bus depot. Just sitting there, staring at her!"

Joseph needed only to endure this conversation in order to get his aspirin. He stayed perfectly still, hoping that if he did not move they might forget he was there.

"Someone ought to go out there and shoot that thing," said Mrs. Drinkwater.

Joseph said nothing, silently urging Mrs. Drinkwater to collect her purchases and leave. He glared at the clerk, trying to catch his attention, but the man just stood there smiling, seeming delighted by the conversation.

"Well, I'm trying to spread the word," said Mrs. Merryweather. "I would just die if another child was snatched."

Mrs. Drinkwater stood aghast. "Another?"

"Oh yes, that was before you were here . . . about four, maybe five years ago—"

Elmira Olsen. The name lit up in his mind, causing a sudden pain behind his eyes.

"— she survived, thank goodness. You know, the Olsen girl?"

Mrs. Drinkwater gasped, then spoke in a lowered voice. "I never *realized*—"

"*Such* a shame," the older woman murmured, shaking her head.

Joseph was no longer listening. Darkness rose up around him and he alone remained in light. A subtle fire ran through his veins, and his headache receded. A sudden pointlessness emerged, surrounding the town, his own life. One thing loomed large before him. He would go now into the forest to hunt the Old Woman. The path lay clear before him.

He thought, *This is madness.* And also, *This is fine.*

HE AWOKE AT DAWN, dressed quietly. His actions felt light, unreal. He was alert and yet he felt as if he had not slept, charged with a kind of nervous energy that drained him as it fed him. He took his bag, packed the night before, from the chair in the corner. He slung his rifle over his shoulder. He took his hatchet off the wall and hung it in its sheath on his belt. Then he donned a hat and closed the door to his room behind him.

In the living room, he was surprised by his father asleep in his armchair by the window. A sudden panic overwhelmed him. He had not expected to see him — had not wanted to see him — before he left. As if he could only leave as long as his father did not see him go. The old man's head leaned forward, the sound of his breathing like a hollow whistling.

By this light his scalp was visible through his thinned hair, spotted and pale. The shape of his skull so revealed seemed inappropriate. The skin of his face sagged like a mask beginning to slip. His expression was not at rest, his brow furrowed, as if his worries hounded him even in his sleep. It pained Joseph that his father should look so tired, and he was annoyed that he would fall asleep in his clothes, in an armchair instead of his bed, and be sore for it all the next day.

Joseph stood in the early morning light watching his father sleep, his heart beating so hard he felt his pulse in his mouth. There was no traffic in the street. The only sound in the room was that of his father's steady breathing.

Joseph took a step backward. Then he turned to leave, closing the door behind him. He descended the stairs on their sides where they would not creak.

Outside, he took an apple from his jacket and started in. It was a clear, bright day, the warmth in the air already beginning to rise. His footsteps rang loudly against the wooden sidewalk. On the other side of the street, a man wearing an apron swept the area in front of his store. Otherwise, the street was deserted. Joseph felt rather small next to the high, plain buildings. He was so rarely out when the street was deserted like this. As he passed an alley, he caught the stale scent of urine and saw a man sleeping or passed out in the refuse.

He came to the end of the sidewalk and the sound of his footsteps disappeared. The buildings ended and a bleak landscape of mud rolled out before him. The trees had been removed, stones pulled from the earth, revealing the raw earth beneath, an uneasy sight, something meant to remain hidden, like the sight of a beating heart.

He would follow the Old Woman into the forest, after the line she had indicated, through the back of Volker Rux's land, and when the road ended he would step into the trees, leaving the town and every man in it.

The sun cast Joseph's shadow well before him, reaching toward the forest ahead. He finished his apple and threw the core overhand into the sea of mud. He followed the road into the trees, his shadow merging with the shade of the forest, and then was gone.

XI

THE OLD WOMAN

--->->

T HE FARTHER FROM TOWN he went, the more pronounced the silence around him became, occupying his thoughts so he was silenced against it, unable to think of anything else. In town there were enough men at their work to counter the living presence of silence, as if the clamour they made was meant for its own sake, to fool themselves into forgetting that unending presence, believing the world was that which they had made instead of that which made them. Among the trees, there was nothing to protect Joseph from perceiving the enormity of this silence. The quiet so disturbed him that he made noise himself by singing, to put a dent in its uncompromising presence.

At midday, in the shade of a cluster of trees, he stopped

to rest and sat chewing some dried venison, looking down on a hill of sparse pine. The sun cast dark shadows behind the thin, feathery saplings. As he sat eating, he thought about turning back. Only half a day had gone by, he could easily go back, explain away his absence. Here in the quiet wilderness, his thoughts screamed out to him so loud they shocked him, and he considered turning back just to silence them. Either he was fixated on the dead silence outside or the unruly racket within. It seemed he could not turn away from himself. The searing flame that had possessed him and sent him out into the wilderness had fled. Suddenly he felt like a child alone in the woods, a boy make-believing.

If he went back now, he might convince himself nothing had been lost. He could resume his life, forget the Old Woman for good, so long as he never submitted to thinking of her again. But he knew that notion was doomed. He need not even think her name, he need only to think of the sleek line of her body, the intensity of her stare, and the desire he felt for her was renewed. He could not turn back. By his own decree he was not allowed.

Joseph realized he had been sitting and staring into space, letting the day get away from him. He heard the call of a blue jay. He had become still as he sat musing, his breathing quiet, his thoughts less glaring. He looked around. The blue jay called again. He could not find where it sat, hidden by the branches. Then, despite the breeze, the rustle of leaves overhead, he heard the mysterious movement of a rock.

He stood, searching into the trees. Nothing more

followed. No other sound aside from his own breathing. He almost believed he had imagined it. But he knew he had heard something, he could hear it again in his memory, the sound of stone shifting.

The slight noise of his preparations to continue silenced the blue jay. The forest returned to its former stillness. Now, as he walked along, he noticed how loud his presence must be, and this might be the reason for the amplified silence around him. He made an effort to step lightly but found he was not adept at walking over the sensitive forest floor. If he made this much noise as he travelled, the Old Woman would surely hear him and he would never see her. This thought stayed with him as he made his way down through sparse trees, then into dense bush. There he clawed his way through tangles of branches until he came upon a field of rock, broken into thick ridges like the plates of armour on the back of a great lizard, moss growing between the epic cracks.

At sunset, he set down for the night in a place with a stone ridge at his back, the forest before him. He scrounged through the brush for dead branches, gathering his wood for the night. Once he had lit a fire, Joseph felt an immediate sense of relief. Though the flames cast a circle of brightness around him, they seemed to plunge the world beyond into further darkness.

He thought again of the shifting rock and could not imagine what had made the sound. He stood and stepped into the trees, the firelight at his back, and stared wide-eyed into the darkness and could see nothing. Without the visual field to gauge what might be lurking about in the night, the immensity of the forest stretched out, far beyond his comprehension, and Joseph became lost.

He tended his fire well into the night, staring into the flames. Though tired, he was unable to convince himself to lie down and close his eyes. The possibility of what existed beyond the fire's reach unnerved him. Firelight lit up the trees facing him, their branches reaching toward one another overhead. The fire's heat warmed Joseph's face and his eyes glistened with the play of shifting flame. As he watched, the fire grew and transformed the pile of gathered wood into a mass of glowing embers.

The fire's dying light roused him from his trance, and he threw more wood onto the dwindling flames. He could not help himself from casting glances into the trees. Even if he had not slept, he had not been totally awake.

Joseph returned to his fire. After staring again into the flames, he began to drowse. This time when the fire dwindled, he did not stir to raise it.

WHEN HE AWOKE, THE air was dark. A cool dampness from the long stay of night surrounded him. He went back to sleep. The brighter light awoke him again. By this light he dug around in the fire pit. A thin tendril of smoke lifted into the air. He smelled the ghostly curl of smoke and a dark wave washed over him.

Not only would the Old Woman know his presence by the noise he made but also by the scent of smoke on the air, the mark of his fire on the earth. She would know him wherever he was. He sat chewing a strip of venison, considering the way through this dilemma, but he could not see the way clearly, as if looking into a murky depth, searching for the bottom that was not there.

When he was packing up to leave he set his hat on a ledge of stone behind him, its dark colour blending well into the forest. Then he hoisted his pack onto his back. A moment later, he set off, the hat forgotten on the stone ledge, as the sounds of Joseph's steps through the leaves diminished and disappeared.

A GROUSE ERUPTED FROM the branches of a tree, wings beating the air. Joseph pulled the trigger and the shot rode through the quiet forest. The grouse fell in a clumsy spiral, its black-edged tail slicing through the air.

He noticed the shift in the surrounding trees, the stillness in response to the unnatural blast of the rifle. Even that short disruption made a large impact, known throughout the forest. Joseph felt the focus of some gaze upon him. He tried to ignore it. He was getting used to the feeling that he was under surveillance. He was not hidden, his presence in the forest was obvious.

He walked over to collect the grouse. Kneeling, he looked into the forest. Trees upon dark trees until his eyes were denied by the multitude of growth, the impenetrable density before him. He chewed his lip, thinking on this unimaginable depth.

Later, he prepared the bird as his father had shown him, plucking the feathers, gutting the small, purplish torso. Finally, he skewered the body and set it to roast over the fire. As the bird cooked, Joseph sat trying to unlock the secret to how he would hunt the Old Woman if she could hear him, smell him, even see him, wherever he went. But he could not think around it. He ate, brooding on this, then fell asleep under a clear, star-filled sky, the firelight accompanying him well into the night.

AN ENTIRE DAY THROUGH dense bush. He fell into it and hoped it would let up, but it just kept going. Hacking into branches with his hatchet was useless. He tired out before he got very far. He tried just pushing through, but there was no space for his body. The forest was too thick. Though he was outside, he felt as if there were no room to breathe. The trees crowded one another, their branches pressing in on him. And the mosquitoes swarmed him. His hands were stung, the skin tight around his knuckles. A mad itch harassed his face and neck. He resorted to crouching, half-crawling, crablike, in order to make his way over the cluttered earth.

He had already left behind some of the things he had brought in his pack. There remained the flint, his knife, a jacket he used also for a blanket, and his tin of salve for burns and cuts, and what ammunition remained to him. He carried his rifle on his shoulder; his hatchet was tied against his thigh. His food was almost gone, despite his best efforts at conservation. All he had was a dwindling slice of dried venison; after that, he would have to rely on whatever he shot, and he would run out of ammo soon enough. He would have to devote some time to hunting.

He had not seen a sign of anything in this bush, panther or otherwise. It seemed to Joseph he was exhausting a large amount of energy just walking through the land. What he was doing now, this clawing through the undergrowth, would cost him dearly. He was hungry already. He would be too tired to sit and hunt when he came out of this. He would just want to sleep. He wanted to sleep now.

His boots were coming apart. At first, he thought it was everyday wear that he had not noticed before, but no, it was this serious terrain, slowly breaking them down. This vexed him in a vague, inarticulate way.

The light of the sky put a panic into his chest.

The bush he was crawling through remained unchanged, with no sight of an end. He paused and wiped his forehead. In all directions the same. Indecision.

He put aside his anxiety with a concentrated effort, trying not to think. But the light was growing dark faster than he was getting anywhere, and he became enraged. An irreconcilable anger worked its way through him, occupying his body. Foolishness, stupidity that he had done this to himself. He had put himself here.

He stopped, breathing hard, contemplating that he might be mad as he lay in a slump, the air clouded with mosquitoes.

He pulled out his hatchet and began hacking away at branches. The earth below him was thick with undergrowth. He tore it up with his hands and threw it to one side, exposing the damp earth beneath. Soon he had cleared a small space for himself. He worked as the light fell, cutting down a few larger branches to make a haphazard shelter. Then he gathered the wreckage of that which he had cleared and heaped it under the roof, stamping it all down into the earth to lie on. By then it was almost dark.

He cast a fire into the pit he had made in the centre of his clearing. Joseph and his fire alone. Unbidden thoughts emerged from the darkness. Without fire, man was just another animal. It protected him from cold, kept nocturnal beasts at bay, and warded off other men. It was like a companion, accompanying him through the dark, and like man could not exist without destroying. They had this in common: a vast potential as protector and destroyer.

At this thought Joseph laughed into the night. He sat staring into the flames. In town, subdued by drink, distracted by the rabble of other men, these thoughts would never come to him. But here he realized the wisps of thoughts that were always trying to reveal themselves, dismissed because they did not show themselves the way other thoughts do. One must almost go seeking them.

When he awoke to the grey, early morning, his fire pit was a cold circle of ash.

The fear of sleeping without the protection of the fire surged through him, but he saw the earth around him was unchanged. Whatever may have passed through in the night had left him undisturbed.

THAT DAY, AS HE walked through the forest, Joseph remembered that he had been dreaming the night before, but as he tried to remember what his dreams were about, the dimensions of his dreams bled into one another and he could not summon the details of any specific one. It was like pulling up handfuls of water. All that he remembered was that he had been searching. He wandered through the forest with his mind stuck on these dreams, as if they were about to show themselves to him, but were constantly turning away.

Everywhere he looked, he seemed to be reminded of his dreams, though he did not know why. He walked without knowing where he meant to go. No matter how strangely familiar his steps might be, nothing was given to him, no insight, no answers came to mind. He went on, glancing into the trees as if he were being hunted.

Now he knew he should turn back. He had been denying himself this thought. But wandering around in this confused, desperate state, he could not ignore it any longer. His body was not comfortable. He was having headaches. He was feeling light, insubstantial. And he found himself obsessing more and more about the other animals in the forest. His thoughts were filled with bears and wolves, and other things that he could not name that remained outside the realm of form, following him in shadow, wherever he went. He knew the longer he stayed out here, the harder it would be to go back.

He would never explain away his absence. Not after being gone for so long. There would be talk and it would only be a matter of time before his obsession with the Old Woman was dredged up. He could hear it now, rumours of an unnatural love, whispers haunting him all the way to his death for some miscalculation as a youth. A great anxiety took hold within him at the thought that he would not be able to place himself back where he had been when he left.

The sun was setting, shade growing into the forest from the ground up. Joseph dropped his pack in a small clearing created by a rough ring of enormous trees. He sat on a rock and untied his boots. A rank stench rose up from his feet. By now his shirt and underclothes stank so unforgivably that if the Old Woman were within a mile of him, she would know where he was by his smell.

He opened his pack to retrieve the flint, preoccupied with how he could hunt the Old Woman without being hunted. As his mind toiled with the problem, his hands worked by themselves to create the fire that would accompany him through the night. Around him, the forest grew quiet.

He looked up when he noticed the silence. At first, he saw the same thick evergreens, the ring of trees, the sky darkening above. Then he saw the sharp yellow eye of an owl in its white-feathered face, glimpsed through the branches of a tree. Joseph grew still, hands paused above his work, watching the owl. The owl stared, unblinking.

With the sound of rustling leaves, the owl vanished and emerged from the branches, plunging toward the ground, the white span of its wings a flash of warning, unmistakable in the dark forest. Joseph only saw the squirrel, brown as the ground of fallen leaves, once the owl snatched it up. The owl turned upward, disturbing a ring of leaves with a gust from its wings, the squirrel grasped in its talons, and disappeared back into the branches.

Joseph sat staring at the empty clearing. The whole

event had taken less than ten seconds. He read on the ground where hunter and prey had left their mark. The upturned leaves, darker brown on the bottom, paler on their tops, were a sign of what had occurred between the owl and the squirrel, and Joseph saw now the flexible nature of the face of the earth could be read for a narrative in space and time. Knowing this, one could know something of the life of the forest, understand what had occurred, what might occur again.

When he came out of this musing, it was nearly dark. He looked down and found himself hesitant to make his fire, to leave such an obvious sign of his presence in the forest. Still, he could not see how he would hunt the Old Woman smelling the way he did, never mind the mark of his fires.

Later he lay staring at the flames, thinking of signs, trying to unravel this knot with his mind, barely knowing what it was, becoming more mystified the deeper into thought he went.

HIS FACE HAD BECOME gaunt beneath his beard, eyes haunted by dark circles. He walked along through spruce, the ground rolling underfoot but otherwise unimpeded except by fallen trees, grown over with a colony of new ones.

He leaned against a tree, breathing hard.

A breeze shifted the treetops. The sun cut through the clouds with a blazing orange light. He believed it would rain.

He thought of his father for the first time since the day he left. He thought of him now, the potential scenarios that would have come to pass in his absence: was he sick with worry, the centre of ridicule, had he gone out to look for him, or rather, more likely, was he going about his days as usual with little change except that occasionally he remembered that his son had left him and he wondered why? Joseph tried to push these thoughts aside, but they glared back at him and he could not turn away. It was the sight before him, the trees glowing golden in the orange light, swept in waves by the breeze. The sound of the movement of the trees. The earthy smell rising up from the forest floor. The beauty struck him so that the only thing he could think was that he wanted to show it to someone. The only person he thought of was his father, and a curtain of sadness descended upon him.

He pressed his back against a tree and ground his palms into his eyes and wept. The sunset cut through the black trees. He wanted to shut it out, but he saw it all the more sharply in his mind. His behaviour seemed cruel to him now, the way he treated an old man who had taken care of him all his life. He was impatient and dismissive because he was frightened by his father, the sight of his age confirming the ever-closing presence of Death. That he had left him now seemed a grave error, and he worried that he would never see him again.

The wind rose around him and he grew cold. The night would bring a deeper cold. But he could not move from the tree. The sun went down, the wind died, and he stayed, sitting against the tree, staring into the unfathom-able forest, as the darkness settled around him.

HE SAT BEFORE THE flames, staring in. He saw the Old Woman walking through short trees in a field of long grass, slipping into the shadows, disappearing into the forest, and then the vision was gone. He could not follow her further.

The vision was so vivid, it was as if he were watching it with his own eyes. He recalled the way she looked, slender, battle-scarred, as if he had seen her before him, and it seemed extraordinary that his mind could have conjured this image from nowhere.

He sat looking into the flames as before, trying to recall the vision, but it would not return. He found this strange.

Joseph dreamed he was being pursued. He did not know by what. But no matter where he ran through the trees, he could not escape. The torment was so great he returned to waking life with a start.

He sat up, gasping like he had been underwater. He felt a sheen of sweat on his neck, his shoulders, and he shivered. Total darkness surrounded him. The faint sounds of movement, unidentifiable, came from all around him. After a few breaths, his eyes adjusted. The half-moon lit the nighttime forest with an inverted light and he could see deep into the darkness.

He thought then of the Old Woman slinking through the bright darkness, moonlight turning her fur silver, illuminating the ghostly whiteness of her face, her eyes reflecting a weird green light.

He tried to imagine what she thought of as she made her way through the night. Did she know he was seeking her? Did she know that he dreamed of her? Did she think of him as she stalked the shadowed forest?

WHEN HE AWOKE AGAIN, the sky was a white sheet above him, the air dark. It smelled like it would rain. He looked beside him and saw that the fire pit was a mound of white ash beneath chunks of charcoal, cracked and smoking. He stared at the ash, its fine texture. He could feel it already.

His hand sunk into the ash so it seemed like its main substance was air. He drew up a handful of it, brought it to his nose, and smelled the bare scent of it. The sight of the ash in his hand meant something to him but he could not call the memory forth. He took the handful of ash and smeared it over his arm like a balm. The white streak left on his skin seemed significant; this is what he was supposed to do.

He began pulling up handfuls of the ash, smearing them onto his shoulders, arms, neck. He covered his torso until he was completely dusted in white ash. Then, smelling of the earth, he stood, feeling like his appearance was now more appropriate.

He took his shirt from where it lay on the ground and held it up. A button shirt of white and orange plaid, thin and faded, pockets on the breast, stained at the neck and armpits. He had bought it from the general store. He had gotten in a fight in it, and his father had shown him how to sew up the shoulder. He had gone drinking in it and

woken up after passing out in the alley behind his building, vomit all over himself, and after that it was no longer
a good shirt.

The smell of it wandered up to his face and he grimaced. Wearing it, he announced himself everywhere he
went. He draped the shirt on a low-hanging branch. It
hung like a flat shadow, a shed skin, casting its translucent
shadow onto the ground. Then he went on into the trees.

WALKING THROUGH THE SUNLIT trees, he pulled off his
pack, looked inside. The pack was empty except for his
thin jacket, the tin containing the last of his skin salve.
He reached inside for the tin, dropped the pack on the
forest floor, opened the tin of salve, saw it too was empty
and dropped it and went on. In a moment he did not even
remember the pack, as if he had always gone through the
forest exactly as he was now: rifle slung over his shoulder,
the hatchet in its leather sheath, fastened to his belt.

He sat watching the darkness gather on the horizon. The
last of the light was seeping from the sky in a wash of red
and violet. He felt the first pangs of apprehension needling
his heart, grasping his throat. He was alone, unprotected by
flame. He was able to see for a long time after the sun went
down, the forest slowly sinking into night.

Even into darkness, he could still see. He thought
that if this was the depth of it he could stand it and
would be fine throughout the night. But the darkness
deepened beyond the point he thought possible, swal-
lowing him whole.

Finally, he could see nothing. He shivered and his hands were freezing. He tried rubbing them together, but they remained numb and stiff. The mosquitoes were impossible to avoid. The sound of their buzzing filled his ears with its constant presence.

Night was an endless plain. With no light by which to perceive the forest around him, his own body was lost. Oneself seemed endless, impossible to contain. There was no retreat from this, no respite.

He worried what might be with him in the darkness. Once he had this thought, he could not send it away and it grew large in his mind. He marvelled that his thoughts were beyond his control, that they could control him, send fear into his heart and distract him with unnecessary perceptions. His thoughts being his, his own thoughts were what he feared. There was nothing in the forest but himself.

He was the only thing lurking in the darkness. He laughed into the night like the strange call of some nocturnal bird.

Joseph burrowed into the forest floor, pulling branches over himself, heaping leaves, and, though he was not comfortable, fatigue persuaded his body to sleep. If he chose, he could stay up, staring into the darkness, swarmed by mosquitoes. Or he could slip away now, into the fold of sleep, submitting to whatever might happen. Huddled against the earth, Joseph slept.

JOSEPH STOPPED AND SAT against a fallen tree, pulling his feet out of his soiled boots. The stench reached out, forcing his head back as if he had been slapped. His socks had turned to rags. The heel of his foot was touched with blood where a blister had been raging and finally broken.

He held up one of the boots. They had not seen this kind of trekking in town and clearly were not made for it. Joseph blamed poor workmanship that they should fall apart. But then he supposed he might as well blame himself for buying a cheap pair over a more expensive pair. Then again, even the best-made boots would not last forever. All things collapsed, all things disintegrated.

These thoughts left him as he had them, flowing away from him as if down a stream. The boots were meaningless. He saw that now. He turned the boot in the air and looked at it from the other side. It would only impede him from going forward.

Joseph stood the boots side by side. They sat on the fallen tree, abandoned amid the hectic wilderness. He glanced back once as he walked away, enjoying his art in the forest. The idea amused him.

His feet on the cool earth, now leaf, now needle, now mud. Barefoot through the wilderness, he made slow progress. His feet were not accustomed to the rough terrain. He could not travel as fast as he had while wearing the boots, and he continued on at a pace akin to a meandering stream. Since he could not move as quickly, he found himself less tired. He went on, deeper into the forest, at times forgetting what he was seeking, completely absorbed in seeing.

He stood studying a tree that grew perched on the edge of a cliff, in the act of falling yet perfectly still. He supposed it was in motion, in a way, at a rate that he could not perceive. One day, once enough earth had melted away beneath it, the tree would come crashing to the forest floor, the end of a decades-long process.

HE COULD HEAR THE air as it flowed through the trees, the entire forest an invisible river. As he walked through the trees he was given a glimpse of the mountain in the distance. He saw the forest growing up onto its rugged base, the white rock tearing through, showing its primal face, and it struck him then that all the forest, all the world, was growing atop the rocky surface of the earth, and he marvelled then how precarious that was. A great wind could blow it away in a single breath; a fire consume it all, born from a single spark.

He stared up at the rock face, contemplating his ascent. It was not a great height but not an easy climb. The way was steep, interrupted by shallow ledges of rock sparsely populated by thin trees. He could not go around, he must go through.

He took the rifle from his shoulder. He held it by the strap and saw its cold weight, its solid, unchanging form. A tool of disastrous capability, multiplying the ability of any man regardless of his skill or the nature of his heart. It seemed a heavy thing to have carried all this way. He almost wondered why he had brought it, the needless burden. He did not need it for where he was going now.

He hung the rifle by its strap from a branch. The branch bowed under the weight of the gun. He stood observing his mark in the forest. He liked the sight of it there, inexplicable, abandoned. Perhaps one day someone would find it in the wilderness and wonder at its meaning.

He looked up the incline and his path lay clear to him. His eyes darted up the rock and he knew each step he would take as if he were in the act of taking it. His hatchet hung from a leather strap he had fastened around his waist, grazing his thigh. He was oblivious to his nakedness. He had stopped noticing.

He found a hand-hold in the rock and pulled himself up. His feet found their way into the stone. As he climbed, he felt no urgency. He had perfect patience for every grip, every breath. The Old Woman was forgotten, and this careful climbing, the blue sky at his back, hand over hand taking hold of the earth, the thin trees brushing past, his hard breathing, his steady heartbeat, were his only thoughts. In this way he could have climbed forever, thinking nothing of the top.

The breeze slid over his skin, the touch of the air reminding him he was one mindless handhold away from falling to his death. Though the rock face was right before him, in hand, he felt as if he were suspended in the air. He was tempted to look down, to judge his distance from the earth, but he dared not look back. The sight of the earth far below might distract him, paralyze him, and he could not afford the pause.

He pulled himself up onto a ledge in the rock face, one shoulder, then a knee. The climb had tired him and he sat, breathing heavy, looking out on the forest roof. It seemed impossible to him that he had come all that way through an indecipherable landscape. Even now the forest was a great secret to him.

He followed the lay of the land down, on one side a wall of rock, on the other dark pine trees. He went with knees bent until the ground levelled out, and through the trees he began to see the wide, meandering body of a river. The sun shone upon the water's surface so it seemed like a river of flame nestled in the wilderness. He went toward it, called by the gravity of water.

The trees grew thick. He pressed through, the needles of the evergreens scratching at his skin. He seemed not to notice. A part of his brain had silenced. Guided by the sound of rushing water, the smell of wet earth, he emerged from the trees and saw the flat river before him. The sun's glare on the water's surface was so bright he had to squint to look on it. In some places, the trees grew right up to the edge of the river and were falling into it, trunks growing out over the water's surface at precarious angles, or submerged in the river, smooth, white branches reaching out of the water's surface like errant plants growing into the air.

His skin was dusty from the climb and his heart pumped in his chest. He was a set of eyes and a mouth. The passage of the water grew louder as he drew near. The commotion of rushing water was totally different from the murmur of the forest, which, he realized now, was the only sound he had listened to for days. He did not hesitate at entering the cold water, even once it rose above his thighs.

The water was brisk but clear. He felt as if his body were

burning the moment he was immersed, and he marvelled at this almost painful sensation, as if he had never felt his body before. A white cloud leached off him into the water, carried away on the current. When the water had reached his chest, he spread out his arms and fell back into the river, floating on his back, watching the sky above, as the current carried him downriver.

Though he felt the sensation of movement, he could see nothing of the shore on either side of him, and it seemed as if he were suspended in space. Above him, the sky was so large he could not fit it all into his field of vision. A falcon flew high overhead. It circled, having spotted the strange creature floating along the river, then headed off, a dark shadow against the pure blue sky. The spell of his solitude was broken. Joseph turned over and the world was set right again.

He stayed crouched in the shallow water, his hatchet cold against him, watching into the forest. A breeze licked at his wet skin, raising gooseflesh along his arms, and he shivered. He looked back on the far shore. The passage of the river filled his ears. Cicadas hummed within the sunlit trees. A sparrow made its quick call. His own breathing seemed loud to him. His heart beat hard in his chest. The sparrow made its call again. He looked into the trees. Golden motes floated in the sunlight that filtered through the scanty treetops. A dragonfly glinted through a shaft of light, disappeared, returned.

Beneath these murmurings he could sense the stillness that presided here, a sincere silence, that touched the dark centre in his breast and filled him with a hesitancy, like he was trespassing on forbidden ground and must tread lightly. This forest would betray his presence more readily than any other forest.

Joseph stepped into the golden trees, the dry leaves crackling underfoot. The sound of his passage over the forest floor dwindled and was drowned in the great space of the forest. An owl made its call, low and furtive, roused by the presence of a hunter.

JOSEPH WALKED DOWN INTO the valley in a daze. He followed the river, a wide path glittering in the afternoon sun. The trees had grown to ancient heights on both sides of the water. The prevailing silence, the thick moss growing on the trunks, indicated that this forest had stood longer than his lifetime, longer than the lifetime of any man living in the world.

He left the river for the trees. The light faded, the air grew cool, and the mosquitoes found him, attracted to the heat of his body as if summoned by an urgent blast from a trumpet in the quiet forest. He walked through the trees trying to rid himself of the swarm, but it was like trying to rid himself of fog. Despite the days spent in the forest, picking up the scent of pine and sap and earth, he could not rid himself of his body nor his blood, which proclaimed his presence. Soon his skin was raw from scratching. He wiped at the back of his neck, hot to the touch, and when he looked at his fingertips he saw the unmistakable kiss of blood.

He heard the sound of water and stood to listen, forgetting the torment of mosquitoes for a moment. He followed the sound through the trees. The earth beneath his feet grew damp. He found a shallow stream meandering through the dark forest over a bed of smooth stones. The stream was calm, reflecting the black lace of the foliage overhead, his own looming shadow.

He waded into the stream and dropped to his knees, cupping the cool water over his shoulders, his neck, and still his skin burned.

Crouched in the shallow water, Joseph noticed the forest around him, the stillness, and held his breath to listen. He continued drawing the water over his face, his hair, as if he had not noticed the stillness. But almost as soon as he became aware of it, he no longer felt the sensation of being watched. Instead, he felt the absence of some presence now that it had gone.

He rose and waded to the other side of the stream. On the bank, he saw the paw print of a panther stamped into the mud. Joseph knelt and looked at the paw print in the mud. It lay underwater and must have been recent since the current had yet to wash it away. He searched the trees to ensure he was not being watched. An invisible mass of crickets pulsed as one. He turned his attention to the mark. The paw print seemed too small to belong to such a formidable panther. He had no way of knowing it belonged to the Old Woman, but he believed it did.

He placed his hand on the print. It seemed to burn. He clutched a handful of mud, destroying the mark, brought it out of the water, and spread it onto his cheek, down onto his neck. The coolness was immediate. He drew forth another handful and smoothed it down the back of his neck. Another handful he smoothed over his chest. He covered his shoulders and the top of his back, his arms, whatever he could reach. He covered his forehead and then his beard, his hair as well. He covered the sides of his torso, the backs of his legs, and the tops of his feet.

When he was done, all that remained of him were his clear, bright eyes staring out of his mud-streaked face. The mosquitoes seemed to vanish. Though he still heard them they no longer landed on his skin to siphon away his blood, unable to contend with the thick coating of mud.

He left the stream, a painted creature, for the night forest.

HE FOUND A LEDGE of stone hidden by a crowd of trees. He investigated the alcove beneath the stone and found it thick with moss. Elsewhere he stood, skinning branch after branch off an evergreen, using his hatchet to shave them from the trunk, throwing them in a pile. Later he brought the branches to the alcove and began crushing them into the corners, weaving them together until they made a layer of insulation, with an opening for the entrance. In the end, he gathered dried leaves and carpeted the ground with them, the sound of them crackling underfoot loud in his ears.

When he was done, the light had bled from the sky. The hum of crickets grew louder as the darkness deepened. He spent time shaping the interior of the lair, carving out a space for himself. There was only enough room for him, a meagre light seeping in from the entrance. He watched as the light collapsed, listening to the flutter of wings nearby. He did not notice when he fell asleep.

HE SMELLED THE SCENT of excreta on the air, unmistakable, and followed it through the trees. A small mound of dark earth, clawed up from beneath the layer of dried leaves, then damp leaves, musty with a panther's urine. Joseph knelt, breathed in the scent. A sharp smell reached his nose—the mark of the Old Woman.

He took up a handful of the earth, smeared it over his shoulders, his chest, like a sash. The prickle of pins swept down his back, his torso. The earth tilted beneath him and he thought he might collapse. He smelled mud, wet stone, the banks of the stream, and he saw the stream as if it were right there before him. He blinked, sniffed. The scent of the Old Woman's mark upon his chest was strong, but even now it faded. He would go through the forest so adorned, undetected, a ghost.

He stepped into the trees, the branches like curtain after curtain. The breath of the wind snaked through the leaves, an endless sigh.

HE WALKED THROUGH BLACK trees, the earth slick with damp. Despite the dark air, the green of the leaves seemed to vibrate, as if the heavy moisture in the air increased the intensity of the colour. Amid the chaos of the forest his eyes were drawn to one tree among many. Bright claw marks bit into the trunk. The marks were recent, perhaps only hours old. He turned, looking into the trees. The quiet forest stood undisturbed around him. He listened, searching for some sign that she was there, but there was none. He reached out and touched the mark of her claws in the rugged bark. She had stood here, where he stood now. A prickling sensation stole across his skin. He shivered at its touch and then he went on through the trees.

JOSEPH AWOKE TO SUNSET, watching the light sweep slowly across the ceiling of roots above him. There was a growing presence that came along with wakefulness. He had gone to sleep chased by hunger and awoken ensnared in its clutches.

He crawled out of his lair and stood, feeling the stiffness in his shoulders, his back. The earth was not a comfortable place for a man to sleep. Without any purpose in mind, he started to walk, the drone of crickets in the air.

As he walked, his body seemed to come back to life but his mind remained foggy, his thinking disjointed. Hunger needled his stomach, kept him walking. There was a dull ache behind his eyes. The realization that he was looking for something to eat was a vague concern, distant.

A mosquito bit him and he scratched at it absently. His skin was crossed with scratches and scrapes. His hands were sore. His joints ached. And now the presence of hunger had become a fixed point in his life. If he allowed his focus to stray, he was harassed by a single notion: he had done madness to himself.

He felt a growing resentment toward the forest, however ridiculous, that it did not know of him or his suffering at all, as if he really were nothing, grasping about on a stony plane. In his state, close to exhaustion, he did not have the energy to dwell on this thought for long, and as he walked the thought diminished and was left behind.

He came to the river and stood among the tall grass on the riverbank. The dark, open space of the river yawned before him. The bank on the other side stood in shadow. The sound of the rushing water told him how the river lay, even into the distance. He stood watching the river, the smell of mud rising from the ground, a breeze lifting off the water's surface. Then he went on.

HE WALKED THROUGH THE trees, arms and legs stained with earth, painted with mud on his shoulders, his face, hair wild, eyes clear and cutting, the hatchet flashing at his side. The forest was bright with sunshine, loud with the call of cicadas rising, diminishing, rising again.

In the base of the tree before him, a dark hollow lay hidden, concealed by bushes. A less discerning eye would have missed it. He believed he had heard the hollow space while walking by. He paused and looked, taking in the immediate vicinity, the rise of land surrounded by bush. He detected a stale scent on the air.

He sat in the entrance, looking in.

The scent had diminished, soaked into the earth. The bones of a rabbit lay scattered within, dull against the earth. He crawled inside. Her scent was lost now. He smelled only the earth, the trees outside the lair. He sat watching the trees through the thin entrance. He rested his head on the earth and fell asleep.

THE SUN ROSE BEHIND heavy clouds. A dark light filtered down from the white sky. Joseph stood stripping raspberries off the spiny branches of a bush. He picked a handful, then went on through the trees, eating them slowly.

He sat in a field, the long grass pummelled by breeze, the flat white sky looming above. A slow sigh seemed to vacate the forest. The clouds rolled in and the sky grew dark. Then the air around him darkened further. There was a sound like ice shifting. It began to rain.

He sat watching the downpour. The rain beating the grass into the ground, hitting the leaves on the trees, was a tremendous uproar. A great tendril of lightning lit up the sky, followed by the rumble of thunder, like mountains crashing to the ground somewhere far away. The crash of crumbling rock heralded a raging wind that blasted the forest, tearing away trees and stone and the river itself. A barren plain stood in place of the forest, the howling wind racing across the empty waste.

He breathed in, feeling the cool air fill his lungs, and when he exhaled, his breath was like smoke into the wet air. Water plastered his hair to his head, ran down his chest, revealing the pale skin beneath his coating of mud. He stayed watching the rain until the sun began to set. The rain abated but did not cease. The clouds rolled apart. Shafts of light plunged down into the dark forest. The crickets awoke and started to whine. The smell of the sodden earth hung thick upon the air. Now Joseph rose and walked through the wet grass, feeling the mist against his skin. The crickets silenced as he passed, jumping away, his presence like a flood, pushing them aside.

The light fell, but he could well see the leaves on the bushes before him covered in drops of water like warts. When he brushed past, he sent a shower to the ground, which set some creature scuttling away through the undergrowth, the sound of its retreat covering the sound of his own passage, and he went on through the dripping forest, a whisper in the shadows.

THE OLD WOMAN'S SCENT in his nostrils, he awoke from sleep, believing, as the ghostly impressions of his dream faded, that she was there with him. He felt her beside him just as he could feel the stones and leaves beneath him. But when he tried to call her image from the dream, it drew away all at once.

He found it difficult to open his eyes to the light. He lay, staring at the roof of roots above him. A cold weight pressed on his brow. He turned on his side and coughed. The coughing raked his throat until his eyes watered and then he slumped onto his side, breathing hard.

Through the entrance of his lair, he saw the orange light of the setting sun. He rose. His head felt full of sand. He emerged from his lair into the twilight. The fiery sky agitated him. He retreated to the trees.

The earth was cold beneath his feet. His skin was filthy, uncomfortable. He tried to walk beyond it, to flee his own discomfort. He was pursued. As the shadows deepened, a wind rose up, whistling through the trees, and he believed he heard voices.

He stopped mid-stride and strained to listen beneath the sound of the wind. He heard whispers through the trees, as if from an invisible crowd. But there was no one. He knew there was no one there.

The wind wrapped him in its cold grasp. His teeth chattered. His feet and hands felt numb. He tried rubbing his hands together and breathing on them, but they were like bone claws, retaining no heat.

He stopped, clutching at the branch of a birch tree. In the shadows before him, he believed he saw the shape of a man, standing still, staring back at him. He knew there was no one there, yet his heart leapt against his chest and his body flooded with the urge to flee.

Though he knew it was unreasonable, he was convinced he had been followed. The townspeople were here, hiding behind the trees. He could hear the mockery in their voices. They had followed him to laugh at him.

He saw himself, the Old Woman draped across his shoulders. He returned home to applause, to the townspeople gathered, as if they had been awaiting his arrival. They gathered around him to see, to touch for themselves the body of that fabled cougar, and to shake the hand of the man who had killed her.

The thought of this made him laugh out loud into the night.

Then he saw himself, returning to town with the body of the Old Woman, but no one would look at him. The townspeople went about their day, either unable to see him or ignoring his presence, marching down the sidewalk one after the other, unseeing. Not only had they not noticed his return, they had been unaware of his absence. And he found that when he went about screaming, he made no sound.

Then a different kind of laughter interrupted his thoughts. He saw his father's face frozen in the midst of laughing. He was laughing at him.

Joseph ran. The ground fell out from under his feet and he slid down a steep slope, grabbing at branches and thin trees, a shower of leaves dislodged by his passage. When he came to a rest, pain flared into his hands and feet where he had tried to break his fall and he let out a howl into the black night.

He took a step. The strength fled from his legs and he stumbled and sat. His throat was so dry it hurt to breathe. He could barely keep his eyes open, but he was too nervous to sleep, as if some electric current circulated through his veins and he was unable to shut himself off.

Above, the moon was a thin crescent. In the faint moonlight, the trees began to change. The tectonic bark of a cedar melted and resolidified before his eyes, and again, in a steady rhythm that was like an enormous breath throughout the forest. His own body was subject to this movement. He lay staring at the moon, the dark tree-line separate from the sky. He saw himself lying where he was, half-buried, his body growing into the forest floor, spreading into the earth, into the trunks, the branches above. Roots became his veins. Moss and stone his skin. His body was the length of a mountain range, his breath the wind that ran through the trees.

He lay seeing this, believing he did not sleep. Then he slept.

HE AWOKE TO THE morning sun. His throat felt full of fire. His body felt made of rock, stiff and disproportioned.

Clusters of blueberries grew on the bushes around him, glistening with dew. He reached out, plucked one, testing its firmness between thumb and forefinger. The berries burst bright purple onto his skin. The taste was sharp. Sour but so pleasing. He sat, gathering them in handfuls, tossing them into his mouth. He poached the entire area, rifling through the leaves to find the ones he had missed.

Then he rose, lurching to his feet, and went on through the trees.

He sat perched on a lone boulder in the afternoon sun. Before him an Outcropping of Boulders sat against the forest's edge, spilling out onto the riverbank. Boulders of considerable size, dappled with dried moss, arranged as if they had tumbled from an enormous hand. He did not know what it was about the scene before him that caught his attention, but he found himself unable to look away, to turn and leave. The faint call of birds from within the trees reached his ears over the passage of the river behind him.

He rose and approached the group of boulders. As he came closer, the sound around him seemed to dwindle, as if the stone absorbed it. He stood looking at the texture of the stone, staring for a long time at the different shades of moss, the new living atop the old, the rough grey stone veined with dark quartz that glinted in the sun.

The mud at his feet called out to him. He knelt and grabbed a handful of the gritty mud. At the foot of the outcropping, he stood contemplating each boulder. He reached out, planted his hand upon the stone, felt the surface of the rock beneath the film of mud, the deep vibration that travelled through his body, into the earth.

He took his hand away and examined his handprint. He walked out into the river and then turned back, looking at his dark handprint on the stone, declaring his presence to all the forest.

Then he went on.

BENEATH THE SCENT OF pine and damp earth, he smelled the now familiar scent of blood. Guided by that scent alone, he walked through the trees, pushing past branches and into a small clearing. It took him a moment to notice the deer.

The deer stared at him from beneath a scant covering of branches which had been arranged not to disguise but as a sign to others. So it would be known that the Old Woman's presence was imminent. Joseph stood looking at the deer. Its hide had been torn back, the grimy ribs revealed, and a dark hollow had been eaten into the deer's torso where the forest cat had gone in to fetch out the organs.

Joseph turned and looked at the rocky hillside behind him, rife with clusters of dense bush and rugged rockfalls. He walked up onto the hillside, at times climbing around the rocks that blocked his way, until he found a clutch of bushes where he settled down upon the warm stone. He lay on his back, one hand behind his head. In his other hand he clutched the hatchet, resting the head on his chest.

A dragonfly drifted through the air and he noticed it in a way that made him believe he had been sleeping until that moment. He lay still, listening, and heard the nearby call of a warbler, long and bright. The sun shone upon the surrounding bushes so that the leaves glinted and even the air seemed to glow. He felt the warmth of the sunlight on his skin like the heat from the forge.

Joseph sat up and peered out through the leaves at the deer in the clearing. The scene remained unchanged. The deer was barely discernible from his vantage point. The leaves on the branches that lay atop the deer whispered in the wind. A subtle quiet bled into the air, and just as he noticed the quiet, a panther emerged from the trees.

Though it had been years ago and only briefly when last he saw her, he could not deny it to himself now: this was she, the Old Woman. He recognized her slight frame, her golden colour, the lightness of her steps, and saw, even from afar, the scar that marred the left side of her face.

His heart beat with a sudden fury and he became lightheaded. He dug his hands into the earth to keep himself steady. He could not suck in breath, as if the air had thinned, become insubstantial. In the midst of this physical reaction, he worried that the panther might hear the beating of his heart through the air, it seemed to him that loud. Even as he had this thought, the Old Woman looked toward the hillside where he sat concealed in the bushes, and though he knew she could not see him, he felt as if she could sense he was there.

The Old Woman began clearing the branches off the remains of the deer, throwing them to the side with a vacant air. Once she had uncovered the torso, she settled down next to it and began tearing out mouthfuls of meat.

Joseph watched as she ate. He was so close he could hear the sound of her teeth scraping against bone, tearing out the meat, as well as the sound of her claws ripping back the deer's hide.

The Old Woman lifted her head, a beard of blood on her face, eyes blazing in her skull, and again looked to the cluster of bushes where Joseph hid. He knew she could not see him. If anything, she would merely smell the mimic of her own scent upon him. Even so her gaze sent a shard of fear through his heart and he had to fight the urge to run.

Then the Old Woman turned and looked into the trees at her back, ears working at the air. She rose to her feet, aimed at the forest.

The birds had silenced. The Old Woman stood, focused on some point Joseph could not see. He sat watching, waiting for her to move, his heart beating hard in his chest. She remained standing, watching the trees before her.

The branches shook as an enormous brown bear galloped out of the trees toward the Old Woman. Joseph's heart stalled at the sight, but the panther maintained her stance, digging into the earth. The bear stopped short when he saw that the Old Woman did not move. He was three times the size of the old cat, but the bear was also old, his fur ragged from age, growing white upon his shoulders, his chest. His eyes were comically small, and he had to swing his head from side to side to keep the Old Woman in his sights.

The Old Woman hissed at the bear, her face dark with blood, stepping over the deer carcass so it lay beneath her. The bear studied the forest cat, taking in her feral gaze, the muscular line of her shoulders, her massive paws. The bear rose onto his hind legs, his belly loose beneath him, then leaned as close as he dared to the Old Woman and gave a sudden roar, revealing his yellowed teeth, his strange, grublike tongue.

The Old Woman stayed low to the ground, ears flattened against her head. She made a piercing growl that sent a cold fire across Joseph's skin. The bear towered over her, the bulk of its mass focusing on her, but the Old Woman was unmoved by this display. She hissed and swiped at the bear. The bear pulled back and roared, shaking its head, as if dismayed.

All at once the bear seemed to know he had lost. This cougar was more trouble than she was worth. Certainly more trouble than a half-eaten deer was worth. He stood, blinking, considering what to do next. He sent an annoyed groan into the air. The Old Woman, staring up at the bear, gave a dull hiss. The bear returned to all fours, staring off to the side, pretending he had forgotten the Old Woman, the deer, altogether, but this too was for show. The bear let out a dejected groan and lumbered back into the trees.

The Old Woman stood watching the bear's retreat, maintaining her stance for so long that Joseph could not be certain she could see the bear any longer. He drew many breaths watching her in this rigid stance. He endeavoured to stay still during this time but found himself fighting the urge to scratch, to shift position.

Finally, she crouched beside the deer and began to eat. When she lifted her head to the falling light, her eyes glowed green through her mask of gore. As Joseph watched her eat, his own stomach churned with hunger.

She sat, licking her chops, looking on the growing darkness. Then she laid her head on her paws and slept. Joseph sat, watching her through the leaves, but soon the darkness became too thick and he could no longer be certain that what he saw in the shadows was indeed the Old Woman. He did not fear her stalking through the shadows, sniffing him out as he slept, and was comfortable falling asleep and slept undisturbed as the Old Woman slept below.

When he awoke in the murk before dawn, he looked out, expecting to find that the Old Woman had gone but she was there, sleeping in the grass, like a barn cat basking in the sun. Joseph sat watching the rhythmic rise and fall of her chest as the sun broke through the horizon and light slowly overwhelmed the shadows.

The Old Woman roused and yawned. She stood and stretched out her front legs, tail slashing through the air. She spread out her paws, licking between each one of her claws. Then she moved onto her shoulders. She performed these actions in a slow, methodic nature, as if they required no thought, as one performing daily devotions. Joseph could not look away.

She spent some time replacing the branches atop the remains of the deer. Then, as if called away, the Old Woman sauntered into the dark trees, a golden shade through the shadows. Joseph could not hear her progress through the trees, so light were her steps, but he could hear the silence caused by her passage and listened as it travelled away.

The sight of the deer in the clearing below called to him like the lone point of light on a dark plane. Joseph climbed down from his niche on the stony hillside, crept through the grass toward the deer. It was not even a question. He knew what he would do. He walked toward the deer without doubt, without thought, his mind silenced against the urge that compelled his body forward. His heart beat as if he were approaching the Old Woman herself. She would know of his presence here. He was certain of it. That was why he did it.

He knelt before the deer, studying its inert face. Then he took up a handful of earth, dark with the deer's blood, and in one stroke passed his hand across his chest, from one shoulder to the other. A sharp smell crept into his nostrils and he felt dizzy. The skin on his palms tingled and he tasted a strange taste on the back of his tongue. Then the smell faded and he was fine.

He set off into the trees, his breathing quick, his footsteps light.

The deer stared after Joseph with its empty gaze, then stared on into the trees as the sun rose into the sky. The shadows of the trees crept across the earth as the sun set and the forest slowly settled into night. The deer stared into darkness even as a subtle silence bled into the clearing. The air sighing through the trees was the only sound to be heard, and the night passed in this unnatural silence. Before dawn, the silence travelled on, and the sounds of the forest resumed.

HE SLEPT THROUGH THE fiery blaze of the sunset into night, when he awoke shivering. Guided in the darkness by his outstretched hands, he grasped through the trees until he came to the river. In that open space the river was darker still than the air and stood out like a path of black stone through a lightless plain.

He felt the approach of the sun in the air, the warmth of the coming light, and he turned and left the riverbank for the trees. The trees stood like hazy shadows in the blue light until the sunlight woke the forest. The green of the leaves emerged from the dusk, as if the trees were slowly catching fire.

He crossed the stream along a string of stones that rose above the surface of the water, mindless of the noise he made. On the stony bank he knelt and splashed handfuls of water onto his face, the droplets flashing in the sunlight. He paused, distracted by the light, the sound of the water dripping from his hand back into the stream.

Almost as it happened, he noticed the silence around him. He felt his pulse at his temples, the tips of his fingers, within his neck. He rose, looked into the trees around him, and she was there. One moment he saw the golden forest, the next he was looking at a scarred, old panther sitting beneath an evergreen, eyes trained on him. He tried not to be amazed by this.

He stood, thin, naked, streaked with mud, but his eyes were clear. He clutched the hatchet in his hand, as if he had brought it along without knowing why and only now that he was here did he know what he must do.

When he looked into her eyes and saw that she was blind, he was astounded. Opalescent cataracts covered both eyes. He had envisioned this second meeting with the Old Woman many times, but his visions had never come close to the truth. There was something disturbing about her stare. He thought, *Perhaps she does not need eyes to see*, and this notion locked him to his spot. Learning of her blindness did nothing to relieve his beating heart, for he knew it gave him no advantage. She knew him by his smell, by the sound he made as he stepped through the old leaves on the forest floor, as he moved through the air.

When she set down a paw, he felt the slight vibration it sent through the earth. A powerful force emanated from her body, like waves of light rushing toward him, rendering him immobile, and he could not determine if his heart beat in fear or in awe.

He had not known wilderness until now. Though he had lived in a town ensconced in vast forest, he realized he had never lived in it. The Old Woman was the wilderness. Though not sleek, her golden fur still gleamed. The white of her chest glowed in the sunlight. The bones of her shoulders, and her ribs beneath her skin, were plain to see, giving her a sharp, naked appearance. The scar on her cheek stood out like lightning in the night sky.

The Old Woman, Mother of Hunters, Queen of Ghosts, whom he had sought through wilderness, and madness. A sudden urge overwhelmed him to step forward and lie down, allow himself to be devoured by her, that he may become a part of her life. He shook the thought out of his head, so great was its strength he feared it would overpower him. But it did not shock him, that he would have this thought. He could no longer shock himself with the strangeness of his own thoughts.

The weight of the hatchet in his hand brought him out of his contemplation. He gripped the haft against the sweat that greased his palm. The Old Woman lowered her head. A low growl crawled out of her mouth, a sound like nothing he had ever heard before. It rode through him like a tremor through the earth. His skin tingled on his neck, down his back.

He saw her sniff the air and she hissed again. He tried to imagine what she must think of him, who had hunted through the wilderness for days, slept where she slept, and smelled like her, yet was totally other.

He raised the hatchet and her gaze followed. Whether she could see some shift in the light or the shadow of his movement he did not know, but he knew he was not hidden from her. She knew all things. He wondered if she could sense the disorder of his thoughts, clumsy and elated, full of dread, and he felt exposed under her blind gaze.

Around them the drone of cicadas sounded like an engine thrumming to life. Sunlight caught the moisture in the air so everything was surrounded by halos of light. He recalled the day he had seen her for the first time, in that dark winter light, how her eyes had seemed to stare beyond him, and thinking of it now he wondered if she had been blind then too.

His breathing was hard. His heart beat inside him like a drum in an empty room. He knew he was distracted by the slant of light through the leaves, the fluid movement of her steps, her opalescent eyes. The Old Woman grew very still. He noticed her pause and he felt a chill run through his veins. She leapt toward him and his heart surged with fear.

He tried to chop into her shoulder, but she twisted out of reach, and the blade caught nothing but air. The Old Woman's scream sent a prickling sensation over his skin. She sprang at him, the force of her attack knocking him to the ground, and he dropped the hatchet in the leaves to catch her in his arms.

He had one hand under her jaw, the other against her chest, but even with all his strength he could only prevent her from getting closer, he could not push her off. Her heavy breath poured over his face. She tried to catch his neck in her jaws, trying one side, then the other, but she could not get her bite in.

The Old Woman rolled away, twisting around to face him. Keeping his eyes on the panther, he felt through the leaves for the lost hatchet. He clutched the haft and stood. He made a savage lunge with the hatchet, but the

Old Woman swatted his attack away as if he were a dry branch, and he was amazed at her strength.

They stood, facing each other, breathing hard. He knew he must not allow her appearance to distract him, and yet it was impossible not to give in to his desire to just stand there and look at her. He believed that she must command forces beyond his comprehension. He even believed allowing himself these distracting thoughts was a trick somehow related to her appearance.

He stepped toward her, hatchet raised, and she shrank away. She hissed and for a moment, before his eyes, she appeared like a snake, all fangs and mouth. He had the thought, *She can change shape*, and dismissed it, knowing he could not spare the attention to consider this notion, and because it terrified him.

He reached in with the hatchet, trying for her side, but the Old Woman batted his weapon away with an easy movement, revealing her hidden strength once again.

She harassed him with her scream, tempting him to strike, but he willed himself to wait despite the fear commanding him to attack. He saw the sudden stillness that came into her body the moment before she pounced. Joseph struck wildly at her face but she twisted aside. The Old Woman reached for his face with both paws and he jumped back, but she wrapped her arms around him, claws into his shoulders. The terror he felt at the closeness of her body was like a wave of nausea. As he pushed her away, her claws dragged through his flesh and he screamed.

The Old Woman rolled onto her feet and backed away, mouth open, sightless stare aimed at him. Three claw marks adorned each of his shoulders. Joseph held out his hands, as if holding the pain itself, breathing short, amazed breaths. The air stung like fire on his raw flesh. He felt the fleeting warmth of blood as it gathered and wept down his arms. The sight of his own blood on his dirtied skin frightened him, the brightness of the colour seemed out of place, a grave warning. His own blood was terrifying to him and yet it seemed this was what he had wanted.

For a moment he forgot the Old Woman, the pain was so great. He heard the whisper of grass. He turned in time to see the Old Woman nearly upon him. She swiped at him as she leapt past, catching him across his thigh. He crumpled to the ground.

He found the bright hatchet in the leaves. He rose without thought and swung his weapon at the Old Woman. The blade bit into her side, behind her foreleg.

The cougar screamed. The sound tore through the forest, echoing through the trees. Joseph took a step and the Old Woman mirrored him; they began to trace an unseen circle. The Old Woman hissed, blood trailing down her foreleg, leaving a smeared red paw print wherever she stepped. Joseph held tight the hatchet, his shoulders burning where she had clawed him, his thigh burning, bright with blood.

The Old Woman froze. She seemed to know what he would do the moment he did. As he swung the hatchet, the Old Woman rose, reached out, and batted his attack to the side. His arm was flung away as if he had struck metal.

Joseph stepped into sunlight as the Old Woman passed into shadow. He wore two sleeves of blood and a stream of blood flowed from his thigh. The Old Woman moved in one fluid motion, never pausing, head low, breathing through her mouth. Her gaze was directed over his shoulder, as if some fearsome sight stood behind him, and he dared not look, unwilling to lose sight of her for a moment.

He felt the pull of the earth, tempting him to lie down. His arms were heavy, his hands throbbed, dark with blood. His heart beat inside his chest like the clanging of a hammer. The air was so bright he had to squint.

Joseph took a step to the right, and the Old Woman followed.

He saw her freeze, the stillness that took over her body, and he knew what she would do.

She leapt, reaching out toward him.

He held up his arm to her, her jaw clamped around his forearm. She had one arm around his shoulders, the other around his head. Wrapped in her embrace he believed he would die. But instead of opening her mouth to devour him, the Old Woman seemed to forget him. She stared beyond him, at some sudden vision, let out a soft grunt, and he felt her grip loosen, her strength suddenly flee.

Then he saw the hatchet wedged into her neck—a true bite.

For a moment he had thought her invincible—that she could sustain such a blow with no effect on her body. But when he pulled his hatchet free, a bloom of dark blood flowered upon her white neck, then flowed forth, and he heard the sound of it dripping on the ground, reaching his ears over her ragged breath.

She let go of her hold around his shoulders and grew

heavy in his arms. Even so, he knew that if he were to loosen his grip, she still had the strength to bite. He tried to hold her up, but the weight was too much, forcing him to the ground. Then he was sitting and she lying across his lap, dark blood flowing from her neck, onto his hands, the ground beneath them. He could not believe the weight of her body, the heat, but of course she was corporeal. He knew he should not be shocked. Still, he was shocked.

Her breathing was the only sound, her slim rib cage rising and falling with the effort. Joseph placed his hand on her rising ribs and felt a current of electricity snap his palm. She felt so thin beneath her hide, just strands of muscle, a frame of bones that weighed nothing more than a bucket of ash, and a beating heart pushing it all through space. How small she was, how simple, and yet the inner workings of her body were a mystery. Studying each part of its function would bring him no closer to the truth. The thing that had powered her through her days was bleeding onto the ground, seeping into the air.

His hand shook in rhythm with his heartbeat as he placed it on her cheek. Then slowly he swept his hand down her side, feeling the warm landscape of her body. He did this again, starting at her cheek, down along her back, unable to stop himself.

After a moment, the Old Woman began to purr.

Her breath came in shallow heaves, her blood staining the earth beneath them. Her bones, her heart, would turn to ash and melt into the earth. He did not know where these thoughts came from. They flowed into his head as if upon the current of some endless river.

He felt her heartbeat struggle. Joseph watched as the Old Woman looked in awe upon the vision before her. Her attention, so rapt, compelled him to look into the trees where she was looking but there he saw nothing.

She took a short breath, then sighed. An unmistakable stillness came over her, the difference was immediate. He felt the sudden presence of Death as clearly as he had felt the presence of life a moment ago.

Her eyes were terrible to behold then. Her entire body struck him in this way. The mystery of her life was separate from the carcass slumped across him, and would never be revealed to him. Not even now.

He looked into the trees and was shocked when he realized how little time had passed. The sun had only now risen. For a moment, he believed the fantastic had occurred and an entire day had been spent. But his beating heart, his burning arms, told him otherwise. Something mundane had occurred. Only a few minutes had transpired since their first glance, and he was astonished.

As if he had just now awoken, he noticed the dark mess of blood that had sprung from the Old Woman's neck. Blood stained her white chest, her front legs, stained too his chest and arms. The ground beneath them was like a red fire pit, the sun lighting up the colour in contrast to the stone of the earth. Joseph wiped his mouth with the back of his hand and a red stain bloomed across his face. His shoulders and arms were dark with the blurry stain of his own blood. He saw the wounds were still bleeding and he was frightened by how much blood he had lost. A vast distance of wilderness surrounded him. He struggled to breathe beneath the weakness of exhaustion. For a moment he had understood, but in the midst of it, he was forgetting.

He sat in the warm sunlight next to the Old Woman's body, the call of cicadas rising from within the trees. He did not know how long he stayed watching her, but as his breathing slowed and his heartbeat returned to a steady beat he became aware of the sudden, unmistakable hunger that threatened to overwhelm him. All other concerns were pushed aside and he became resolved.

He picked up the hatchet and dug into the Old Woman's torso with two swift chops. Two lines of black blood appeared on her white belly, began creeping toward the ground.

He reached his hand into her still-warm body, like reaching into a forbidden nest, his skin prickling as if he feared being bitten, and therein grasped among the unprotected organs. He pulled out a gruesome morsel, the dark meat seeming to vibrate in his hand. In this light, the meat looked purple and he did not believe he could eat it. But he brought it to his mouth and took a bite. The texture was beyond anything he had ever eaten, raw, nothing hidden. It was unlike eating food. He almost vomited. Then he clenched his eyes shut and swallowed. His heart beat like a flame flares when the coals beneath it are stoked. He felt the fire of his own blood as it coursed through his veins, filling him with a dizzying strength.

He opened his eyes. Around him the forest had grown bright. The sun reflected off the particles of water in the air and he watched their continuous motion, the invisible currents revealed. The veins on the leaves stood out to him like they were etched in light. Each leaf, as his eye fell on it, seemed to be the centre of the forest. He blinked, not believing, but the vision stayed. The earth beneath him was cool and full of darkness, and he dug his hands in and brought up handfuls of stone and soil and old leaves and looked into the endless vision in his hands.

The light had faded. He looked up to see if a cloud had passed overhead, but the sky remained unchanged. Then the light was rising fast, as if day after day were passing around him. He saw the forest aflame, the fire blown out by a great wind.

Finally, he awoke.

He looked on the Old Woman's corpse in the twilight. His presence here seemed somehow inappropriate. The process of her decomposition must not be attended. It required some privacy, and he knew now that he must leave her.

When finally he rose and took a step, he was uncertain, ill-balanced, as if it had been many years since last he had walked. Before he stepped into the trees, he looked back. The circle of blood beneath her appeared black in the fallen light. Then he turned to leave, wanting to be away from this visceral scene. He walked without thought, disappearing into darkness, and did not emerge from the shadows for many days.

JOSEPH AWOKE WITH A shiver. He lay in the long grass beneath a clutch of bushes. A spider's web stretched between two branches above him, the fine threads lit up like filaments of pure light. As the sun rose higher, the angle of light shifted and the spider web disappeared.

Joseph sat among a cluster of boulders on the scree fringing the mountainside, a cold wind rifling his matted hair. The skeletal frame of a dead pine tree jostled in the wind. A few of the highest branches still had sprays of green needles, but the lower branches were bare, the bark grey and worn by years of weather. The same tree alive and dead at once. This seemed to him an irreconcilable state of being.

He walked down to the river's edge and into the water. On the swim across he felt his heart beating hard inside his chest. The sound of his own breath rushing in and out of his lungs was tremendous. The torn skin on his shoulders stung at the water's touch. He felt the claw marks like scars of light, bright and painful. He emerged from the river, water streaming from his body onto the earth. His coating of mud washed away. Wisps of steam rose off his skin, ghostly in the sunlight.

If he thought back, he could not remember how long it had been since he left the Old Woman behind. At times he doubted the veracity of his own memory—what he considered memory—and he wondered if it had been a dream. It seemed an unreal thing to have happened. He did not believe himself. But he did believe the claw marks dug into his shoulders, now turning black as the wounds scabbed over.

He felt like nothing more than a set of bones and was shocked when he felt his heart beating at points beneath his skin. It amazed him that he was not dead, and he felt he could die at any moment, his existence was that precarious. Yet somehow his death did not concern him. Whatever injury he had sustained during his stay in the forest, any damage to his body, was meaningless. The suffering of his body was meaningless. He himself could not be destroyed.

He no longer carried the hatchet. He did not remember where he had left it. He tried to picture it leaned against a fallen tree, lying in a bed of brown leaves, dropped in the grass by the river, but he could not bring the image to mind and so believed the hatchet to have disappeared from the face of the earth.

At night, the sky was a field of stars so bright he walked by their light alone. He came to flat land, which had once been a bog. Now the skeletal shards of tree stumps stood white, awash in starlight, amid a lake of tall grass. The trees had stood sentinel as the land flooded and drowned them, their branches shed, their trunks washed smooth by the rain. He trekked through the waist-high grass, past the dead white trees, into the trees beyond.

He had never been so silent in all his life. At times he tested his voice in toneless, meaningless calls, as if he had forgotten words. There was no one to hear them so there was no use for words. He made sounds simply to see that he still could, a language of his own invention, and went bleating through the forest, naked and alone, like some mad beast.

He went on, forgetting, then remembering, the town to which he knew he must return, the town that now seemed unknown to him. The nights were growing cold.

He had slept the last few nights under the branches of an evergreen, heaping the dry, brown needles over himself for warmth, only to awaken uncovered, shivering, the distant sun shining slantwise through the trees.

He continued toward the town with a somnambulant determination. He had no thoughts of his father or other people, only the shelter it meant to his body, an end to discomfort. He needed rest. Some form of oblivion. He had no choice. The forest was pushing him out, sending him back. He did not belong here.

He awoke on a hillside curtained with fog so thick he could not see the earth around him but for a small realm. The ghost of a tree was the only indication of any presence other than his own. Then he sensed there was something moving. At first, they were just shadows in the ether, suggestions. He waited. They emerged, a herd of deer wading through the fog on slow, quiet feet.

He sat up and watched as they passed. The deer did not seem to consider him a threat. They passed by him on either side as if he were a tree, or another deer. The herd went on into the dusky fog, he did not know how many, until they were shadows once more, disappearing before him, and then he was alone.

HE BEGAN TO ENCOUNTER and avoid the dwellings of men. He could tell where they lived by the silence surrounding the cleared land, and he circumvented these areas so as not to appear outside the cover of the trees, so as not to be seen. He saw men from afar and he watched them at their work, tiny limbs raising tiny implements, trails of smoke from their homes like streams into the sky.

At the road he waited within the trees as a man on horseback rode past. The horse pulled a cart stacked high with barrels secured beneath a tarp. Neither the horse nor the man had any knowledge of his presence, and he stood watching them directly, never taking his eyes off the pair. Man and horse went on, the racket of their cart on the dried mud road drowning out the breeze through the treetops. He stared after them for a long time, listening to the sound of their progress diminish, replaced by the sound of the wind through the leaves. Then he went on.

He stood in the trees surrounding a small clearing where a cabin sat secured against the forest, a stream of black smoke rising from the chimney. He could hear the sounds of movement from within: the clatter of crockery, the soft echo of footsteps, murmured words. The door opened and a young girl emerged, carrying a bucket. She walked to the pump at the side of the house, placed the bucket beneath the spout, and started pumping. Despite her small size she operated the pump like one who had performed this action many times. Though the silence of the birds gave him away, the girl seemed not to notice. He watched as she walked back to the house, holding the bucket to the side, her slight frame contending with its weight, closing the door behind her.

The dwellings grew more frequent. Cleared land, at first glimpsed through the trees, became impossible to avoid. With fewer trees, the face of the earth was revealed. The open space made him nervous, and he was hesitant to venture into these areas. He stayed within the thin swaths of trees dividing one man from the next. He followed no path, believing he wandered without direction, when in fact he was slowly gravitating toward his inevitable destination, however unknowing, like water flowing downhill, until at last he came to the edge of the trees surrounding the town.

Streams of smoke travelled upward from the chimneys of the rash of buildings below. From where he stood, he could not see any person but he could hear the hum of people moving around within the town. The closeness felt alien to him. The sounds of cars and carts along the main road reached him where he stood. He heard the backfire of an engine starting, the racket of hammers in construction, the voices of men. A shout in anger or jest, he could not discern. He recalled the sound of language and it was like finding old clothes he had not seen in years, only now they appeared strange and unfamiliar to him.

He had not laid eyes on such a sight in many days and his mind stalled from the thought of how he would get himself back into town. He stood, watching from within the trees, his heart beating hard in his chest, mouth dry, and he realized he was afraid.

Only now did he think of his appearance; his beard a matted mess, his hair wild and unkempt, his skin unwashed, rough, and torn. His nakedness, which he had grown so comfortable with, which he had so recently loved, now stood out to him like some grave and shameful error. His arms and legs were stained from having slept on the earth. The Old Woman's blood was still embedded under his fingernails, which he had wanted to preserve. Even his own blood contributed to the grime on his body. The claw marks on his shoulders had turned black, the skin bruised bright purple, green, and yellow. He knew he did not resemble the man he had been when he left.

He thought of himself going into town appearing as he did now, thought of himself being seen by other men looking as he did, and he did not know how it could be done. Not looking like other men was a great obstacle, and he knew he could not walk among them. They may fear him, or they may not believe he was a man.

He stood within the trees, staring at the town. Now that he had seen it he felt a vague urgency to return. He could not stay in the forest, however much he might want to. In a distant region of his mind, he knew he was unwell and that if he returned to the town he could stave off discomfort, evade Death a little longer.

He had not anticipated that this anxiety would affect him when at last he returned to town. In fact, he had not thought of returning to town at all. He had gone whole into the forest and his body had returned abandoned — the flesh returned but not the man — and now here stood this cold wisp of a creature looking on the town like some derelict bird returned from an errant flight.

As the sun went down he stood watching the slow shadow of the trees reaching across the town. The windows lit up and glowed through the dusk while overhead the stars grew in strength. The smell of fires burning reached out to him from across the sea of grass, and he remembered with sudden clarity the sight of firelight on the faces of other men, the smell of baking bread, the sound of flames crackling as he lay, wrapped in blankets, secured against the night.

The call of an owl wafted through the trees behind him. The cool air brushed his burning face, and for a moment the task before him was forgotten. He felt at ease. It did not matter how to get back into the town, he was already here.

The murmur of crickets rose up from the moonlit grass. His breath stood out upon the air before him. The air was cold, but he was warm, his skin burning in the darkness. He felt his heartbeat in his neck, in his fingertips, like the steady beating of a hammer against an anvil. Again the owl sent forth its call, and it was then Joseph stepped out of the trees.

XII

PSYCHOPOMP

➵

T HE OPENING LIGHT ROUSED him from his sleep. Something tugged at his memory. He had been searching for something. He found himself looking at the dresser, long and low against the bedroom wall, the mirror above it reflecting an old man tucked up in white sheets, bright eyes staring out. A vague notion washed over him. He remembered now, coming to the edge, but he had been pulled awake too soon. He realized he had been dreaming. It was just a dream he was remembering. And he began to forget.

He sat on the edge of the bed, adjusting to the effects of gravity. He took a breath, stretching his neck, his shoulders. It was in his joints, those points of connection, that was where he felt the wear after so many years. He reached for his walker and pulled himself up, then stood a moment, gaining his balance. Coming out of sleep was something that had to be done gradually, otherwise the disorientation was too great. He set off for the kitchen, ankles popping as he made his way down the carpeted hallway.

Already the apartment was growing hot. He turned the air conditioning up a few degrees using the control unit mounted on the wall by the front door. He could barely think in this heat. Winter was bad too. It did not matter what he wore, he was always cold. The wind cut through him like he was a leafless bush. Given the choice, he would probably choose summer as the more bearable of the two seasons, but it won out only by a small margin.

He turned on the tap and filled his coffee pot to the sixth line, poured the water into the top of the coffee machine. He doled out six tablespoons of ground coffee and pressed the Start button. Then he stood, waiting in the kitchen, looking into the living room.

The memory of another morning came to him, unbidden. Perhaps a similar slant of light, the same posture assumed, had summoned the memory from the depths of his mind. Or perhaps it was random. A misfire between brain cells that called up this memory instead of thinking about the day's errands. It was the sound of running, two sets of uneven footsteps, his daughters. Then the slight, sure-footed steps of his wife following close behind.

The coffee machine beeped, pulling him out of his thoughts. With perfect patience he waited for the last drop to fall. Then he poured the coffee, picked up his cup, and blew over its surface before taking a sip. He looked at the blinded windows, watching the light as if some beast were lurking outside instead of the sun.

He opened the refrigerator and took out an orange. Today was his shopping day. There was no question as to what he would buy. He always bought the same thing. The same thing was always there to buy. There were no decisions required. All he need do was fulfill the mechanical actions required to achieve this goal, as he had every week for what now seemed like a lifetime. He shut the fridge door and stood, quietly peeling his orange.

He returned to his bedroom to dress. He had a cleaning woman come in twice a month to maintain the status quo. He took care of the dishes and his laundry. In the basement of his building, he would load his clothing into the washer, wait until the cycle ended, then he would move the load into the dryer and wait until that cycle ended. He had his walker, so he would sit while he waited. Sometimes he fell asleep sitting upright. People did not seem to want to talk in the laundry room. They were a bit disturbed, a bit put off, by his presence. Sometimes Joseph pretended he was sleeping to make them feel more at ease. Sometimes he was in fact asleep.

Often Joseph found himself alone. He would sit in front of the washer, watching his clothes tumble over and over in the soapy water. It was somehow peaceful, sitting among the machines, all in perfect working order. Though the sound of their operation was almost deafening this was the sound of normal functions.

He slid open his closet door and took out a blue button-up shirt and khaki-coloured pants, both baggy around his thinning frame. He did not want to iron, and really no one minded his appearance. No one was paying attention.

The sets of scars on his shoulders were so faded now they barely stood out. He would forget he had them, until he caught his reflection in the mirror and saw the faint lines where she had laid her mark into his flesh.

He applied sunscreen to his face, his skin looking like the hide of a speckled lizard. Then he sat on the edge of the bed to put on his walking sneakers. If he did not have them on, he would not get far. The sidewalk was not reliable, uneven in parts. It was important to have the proper equipment. He patted down the Velcro straps and stood. He took his keys and wallet from the night table and stuffed them in his pockets, then pushed his walker into the hall.

He turned down the air conditioner, since he was going out. He would turn it up again when he got home. He grabbed his hat by the door, the red band faded and fraying. He put on his sunglasses and looked at his reflection in the mirror. A bespectacled old man stared back at him. Then he left his apartment, locking the door behind him.

The hallway was made dark by his sunglasses. Joseph pushed his walker toward the doors at the end of the hall. He pressed the round metal button on the wall and a faint buzzing sounded as the doors eased open. Sunlight flooded into the hallway. Squinting against the light, Joseph stepped outside.

T HE SUN BURNED IN the sky overhead. Joseph worked his slow shuffle down the street. Heat shimmered over the sidewalk in the distance like the vaporous breath of the earth itself seeping up through the concrete and rising into the air. Maple trees stood ensconced in concrete planters at measured, equal intervals. The shade cast by their branches did nothing to alleviate the heat from above, nor the heat that seemed to radiate from the asphalt below. His hat shaded his face and his sunglasses saved his eyes from the glare. Without them, it would be impossible to see during the bright day.

He walked along beside a line of multiplexes, each one six storeys tall, each with an identical lawn populated with manicured yew bushes. Beside him, a car drove past. Sunlight reflected off its windows, the chrome detailing on the car windows, the hubcaps, and the flash of light reminded him of the heat against his face while as a child he watched his father work at the forge. The ping of a hammer against molten metal rang through his ears.

A car horn blared. Joseph was seized by a sudden dread. A vehicle had changed lanes in the intersection, nearly hitting the car already occupying the desired lane. Both the offender and the offended were well down the road now. Joseph's heart beat hard in his chest. He felt annoyed, as if he had been rudely awoken, severed from the thread of thought that had entangled him from so many years ago.

At the intersection, he pressed the button to indicate he wanted to cross, then stood waiting for the light to change. The light turned green and the little man glowed to life. Joseph pushed his walker into the street. Beside him, the line of cars sat vibrating. Waves of heat rose from their hoods as he shuffled across. He was not yet halfway through the intersection when the light turned amber and the counter started counting down. He thought he could sense the cars on his right inch forward, and he was filled with a mild anxiety that he would be mowed down. As if they could not see him, the drivers of the vehicles could not recognize him as a living being since he himself was not operating a vehicle. He was instead like a chipmunk, or a type of bush. It seemed he had barely stepped onto the sidewalk when the line of cars set off with the panicked roar of acceleration. Joseph stood feeling his heart beating in his chest, the traffic coursing by behind him.

A group of youths walked toward him. Joseph grew a stern expression and tried to look unapproachable, pushing his walker along as if he did not see them. They passed by on either side, parting to let him through, emitting distortion from some unseen source within their garb.

Youth seemed fearsome to him, a new kind of man who lived elsewhere, in another world, not the physical world in which he lived, and they would end up somewhere other than he would, a destination he could not imagine.

Though he lived among a great number of people, at times it was as if the world had become deserted. For all the many houses packed together in the convolution of the suburbs in which he lived, he barely saw anyone. But he knew they were there, and their secret numbers frightened him. He sensed their presence, the sound of thousands of living bodies, the sound of their many breaths seeping into his daily thoughts, his dreams at night. So that when he was confronted with strangers, he felt alarmed, as if coming across unknown creatures, other predatory animals. He was no longer used to encountering other men. They had become strange to him.

A plane droned by overhead. He looked up at the mechanical body propelling hundreds of men through the sky. He considered this a fantastic feat though the world was populated by such machines now. That was the natural world. He himself had devoted his life to maintaining these machines, a convert to the mechanical life.

Joseph watched the plane as it flew by. Then he went on.

H E ENTERED THE CAVERNOUS Superstore. A network
of pipes and ducts ran across the ceiling, inseparable
from the structure of the building, lining the walls,
reaching down into the earth, where they met with the
network of systems belonging to the city. The sounds of the
heating and cooling system reached the shoppers below, a
continuous, dull hiss. So Joseph, shuffling along the white
aisles, began to feel a vague fear, the same response he
might have to hearing a snake slithering through the grass.

From behind his sunglasses Joseph observed the other
shoppers. He watched their slow movements, furtive glances,
as if they were trying not to draw attention to themselves
as they picked over the produce, inspected blueberries from
the U.S., avocados from Mexico, bananas from Colombia.
Perhaps they were hesitant because they knew they were
being watched. Planted in the ceiling, identical rows of black
eyes gazed down, unblinking. The shoppers were constantly
monitored but this did not seem strange to them.

Aisle after aisle of everything a man could imagine. The
aisles seemed like an endless labyrinth, not because they
were constructed in a confusing way but because shoppers
might become so distracted by looking at the multitude of
products that they might never find what they were looking for, forgetting they were meant to be shopping at all.

Joseph fell into this trap himself, searching the aisles

without purpose. Browsing, to see what was there. He picked up a package of white rice and read about its unique sweetness and enticing aroma, each grain harvested the same as rice had been harvested for centuries. A pleasant notion, though he doubted it was true.

Joseph stood staring down the aisle with the peanut butter. He studied the variety of jars with different-coloured labels, arranged in neat lines, all facing front — but he could not find his brand, the peanut butter he wanted.

A stockboy turned into the aisle, followed by a four-car trolley stacked high with cashmere-soft toilet paper.

"Excuse me." Joseph held up a hand to flag the boy down. He had white cords leading into his ears, and Joseph feared the boy might not stop if he were only to speak to him. The boy pulled out one of his earbuds. He was young, of a small stature, so Joseph had trouble placing his age. He had a weary look to him despite his youth, with a smattering of acne on his cheeks and around his mouth.

"I'm looking for my brand of peanut butter . . . the one with the squirrel?"

"Oh." The boy looked at the shelves beside them, reading the information posted below each product as if trying to decipher a code. "I think we're sold out of that right now."

"Sold out?"

"Yeah, look there." The boy pointed to a spot on the shelves where indeed there was an empty space, the bright orange sticker below advertising the sale price.

It did not seem possible, with all this selection, that they should be sold out of the peanut butter he wanted. He was so dissatisfied with this idea that he considered not even buying peanut butter, that was how annoyed he was. But then he thought, no, he did not want to go without.

"Would another kind do?" the boy asked.

"I guess so . . ." said Joseph.

"What kind do you like?"

"Nothing fancy."

The boy picked one of the jars off the shelf and handed it to Joseph. The label was made of thick paper. A bold font declared the brand; an illustration, in vivid colours, showed good-looking peanuts spilling out in a warm light. At the top and bottom of the jar, a stripe of the creamy peanut butter was visible, fine bits of crushed peanuts sprinkled throughout.

"How much is this one?"

The boy scanned the labels on the shelf. "Seven ninety-five."

Joseph grimaced. "Oh, no. Something cheaper."

The boy grabbed another jar. The solid yellow label was printed on thin paper, its black block letters declaring the word *peanut butter*, the word *smooth* below that.

"How much is this one?"

"Three ninety-nine."

Joseph nodded. "That will do. Thank you."

"No problem."

The boy replaced his earbuds and continued pulling his trolley of toilet paper down the aisle and out of sight.

Joseph set the yellow jar into the basket attached to his walker and went on, feeling somehow unsatisfied with his purchase.

A long, frozen corridor made of many doors. The doors

were big enough for a man to walk inside. Joseph imagined himself reaching in, the door closing shut behind him, and then being trapped and freezing solid. He imagined the other shoppers walking by, opening the door next to him, grabbing a pint of black cherry ice cream, closing the door, and going on with their day, Joseph's frozen expression staring after them.

He turned the corner and saw a sign above a cooler of chicken that read "$2.99." He did not think, he pushed his walker toward the cooler in haste. Chicken for $2.99 did not seem right, he knew. It must be expiring, Joseph thought. That was all right, he could eat it today.

He saw the indiscernible chunks of chicken sitting in their plastic bags of pink water. He leaned over to inspect the chicken and saw that the packages were marked from $8.45 to $12.28, priced according to weight. His brow furrowed. Then he looked at the sign again and saw the canisters of breadcrumbs stacked above the cooler.

Clever, Joseph thought. *They tricked me.* He laughed out loud that he had scurried over here so quickly. He laughed, ignoring the curious stares he drew from his fellow shoppers, amused that he had fallen for the ploy, that it may even have worked on some, laughed that this was how you got meat, laughed that there was so much of it, though it was not really funny. He thought it was funny that he had been tricked, was all. What a ploy.

He looked again at the chunks of chicken soaking in their pink juices in the plastic bag, the mound of them; the sight of the flesh plucked of its feathers prodded his memory and he thought of his father.

His father would buy a chicken at the market and carry it home, tucked under one arm, Joseph walking along beside him on the mud road. Joseph remembered now the old place where they lived before moving to the apartment in town, remembered walking around the muddy yard wearing a sweater that was too big for him, sitting on the very table his father used as a cutting board, his father's hands; he remembered those hands almost like they were his own, for he had so often watched them at work, and he remembered the knife with the mother-of-pearl inlay, which his father used to slice apples and decapitate chickens. The brim of his hat hiding his face but for the edge of his bearded chin. Joseph watched as his father laid the blade into the chicken's neck. In his memory, he saw the dirt rimming his father's thumbnail, the scars in the wooden bench where many chickens before had lost their heads, and the knife that his father forever carried with him — where had it come from? Who had given it to him? He had never asked.

Shaken by the intensity of this thought, confused and maddened that it came to him now, suddenly Joseph felt a great longing drain through him, a longing to return, and somehow a longing for rest, and he began to cry. Hard tears fell from his eyes and he wiped them away behind his protective sunglasses and squeezed his eyes shut, to keep the tears in. He reminded himself he was in public. Hardly the place for emotion.

At the checkout, his cashier, a young girl who could be no more than fifteen, scanned his purchases and placed them in a bag. Joseph inserted his credit card, punched his code into the machine, but something was wrong. He leaned in close, trying to read the dim digital screen.

His cashier turned the machine around to read what it said.

"Sometimes it just takes a minute . . ." she told him.

Joseph nodded, smiling from behind his sunglasses, feeling impatient because of the wait, but he knew it wasn't the girl's fault.

He thought of himself at fifteen and the memory that came to him was of the day he had first seen the Old Woman. The details had blurred, like an old drawing, faded from the years. He could just recall the sight of the Old Woman, sitting there on the cliff across from him. There was a strange darkness to her eyes that he could not account for and they had a strange magnetic quality which he did not remember them having in life.

"Thank you, sir."

He shook the vision away. The cashier was holding his receipt out to him, her impatience thinly veiled.

Joseph placed his bag of groceries in his walker basket and set off toward the exit.

The doors slid open before him. He could hear the rumble of the hot world outside, the hollow sound of the store behind him. He stepped out into the heat, sweat bloomed on his skin, and the doors slid shut behind him with a sigh.

A man sat begging on the sidewalk outside the grocery store and their eyes met. He was younger than Joseph, though still an old man. His skin was weather-ravaged, his hair had the colourless appearance of fibre-optic filaments.

His left eye was surrounded by mottled skin and the eye itself was clouded white. This gave Joseph a chill despite the heat. He felt as if a shadow passed over his head. He almost looked up.

When the man held out his hand, Joseph muttered an apology and went past. He had no change on him. Not a coin. He no longer carried money.

Joseph was amazed that the man could live outside, exposed to the crushing heat. How he survived the harsh breath of winter seemed a mystery. He was bewildered by the notion of living outside. It seemed to him a supernatural skill.

T HERE HAD BEEN A time when Joseph had known every vehicle, and the owner of every vehicle, in town. Now he could not even guess at the number of vehicles in town. Probably tens of thousands. He tried to imagine all the cars in all the world at this very moment. But he could not imagine this number and instead became swallowed by this thought, so large that he was diminished against it.

Joseph walked home along the storefronts on the south side of the street, in the shade of the buildings. The sidewalk was white and newly made, a sign of healthy infrastructure, people at work. Joseph cracked a smile. Even this would have to be remade in no time, a hundred years perhaps. A hundred years was nothing. No time at all. Whatever man constructed seemed fated to be crushed against the indomitable face of the earth. It would all crumble to dust. He shook his head, strangely amused.

Joseph saw buildings rise up on this spot, decay, then fall, like the trees of a forest. Rising and falling like the cycle of growth in a concrete forest. But he was not at all disturbed by this vision. He knew this was beyond him, he would be long dead when this occurred, and knowing this was a great comfort to him.

Joseph stopped to catch his breath. He looked into the window display of a large store. A mannequin family sat in fold-out chairs around a fold-out table set for dinner with plastic dishes and plastic cutlery. The father, mother, and two children—a boy and a girl—all wore appropriately outdoorsy clothing: plaid shirts, khaki shorts, fashionable waterproof vests, and sunglasses to match. All of this from within the protective netting of something called an outdoor room.

Beside the family, a more serious scene. Joseph looked at the bright orange jumpsuits on two male mannequins, their puffy camouflage-print jackets. They both wore deer-hunter caps. One mannequin was fitted with binoculars, or what might have been night vision goggles, while the other held barbecue tongs in one hand and a drink in a Styrofoam sleeve in the other. At his feet was a smart-looking, portable stove, complete with orange cellophane flames, coaxed to life by a strategically placed fan.

Face the Wilderness! proclaimed the neon sign; an enemy to be conquered.

Joseph was seized by an uncontrollable fit of laughter. He laughed so hard at first no sound escaped him, only a hideous grimace contorted his expression. Then a wheezy breath that resembled laughter seeped out from between his teeth.

One of the employees inside the store noticed Joseph standing around laughing on the sidewalk and gave him an annoyed look, hooking his eyebrow. Joseph dismissed him with a wave of his hand, turned back to his walker, and went on.

There was a parking lot coming up on his right and Joseph walked out of the shade, into the full sunlight.

Stepping into the sunlight was like stepping into a furnace. Even breathing in the hot air seemed harder. The heat pulled perspiration from his body; a line of sweat appeared on his back, staining his shirt. Even so, he kept laughing.

Joseph spotted a bench in the shade of a maple tree and steered his walker toward it. He took a seat and looked across the road. Before him was another bench, sheltered in the shade of a maple tree. Behind the bench was a playground, the bright blue and red metal structures of swings, slides, and monkey-bars blazing in the summer sun. Beyond that stood a row of houses, their yards protected by an unending lattice-bordered fence. Joseph frowned. He looked behind himself. A playground, bright blue and red metal structures gleaming in the sun. Beyond that a row of houses behind a lattice-bordered fence. He looked back across the road. He half-expected to see a reflection of himself, seated on the bench in the shade, staring back at him.

The Old Woman stepped into his thoughts. He saw her slip out of the shadows, moonlight glinting off her smooth hide. Then, she disappeared back into the shadows and he saw only darkness.

Throughout his life, he had gone years at a time without thinking of her. But always she returned, sauntered back into his thoughts, and he was powerless against remembering. He indulged this thought now, recalling the sleek lines of her body, and he remembered how he would give himself over to thinking of her secret life in the forest, the hold she had over him, his total devotion to her, which, he was willing to admit now, was somewhat akin to fanaticism.

It had been almost eighty years since he had gone seeking into the wilderness in pursuit of the Old Woman. His memories of living in the forest were like the details of a barely remembered dream. His altercation with the Old Woman had become pared down to a single moment, when they had been wrapped in each other's embrace, facing one another. Such a brief moment to hold such weight in the long life to come.

He barely knew what any of it was — only his next breath concerned him, his next step. What was the purpose of this bare existence? Why had he lived only to wallow in loneliness? And what kept him here while others floated away like dandelion spores on the slightest breeze?

At times he feared he might live forever, and he longed for the hunter who would come for him from out of the forest. He suspected that he was supposed to know something by now, about why he had survived this long, but he did not feel like he knew anything more than he had fifty or sixty years ago, and he began to believe he never would. At other times, he feared he had known something but it had been forgotten.

If he tried to think of it now, the reason he had gone into the forest to hunt the Old Woman eluded him. Sometimes he remembered the line of thought that had brought him to the conclusion that he must follow her into the forest, but always the path grew dim once he set upon it and disappeared before he reached his destination. It seemed like it had been clear to him while he was in the forest, but left him once he had returned to town. As if the knowledge could not be taken with him out of the forest. Like a dreamer who on waking is robbed of some imperative understanding, unable to take it with him into waking life.

He thought about the Old Woman ambushing him from preposterous hiding places. He imagined her pouncing on him once he pulled back the shower curtain in his own bathroom, leaping at him from behind a row of garbage cans on the street, launching out of the bus as the automatic doors opened. He imagined her ability to hide in thin air and saw her attacking him as he sat down in his armchair, from underneath his coffee table, when he opened the linen closet to grab some towels. And he did not know why he saw these things. The images came to him, from the air it seemed, and he allowed himself to see them. But whenever he came out of these reveries, he could not help but feel a twinge of sadness for having had them, for he knew no such cougar lived in the city.

He had thought about visiting the place where he had killed her in the forest, but he dared not make the journey for fear of what he would find. The river had been diverted into a concrete channel years ago, surrounded by a grid of repeating houses, like a planted crop waiting to be harvested. He would find a fountain surrounded by a manicured lawn, concrete benches for sitting, a few trees planted into the ground, cement borders around them.

Joseph hauled himself up and continued on his way down the baking sidewalk. He came to a stop at an intersection. The countdown on the crosswalk still showed "9," but he knew this was not enough time for him to cross the four lanes of traffic so he waited for the next light.

A young man coming down the sidewalk glanced at the count and, clutching his messenger bag under one arm, dashed across the street. It took him no more than half a dozen long, easy strides. He reached the other side of the intersection with a "3" still on the counter.

Joseph watched the young man, the movement of his body seeming uninhibited by the physical world, and with sudden clarity he recalled the sensation of running, of kicking up dust in his wake, ducking tree branches through a shaded forest, leaping over creeks and the embarrassment of failing, leaping over creeks and the triumph of success, across the wet sand on the lakeshore, slick stones glinting like coins of light underfoot.

The light changed, and Joseph pushed his walker onto the road and across the intersection. Cars hurtled past beside him, the stream of metal pushing out waves of heat that crashed against him like the waves of a vile sea.

J OSEPH UNLOCKED HIS APARTMENT door, the jangle of his keys breaking the silence in the quiet hallway. He breathed in the familiar scents — coffee, washed dishes, dust — and shut the door behind him. It was nice and cool in here. He could not take the heat. He had become so used to the controlled temperature of the indoors that now he could not survive without it. Without air conditioning, the days would be intolerable, the nights worse. It might be enough to push him over the edge, the torment of relentless heat.

He went to the living room to sit for a moment and catch his breath. He could not help but feel the summers were crueller now, unbearably hot. Not like they used to be. The heat had never bothered him as a young man. He remembered spending entire afternoons with friends fishing out on the lake, wearing a hat but no shirt, the sunlight from the sky and the reflected light from the water roasting them in between. He remembered the fresh heat in the morning; the slow heat of the afternoon, thick with the smell of pine, the song of cicadas in the muggy air; the hot scorch before the twilight; the warm embrace of evening; the heat of darkness. He thought of his wife, of how they had met.

The air conditioner humming to life roused him from his thoughts. Thinking of his wife in this way, their shared life, filled him with a deep longing, now thirty years old. He shook off these unbidden thoughts and stood to unpack the groceries.

HE TOOK THE CARDBOARD box out of the refrigerator and stood reading the instructions on the back, a pained expression on his face. He opened the box and emptied its contents onto the counter. Three coloured packages spilled out: one white, one green, one black.

Joseph snipped open the white package with a pair of scissors, squeezing the lumpy log into the microwave-safe container. Cubed chunks of white meat sat shiny in a gelatinous, herbed gravy. He cut open the green package and sprinkled the tiny uniform squares of green, yellow, and orange freeze-dried vegetables into the container. Finally, he opened the black package and squeezed out a thick brown sauce that smelled sweet and savoury at once, smothering the cubes and squares in the container.

He opened the microwave door, popped the container inside, covered it with a splatter guard, then punched in eight minutes and pressed the Start button.

The microwave sat glowing on the counter, slowly heating the food.

While he waited, he took his pills.

Soon the sound of sizzling could be heard over the continuous hum of the microwave and it set Joseph's mouth watering. He stood waiting, staring at the illuminated box on the counter in the semi-darkness of the kitchen. The microwave ended with an insistent ding. Joseph opened the door and the scent of the cooked food wafted toward him. He took the sizzling tray out of the microwave and placed it in the basket of his walker, careful not to scald his fingers on the steam escaping from under the plastic film.

In the living room, Joseph transferred his dinner tray from his walker to the small table he had set up beside his armchair so he could eat and watch television. Then he sat down, turned on the television with the remote control, and started flicking through the channels.

The screen was black after a commercial break, then the picture faded to white and emerged as a calm winter forest scene, trees covered in snow, unbroken blue sky above. The picture changed to show a pair of falcons sitting on a naked branch, then changed again to show the birds in flight.

The host, wearing a red toque and sunglasses, stepped into view in front of a scene of snow-covered evergreens and the sound of the studio audience's applause rose to life. He smiled a lupine smile into the camera for the viewers at home. They were in Algonquin Park, where two thousand black bears made their home, and today they would accompany a team whose job it was to track the bears down and count them.

Adventurous music set the tone. The camera flew over the park, showing scenic winter views: a vast forest of black trees blanketed in white snow, a placid river snaking through the frozen wilderness. They came upon the inert carcass of a moose surrounded by a pack of wolves. When the camera zoomed in, the wolves ran away into the trees. At this, a soft chuckle issued from the audience.

Next, they showed the helicopter landing. The host and

his team jumped down and ran for the trees, implying the serious nature of the task ahead, mimicking the intros of popular police dramas, or medical soap operas.

The music had come to an end, and the team was trekking through the snowy forest, each person loaded with packs or equipment of some kind. Some carried shovels. An up-close shot of a horned owl sent a shiver down Joseph's spine. The bird's stare was unflinching, looking directly into the camera. Joseph felt he had made eye contact with the bird, though it was merely a reproduction of the bird's stare. There was something familiar in that stare, encountered suddenly.

Using his tracking device, the doctor led them to the first den. They approached a snow-covered fall of tree trunks, the dark entrance. As the team used shovels to dig out the entrance, the host became overwhelmed by the notion of encountering an actual bear.

When the camera looked inside the den, the bear's brown eyes came into focus, and the audience cooed. Then, a shot of an attractive blond assistant preparing a shot, explaining to the camera that they were giving the bears their annual dose of antibiotics so they wouldn't get sick.

Once the entrance had been cleared, one of the team members leaned into the den and shot the bear with a tranquilizer gun, *phut! phut!* Then they reached in and dragged the bear out into the snow. She wore a white collar around her neck. This was how they kept track of the bears, so they knew where they were at all times. The bear's tongue lolled out under the effects of the drug. Music played in the background, so the audience knew there was nothing to be afraid of now that the bear had been drugged.

As Joseph watched, he began to feel uncomfortable at the way the team handled the bear. She lay limp in the snow, belly exposed, limbs splayed out, the black pads of her toes visible, the bone-coloured claws. They opened her mouth to look at her teeth. They opened her unconscious eyes and shone a light on the black pupils. He was reminded of his younger days in the shop when he would need to test the systems of a car to ensure they were functioning.

As the team worked on the mother bear, the camera cut to the bear cubs, who were still huddled together inside the den, groggy bundles of fur. They pulled the bear cubs out into the freezing light. Suddenly, the host was overcome by sweetness. The music changed to a light-hearted, sentimental melody. The cubs squawked at these strange visitors, who cuddled them, speaking in high-pitched tones. The cubs had pink tongues, milky-blue eyes. The stretched-out image of the cameraman was visible on the cub's eye as the perspective zoomed in for a close-up.

They weighed the cubs, took measurements of their heads. This was important. Measuring the heads of the bear cubs would give the team a deeper understanding of their lives, and therefore their environment and thus nature as a whole. They must know this. There could be nothing that was considered unknown. Such a thing was unacceptable.

They did the same for the mother bear, taking her measurements, measuring fat content. They equipped her with a new collar. The batteries only lasted a year so it was time to replace it. Then they gave her an injection, the antibiotics the student assistant had prepared.

The notion of this injection made Joseph suspicious. He wished they would tell the viewers exactly why they were giving the bears antibiotics. But the picture moved on, focusing on the attractive student assistant, her blond hair stylishly peeking out from under the toque placed just so on her head. This was the image of nature people wanted to see, a young woman garbed against the elements, having a wonderful time in her equipment, smiling even from behind her sunglasses. Her appearance indicated she was not threatened by the wilderness, she was at home in the wilderness, and so was the viewer by extension, through watching her.

The team placed the drugged mother bear and her squawking cubs back into their den. They replaced the branches and snow in front of the den so when the bear woke up she would think she had been visited only in a dream.

Joseph flipped through the channels, feeling the tension brought up by the bear program diminish with every click. He stopped on a channel that showed a man on a ladder and a roof full of snow slide down in one complete sheet, knocking him off the ladder and burying him. The audience laughed. The tension in Joseph's chest drained away, and he forgot his concern, sitting in the bright embrace of the television.

———

HE WAS NOT WATCHING the television but sitting with his eyes closed, dipping in and out of sleep. His back was sore from sitting. His knees ached from his walk. He took up the remote and clicked off the television, turned off the lamp. He brought the walker around and hauled himself up. For a moment, he stood in the darkened room as his eyes adjusted. The headlights of a passing car swept over the living room. He saw the contours of the room in the shifting light, his shadow cast large and distorted by the angle of the headlights. Then, in darkness once more, he pushed his walker down the hall to the bedroom.

He threw his clothes in the laundry basket and changed into his night clothes. Tomorrow, he would do laundry. He thought of sitting by the washer in the subterranean warmth of the basement, listening to the sounds of the machines. He thought of going for a walk, finding some shade in the park, sitting and watching people walking their dogs, riding bicycles with their children. He thought of drinking coffee, reading the paper, watching television.

The harsh light of the bathroom flickered on, revealing his reflection. He inspected himself in the mirror. A web of wrinkles fanned out around his eyes. His cheeks were thin, hollow against his skull. His skin was spotted on his forehead and scalp. Only the eyes remained familiar. This consoled him, this sameness.

He stood in front of the mirror brushing his teeth. He gave no thought to this mechanical action and his mind began to wander. He travelled backward, landing on a time when he and his two daughters stood brushing their teeth together in front of the bathroom mirror. They were very young. He was his younger self, with tanned skin and flesh in his cheeks, though by then his dark hair had become shot through with silver. The girls each stood on a stool so they would be tall enough to see into the mirror above the sink. They were on either side of Joseph, looking up at him with serious eyes, dark eyes like their mother's, toothpaste foaming at their mouths. A moment passed in silence. Then Joseph pulled a face, fangs bared, wide-eyed, and snarled like a wolf. He held up his hands like claws amid the amused squeals of his daughters. Soon all of them were pulling faces at one another and snarling until their mother called from downstairs, *What's going on up there . . . ?*

He could hear her voice now, in the quiet of his solitary bathroom, hear it clearly in his mind, exactly the way she would have said it, as if she had indeed spoken just now.

Joseph laughed out loud, sounding to himself like an old recording that had been played so many times it had begun to warble. Thinking of his younger self, compared to the man staring back at him, he thought, *how strange I look*, and, *strange that I look strange to myself.* Yet the same. No sudden change had occurred. It had been a gradual decay.

He took the towel from the rack and laid it next to the sink, then ran the water and washed his face of the toothpaste foam. He dried his face on the towel and hung it back on the rack to dry.

He turned off the light and shadow flooded the room. In the absence of light, he felt a wave of dizziness wash over him, and he gripped the door frame so as not to lose his balance.

He looked to the farthest corner of his bedroom and saw his eldest daughter standing there, as she would have appeared at the time of her death. She stood, hands folded in front of her. Her face was torn away along her jaw, ripped open at the mouth, so he could see the bright bone beneath. The skin on her hands was shredded, her clothes stained black from sliding over the asphalt, stained dark with blood, made all the more noticeable because her shirt had been white. He knew that shirt. He had seen it many times before he had seen her wearing it in death. She stood looking at him directly. Her expression was not menacing. She did not mean to frighten him, only to show herself to him.

He closed his eyes on this vision, and when he looked again at the shadowed corner, she was gone.

Joseph threw back the thin blankets and positioned his walker by the side of the bed, ready for him to use when he awoke. Then he got under the covers and lay down. After a moment he reached up and turned out the light.

Darkness surrounded him, then he saw within. With each breath he felt a swelling lightness fill his body. His heartbeat seemed loud in his own chest, a pronounced loudness that he could not account for, as if his hearing had suddenly become more sensitive, but this was only a brief notion before he fell asleep.

H E WALKED DOWN THE darkened hallway of his apartment building, squinting at the dim light coming in around the edges of the doors ahead. They opened as he approached, and he did not find this unnatural.

Outside, the sun had yet to rise. The sky was overcast. There were no cars, no other people on the street. It was from this prevailing sense of static that he understood the street had been abandoned long ago. The stillness here was the stillness of many years of lifelessness.

Where in life there stood a reflection of multiplexes across the street from his apartment building, there was instead an impenetrable wall of forest, the trees taller than any he had ever seen. Joseph crossed the street and waded into the long grass, toward the line of trees. As he walked, the stalks reaching over his head, he noticed the unearthly silence, the day more quiet than seemed possible, and he noticed there was no life underfoot, no mice, no crickets. Even this activity had long since ceased.

The trees stood together in a mad press. There seemed no way to get through, but he knew he must go in. He thrust his hands into the needled branches and pushed his way between two trees and entered a thin corridor, which he followed, fighting the branches as he went. As he forged a rough passageway, the needles tore at his night clothes, catching and ripping the material, until trails of threads led away from his body, strung across the branches like a strange webbing. And when his clothes had been unravelled, the needles scratched at his skin until his flesh too had been torn away and the body beneath revealed to be true, so when at last he emerged from the trees he was a young man — though not the young man he had been in life.

In his hand, he held the hatchet forged by his father, the same hatchet he had taken into the forest and left behind. But the blade was not dull and weathered, the way it should be wherever it lay, but sharp, freshly hewn. When he saw the hatchet grasped in his own hand, he knew what he must do.

He was barefoot through the forest, over ground littered with brown needles, roots erupting from the earth, beneath fallen trees the size of autobuses, their decay lasting longer than a man's lifetime. Fog threaded the trees, their tops lost in the white ceiling above. The air was cold against his skin, but he felt immune to its touch, unaffected by this superficial discomfort. This was old forest. And she was here, stalking the ancient trees. He felt her presence on the air.

He studied the forest floor searching for even the slightest sign that would tell him of her presence. He caught her scent and found it was still familiar to him. While he was briefly distracted by the memory of her scent he was aware this meant she would be able to smell him as well.

Despite the cool air, he felt the warmth of his own blood beneath his skin. His cheeks burned, likewise his thighs, his chest. He paused to listen but all he heard was endless forest, deep in silence, no other animal resided here. They two were alone. No other breath was permitted here.

He stood scanning the tangled mess of forest, his hand against the rough bark of a tree. He closed his eyes, reaching into the forest with his ears. His own breathing was noise to him.

Then he heard her. As her tremendous footfalls echoed through the forest, so drummed the beating of his heart.

He slipped into the trees.

He felt it before he heard it: a low, continuous rumble. He stopped and listened, then knelt to lay his hand upon the ground. In all the forest, this was the only sound. He stood and went toward it, gripping his hatchet, a trail of breath rising from his head. The sound grew louder as he drew near.

When he came out of the trees he saw a white waterfall rushing over black rocks, crashing into the water below. A cloud of spray rose from the base of the waterfall, mingling with the fog. Joseph cast glances into the surrounding trees as he made his way down to the pool of water at the base of the waterfall.

He saw his reflection on the surface of the water, his eyes glowing like molten metal inside his shadowed skull. He held his breath and listened, but he heard nothing. She was watching him now. He could feel her gaze on him as if he had been touched. He walked through the cloud of spray, clutching the hatchet, eyes searching the trees. The spray dampened his hair, his skin. The sound of the waterfall was tremendous behind him, and he tried to focus his hearing into the trees, as if the sound was impeding his vision.

Then, as the fog shifted and thinned, he saw her in the distance.

She emerged from the pale landscape, her unflinching stare devoted to him. Though he saw her through the fog, the wafting spray, still the sight of her sent a prickling sensation along his skin, like his nerves had grown out beyond his body and into the air and had brushed against a cold fire.

She leapt down from her perch. As she met the ground, leaves rose up, floated away, and settled in a perfect circle. She ran toward him from out of the white shadows, the sound of her footsteps loud to him, and now, caught in the direct line of her gaze, he could not move.

Seeing her lean figure through the fog had a hypnotizing effect on him, and for a moment he was caught noticing her beauty. But as she came closer, he suffered a sudden shock, for he saw she was a giant, a cougar of gigantic proportions. Her eyes glinted with a strange darkness in the muted light, and the sight of her, sharpening as the distance between them closed, sent a wave of fear through him that caught his breath and turned his fingers cold.

His feeling of relief at seeing her was immediate, so much so that he became overwhelmed. Looking on her body, the sight of her deeply missed in all the years since he had last seen her, filled him with an inexplicable urge. Though he knew she meant to kill him, he was afflicted by an urgent desire to run toward her.

The Giant Cougar halted a short distance away,

looming over him. Up close, he saw that her eyes were two black diamonds set in the sockets of her skull, a dim light shone out of them, and he knew that she saw with a different sight. This vision in no way hindered her perception of him or the forest around her. He knew he should not look into those eyes or else become arrested by contemplating their nature, but he did anyway.

She walked a perimeter around him, her massive shoulders rising and falling in a fluid motion. Again he was struck by her beauty, the construction of her body. He imagined the sacred frame of her bones working beneath her flesh. She had been restored to the fullness of her youth, but her posture, the way she took her steps, betrayed an ancient existence. Her fur was dark gold, her white chest glowed. Her mouth hung open and he saw the deadly teeth within. There were no scars on her body. Her gigantic size was an indication of her passage into greatness. That and the strange eyes, which seemed ornamental, acquired through some process he did not understand.

She stopped and stood before him, breathing gently. Joseph stood ready, desperately waiting for her to move, his heart hammering inside his chest. The Giant Cougar sat, staring at him with those black diamond eyes. The forest seemed to hold its breath. Then she lowered her head and hissed, ears flattened against her skull. The sound pulsed against him. He stared into her open jaws, large enough to consume a man whole.

The Giant Cougar pounced. Joseph leapt out of reach, never letting her leave his sight. The Giant Cougar twisted around to face him. She opened her mouth and screamed.

It was not the chilling scream he remembered, though; instead, it sounded like the breath of the wind through the trees.

The Giant Cougar inched around him, her massive tail flicking. He felt his gaze locked to her bewildering eyes. He tried instead to focus on her body, its passage through space connected to his own. He wanted to stand and watch her. He wanted just a moment of pause that they might look on each other. But he knew that time would not allow it. They could only know each other through transitory touches.

He raised his arm, clutching the hatchet. The Giant Cougar reached out. He ducked her outstretched paw and planted the hatchet in her chest. It sank home, into the thick meat of her breast, but it was an insignificant injury. The Giant Cougar screamed and twisted, dislodging the hatchet. She swiped at him again, her claws catching his right forearm. He barely felt it, but he knew it was a true cut as the warmth of his own blood crept down his skin.

The Giant Cougar tackled him, wrapping her forelegs around him, and he dropped the hatchet. He shrank into her embrace, pressing against her warm chest, and she was unable to bite him. He squirmed out of her grasp and scrambled over the forest floor. He found his hatchet amid the leaves and turned and plunged it into the Giant Cougar's shoulder. She hissed and twisted around, knocking him aside. He tried to hold on to the hatchet but instead lost his grip as he was thrown through the air, landing hard on the cold, leaf-covered ground.

The Giant Cougar pounced, her jaws descending upon

him. He latched on to her face, a handful of her flesh in his hand, and yanked the hatchet out of her shoulder. She rose, screaming. He drew back his arm to strike again and in that moment caught his own reflection in the surface of her black diamond eye. He saw his own distorted expression on the surface of her eye, and then he saw within: he saw the extent of her life from the beginning right through to the end, and his too within it, and this great distance was traversed within the span of a single breath.

As he paused to witness this, the Giant Cougar grabbed him between her massive paws. He chopped into her paw and she dropped him. He planted the hatchet into her front leg and she screamed, the sound of wind again. Then she swiped at him and he raised his arm to shield himself and her claws tore deep gashes into his forearm. He dropped the hatchet, unable to hold on against the pain.

The Giant Cougar reached out and slashed him across his left breast, tearing streams of blood across his skin. She caught him in the face and ripped through his cheek. He felt his own blood weeping down his neck.

His skin had been torn open, exposing him to the stinging touch of the air. He could feel the forest floor and through this the trees of the forest. It was painful to feel it all, his body open to the air, but as well as this pain he felt the Giant Cougar, and beyond that the body she had had in life, Mother of Hunters, Queen of Ghosts.

He was not upset by the destruction of his body. Whatever damage was done to it was not done to him. Each time the Giant Cougar struck him, she tore away strips of his flesh, his own blood drenching him red in the pale forest. He knew the destruction of his body was a necessary process. It could not go beyond this point.

Finally, he no longer resembled himself, scored with wounds, dark with blood. Only the bright eyes remained intact. The Giant Cougar tore a slash down his back. He believed he felt her claw nearly tear through his chest. He took a struggled step forward and sank to the ground, the pain crushing him beneath its weight. The earth had never seemed more beautiful to him. He felt its touch penetrating deep within him.

The Giant Cougar appeared at his side, brought her face close to his. As she breathed, gusts from her nostrils rushed over his tattered skin. When she opened her mouth, he felt her warm breath wet his face.

He opened his mouth to scream as she bit down into his neck, but no sound came out. He could no longer make any sound. When he felt her chewing into his shoulder, he no longer tried to scream. He watched, impartial, as she began to devour his body. Her teeth ripped through his flesh, but he was not concerned by this; instead, he wanted to watch her as she ate him, to see into her eyes, but her eyes were hidden by her golden eyelashes as she looked down, concentrating on her work. As she began to eat his chest, clawing back his bones to get at his heart, he closed his eyes, submitting himself to her hunger, and a deep sense of calm spread through him, all the tension released from his body, as if the rope anchoring him to the earth had been cut.

He felt himself drifting, as if travelling down a gentle, black river. Though he knew he had been consumed by the Giant Cougar, and he believed he must now be within her, he sensed a vast openness coming to greet him. He felt himself begin to spread out, stretching farther and farther, until at last he sensed only darkness and that he was approaching a great precipice which he could neither see nor hear but knew was there, and he could feel from the vibration that he was about to meet it, and even this was but a fleeting thought, a bare moment.

A GREEN JEEP ROLLED into the parking lot on Sunday morning and parked in one of the reserved spots behind the triplex. An older man got out of the jeep and crossed the parking lot, searching his wallet for the passcard that would let him in the back door. The doors slid open, and shut behind him. Once inside the darkened hallway, the quiet coolness of the building was a glaring difference from the sweltering heat outside.

He was here on a different matter, which had occupied his mind all morning, but as soon as he passed Joseph's apartment door, this matter was forgotten. It was as if something had brushed his cheek, like the wing of a bird, or he had heard his name called from the other room. He stopped and looked at Joseph's door. It looked the same as all the others, yet it stood out to him, as if it glowed.

He knocked on the door, calling his tenant's name, and waited. He heard no movement from the other side; in fact, a distinct stillness seemed to occupy the rooms within. He knocked again, calling louder, but still in a polite tone. He took out his cell phone and called his tenant's number. Inside, the phone rang and rang, echoing in a strange way, like the ring of ice inside a hollow cave.

He decided to enter the apartment.

Later, he would say, his tenant was elderly and should therefore be checked on, as a way of justifying things to himself, and he told himself again and again, *I was right to check*. But really there had been no outward indication, nothing extraordinary that had caused the landlord to check on his tenant, Joseph Brandt.

Sighing, he sorted through his keys to find the master key that would open Joseph's apartment.

He unlocked the door. The apartment was lit by outside light only, which crept in through the drawn blinds, casting a shadowed light onto the cream-coloured carpet. The air conditioner was running, and the landlord felt the sweat he had gained on his back while outside begin to cool and he gave a sudden shiver. He went to the thermostat and turned down the air.

"Mr. Brandt?" he called out.

He surveyed the apartment. A man by himself, more like a hotel room than a living room. The photos on the walls, the few belongings were completely removed from meaning for him, relics of an unknown life. Except for the well-worn armchair sitting in front of the television. This he could relate to.

"Mr. Brandt?"

He walked the short hallway toward Joseph's bedroom. It was only once he drew near the door that he wondered if something might be wrong. He pushed it open but did not enter the room.

Joseph lay under the covers, on his side, facing the wall. At first, the landlord thought he had disturbed the old man in his sleep, and felt that he had been wrong to enter the apartment, but when he saw the stillness of the body, that the sleeper did not stir at the approach of another, he realized the old man was not sleeping. And once he realized that he had come into the presence of Death, that he was alone with the dead, the familiarity that was Joseph Brandt, the man he had known, vanished. All that Joseph had been in life was stripped from the body before him and the truth of nothingness struck a deep fear within him.

He could not look away from the body lying in mockery of sleep, the inert pose somehow obscene, a rude joke. His own body was repulsed by the presence of a thing dead, decomposing, and he turned and fled.

He felt uneasy with his back to the body and even looked over his shoulder as he made his retreat from the apartment, not even closing the front door, down the hallway. He hit the button and the front doors eased open. He walked at least ten paces before he stopped. His dread had followed him outside into the glaring heat, where it was burned away in the sunlight as he stood breathing, hands on his hips, heart pounding in his chest.

He stood on the sidewalk, looking at the windows of Joseph's apartment, blinds closed to the world, and wondered when it had happened, how long had the body lain waiting to be discovered. The thought gave him a chill, despite the heat.

He waited a while for his heartbeat to calm down before venturing back into the building. But the feeling of dread did not return when he looked again upon the dead body. Instead, the landlord found himself staring at the remains of his tenant and, not without a note of genuine regret, felt compelled to comment.

"Well, shit."

AFTER THE OLD MAN'S daughter came to pack up and clear out his belongings, the landlord hired a professional to give the apartment a thorough cleaning. Then he started his renovations. He ripped up the carpets and replaced them with laminate flooring. He replaced the old blinds with drapes, and he replaced the faucets in both the kitchen and the bathroom. Then he painted all the rooms the same colour, called haystack. This work took him a few months so he did not begin to advertise the place until late November.

In December, he showed the apartment to a young couple. It was not a big enough apartment for a family, but a young couple might stay for a few years, at least until they needed more room or could afford something better. The space was really more suited for a single person, but the couple was very interested and he liked the look of them. After checking their references, their credit history, and confirming their letters of employment, he offered them the lease.

The couple moved in on the first of January. All their possessions fit into one cube van. They were being donated a bed frame, a dresser, a kitchen table with a matching set of chairs, but this was not scheduled to arrive until a few days later. It was a sunny day, no wind, even though it was winter, for which the couple was grateful as they began to unload the contents of the van into their first apartment together.

The first thing they moved in was their silver tabby,

setting her carrying case down next to her litter box in the bathroom and unzipping the entrance. But the cat did not move, despite much coaxing. They set down the cat's food and water bowls and closed the bathroom door, so she would not be disturbed as they moved the rest of their stuff inside.

They made short trips from the vehicle to the ground-floor apartment, smiling as they passed each other in the hallway, as if recently bestowed some new and exciting secret. There were only a few items they had to carry together, the mattress, their loveseat and coffee table, but there was one item they struggled with — the television stand, a brutal block of wood they had been unable to disassemble but managed to negotiate into the building, down the hall, and through the apartment door with only a modest amount of cursing.

Once all of their possessions had been unloaded, they opened the bathroom door, but the tabby stayed, hiding in her carrier. Later, when the couple was not looking, the cat crept out of her case to hide behind the toilet.

The first night, they slept on their mattress in the middle of the living room, surrounded by the disarray of their possessions. They had stacked the boxes against the walls, a vague organization based on the destination of the contents of each box. As they slept, beams of car headlights swept across their apartment walls, like the languid pulsing of a distant lighthouse.

The next day, they sorted through the boxes. While organizing the chaos, inspired by their newly acquired territory, they made love on the loveseat in its temporary resting spot in the hallway. From beneath an armchair sitting in limbo between the hallway and the kitchen, the couple's silver tabby sat like a regent observing an unamusing jester.

Slowly, the couple's possessions migrated to their rightful locations. Long, thoughtful conversations were had about the best way to fulfill the function of a certain space, set up a room, display collections. An argument about the organization of vinyl records occurred, which ended in tears and slammed doors, and resulted in murmured apologies and more love-making on the loveseat, now in its rightful place in the centre of the living room.

At night, the woman dreamed of a fire raging on the horizon. The fire drew ever closer, threatening to consume the whole world, and when it reached them there would be no escape from the flames, burning the hair upon their bodies, the flesh upon their bones, their bones to ash, and the earth itself scorched to charcoal, and over all the earth a cold wind driving the black ash across nothing but barren plains.

She awoke from this dream, the words emerging from her lips already forgotten, the details of the message fading. Roused by her unrest, the man pulled her close and held her until her breathing slowed, and they both returned to sleep.

Disturbed from her sleep, the tabby rose and stretched out her front legs, then her back legs. She leapt down from the bed to go on her nightly stalk. Silent across the laminate flooring, she watched into the shadows as if witness to another order of events, then looked away, unimpressed by these visions. She patrolled the entire expanse of her small territory. Then, as she often did, she settled down in the living room where Joseph's armchair had been. The headlights of a passing car swept across the room and the cat's eyes reflected the light like two chips of green fire in the darkness, as she sat watching, waiting.

ACKNOWLEDGEMENTS

I WOULD LIKE TO THANK the wonderful people at House of Anansi Press, with special thanks to Michelle MacAleese, Maria Golikova, Alysia Shewchuk, Gemma Wain, Sonya Lalli, Laura Brady, and Debby de Groot.

Samantha Haywood, for her faith in me and her dedication to getting this novel into the right hands.

Michael Redhill and Heather Sangster, for their thoughtful editorial guidance.

I am grateful for the support of my friends and family, and to my early readers, Serena D'Souza, Jane Hodgkinson, and Ian Sattler.

PAMELA KORGEMAGI is a graduate of York University's creative writing program. *The Hunter and the Old Woman* is her debut novel. She lives and works in Toronto, Canada.